Just before I left the office to return home, I was slipping on my coat when my eye caught a fleeting shadow of movement from the front windows. Had someone been looking in at me?

It was just starting to get dark. On edge, my heart began to race. I quickly made my way to the front room and looked out the window just in time to see a figure in a long black coat disappear around the side of the building. I had not been quick enough to see if it was a man or a woman, and suddenly I was too afraid to step outside and try to chase the person.

My cell phone rang just then and startled me further. I hurried back inside to answer it. Grant was calling, so I picked up. "Hello?"

"Bridget ... are you still at work?"

"Yes."

"I need to see you. I want to apologize for yesterday."

I set my purse and coat down and took a seat at one of the desks in the front room. "Grant, I'm a nervous wreck right now. I need to get home."

"What's wrong?" he asked.

"I'm not sure. I think someone was spying on me."

"Get out of there," he ordered. "*Now.*"

Other Fiction by Ann Ulrich Miller

Rainbow Majesty (Romantic Suspense)

Sonata Summer (Romantic Suspense)

Non-Fiction

Throughout All Time, A Cosmic Love Story (Memoir)

Stepping Forth,
   An American Girl Coming of Age in the '60s (Memoir)

Titles published under the name Ann Carol Ulrich

Night of the November Moon (Romantic Suspense)

The Space Trilogy:
   Intimate Abduction

   Return To Terra

   The Light Being

      (Sci-Fi/Romance)

The Annette Vetter Mystery Series (1968-69 period)
   The Mystery at Hickory Hill

   The Secret of the Green Paint

   The Pouting Pumpkin Mystery

   The Legend of the Lantern

   In the Shadow of the Tower

   The Ground Hog Mystery

   Spring Break at the Lake House

   Prom Night

The Root Cellar Mystery (pre-teen)

See more at **AnnUlrichMiller.com**

THE
DREAM
CHASERS

ANN ULRICH MILLER

Earth Star Publications

THE DREAM CHASERS

Ann Ulrich Miller

Earth Star Publications
P.O. Box 267
Eckert, CO 81418

www.earthstarpublications.com

FIRST EDITION
November 2018
2nd Printing November 2023

ISBN 978-0-944851-56-2

Printed in the United States of America

Front Cover photograph by William Rochfort Jr.

To Ryan

1

The dream came again. I heard my sister's voice in the distance. *"Help me, Beej!"*

We were in a dark place, cold and damp. I sloshed through shallow water in a dark tunnel and the wind blew my bangs. "Liz! I'm here!" I shouted. "Liz, hold on!"

"Beej! I beg you!" she pleaded.

Frustrated, I had no idea where to turn. But before I could make any decision, the alarm went off on my cell phone.

Relieved that I had been saved from my sister's anguish, I reached for the phone and fought the desire to fall back to sleep. It was seven o'clock and I had to get ready for work.

I was in the bathroom washing up when my iPhone started playing *All My Ex's Live in Texas* by George Strait. The word CONNIE appeared. I grabbed my phone and answered it. "Hi, Connie," I said, reaching for the towel.

"Oh, did I wake you, hon? I know it's early." Connie's voice with a touch of Texas spoke more rapidly than usual.

"It's okay, I'm up." I glanced at the gray light growing brighter from the bathroom window.

Connie squealed slightly. "I wanted to catch you before you left for work. There's a couple that wants to see yer house, darlin'."

I released a sigh. "I thought we already discussed this."

"Oh, B.J., come on," Connie pleaded. "They could be the ones! I know you said you didn't want to renew our contract, but I have a feeling about this couple. I declare, I do believe they're gonna be the ones to put an offer on your house."

My house was not in shape for a showing. "I still have last night's dishes in the kitchen sink," I told Connie. "My laundry is in heaps. Can't you just tell them tomorrow would be better?"

Connie went on to explain that her clients were only going to be in Dexter one day. "I know we talked about taking yer house off the market for a coupl'a months, but I don't think they're gonna mind a little mess."

After a little more convincing, Connie finally got me to agree to the showing, and we ended the conversation. I quickly got dressed while my coffee was brewing. Then, I couldn't help it, I just had to rinse my dirty dishes and stash them in the dishwasher, hoping nobody opened it. I scurried around, doing a quick pick-up, all the while grumbling to myself that this was what I wanted after all. But after six months on the market with hardly any interest, last week I'd decided that maybe selling my house was not such a good idea. Besides, what was I supposed to do if it *did* sell? Where would I go?

I drank my coffee and blended a smoothie for breakfast. Too soon it was time to leave for my job at the *Dexter Chronicle,* our small-town newspaper. There was no use even hoping that things could change for me. I'd worked at the *Chronicle* for fifteen years and had made my way through just about every position, from receptionist to typesetter, to proofreader, to paste-up, and copy editor. I had delivered papers, I had sold ads, and in the last year I had been assigned work to the website, on top of my usual duties in the production department.

As I wound through the residential streets toward downtown, I had a flash of memory from that snippet of a dream. My sister Liz had died two years ago in Blanca Hills, a town in southern Colorado. Unlike in most families, Liz and I had *not* been close. As girls my younger sister and I had competed for our parents' attention. We had fought a lot. Where I had excelled in school and been the straight one in the family, Liz had deviated. She had gotten involved with the wrong crowd at an early age and had not finished high school. She ran away from home at 16, only to return a few years later to cause trouble that ended my short marriage to Dirk Martin.

Liz and I had not spoken in years. She had been attractive in an alluring way, slender and tall. Her hair had been lush and dark like mine, and she had flashing brown eyes where mine were blue and more demure. She became an alcoholic, a drug addict, and had served some time in prison.

I kept my distance from her. She had never attempted to ask for my forgiveness until two years ago, when she tried several times to contact me. I didn't answer any of her calls or messages, and I begged my son, Jason, to have nothing to do with his aunt. As far as I knew, he only remembered her as the wayward woman of the past, who for some reason unknown to him, had turned me against her.

Work was busy and we were in production for the next issue. I had little time to dwell on what may or may not be transpiring at my humble house on the edge of the mesa, nor did I think about Liz, although it had developed into a pattern that she would appear in my dreams from time to time, as if beckoning me. That day, I shut her out of my mind because there were other concerns that sprang up.

I was typing corrections and laying out the classifieds page toward late afternoon when the managing editor, Zach, walked in and interrupted me. "Hey, Bridget, can I have a word?"

I glanced up at the tall, thin thirty-something man with short brown hair, glasses and bushy eyebrows. He squatted beside my chair. "What's up?" I asked, typing on as if he wasn't there.

Zach scratched his head, then sighed. "You know the web editor position you applied for?"

I stopped typing and blinked at him with a hopeful smile. "Yes?"

Last week I had brushed up my résumé and submitted it to the publisher because the *Chronicle* was planning to hire a full-time web editor for the paper's website. For the last year or so, I had formatted the stories and pictures from the print issue and kept things current on line. It had become obvious that the job was time consuming and required a full-time employee. The higher-ups decided they wanted to see what profits they could reap by developing the paper's Internet presence.

Nobody else seemed interested in doing such hard work, yet I had stepped up to the plate, mostly because Merle, my techie ex-boyfriend, had taught me a lot about formatting and designing web pages. I was quite sure I was a shoo-in for the position. Of course, it would probably mean that Sally, my production manager, would have to find another assistant.

Zach turned his eyes away from me—*not* a good sign—and let out a huge sigh. "We've hired someone," he said.

"Oh?" I stared at him.

3

"His name is Stan Hammer and he's got lots of experience. We're negotiating a contract with him as we speak."

Negotiating a contract? I was floored and had stopped typing. Now I stared at the screen in front of me, not wanting to show my disappointment.

"Stan runs a business," Zach continued, drumming his fingers against a knee. "He works from home, maintaining other websites."

I looked at Zach and cocked my head.

"So ... we were wondering if you'd still be interested in helping out with the website," he said.

"What do you mean?"

"Well, we will still need you to convert all the stories each week and handle the images. We'll leave the high-end technical expertise and marketing angles to Stan. He seems to think we can increase our revenue considerably in the next six months to a year."

I swallowed. "That's ... great," I managed.

"So you'll still have your hours," Zach added, standing up.

"When does he start?" I asked.

"I'm not sure yet. He's driving up from Junction tomorrow to look at our set-up, but we've agreed to let him work at home. That commute from Junction five days a week isn't necessary."

"He lives in Junction?" I asked. Junction was fifty miles northwest of Dexter.

Zach nodded. "He and his wife have two young children, and his wife works, so Stan prefers to stay at home with the kids."

As he walked back to his office, I turned to Sally, who was working at her computer and had caught every word. She stared at me and raised an eyebrow. I sighed and went back to what I was doing. Oh well, at least now I didn't have to deal with Sally finding a replacement for me in production. She must have known that I had asked for the web job, but she made no comment.

Five o'clock came just as my tasks were completed. Sally dismissed me, reassuring me that she had already begun sending the pages electronically to the printers in Junction. By tomorrow, the *Chronicles* would arrive on a truck for processing, mailing and delivery.

When I pulled into my driveway ten minutes later, Merle Franklin was waiting for me on the front porch. My house was a white 1940s vintage two-story, solidly built, with a prominent covered porch that

4

extended across the entire front. Shrubs and rose bushes that wouldn't bloom for a couple of months yet grew along the wrap-around trellis.

Tall, lanky and red-haired, Merle sported a modest pointy beard that contrasted with his silver wire-rimmed glasses. He leaned against the porch wall with a toothpick in his mouth, watching me park and get out of my car.

"Hey, Merle," I called to him.

"Hey, yourself," he called back in a deep voice. Thin lips curled into a half smile.

"What brings you by?" I climbed the porch steps and he waited for me to unlock the front door. The real estate company's lock box banged slightly as I pushed open the door and Merle followed me inside.

"Just thought I'd stop by and see how things are going," said Merle.

I set my things down on the small table in the foyer and looked around. "Good," I told him. Merle and I had dated after we met more than two years ago. The relationship had been more of a friendship than anything else. I had this habit of starting a relationship and then backing out, concerned that my ex-husband would try to use it as a means to separate me from my son. Now, even though Jason was in college, I still resisted commitments.

We wandered into the kitchen and I picked up the business card off the counter that Connie had left earlier, which confirmed she had shown the house.

"Any luck with your house?" Merle asked, eyeing the card.

"Connie showed it today," I said.

Merle looked around and said, "Maybe they'll make an offer, Beej."

I sighed and opened the refrigerator. "Wanna beer?"

"Sure," he said.

I reached in and grabbed a bottle, handed it to him, and then pulled out a bottle of lemon-flavored iced tea. "I didn't get the web editor job," I told him.

"Well, why not?" Merle opened his bottle and took a sip of beer. "You're qualified. Who'd they give the job to?"

I grumbled. "Some nerd kid from Junction. And get this ... they're letting him work from home."

"That's not uncommon," said Merle.

"But at least they still want me for the grunt work." I smiled.

Merle took a longer sip of his beer, then looked me in the eye.

"Janie wants to get married."

"Wow, that was rather sudden, don't you think?"

Merle squirmed a bit and wiped some beer from his lip. "She doesn't think so."

"Are you going to accept her proposal?" I asked.

"Probably," said Merle. "It seems like a good idea right now."

"Well, Merle, it's time you settled down."

"I just wanted to make sure you didn't mind." Merle looked at me in a funny way.

"Not at all." I watched as he sheepishly stared at the floor. "Merle, we're still friends. Yes, we had a relationship. But that part is over. We agreed."

He nodded his head and smiled at me. "She wants kids," he revealed.

I laughed. "That's okay. You're still young enough to be a dad, for goodness sake. Heck, you're younger than I am."

He was about to say something more when my cell phone rang. I grabbed it and saw that it was the real estate agent. "Hi, Connie," I answered.

"B.J., good news. The people I showed your house to are making an offer."

"You're kidding. Really?" I perked up.

"We wrote up an offer this afternoon and I'd like to bring it over to you to sign."

"Wait a minute." I turned to Merle. "There's an offer on my house."

Merle gave me a thumbs up and took another swig of his beer.

"Connie, before you come over here, tell me what their offer is," I prompted.

"It's a hundred thirty-five thousand," she revealed hesitantly.

I frowned. "That's crazy," I told her. "I can't accept a low ball. I have to pay off my mortgage, for heaven's sake. And you need your commission. What the heck?"

"I know it's low," said Connie. "But you have to consider the age of your house."

"No, Connie. Don't insult me." I watched as Merle slowly shook his head from side to side, obviously amused at my defiance.

Suddenly, Connie erupted in giggles. "Girl! I'm only joshin'," she exclaimed so loud that I had to move the phone away from my face.

"They're payin' full price."

"What!" I shrieked. "What did you say?"

"They like the house," said Connie, "and they're from Texas. An older couple looking to retire in western Colorado. They said the house was perfect. They're givin' you yer price, B.J. And I'll email the contract to you tonight. Don't worry, I'm not comin' over with it. You can go through it and sign everything electronically."

Later, after Merle left, I felt like I was still in shock. My house had sold! What was I going to do now? Suddenly, I had to make some plans. I had to make a decision. I would also have to start packing.

"Mom, that's awesome," Jason told me over the phone when I called him later that night. He was away at college in Boulder. "How soon do you have to find another place?"

I had received Connie's contract and had spent an hour reading it and signing electronically on line. "The closing is supposed to happen in May," I told him. "I've got sixty days to pull myself together."

"This is what you've been wanting, Mom," my son told me. "Right?"

"Uh ... yes, I think so."

"Mom, are you going to stay in Dexter?"

"Well, it's where my job is," I replied. "I'm not going to be independently wealthy, you know. By the time I pay off the house ..."

Jason interrupted me. "Mom, what about your dream?"

For a few seconds, I was lost in thought.

"Mom?" Jason prompted.

"Uh ... When is your break?" I asked to purposely change the subject.

"In three weeks."

"Are you planning to come home?"

"I haven't decided yet."

"Are you going to your dad's?" I asked.

Jason cleared his throat. "Come on, Mom. Are you serious?"

"Well, Utah's gorgeous in the early spring."

"I might take off with a couple of the guys on campus," said Jason. "They're thinking about a backpacking trip."

"There's still snow in the high country," I protested. "Where were they thinking of hiking?"

"Baja."

"Oh, Jason, can you afford that?"

"Nope." He chuckled. "But seriously, Mom, I think you should consider doing something outrageous with your life when you sell the house."

"I don't know what you're talking about."

"Just think about it," he replied. I heard male voices in the background. "Well, I gotta go now. Talk to ya later."

He hung up before I could say another word.

I spent my weekend cleaning out the spare room. The basement was going to be a nightmare and I was on my own with all of this. I didn't want to think about buying another house right away. But I knew I'd have to at least find an apartment to rent or a condo.

It was about two weeks later when we were notified at work that pay increases were coming. The owners were sporadic about giving raises, so everyone was excited. I had continued my website work for the paper and had been introduced, finally, to Stan Hammer, the newly hired web editor from Junction. He was quite young—in his 20's—and was brimming with plenty of ideas to improve the cyber presence of the *Chronicle*. I took notice that Stan wanted me to continue doing all of the detailed tasks of formatting articles and converting the photos. I didn't mind the nitty-gritty of all the work as I was used to slaving away for hours and I hoped for a decent reward for my efforts when the envelopes got passed out.

A couple of days later, I was typesetting in the production room when the office manager dropped off the white envelopes. I finished the article I was typing, then took a sip of tea that was on my desk before opening mine. At first, when I read it, I thought it was a joke. My hourly wage was being raised twenty-five cents an hour. *Twenty-five cents an hour!* It was a slap in the face. I was outraged.

Sally had been watching me from her desk as she worked at laying out the next edition on her wide screen computer. "Beej, is something wrong?" she asked.

I was practically hyperventilating and must have turned beet red. Slapping the paper down on my desk, I blinked my eyes and stared across the room at her. "No. Nothing's wrong," I lied.

Then, very calmly I stood up and walked off to the restrooms in back. Inside, I stared at my face in the mirror and watched as tears welled up in my eyes. I wanted to scream in humiliation. A lousy twenty-five cent raise while Whiz Kid, not even 30 yet, had waltzed in and gotten the position I'd wanted, and then he didn't even have to show up for work?

Sally met me as I came out of the bathroom. "Beej, I can see that you're upset."

I folded in my lip and blinked at her. "I don't have anything to say."

"Well, okay, I won't pry. Can you do the corrections on the obits?" she asked. "Marissa left the proof on your desk."

"Sure."

I was trying to concentrate on my work when Marissa, one of the advertising reps, came into the production room and started a gossip session with Sally. I found it hard not to overhear what they were saying, and my ears perked up when I heard Stan's name mentioned.

"They're paying him fifty-five grand a year is what I heard," said Marissa.

Sally gasped. "Really? Are you sure? I mean, I don't think Zach makes that much."

"It's absurd!" cried Marissa. She turned to me. "B.J., do you think if you had gotten the web editor job, they would have paid you fifty-five grand a year? Plus ... he gets to work from home."

I faked a smile, then buried myself in my work, all the while fuming inwardly. While I was the one doing all the grunt work, twenty-something Stan Hammer got to wear the label of "Web Editor" of the *Dexter Chronicle* while working from the comfort of his home fifty miles away. While I slaved away, he was tending to his other business customers and getting paid high dollars for being, virtually, a consultant!

I wanted to cry, but I held it back. I wouldn't give Sally nor Marissa the satisfaction of knowing how bitterly disappointed I was, and how my ego had just been badly bruised.

That was the turning point for me. I decided right then and there that I needed a change. I was disgusted with the *Chronicle* and I knew it was time to make a fresh start somewhere else. After all the years I had given them, all I had to show for it was a lousy twenty-five cent an hour raise. It was time to follow my dream.

2

March rolled into April. Dexter tulip patches erupted in neighborhood lawns. It was still too soon for the trees to bud out, but the arrival of robins and other songbirds declared that spring was here. Late winter snowstorms had swept the Rockies, and even our small town west of the mountains got dumped more than once with the heavy white stuff, making roads miserable.

Jason called to tell me he was coming home for a few days during his break. He had sacrificed his trip with his college buddies to Mexico, in order to spend some time in Utah with his father and Alicia, his stepmother. I figured my son was short on cash and needed to suck up a little to Dirk.

I was enjoying my morning coffee on Saturday morning when Jason's car pulled into my driveway. When he entered the house, he set his pack down in the living room and grinned when he saw me at the kitchen counter. "Hey, Mom!" he called.

"Jason, I didn't expect you this early. What did you do, drive all night from Salt Lake?"

He shrugged as he shuffled into the kitchen, dressed in a gray hoodie sweatshirt and baggy pants. "I can only stand so much at Dad and Alicia's," he commented. He walked over and gave me a quick hug. "Besides, I wanted to spend some time with you before heading back to Boulder."

"Want some coffee?"

"Sure." Jason got a mug out of the cupboard and walked over to pour himself a cup of coffee. Then he pulled out the other counter stool and sat down beside me. He gazed out the window that overlooked the backyard. "I'm sure gonna miss this place."

"I know, so am I." I took a sip from my coffee.

Jason looked around, then asked, "Where are all the boxes? I thought you'd be mostly packed by now." My son had his father's looks, brown eyes with a strong nose and chin. He pushed a strand of dark brown hair off his forehead.

"I've been kind of busy. I'll get around to it." But the truth was, I dreaded moving.

"Did you find a place yet?" Jason asked.

"No. Not yet," I admitted.

"You've only got about a month, right?"

"I'll have to rent something soon," I said. "There just hasn't been a lot of rentals available in the paper."

"Craigslist, Mom!"

"I don't think so," I told him with a warning look. Then I sighed. "But you're right, I'd better think about getting a storage unit, at the very least."

"I thought I'd help you get started," said Jason. "You know, packing up stuff."

"Oh, that's kind of you, Jason. Thank you." I stood up and took my coffee and plate to the sink.

"What's this?" he asked, fingering the blue notebook.

"Just something I've been working on," I said.

He grabbed the notebook and opened it. I glanced at him hopelessly. There was no sense in hiding things from him. He paged through it, then smiled. "Are you taking classes?"

"A class," I replied and turned on the faucet to rinse some dirty dishes.

"Where?" he asked.

"The Vo-Tec," I revealed. "I'm taking a course on how to write a business plan."

"Sweet." He closed the book and grinned up at me. "This can only mean ..."

I turned off the water and looked at him. "Okay, I've made up my mind. I'm going to see if I can get a loan and start a shopper in the Lower Valley."

"That's awesome, Mom." Jason twirled around once in his chair. "I mean, how many years have we talked about this? Are you really going to go through with it this time?"

"Only if I can get a loan," I said. "The sale of the house won't be enough money to start a new business. Plus I'll need a place to live. I'm thinking I could find a place that I could use as an office with living quarters in the back ... or upstairs."

"This is so epic," said Jason. "Have you told them at work yet?"

"No!" I shot a warning look at him. "And don't you say a word to anyone. Not yet. I still have a lot of research to do and projects to line up. This is a huge undertaking, not just a hobby or a hare-brained scheme."

"You're going to be a big success," said Jason. "The valley needs a shopper, and not just any shopper ... your paper is going to help people, and maybe lift some of them out of poverty."

"Oh, Jason ..."

"I mean it, Mom. When I was down there in southern Colorado those two years, going to Blanca State, I could see it. There are so many low-income people, and if they had a means to sell stuff, and maybe advertise for work ... I think it could make a difference."

I smiled at Jason. "I do want to make a difference," I said. "Well, we'll see."

Jason gave me a hug. He had been the one who, three or four years ago, had asked me when I was going to start a shopper in Blanca Hills. At the time I thought he was joking. It had been a fall day when we were driving over Buffalo Pass. I was taking him home for the weekend, and the beautiful national forest of that part of the state had been in fall colors, the golden aspens glowing in the sunlight.

He had planted a seed in my mind that day. At the time, I had dismissed the idea as a pipe dream. But over the months ahead, that seed had grown inside my imagination. The idea of running my own little paper really got the juices flowing. I had gotten my degree in journalism, and I had worked at various newspapers and magazines for the last umpteen years. I began to feel confident that this was something I could do and possibly succeed at—not just for myself, but for the communities in the Lower Valley. Jason's observation was right, the area was a little depressed. It needed a shopper.

"Where do you want me to start?" Jason asked, looking around.

"Wherever you want." I shrugged, then turned back to the sink to shut off the water.

Jason decided to clean out some closets. First, he drove around town and brought back a supply of cardboard boxes he'd confiscated from behind liquor stores and the local grocery. We pulled out more than ten years' worth of stored papers, junk and keepsakes that I had stashed and forgotten about. I had to give my son credit, he could be a diligent worker when he set his mind to it.

It was around seven o'clock that evening when I was ready to quit. I felt completely worn out and went into the kitchen to grab a soda to pep me up. Jason called to me from the hallway, "Hey, Mom, I found the family album."

I wandered in and saw him next to a pile of books and collectibles from the hall closet. He had opened a picture album and was slowly paging through it. "I don't think I've seen this before," he said. "Was this you as a girl?" He lifted it toward me.

I knelt down beside him and saw a color snapshot of a skinny, dark-haired girl posing in front of a large red rock. There had been a field trip to Canyonlands when I had been in the fifth grade. "Yes, that was me. I must have been about 10 when that was taken."

Jason paged through more of the book as I gazed around at all the boxes he had started filling with my stuff. I couldn't believe I had hoarded away so much junk in the last several years. I started picking through some of it.

"How come there aren't pictures of Aunt Liz?" Jason asked a few minutes later.

"There might be one or two of her," I replied nonchalantly. "Maybe in a group shot."

After a moment's pause, Jason asked, "How come you never talk about her?"

I let out a sigh, not sure I wanted to go there right now. I'd had another fleeting dream the night before, in which my sister had made another ghostly appearance. What should I say to my son about the woman who had come between his father and me seventeen years ago? "Liz and I didn't get along," I finally said. I rummaged through a bunch of documents, wanting distraction. I had no idea why I had saved everything.

"Mom, you always say that," Jason challenged. He closed the picture album and faced me. "I've got to tell you, when I was at Dad's this last week, the subject came up, and I asked them about her. They explained to me what happened. But ... I'd kind of like to hear what you have to say."

My pulse immediately quickened and I frowned. "Before I do that, maybe you should tell me just what your father said to you." I put down the box of papers.

Just then, my cell phone rang in the kitchen and I got up to go answer it. Connie was calling.

"I meant to phone you yesterday," she told me. "The appraisal is scheduled for Monday. You don't have to be home, of course."

"Well, do I need to clean up?" I glanced around at the mess Jason and I had created.

"No, that doesn't matter, B.J." Then she asked, "How are things going? Have you found a place yet?"

"Nope. Jason's here this weekend."

"Oh, your son ... well, that's terrific."

"He's been very helpful," I commented. "I'm making progress."

"Well, don't you worry, hon. There's still plenty of time ... you've got time."

Just as I hung up, another call came in right away. This time it was Merle. "Hi, Merle," I said into the phone. "What's up?"

"Beej, just checking in to see how it's going," he said.

"As well as to be expected." We fell into a conversation that lasted ten minutes, and then after we hung up, I realized how late it was getting and fixed grilled cheese sandwiches and served Jason some left-over potato salad from the deli.

With all the distractions, we forgot about the conversation involving Liz. One of Jason's high school friends had found out he was in town, so the two of them decided to go out and do some partying on his last night of spring break. Too tired to do much else, I settled for a TV movie and a glass of wine, but ended up nodding off before the story ended. I turned off the set and dragged myself to bed.

Jason must have come home sometime later. I let him sleep in the next morning. I knew he'd be heading back to the university that afternoon.

The rest of April passed quickly. My many hours of research resulted in a catalog of files on my computer, in which I had created a database of potential advertisers in the Lower Valley. These comprised several small towns with Blanca Hills the most prominent.

My goal was to cover all of the towns in the valley. In my research, I followed the advice of my instructor and studied potential competitors. There was only one that stood out as a rival, and that was *The Mountain Sentinel*, a daily newspaper in Blanca Hills. It had been around for decades and had a wide circulation. But I might have an advantage because I hoped to deliver my shopper to everyone in the Lower Valley for free, while the *Sentinel* delivered only to paying subscribers, which were a small part of the population.

I invited Merle and his fiancée, Janie, over one evening in late April, with the purpose of letting Merle read the first draft of my business plan. It had taken me two weeks to put together all the details. While we sat out on the enclosed back porch with dessert and coffee, I proudly presented it to him. Janie craned her neck as she watched him slowly page through the bound document.

I sipped coffee while studying the two of them. Janie was a blonde, who wore heavy eye makeup and had on a silky, copper-colored blouse, black stretch pants and matching sandals. This contrasted with Merle's rather sloppy jeans, running shoes and casual button shirt. She wore fashion eyeglasses and had a narrow nose and a light complexion in contrast with dark lipstick. Every so often her squinty brown eyes would scrunch up while she smiled at me, as if to show off the fact that she was the one who was going to marry Merle. I found it rather comical. Even though Merle and I had a relationship at one time, it was pretty clear to us both that we were not well suited as a couple. At the same time, Merle was the best friend I had at the moment.

"Why is it called the *Buffalo Billboard*?" Merle asked me. "How did you come up with a such a name?"

"It's because of Buffalo Pass," I told him.

"Where's that?" asked Janie.

"Buffalo Pass is between here and Blanca Hills," I replied with a smile.

"It's B.J.'s favorite pass in Colorado," Merle explained as he continued to browse the plan.

"I thought it had a ring to it," I said. "It's a shopper, so *Billboard* seemed appropriate." I sipped my coffee.

"Do you mind if I take this home tonight?" Merle glanced up at me and pushed his glasses further up his nose. "I'd like to study it and maybe I can offer a few suggestions."

Janie looked surprised. "Merle ..."

"Sure, if you want to," I told him, ignoring Janie.

"I'll get it back to you tomorrow. Will you be at work?" asked Merle.

I sat up straighter. "Uh ... I'd rather you didn't bring it to me there." I pushed some bangs out of my eyes. "I haven't told anyone at work."

Merle nodded in understanding. "I see. I'll drop it off here then."

"Mmm ... B.J., this rum cake is scrumptious." Janie spooned another forkful into her mouth and smiled. "You must give me the recipe."

"I bought it at the deli," I confessed.

Later, after they left, I called Jason to see how he was getting along. It had been a couple of weeks since we had last talked. But all I got was his voice mail. I decided not to leave a message. He was probably out with friends or busy with one thing or another.

That night I awoke from a disturbing dream that left me rattled and shaking. In it, my ex-husband Dirk and his wife, Alicia, had dominated the dream with their angry voices blaming me for all of my sister's wrongdoings. I was paralyzed with the shock of having to deny their false allegations, as if I had been the one convicted. In the dream, I tried to get away from them, but couldn't.

What made it worse was seeing Jason as a small child, crying and reaching his little arms up at me and sobbing, "Mama! Mama, why did you do it?" Then a cell door slammed in my face and I turned my head to find my sister, Liz, dressed in an orange jumpsuit, grinning sadistically right at me.

I got out of bed and slipped into my bathrobe. Sobs erupted as I headed into the kitchen for some water. I really wanted to call Jason right *now*—in the middle of the night—and ask him to tell me what those two had discussed with him a few weeks ago involving my sister. I could only imagine what awful lies Dirk had told my son.

Flicking on the stove light, I opened the cupboard and took out a mug, then made myself a cup of tea. Sitting at the kitchen counter five minutes later, I slowly dunked the teabag and allowed myself to remember some of those treacherous times in my past.

I'd chosen to have little to do with Liz after she dropped out of high school her junior year. By then I was a freshman in college, not sure what my major should be. I met Dirk Martin through some friends in my circle on campus. He came from a well-to-do family in California and was having the time of his life with his frat brothers. We hooked up and then we eloped during our last year at the university. Whenever I asked when I was going to meet his parents, he'd shrug and change the subject. So much for my childhood fantasies of an elaborate wedding.

To make things worse, Dirk's parents were mortified when they learned he had married me. There was no hiding the fact that I was not up to their standards, and when I found out I was pregnant the winter before I was to graduate, there was no financial assistance from them. They almost disowned Dirk, who was still working toward his degree in business. He had to get a part-time job, which he resented me for. We lived in campus housing and I worked part-time as a typesetter for the college newspaper, which hardly paid anything at all, except a stipend. But it was a foot in the door for my career in journalism.

Jason was born that August. Dirk and I had both graduated in the spring, and he managed to get hired by a high-end firm, thanks to his parents, who finally came around to half-way accept me because of their new grandson. The next couple of years seemed promising. We moved to Colorado and were able to buy an upscale home in one of the Denver suburbs. Even though I detested living in a metropolis, I didn't have to work. In fact, Dirk insisted that I not work. My job was to keep house, care for our son, and attend business parties that helped propel my husband to the next level of his career. I dreaded those parties. I was always looked down upon and I felt out of place.

I realized that if I didn't do something, the education I had invested in my chosen field, journalism, might go to waste, plus there were student loans to pay back, and Dirk refused to help with those. He had enough on his plate, climbing the corporate ladder and pleasing his family back in California. So I started finding free-lance writing jobs on the side. I learned not to tell Dirk about these because I knew he wouldn't approve. He wanted me home with our child, period. But I felt I had to get out, to interact with people and use my skills as an investigative reporter. I managed to get a bank account in my name that Dirk didn't know about, all the time hoping that things would get better between the two of us. Unfortunately, our relationship was deteriorating.

Liz showed up out of the blue. She had been in and out of prison for various crimes. At first, she convinced me that she was a changed person. I wanted to believe that my sister could be an upstanding citizen and not the loose, selfish teen-ager she had been, sleeping with anyone who would help her get drugs. She was toxic to be around. Friends I had in high school would keep their distance from me when Liz hung out with us. I grew to resent her, yet she was my sister and I hated myself for it.

Jason was two years old when Liz showed up on our doorstep, looking sophisticated and reformed. She may have fooled Dirk, but she didn't fool me. Yet Dirk insisted that we take her in. He felt everyone deserved a second chance. Never mind that Liz had already used up a dozen or more second chances in life, and I didn't believe for a moment that she wouldn't return to her old ways. Yet, I agreed to let her stay until she could find a job and get an apartment. She also was delighted with Jason and he seemed to like her as well.

I sipped at my tea, remembering those dream voices that had yelled at me—Dirk and his present wife, Alicia—accusing me of crimes Liz had committed, *not me*. And the child Jason in my dream, reaching his little arms out to a sister who betrayed me.

Dirk had finally permitted me to go on some assignments, since Liz was staying with us and could watch the baby. I eagerly took jobs to write extensive articles—sometimes a series of them —for various magazines and papers not just in the Denver area, but all over the country. I was beginning to feel confident again and I was gaining valuable writing experience in the publishing world. But after six months of that, I came home one afternoon to find Liz in bed with my husband.

That was the day I packed up some belongings, grabbed my toddler son, and left Dirk. I will never forget the evil sneer on my sister's face, her arms crossed as she stood at the front door of my home and watched me put my son into the car and drive away, sobbing. She and Dirk had been having an affair since the week she had come to stay with us. I was angry, hurt and devastated. It wasn't so much that Dirk had cheated in our marriage, because our intimacy had been dwindling for more than a year. But it was the idea that my own sister had wheedled her way into our home, hoodwinked me into believing perhaps she wasn't a totally bad person after all, and then had committed adultery with my husband, in an ongoing affair right under my roof.

I took the advice of a few friends and sued for divorce and full custody of Jason. I had a good lawyer, but she wasn't good enough. Dirk's family's influence took immediate control of the situation and he won the court battle. His attorney did convince him to give me a monthly appeasement, which he grudgingly gave, but it was not enough to live on. As for Jason, Dirk's attorney convinced the court that our son should be in his father's custody because he had the financial means to care for him.

I remember crying afterwards and pleading with my lawyer, saying, "What about the best interest of the child? Why doesn't the judge take Jason's needs into consideration?" I was, after all, the injured party. And my lawyer told me in a low voice, "This case is different, Bridget. The court appears to believe that the male parent has better means for providing for your son."

"You mean money talks!" I fired, now livid.

She gazed at me sadly and nodded, her eyes darting to the hallway, where Dirk and his parents were laughing and hugging, congratulating themselves for his success. "At least you're getting some kind of settlement," she added.

I didn't see my sister again for many years. She left town. I found another lawyer a couple of years later, and we motioned the court for a change in custody. This time, I discovered that Dirk was willing to compromise. Apparently, he had found out how hard it is to have a burgeoning career in business and raise a young child by himself, even with a live-in nanny.

We compromised and agreed to joint custody of Jason. However, I would not receive any child support. I moved to the Western Slope and rented a duplex, got a job at a newspaper, and began to heal from the wounds Dirk and my sister had inflicted on me and my son. Eventually, we moved to the small town of Dexter and I bought a modest house in a nice neighborhood and went to work for the *Chronicle*.

I knew that Dirk had people watching me. He had strict rules for the "joint custody." I could have Jason most of the year as long as I did not have live-in boyfriends or act in any unethical manner. If he felt I had violated his trust, for the sake of Jason, he would make me go back to court over custody.

Meanwhile, Dirk remarried after Jason and I moved to Dexter. He married Alicia, who was from Salt Lake City, and Dirk's business was now in the state of Utah. Alicia had a daughter, Avery, who was a few years younger than Jason. It seemed that whenever Jason had visitation with his dad, Avery was off somewhere, going to boarding school or visiting relatives. Yet he said he had met her and talked to her a couple of times, and that she was a raving beauty with long black hair and hazel eyes. Dirk and Alicia did not have any more children.

As I finished the last of my tea, I felt exhausted from recalling all of that horrible past. Yet I considered it fortunate that I had been able to raise Jason myself rather than lose him entirely to the clutches of the Martin family and their obscene wealth. Thankfully, Jason seemed to have a level head and could see the hypocrisy of his father and stepmother, who hadn't come from a wealthy family, but certainly acted like it at times.

I dragged myself back to bed, not wanting to think any more. I did not want to dwell on the fact that my sister, Liz, had been found dead in a motel room in Blanca Hills two years ago.

3

There it stood. Buffalo Pass. My Camry emerged from the winding canyon and began to command speed as the highway stretched eastward before me. The domed mountain ahead never ceased to stir excitement in my breast with its majestic mound clothed in an evergreen cloak.

Still twenty-five miles in the distance, its magical presence captivated me. The Colorado blue sky glowed vibrant on this May morning, and wispy clusters of white clouds drifted near the surrounding ridges. Glancing to my left, the more barren mountain range made mostly of adobe clay, darted in and out of view.

As I listened to relaxing, inspiring music from my satellite radio, I had no doubt that today's journey would result in success. This was the day that I would be opening the door to a new life and, hopefully, fulfillment of my dream. I had never felt so free as at this moment ... cruising on this lonely two-lane highway, soaking up all the positive energy from Buffalo Pass.

The morning after my terrible dream, I called the president of Valle Viento State Bank and made an appointment for two o'clock the next day. Valle Viento was the small town just west of Blanca Hills, and I had decided that town would be the headquarters of my valley-wide paper.

In a briefcase in the back seat, I had my business plan, my résumé and references. Sally had granted me the day's leave, not knowing that I was planning to give my notice very soon. If everything worked out the way I hoped, I would give thirty days' notice before quitting my position at the *Dexter Chronicle*. No one from work knew my intentions. I had to keep it that way, in case this didn't work out. After all, there was still the chance the bank would not give me the loan. I wasn't ready to burn any bridges yet.

Gazing out the windshield at the gorgeous Buffalo Dome only added to my assurance that this was my destiny. Under ordinary circumstances, I should have been nervous, but for some reason I wasn't. This new feeling of freedom felt good and overpowered all of the negative "what ifs."

"Mom, I was afraid you were going to chicken out," Jason had told me on the phone last night when I'd called him. "I hope everything goes well for you."

"I'll call you when I know something definite," I had told him, then asked, "Have you heard anything more from your father?"

There was the usual short silence and then the laconic response, "Uh ... yeah ... we talked last weekend."

"And?" I had to pump it out of him sometimes.

Jason sighed. "He wants me to work in Salt Lake again this summer." He did not sound enthused at all.

"I thought you were taking summer classes," I commented.

Jason sighed again. "I need a break from school."

Then I had quickly asked, "What did your dad and Alicia tell you about your Aunt Liz? I have to know."

There was a silence, and then my son let out a sigh. "Mom, I've got finals to study for. I'd better go." It seemed that he wanted to cut our conversation short.

"Okay, darling. I'll talk to you soon," I said, then I nervously added, "Jason ... we really need to talk about that."

"Don't worry, Mom," he promised. "But I really have to go. Bye." The call ended.

I couldn't blame Jason for wanting to cut the conversation short. It obviously was not the right time to spring that on him. I only hoped he hadn't said anything to Dirk about my plans. Jason knew better than I did how anal Dirk could be, and in particular how critical his father was of anything I strove to accomplish.

Out my windshield I marveled once again at the enormous dome-shaped mountain drawing nearer. The road climbed and I marveled at the Ponderosas and mix of Douglas fir and Engelmann spruce. Thoughts of Liz and my dream faded as the Camry climbed the winding highway over the Buffalo Pass summit.

The air felt much cooler and the beauty of these mountains,

contrasted with the sunshine and early buds of aspen trees in spring, ignited more sparks of hope inside of me. I would reach Valle Viento in another hour and a half. A glance at the clock on my display panel reassured me that I still had plenty of time.

Content and confident, I left the summit and headed back down the highway toward my destiny.

It was five minutes before two when my car cruised slowly up the streets of Valle Viento. I gazed around at the buildings and various businesses, thinking about how my newspaper was going to help promote and enrich them in the near future. I pulled up in front of the bank, where there was an empty spot waiting for me, and I smiled to myself, taking note that there were no parking meters in this town.

Gathering my briefcase and my iPhone, I grabbed my purse and keys and climbed out of the car. I felt comfortable and at ease in a blue sleeveless summer dress and white sandals. My dark hair was pulled back in a swishy ponytail as I headed up the sidewalk toward the building. A cool breeze softened the kiss of heat from the sun on my bare arms.

When I entered the bank, I found myself in a small, but elegant lobby. I approached one of the two tellers. "I have an appointment with Mr. Starkmore," I said. "My name is Bridget Martin."

The girl, tall with black tousled hair and heavily lashed brown eyes, smiled at me, then glanced off to her right. "If you'll have a seat, I'll tell him you're here."

I strolled over to a waiting area and sat down, feeling a little fluttery for the first time. An older woman came into the bank and had business with one of the tellers. I fingered the magazines on the table beside me, but before I could decide to pick one up, a man called to me, "Ms. Martin?"

The president of the bank, Mr. Starkmore, stood at the door to his office, a cordial smile on his round face. He was bald with wire-rimmed glasses, wearing an olive green shirt and brown dress pants. No suit, no tie. This was definitely a small town. I stood up and walked over, then shook his hand.

"Pleased to meet you," I said.

He led me into his office and motioned toward a seat in front of a large shiny desk. I sat as he settled down into his big chair. Folding his hands on top of his desk, he gazed at me and asked, "What can I do for you, young lady?"

"I am starting a newspaper in your valley," I said, gripping my briefcase, "and I would like to apply for a business loan."

Mr. Starkmore nodded, puckering his mouth a little as the idea seemed to run through his head. "Very good," he said. "Tell me about it. What are your plans?"

I opened my briefcase and pulled out the carefully formatted folder with the title on the cover, "THE BUFFALO BILLBOARD—Business Plan." He carefully took it from me and crossed his legs as he sat back in his swivel chair, then opened the report.

I sat upright in my seat and stared out the window at traffic moving slowly up and down Willow Street. The bank building was on the corner of the main drag, which was actually the highway that connected one end of the valley to the other, east to west. I had visited the area on several occasions and had always been enchanted by its charm, its people, most of whom were descendants of Spanish heritage with some Native American mixed in. One of the oldest Catholic churches was in one of the valley's towns thirty miles south, and a small state university was in Blanca Hills, just fifteen miles east.

Jason had actually started out as a freshman at Blanca State University, but had transferred to Boulder the following year. I loved the area, the beauty of the mountains, the friendly people and their heritage and cultural influence. It was not an area of the state that had great affluence, but that was probably the reason for the population not growing as quickly as other places in Colorado. I was drawn here time and again, and now—with any luck—I would be starting a new life and hoped to offer something lucrative and exciting for the community.

Mr. Starkmore took his time reading through my entire presentation. I had spent the last two weeks tweaking it, and utilizing the skills I had picked up in the course I had taken at Dexter's community college. I had memorized my talking points and was looking forward to answering the bank president's questions.

Finally, he set the booklet down on his desk and looked at me. "I must say, I'm impressed with your plan," he said. "You've put a lot of effort into this, and I can see by your résumé that you have plenty of experience in the newspaper field."

"I know just about every job there is that has to do with publishing a paper," I told him. I explained how I'd worked as typesetter, proofreader, reporter, assistant editor, production manager, as well as in circulation and distribution. I'd worked for five different papers and a couple of magazines since graduating with my journalism arts degree in college.

"Why here?" asked Mr. Starkmore. "Why did you choose Valle Viento, of all places?"

I told him. I explained about the many times I had come here just to experience the beauty and the homeyness of a small town community. I explained how my son had attended college in Blanca Hills, and how I thought that bringing a small town newspaper—a shopper—might help boost the economy in not only Valle Viento, but the entire valley as I planned to distribute to each town.

"Will you have subscriptions?" he asked me.

"No," I said. "I'll mail it free to every address. The wide circulation will ensure that everyone gets a paper every week, and the advertising will pay for it all."

He opened the plan and paged through it again. "I see you have listed the businesses in the entire Lower Valley. How are you going to get them to advertise?"

I explained my intention of hiring a couple of ad sales reps who would work on commission alone, at least in the beginning, and how our first month would offer half-price advertising. Once the community saw the paper, they'd feel prompted to get involved. Being a shopper, anyone could place classified ads, which would cost very little and in some cases would cost nothing at all. I stressed the popularity of local shoppers across the nation, and how I had gotten my first job as a teenager, delivering papers at the shopper in my home town.

"What about the competition?" asked the bank president.

"I know about the other papers in the valley," I told him. "I've studied them. I think this valley needs some new blood. It definitely needs a shopper. People love them ... and they're *free*."

Then I remembered the magic words the instructor at the business course had told me to use. "And I'll be hiring people to help put out this paper," I said. "It's the multiplier effect. The *Buffalo Billboard* is going to bring prosperity to Valle Viento and the neighboring towns." I looked directly into the bank president's eyes. "My paper is going to make a difference."

Mr. Starkmore nodded his head, still studying my plan. "And how much money do you think it will take to get your business off the ground?" he asked.

I was prepared for this and had thought everything through carefully. I told him the amount I wanted to borrow, and then he asked me about collateral. I told Mr. Starkmore about the pending sale of my property in Dexter and pulled the copy of my contract out of my briefcase. He scanned the papers and nodded in approval. "A major portion of that money will go into a holding account," I added.

"Well, Ms. Martin, let me give this some serious consideration," said Mr. Starkmore. He handed back my real estate contract. "May I keep the business plan?"

I nodded. "Yes, of course. I have a copy."

"Of course you do." He chuckled. "I'm impressed with your presentation, and I will give you a call tomorrow afternoon about the loan." He pushed his chair back and stood up. I rose from my seat and he offered his hand once again.

"Thank you, Mr. Starkmore," I said, pleased that everything had gone well, even though I couldn't be sure yet if I was going to get the business loan.

I felt pleased with myself after I left the bank. My spirits soared. Instead of getting into my car right away and heading back over the pass, I decided to walk down Willow Street and bask in my optimism. Mr. Starkmore had been impressed enough to possibly give me the loan I needed, and I already felt a part of this town. When I passed someone on the sidewalk, I couldn't help but smile. They smiled back at me. Everything was rosy.

Before turning around to go back to my car, I passed a building that was on the other side of the street. It was empty and had a sign on the door that read FOR RENT. When traffic cleared, I crossed the street and walked up to peer inside the windows of the building. It looked like it had been a storefront of some kind. There were windows with vertical shades, so I couldn't really see what was inside. But it was large enough and perhaps there were rooms for offices.

Excited, I jotted the phone number down, then pulled out my iPhone and made a call.

A man with a foreign accent answered and said, "Hay-lo."

"Hello," I said into my iPhone. "My name is Bridget Martin. I'm calling about the building you have for rent on Willow Street."

"Oh! Ya. You need an office?"

"Yes," I told him. "I'm opening an office fairly soon, and I need a place to set up a new business."

"What kind of shop will you haff?" he asked.

"It's a newspaper."

"Oh! *Goot!*"

"I need to ask ... does the building have any rooms in the back?"

"Ya! It hass. Five rooms it hass."

"Is it possible for me to see it?" I asked. "And, how much are you asking for the rent?"

The man on the other end of the line let out a big sigh as he pondered, but then he said, "I ask five hundret."

"Five hundred dollars? For a month?" I hoped he wasn't going to say five hundred a week.

"Ya ... *und* five hundret deposit."

"Of course."

"When you wanna see?"

"Well," I said, "I'm going to have to head back to Dexter shortly. I could make an appointment to see the building the next time I'm in town."

"Why not see it now?" he asked enthusiastically. "Where are you now?"

I told him I was standing in front of it.

"I come show it now," he told me. "You'll see it is goot price."

"How soon?" I asked.

"I will be there in half an hour," he said. "I live in Blanca Hills."

"Oh, I see. Well, okay then, I'll see it today. Uh ... what is your name?"

"Otto Breitbart."

When we ended the call, I looked around and decided to find a café where I could get a sandwich. I hadn't had any lunch and I was suddenly quite hungry. On my way back to my car, I passed a little café across from the bank and stepped inside. It was quiet in the middle of the afternoon and I took a seat near a sunny window at a small table. A waitress brought a menu and a glass of water, and I ordered a chimichanga with a glass of iced tea.

Wouldn't it be amazing, I thought, if the building turned out to be the one for my office? After all my research, I had selected the town of Valle Viento because of its proximity to the other towns in the valley. Blanca Hills, of course, was the county seat and a larger town with more businesses, but I liked the quaintness of Valle Viento. It was possible to call any of the other surrounding towns without having to pay a long distance land-line charge. It was necessary to cut costs as much as I could.

Jason crossed my mind as the waitress brought my drink. I sipped it, waiting for the food. I knew my son was cramming for exams right now. Next week he'd be done with school until the fall. Would he follow his father's advice and return to Salt Lake City all summer? He could have stayed on campus and taken summer classes, but apparently he was getting burned out. I remembered all too well how it was when I was 20 years old and in college.

My son had been an easy child to raise. As an infant he had never given me any trouble, and he had been calm and wise even as a toddler. There had been no "terrible twos," and the only problems stemmed when he spent too much time around Dirk and Alicia.

Jason had been the focus of my life for the last two decades. He was my world, and I had spent my time and energy making life easier for my boy. I had to feel proud. Jason had grown into a well groomed, well educated and well mannered young man. I tried not to let it irritate me whenever Dirk, and especially Alicia, bragged to others about my son, claiming responsibility for his poise and intellect.

The waitress brought my chimichanga and a dish of tortilla chips and salsa, pregnant with cilantro. I dug into my meal, wondering if the bank president was going to help me fulfill my dream. Well, I would know by this time tomorrow, perhaps. And here I was ... chewing a chimichanga in a little Mexican café in Valle Viento, having applied for my business loan, and about to meet a German man who might become my landlord.

I quickly finished my food, drank the rest of my iced tea, and touched my mouth with the napkin. When the waitress brought my tab, I paid it and left a couple of dollars on the table for a tip. A glance at my iPhone said that in five minutes Mr. Breitbart would arrive at the office building. If everything looked okay, I would agree to rent it ... contingent on getting my loan, of course.

4

An older Ford 4x4 truck had pulled up in front of the office building that was for rent. As I approached, a tall man with gray tousled hair, bushy eyebrows and a gray beard stepped out. He was dressed in plaid shorts and a white V-neck T-shirt that did little to hide a bulging belly. Gray hair grew on his forearms and his bare legs. Slip-on red sneakers with no socks indicated he'd probably just jumped into his truck to drive over from Blanca Hills.

"Are you Mr. Breitbart?" I asked, stopping a few feet in front of him.

"Otto. Call me Otto, please," he said with a warm smile. He extended his hand and I shook it. "Come inside. Look around." He ushered me inside the office building and turned on the overhead lights.

I found myself in a large empty room carpeted in beige. The building was old with dark paneled walls, but it appeared clean. Large blinded windows took up the front, and I noticed right away a small office that opened into the room to my left. I walked over and glanced inside. There was no door between the office and the big room, but there was a second entrance on the side. The room was adequate for my needs, although I would have preferred a door I could close for privacy.

He beckoned me out and we walked to the rear of the large room. A privacy wall separated the room and revealed a kitchen area with a counter and a short hallway that led to a storage area and a single bathroom. Peeking inside, I saw the stool and sink, but no shower.

"Are there any other bathrooms?" I asked. I had seen another door we had passed, making our way to the kitchen.

"No," he replied. "Follow me." He then led me back through to the door that opened up into a second large room. There were no windows, but the room appeared large enough for storage needs and I noticed a door that was probably a closet. Opening it, I peeked in, but it was dark and narrow. Thinking it was just a closet, I closed it up and followed him back out into the main room.

"This used to be a store," he told me.

"Oh, what kind of store?" I asked.

Otto shrugged. "I don't know ... some kind of clothing shop. The built'ing has been empty for a lot of months."

"I see. Well ..." I looked around again and started imagining where desks could be placed and where I would set the light table and file cabinets. The building was certainly large enough for a newspaper office, though I had hoped the bathroom would have a shower. I planned to stay there during the preparation period. At some point I would look for an apartment to rent. Otto walked around, checking things while I pondered and strolled back into the kitchen, then the small office without the door.

"Okay," I finally said. "If you don't mind, I'll need to give you my answer in a few days." I had to be sure the bank would be giving me the loan before I committed to renting an office.

Otto nodded his head and followed me out, turning off the lights as he locked up. We exchanged information and then he climbed into his Ford truck and I walked back down the street to my parked car in front of the bank. My head was swirling with thoughts. The building was centrally located, which was good. It was large enough, and it had a back room and plenty of parking out front. I knew it was probably a good find. I had been studying the local newspaper's classifieds lately and there hadn't been a lot of commercial rentals.

When I got to my car, I sat inside for a couple of minutes to reflect. It seemed surreal. Here I was in Valle Viento, on the verge of having my own business—my own newspaper—and it was like a dream come true. But what if Mr. Starkmore called me up tomorrow and said he couldn't give me the loan?

What was scarier to me right now was ... what happened if he did?

The trip back to Dexter over Buffalo Pass was relaxing, and my mind was filled with possibilities as I put on some music and decided just to enjoy the beautiful mountain scenery and not worry about the future. By the time evening shadows were settling over my town, I pulled into my driveway, tired but excited about what prospects tomorrow would bring.

A t work the next morning, Sally asked if I had enjoyed my day off. I smiled and told her yes, but offered nothing more, and she didn't press me for details. It wasn't in Sally's nature to talk about anyone's personal life unless they brought it up first. She never talked about her own life, unless asked, and even then, she didn't say much about it.

She usually just sat at her big desk by the window, focused on whatever task that was before her. I had always had the impression that my supervisor felt she was above everyone else at the *Chronicle*. Sometimes even Zach, the assistant editor, who was a lot younger than the two of us women.

I went home for lunch that day, mostly to check my answering machine, in case the bank had called and left a message on my land line. I had given both my cell and home phone number. There were no messages. After I returned to the office, I worked on some data entry in the circulation department and around three o'clock, my cell phone buzzed. I saw that it was from an area code from the Lower Valley and answered it.

"Hello, this is Bridget."

"Good afternoon, Ms. Martin," said the voice of the bank president from Valle Viento. "This is Edward Starkmore at Valle Viento State Bank. How are you?"

"I'm well," I replied, my heart starting to race. What would the answer be?

"Good," he chuckled, "because I have good news for you. The bank is going to lend you the money to start your newspaper."

I gasped, excited. But before I could comment, he spoke again.

"However … we can't give you the full amount you requested."

"Oh," I said, my eyes darting around the room to see if it was safe to talk. I instinctively stood up from my desk and headed for the back door. I wanted to keep my conversation private.

"I believe we can give you at least 75 percent of what you asked for," continued Mr. Starkmore. He began explaining the details of the loan, including the amount I would borrow, as I stepped out the door and was greeted by the hot afternoon sun. "All of this depends, of course, on you investing a percentage of the pay-off on your house sale as collateral," he concluded.

"Thank you," I told him, my hand on my heart.

"Now when is your closing?" he asked.

"In two weeks," I said.

"Fine. I'll draw up the papers. When are you coming to the valley again?"

We discussed the details. I realized that from this point on, there was no turning back. I was committed. I would have to give notice to the *Chronicle* sooner than I had anticipated. It also meant another trip to Valle Viento to set things in motion. We ended the conversation and I went back inside the office. It was hard to concentrate on my work the rest of the afternoon, but I managed to keep from showing my emotions and left the office at five.

I tried calling Jason first, but it went right to voice mail. I left him a message to call me when he had a chance, and then I phoned Merle. I got his voice mail as well, but I left a short, excited announcement before driving home, so happy that I giggled and sang along to music on the radio.

There was suddenly so much to do. I had to get papers filed with the Secretary of State, register my trade name, call Otto Breitbart to secure the office rental, order supplies, hire employees! I hardly knew what to do first. Suddenly, I wished more than anything I had someone to help me, to be my second-in-command, to lean on for moral support. For the first time, I realized I was on my own. I would have to do everything myself until I got the ship up and running. I was about to face the biggest challenge of my life.

5

Merle was the first to offer me congratulations. I had left a message on his cell, and when he phoned me that evening, I could tell he was genuinely thrilled for me.

"So how come you're not getting the full amount you asked for?" he joked.

"It doesn't really matter. I'm going to make this work," I insisted.

"You're going to need a website," Merle suggested.

"Well, I've actually been toying with a theme," I said.

"Mind if I help? I won't charge an arm and a leg."

"I was hoping you might say that." I laughed. "I'm going to need somebody to manage the on line presence." Then I heard Janie's voice in the background.

Merle put his hand over the microphone and a few seconds later said, "Gotta go. Bye, Beej."

"Later, Merle." I hung up.

I spent the evening packing and thinking about all the tasks ahead of me. I'd decided that my shopper would publish its first issue in early August. That gave me less than three months.

Jason called me when I was preparing for bed. "Mom, I'm sorry I didn't call earlier," he said. "I finished my finals today. I'm happy you got the loan."

"Thanks, Jason. When's your last day in Boulder, or are you taking summer classes after all?"

"Nope." He sighed. "Dad still wants me in Salt Lake, but if I get a job *elsewhere* …" He lingered, waiting for me to fill in the blank.

I immediately picked up on his thought and let out a gasp. "Jason! Why don't you come and work for *me*? I'm going to need someone to be my distribution manager, and you know the Lower Valley really well."

"That sounds like something I could do," he said.

Then I added, "I can also teach you how to design ads. With your computer expertise and artistic ability, you're exactly what I need."

"Hey, yeah ..." I could tell he was growing more enthusiastic about the idea. "When are you moving down there?"

"Actually, I found some office space to rent in Valle Viento," I revealed. "Now that I have the loan, I'm going to call Mr. Breitbart and rent it from him. There are rooms in back where we can stay until we find an apartment to rent. How does that sound?"

Jason sounded relieved and excited. We discussed a few more things and then ended the call. I felt recharged with the idea of Jason joining me on this venture. It wasn't until later that evening, as I was preparing for bed, that I remembered we still had not discussed what Dirk and Alicia had told him about my sister Liz. I had to make a point of getting Jason to open up about that.

The next morning at work, I invited myself into Zach's office and asked him to call Sally to join us. He raised a dark eyebrow as he paged her, and I made myself comfortable in the chair in front of his desk. Two minutes later, Sally walked in with a smile and stared at me curiously. Zach motioned to her to take a seat.

"Now what's up, B.J.?" asked Zach, his hands folded in front of him on the desk.

"I am giving my notice," I said with a smile. I watched as both their mouths opened in surprise.

"Why?" asked Zach.

A second later, Sally asked, "When?"

"I am moving to the Lower Valley," I told them. "I am starting my own paper there." When neither one of them responded, I continued, "It's time for me to start living my dream. For a long time I've wanted to start a shopper in that area. I've spent months doing the research and now it's happening."

"When are you leaving us?" Zach sounded worried. Sally merely smiled.

"Well, originally I was going to give a month's notice," I confessed, "but with the circumstances of the sale of my house here in Dexter, I'd like to move down there in two weeks."

Both of them were silent for a few seconds as the news sank in. Then, Sally sighed and said, "We need to get a help wanted ad in the next paper." She stared at me. "Who am I going to find to replace you, Beej?"

Zach leaned forward on his desk and held his dark curly head. "Who is going to do the coding on the website?" he asked, more to himself than anyone else.

"How about your new web master?" I asked with a straight face.

Sally smiled smugly, her arms folded, and she looked from me to Zach. "Stan should be able to do it," she said.

"But ..." Zach shook his head in frustration. "Oh wow... you're going to have to show Stan what you do," Zach told me, looking worried.

"I thought he knew everything," said Sally, for once taking my side. "After all, isn't that why you hired him?" She stood up and headed for the door. "I have to get back to work."

I suppressed a smile and stared into Zach's brown eyes. "Of course I'll show Stan how to format the stories. I'm just surprised that ... well, that's neither here nor there, now is it?" I stood up.

"Okay. Thanks, B.J." Zach nodded at me as I turned to walk out the room. Then he called out, "We're going to miss you. I mean sorely."

I returned to the production room to continue my work for the day, and soon the office was buzzing with the news that I had given my notice. People from other departments came in, one by one, to ask me about my new venture, but I gave little information. I had work to do, and Sally was on the phone a lot, sounding worried. I knew I had caused a disruption, but there was little I could do about it now.

On Saturday I drove the 200 miles to Valle Viento. I had called Otto Breitbart and we met at my new office building to sign the lease. I wrote out a check for the security deposit and first month's rent. Now that he had some money in his hand, Otto had a twinkle in his blue eyes and took me through the rooms once more, pointing out the air conditioner, explaining the heating system, and other details. I learned that there were other offices on the other side of the wall behind the building. I hadn't realized this.

"Don't worry," he said. "They all haff their own entrances." One was a jewelry store, another a thrift shop, and a small insurance agency, all with storefronts on the adjoining road. I was just relieved that Otto would be paying my utilities, except for the phone and Internet.

"Do you know someone in the area who makes signs?" I asked as we walked back out front. He wrote down a name on a slip of paper and gave it to me. I also told him I needed to find an accountant, and he knew of one in Blanca Hills. With a smile, Otto wished me well and left the building.

The rest of the day, I pored over office supply catalogs, making a list of the furniture and other things I needed to set up my business. I was tempted to go all out and lavishly furnish the office, yet I knew I had to stay within budget. I did not want to make the mistake of overspending without knowing if this was going to be a success or not. On Monday I would call the phone company and local Internet service, set up an on-line banking account, and start designing forms and promotional materials.

On the drive back over Buffalo Pass, a deer startled me and I had to slam on the brakes. Fortunately, I missed the doe, who quickly understood she needed to get out of the way. My heart was racing and I said a prayer of thanks for being lucky enough not to have hit the animal. My mind had been on Jason and how he was going to handle this decision with his father.

I cruised more carefully down the west side of the pass, my pulse returning to its normal rate. Music from the radio was playing old classics from my high school years, and I listened as one brought to my mind an image of my sister, Liz. It was while we were still young enough to not have differences. She had been wild even in her pre-teen years, yet we had suffered our disagreements on a more innocent level. I smiled as I recalled that we had actually had fun together a few times during our childhood.

Then my mind shot ahead to two years ago, when Liz had been living in Blanca Hills. She had moved around a lot, been in relationships—most of them disastrous—and ended up dead. The official cause of death had been "accidental overdose," yet I could not forget the disturbing phone message Liz had sent me two weeks before she was found. She had reached out to me for help. She had said she didn't feel safe anymore, and that she needed to talk to me about something important.

Now I sighed with regret. I had long written off my sister as a hopeless case, especially after her affair with Dirk which led to the divorce. I couldn't forgive her, especially with all the legal hassles that ensued with Jason stuck in the middle of it all. She had never apologized for the affair, nor had she bothered to contact me all those years in between, which had been fine with me. Still, the phone message gnawed at me. I had disregarded it at the time. Yet I had often wondered, what if I had reached out to my sister in her desperate time of need? Would it have made a difference? Would she still be alive today?

The week passed swiftly with all of the things I had to do, not just for my impending new job, but also with the closing coming up on my house. I rented a storage shed, hoping I would only need it for a month, or two at the most. Then I started moving the smaller boxes over.

Sally let me have Friday off, so I once again drove to the Lower Valley. There were some things I needed to take care of that couldn't be done on weekends. It was a warm day, now mid-May, and I had appointments lined up with the accountant, the sign maker, and some bank business.

It was after three-thirty when I pulled into the parking lot of *The Mountain Sentinel* in Blanca Hills, the daily newspaper that served the entire Lower Valley—my competition. The large, two-story brick building was on a side street off the main highway. The parking lot had trees for shade as I found a spot between a black pickup truck and a silver Porsche.

The newspaper office was not as busy as I'd expected. Two front office girls were at the reception desk, one on the phone. The other, a tall redhead with glasses, smiled at me in greeting. "May I help you?"

"I need to place some classified ads," I said.

She reached under the counter and pulled out a pad with forms for filling out classifieds. I stared at it as she handed me a ballpoint pen. It was rather drab in design, I noticed with criticism. I had already designed what the *Buffalo Billboard's* classified forms would look like, with the logo of the buffalo in the top left-hand corner. The girl directed me to a seat against the wall, and I sat down to write up my ads.

"When is your deadline?" I asked.

"Two o'clock for the next day's edition," she told me. "Your ad won't go in until Tuesday."

I was looking for ad sales people and a receptionist for the *Buffalo Billboard*. I did not want to reveal the name of my business in the ad, but did include that it was for a weekly newspaper starting up in the valley. When I finished writing out my ads, I handed them to the girl at the desk, who read through them as I pulled out my credit card.

She looked at me curiously, flashed a smile, then counted the words and gave me the price. I told her I wanted to run the ad for a week, then gave her the credit card. She printed out the receipt, then grinned at me. "Good luck," she said with a wink.

I left the building and headed back to my car. A man was standing next to the silver Porsche, staring at my Camry. He was tall with a slender build, light-colored hair, probably in his late 30's. He was dressed in a light blue short-sleeved shirt and wore a navy tie and gray slacks. He turned to face me as I approached.

"Hello," I said with a polite smile.

His green eyes swept me from head to toe and his return smile was friendly and included a dimple. "Is this your car?" he asked.

"Why...yes, am I in a reserved spot?" At once I was concerned.

His hand, large and strong with a brush of light body hair, stroked his chin as he glanced at my wheels. "Did you know you have a low tire?"

I saw that my left rear tire was a bit low, but not flat—not yet. I sighed. "Oh, great ..."

"There's a tire shop just down the road," the man told me, still smiling as he regarded me closely. "They'll check it out for you. You probably have a slow leak."

I smiled. "Thank you."

"Uh ..." He gestured toward the building. "Are you here to apply for the job?"

Baffled, I looked up at him and shook my head. "No, I just came in to place some classified ads."

"Oh, I see." He nodded, somewhat disappointed.

"What job?" I asked out of curiosity.

"Copy editor," he replied.

"No," I said with a smile. "Are you applying for the job?"

"No, I'm already employed," he said modestly, sweeping a lock of light-colored hair that had fallen over his right eye.

I smiled at him again and opened my car door. "Well, thanks for the heads up about my tire."

"Anytime," he said, still standing in the same spot, gazing at me. "I take it you're not looking for a job then," he added.

"No. Why?" I gazed at him curiously before I climbed into the driver's seat.

"Because if you were, I'd probably offer you the position."

I looked at him in surprise. "You?" I looked over at the newspaper building. "Well then, you must be ..."

Before I could finish the sentence, he thrust his right hand out toward me and said, "I'm Grant Tucker. I own *The Mountain Sentinel*."

Immediately my pulse quickened and I tried not to show my surprise as I slowly shook his hand, staring into his face. This was my competitor! "I'm ... I'm Bridget Martin," I finally said with a smile.

"Nice to meet you, Bridget. I'm looking for a copy editor," he disclosed, studying me more closely.

I couldn't help chuckling as I stared at the ground. "Do I *look* like an editor?"

Grant's mouth puckered a little and then he shrugged. "No ... you don't," he finally replied.

I couldn't help laughing a little as I opened my car door. "Well, I guess that says it all," I told him, wondering how he thought an editor should look.

"Well, I'm sorry, but we really need to find someone," he said with a smile. "I thought maybe ..."

"Good luck," I told him, repeating what the front desk girl had said to me. Then I climbed into my Camry, started the engine and shot him another smile as I slowly backed out of my parking space.

I was aware of him watching me the whole time I drove off. He had taken me by surprise. I hadn't expected to come face to face with the publisher of the *Sentinel*, and such a handsome one at that! I almost forgot that my tire was low and, just in the nick of time, pulled into the tire shop half a block away.

6

Jason called that weekend. He had moved out of the dorm and was now in Salt Lake City, visiting his father. He wanted to break the news to them in person that he had decided to work for me in Valle Viento. I was surprised to learn that Dirk had applauded his decision.

"I'm just as surprised as you are," Jason confessed. "I think at first they were skeptical. Dad seems to think you're destined to fail."

"Oh, so they're thinking we'll both only be there through the summer," I surmised. Then I asked him, "When are you coming to the valley?"

Jason said he planned on spending the week with them and would travel back to Colorado the following weekend. "Avery's supposed to be coming home," he added. "I always seem to miss seeing her, so this is my chance. Did you know I haven't seen Avery since I was in high school?"

After we hung up, I thought about the mysterious Avery. She was Alicia's daughter, yet Dirk had adopted her when they had gotten married, so Avery's last name was also Martin, yet she was a stepsister to Jason and about two or three years younger. Why they had sent her to boarding school on the East Coast had always puzzled me. I had decided that probably her birth father's relatives were helping raise her. I couldn't think of any other plausible explanation, plus I had never met her face to face.

Well, I was glad that Jason would get a chance to see Avery, and maybe get to know her better before moving to the valley. Then I remembered that Jason and I still had not discussed what Dirk and Alicia had told him about Liz. It had become quite the elusive topic.

In fact, that very night I dreamed again about my sister. This time she was in Salt Lake City, visiting Jason, his father and Alicia, and they treated her in a welcoming manner, as if she were a trusted old friend who had dropped in to spend a night or two in their elaborate home with its swimming pool and view of the Wasatch mountains.

In the dream, she and Jason were laughing and talking in their large living area, and I was there in the corner, merely as an observer. No one paid any attention to me. Then, when the doorbell rang, everyone stood up in excitement, and Alicia announced, "It must be Avery!" We all moved into the foyer to greet her, but I woke up at that point.

Because I did not want to go back into that same dream, I got out of bed, turned on my bedside lamp, and walked through the house in my robe, trying to wipe the dream memory from my mind. Boxes were piled in every room now. I had mixed feelings about leaving Dexter. After the coming week, I would say goodbye to my secure job at the *Chronicle*. What was I getting into? Was I going to make a success of the *Buffalo Billboard?* What would happen if, like Dirk predicted, I failed?

That thought was unthinkable. After all, months had gone into planning and preparing for this upcoming venture. I had experience in every aspect of the business, except perhaps the bookkeeping end, but I was hiring a good accountant to do all of the tax work, payroll and reports. But the responsibility! I would be the sole proprietor and responsible for everything happening from this point on. Still, what if something went wrong?

I wandered through all the rooms of my dark house, feeling suddenly insecure. The towering boxes stacked against the walls seemed overwhelming. Finally, I decided I had to go back to bed. But then I lay awake for a long while, wrestling with the intruding thoughts that scolded me for daring to change my life so drastically. What had I been thinking?

At some point, sleep won out. I slept without any more dreams of Liz.

The next morning I had my coffee out on the back patio. The sun was warming up the day and birds were singing in the neighborhood. I realized this was the beginning of my last week in my cozy house. One week from today, I would be sleeping in the back room of my office in Valle Viento. Office furniture that I had ordered would arrive the following week. Thankfully, Jason would be there to help me set everything up.

My cell phone rang later that morning, after I'd cleaned up my breakfast dishes. I answered it, having noticed the area code from southern Colorado.

"My name is Peg Espinoza," the woman on the other end told me. "I saw your ad in *The Mountain Sentinel*, and I'm curious about the job."

I thanked her for calling, then grabbed a pen and notepad off the counter, so I could take notes. "Do you have experience?" was my first question.

"As a matter of fact, I do." Peg laughed. "I used to sell ads before I moved to Blanca Hills from Arizona. I have references. Tell me about your weekly."

Our conversation lasted about five minutes. Peg was easy to talk with, and we arranged for her to come by the office after next weekend. I took down her information and sighed with relief as the call ended. She was the first person to respond to the help wanted ad for sales. Later in the week, I had three other calls from women who wanted a chance to interview with me. One of them wanted the receptionist job.

The closing was Friday of that next week, which was also my final day at the *Dexter Chronicle*. I met Connie, my agent, at the title company that morning at ten o'clock. The new owners were there as well. Fortunately, it didn't take long. The couple, from Texas, were middle-aged and excited about moving into my house, which suddenly was no longer my home. The movers were coming the next morning to clear everything out and take my furniture and most of the boxes to the storage unit in Dexter.

The proceeds of the sale were wired to the bank in Valle Viento, most of which were going into the bank's collateral account for my business loan. I had my hands full, tying up loose ends and packing my car with what I'd need to start a new life.

Merle and Janie had rented a small truck, and we loaded my bed and a few other pieces of furniture I wanted to take, so that I could set up temporary quarters in my office. We had just finished loading my house plants and what was left in my refrigerator when the new owners showed up to claim the house. I suddenly felt sentimental as I handed over the keys and looked at the house where Jason had spent his growing-up years. There had been some happy times, some lonely times, but mostly security. Now I was leaving for something entirely new, and I didn't know when or where I'd have a house again.

Janie decided at the last minute that she wanted to ride along with me to Valle Viento. Merle drove ahead in the rental truck, and I followed, glad that I had Janie to keep me from feeling sad. But after half an hour, her constant chit-chat started to annoy me. She loved to gossip, and I always made it a point not to tell her too much about my personal life, even though she wanted to pump it out of me.

Four long hours later, we reached our destination. It was late afternoon and we unloaded the truck first. Then, I treated my friends to dinner that evening at a small restaurant in Blanca Hills. We were all tired, and I thought Merle would want to get a motel. Instead, he and Janie decided to drive back to Dexter that night. I thanked them for all they'd done to help me, and promised Merle I'd get him what he needed to start setting up the *Billboard's* new website.

"Be careful going over that pass," I warned them, remembering how animals loved to cross the highway at night.

I walked into my new office and suddenly felt nervous. The first thing I did was lock the door and secure the deadbolt, then I went to close all the blinds on the windows. I gazed around at the empty big room, then wandered through the hallway to the kitchen area, where I had set my microwave on the counter, and made sure the small dorm refrigerator was cooling.

In the back room, we had set up the bed and a small chest of drawers. I had some unpacking to do, but I was too exhausted right then and needed to settle in for the night. I turned on a small table lamp and got into my suitcase, searching for my toothbrush. Not having a shower in the office bathroom meant that I would have to buy a pass at the local gym, where I could go to grab a shower at least. I had already checked into the cost and it was reasonable.

"Tomorrow is Monday," I said to myself as I slipped under the covers of my bed a while later and reached for the book I was reading. Peg Espinoza was supposed to come in around noon. On Tuesday I was having some more interviews of prospective employees. Jason would arrive either the next day or Tuesday, I wasn't sure when. "It's really happening." I smiled, looking around at the stark concrete walls and feeling cozy for the first time, even with all the boxes piled around me. "I'm living my dream."

The delivery truck arrived Monday morning with my new office furniture and supplies, including computers and printers, filing cabinets, telephones, office chairs and a reception desk. I would put Jason to work assembling everything once he arrived. Meanwhile, I had to get ready for prospective employees I needed to interview that day.

I walked up the street to the little café and ordered a breakfast burrito to go. Back in the office, I made a pot of coffee and ate while going over some points I would discuss in the interviews.

At ten o'clock a woman walked through the front door, wearing a denim skirt with rhinestones, a matching denim jacket over a white tank top. Her honey-colored hair was gathered in a ponytail and green eyes smiled at me as I stood up to greet her.

"Peg Espinoza?" I reached out and shook her hand. She grinned. Her face was pleasant with high cheek bones, and she wore no makeup.

"Yes, I am," she said, then set her rhinestone handbag down on a chair and gazed around the room. "So this is it ... nice!"

I had to laugh. "It may not look like a newspaper office yet, but it will." I invited her to join me at one of the tables I had set up that was piled with unopened office supplies.

"Oh, this is exciting." Peg's eyes gleamed as she took a seat and grinned at me. "I like it already." She studied me a moment, then asked, "What should I call you?"

"Bridget," I replied, then added, "or B.J."

"I like B.J.," she said. "What does the J stand for?"

"Jeannette," I disclosed.

"Ah." Peg rested her arms on the table and then asked, "When is your first paper coming out?"

"August sixth," I replied, wondering what I should ask her first. But before I could interview her, Peg pulled a small notepad and a pen from her handbag and started jotting notes.

"Now tell me, B.J., what are your ideas for ad rates, and what sort of commission are you offering your sales people?"

I had my ad rates already on a card, and fished them out of my pile of notes. She studied them intently while I explained that I would be offering 35 percent commission on display ads along with a gasoline allowance while on the job.

Peg smiled and nodded, writing it all down. "I know how newspapers work," she told me. "That sounds fair. Paid by the week or by the month?"

"Biweekly," I replied.

"You're doing a shopper," she continued. "What will you be charging for classified ads?"

I told her the figures I had come up with, then showed her my list of classified ad categories. I emphasized to her that the classifieds were the "meat and potatoes" of the publication and that we would need to gather as many classified ads as possible for the first few issues, until people began to take advantage of the service. "And so I believe we should offer all classified ads for free for the first month," I concluded.

Peg grinned and I was pleased with her genuine interest and smiling face. She reached over and grabbed my hand, and said with a wide grin, "B.J. Martin, you are a genius! This venture of yours is going to be a tremendous boon to this valley." She then asked if I would show her around the building.

I was impressed with Peg and couldn't help liking her, despite her forward personality. She was obviously a go-getter and the perfect person for the sales position. She was experienced and worldly, and I learned that she had worked in a middle school as a substitute teacher when she and her husband had lived in Arizona. They had no children, but they lived on the east side of rural Blanca Hills. She was about my age and I already felt we'd been longtime friends.

Before she left, she turned to me with a serious face and said, "I think you should hire more than one salesperson."

"Well," I replied, "I had thought about maybe hiring someone else."

"No," she said, "you need to hire a *lot* of them. If we are going to compete with *The Mountain Sentinel*, we need to infiltrate this valley."

"How many do you think I should hire?" I was worried about my costs.

"B.J., at least three more. At least!" She started out the door, then turned around. "I'll come in tomorrow and help you get things organized. And then we'll see about finding some other people for you to hire."

"Uh … sure." I couldn't help smiling as she left the building. She had a domineering personality, but I liked Peg. She was genuine, even if she was a tad overbearing. I needed someone like that to get my business off the ground.

That afternoon, I hired Aspen Collins to be my receptionist. Aspen was young, just a couple of years out of high school, and already had a toddler. She really needed the job as her husband drove truck over the road, and she was basically supporting herself and her child until work picked up for him. Aspen's family had roots in the valley and were of Spanish heritage. She appeared to be a bright girl, small in stature but with intelligent brown eyes and soft, reddish brown hair that she kept short and well styled. She was good with numbers and could type. She seemed eager to learn new things and was willing to put in five days a week.

Another woman came by to interview, but I had already made up my mind to hire Aspen. I still went through the interview with her and told the girl I'd let her know. She was also young and much quieter than Aspen, though she too insisted she needed a job.

It was getting toward the dinner hour when Jason pulled up. I was relieved that he'd arrived and helped him bring his things into the back room. He was going to fix up a corner for himself until we decided what to do about an apartment or a house. He had driven straight from Salt Lake City, having left that morning.

"You look tired," I told him. "I've got some cold cuts in the fridge. I'll make us a sandwich for supper."

"It was a long drive," said Jason. He pulled out one of the two folding chairs I'd provided and sat down at the small table that I'd moved into our kitchen area.

"How is Avery?" I asked, getting bread out of the box I'd set on the counter.

"She's anti-social," said Jason.

"Really?" I looked at him, reaching for a paper plate. "What's she like?"

"Quiet. Reserved. Doesn't talk much. Got any soda in that dorm fridge?"

I opened the little refrigerator and took out a can of cola for him. "Did she talk to you?"

"No, not much," admitted Jason. "She doesn't seem to relate much to Dad or Alicia either."

"Hm, that's strange," I said.

"Yeah, I thought so. Avery was on her cell phone a lot with her girlfriends. She spent a lot of time in the guest room and didn't come out much, except to eat."

How bizarre. Again, I had always thought it was weird that Dirk and Alicia had sent the girl to boarding school out East.

"I mean … she's pretty and everything." Jason popped the lid on his soda can. "She's got this beautiful dark hair and a lovely face … and figure." Then he smirked and looked at me. "Kind of looks like you, Mom."

I figured he was joking and laughed at him. "Yeah, right …" I finished making his sandwich, then sat down at the table with him. Folding my hands in front of me on the table, I looked him in the eye and said, "This is a good time to talk about what your dad and Alicia told you about Aunt Liz."

7

This time Jason didn't try to evade the conversation. "Okay," he said, taking a bite.

"I want to know exactly what they told you about her," I prompted.

Jason chewed a bit, then after he'd swallowed, he said, "They told me she was trouble as a girl growing up. I get that. But they said she came to stay with you and Dad after she was reformed. In fact, she took care of me so you could work."

I nodded in agreement. "And?"

He sighed. "They told me you sent her away. You got into a fight with her and made her leave. Then nobody ever heard from her again."

I stared hard at my son. "And do you believe that?"

Jason blinked and shrugged, then took another bite of his sandwich.

"Obviously, nobody told you the full story," I said. "Your Aunt Liz was an addict."

"I know, they said that," said Jason.

"She also betrayed me ... and so did your father." I looked him in the eye.

"Oh." Jason looked momentarily startled. "She did? You mean, Dad ..."

I nodded my head and crossed my arms. "My sister was the cause of our divorce."

"How come you never told me that?" asked Jason. "All these years ... I believed ..."

"I tried to put it all behind me," I confessed. "I didn't think you needed to know the gory details."

"I knew you and Dad split up because there was someone else," said Jason, "but I didn't know it was Aunt Liz. Oh, shit ..."

"She never apologized to me," I added. "We left each other alone for all those years." I stood up and grabbed a bag of veggie chips on the counter, then handed them to Jason.

"Until she died?"

"Yes." I nodded. "And the ironic thing is, she died in Blanca Hills."

"Yeah, I remember that," he said, opening the bag of chips. "I'd already transferred over to Boulder. Why did she come here to the valley, do you think?"

"Nobody knows," I said with a sigh.

"That's weird," said Jason. "Mom, I'm sorry."

"No need to be," I told him just as my cell phone rang in the main area of the office. I got up to answer it and it was the local phone company wanting to come out the next day to install the Internet and telephone service.

The next morning, Jason and I drove to Blanca Hills to look at a Suburban someone had advertised for sale in the *Sentinel*. It was a large black SUV that had some age on it and a few dings, but the price was modest and Jason agreed it would be a good vehicle for transporting bundles of papers.

I attempted to bargain down the price, but the owner made it clear right away that he would only accept his asking price, then emphasized repeatedly that it was in excellent condition for its years. I ended up purchasing the Suburban for the *Buffalo Billboard*, and Jason drove it back to Valle Viento after we swung by the courthouse to get plates and registration. I'd arranged to add the Suburban to my insurance policy by phone and they faxed proof of insurance over to the DMV.

"How does it ride?" I asked Jason after he'd parked the Black Beast next to our two cars in front of the office building.

"Sweet!" he said with a grin. "It's got a super sound system." As we returned to the office, I glanced at the new arrival and couldn't help but shudder a little. Jason had a knack for choosing cars based on their speakers and not the important factors, such as brakes and engine function. I had a fleeting thought of dread, but shook it off as we went inside.

Peg showed up a few minutes later, enthusiastic and full of ideas. Jason went to work assembling and arranging furniture while I went over potential advertising clients with my new sales representative. The more I interacted with Peg Espinoza, the more I liked her, and the excitement she conjured up was infectious.

She had come in contact with a woman she knew who wanted to sell ads. Colleen Hollenbeck came into the office that afternoon for an interview. She was small and dainty with short black hair and a friendly, outgoing personality. She sat down with Peg and me, and we chatted about the work we hoped to accomplish. Bright-eyed and curious, Colleen asked lots of questions, mostly directed at Peg, who answered them while I sat and stared from one to the other.

Finally, Peg stood up and beckoned me into my inner office—the room without the door—and she asked, "Well, what do you think?"

"I like her," I told Peg. "But she doesn't have experience. She's never sold ads before."

"Yes, I know." Peg sighed. We both looked out the door at Colleen, who was seated at a table, checking her lipstick in a compact mirror she'd pulled out of her purse. "But she can learn."

Then I came up with an idea. We walked back into the main room, where Colleen smiled up at the two of us as we sat down. "How would you like to write some short articles?" I asked her. "You could approach some of the advertisers and offer to do some interesting write-ups about them."

"Hey, yeah!" Peg beamed, patting me on the back.

Colleen's cheery face brightened. "I think I could do that. Yes, that would be fun."

Aspen started her job the next morning. She was going to work half-days until we started production. I taught her how to use the computer and set her up with some templates so that she could type classified ads into the program Merle had helped develop for us. I also showed her how to enter customers into a database, and perform simple correspondence. She learned quickly and was fairly good at typing, which was a blessing. Her best asset, however, was talking on the telephone. She practiced the greeting and programmed the answering machine. She was willing to take on any menial tasks I could come up with to fill her time.

On Friday morning, Jason started learning how to design display ads, and I was teaching him some basics of our chosen program on the computer when a man in his 40's walked into the office, dressed in a white shirt and tie. He was clean cut and had a dark complexion with Middle Eastern features. I smiled and introduced myself, wondering what he wanted.

"The Work Center sent me over," he said in a pleasant voice. "They told me you need sales people. I'm an experienced salesman."

"Oh." This was a surprise to me. Obviously, Peg had taken it upon herself to visit the local Work Force and had left information about the *Buffalo Billboard*. I had forgotten the conversation, but now I recalled that she had mentioned she was going to try to find some more prospects. I introduced myself and asked him to sit down.

"My name is Rodney Rankar," he said. "I've worked in sales before and I've lived in the valley for six years."

"Do you have a résumé?" I asked.

He shrugged. "Not really. But I promise you, I'll deliver. I'm very good at what I do."

Rodney had the gift of gab and he was quite charming. I was a little concerned about his background, but he kept on talking and I could see that he was very persuasive. He also agreed to the consignment I offered and said he could start getting ads right away. Peg had just come through the door after picking up the mail, and she immediately took over the interview. I sat quietly and watched their interaction, and then Peg looked at me and I nodded.

"Does this mean I've got the job?" Rodney grinned.

"You most certainly do." Peg laughed. "You can start tomorrow."

Rodney left the office, chuckling, and I saw him do a little dance on the sidewalk as he made his way to his beat-up old car parked on the street. I looked at Peg and sighed. "Do we have enough now?"

"No," said Peg, "but really, that's up to you, B.J." She winked, then handed me some envelopes to open. I took them into my inner office and listened as Aspen and Peg chatted. I sure wished I had a door I could close, to shut out the noise. I had a lot to do in the two weeks that remained before we had to put our first issue together.

"Mom, how do these look?" Jason popped his head through the doorway and showed me some print-outs he had made of practice assignments for ads. I took them and studied them, a smile curling as I handed them back to him.

"Jason, you're learning quickly. I knew you would."

Later, Peg stuck her head in my office and said, "Hey, B.J., Colleen and I are going to the farmers' market tomorrow morning. They have it every Saturday in Blanca Hills. We thought we could pass around some of these classified ad forms ... maybe talk to some people about putting in free ads."

"Peg, that's brilliant," I said. "We're going to need to get some ads."

"Aspen's making signs," she added. "We can even set up a table and drum up some interest."

I thanked my lucky stars for Peg Espinoza. She was a spitfire of enthusiasm and ideas. And I had to smile as I went back to my work, remembering how Colleen had talked to me after her interview and had disclosed to me, "I really like your boss. She's funny, don't you think?"

Instead of correcting Colleen, I had rolled my eyes and put my hands on my hips. "She's certainly that," I agreed. Later, when Peg told Colleen that I was the boss—not her—Colleen had gasped and turned bright red. But when she saw it made no difference to me, she relaxed once again.

Merle had come through with a website design for the *Billboard* and I spent time on the phone, discussing changes with him. We had a cyber presence, at least, and he was going to design a submission page for classifieds so that we could get more ads for the paper. I had paid for some local radio spots to advertise our new shopper, and we were busy getting a bulk mailing ready to send to all of the advertisers I had gathered through my research. Soon everyone in the valley would know that we were starting up on August sixth, and they could, if they chose, be included in the premier issue at half price.

Jason and I continued to sleep in the back storage room, in our separate corners, and we had been too busy to try to find other living arrangements, but I knew it would be necessary soon. I was not happy having to go to the local gym in Valle Viento to get a shower every other day. We hoped that if we placed an ad, looking for a place to rent, someone would contact us after the paper came out.

On Saturday night, we had retired to the back of the office and I was lying in bed, reading my book, when suddenly I noticed blue flashing lights coming from the front office. I had left the door slightly ajar between our living quarters and the rest of the building. Jason climbed out of his bed, which was basically a futon mattress on the floor, and stepped out to see what was going on.

"Mom, the police are at the door," he said in alarm.

"What!" I immediately grabbed my bathrobe and slippers, then followed my son into the front room. A squad car out front had its lights rotating, and two officers with flashlights were peering inside. I immediately switched on the kitchen light and we approached the door.

"Unlock the door and let them in," I told Jason, which he did.

One of the officers stared at us, shining his light on us. "Sorry to bother you, ma'am," he said, "but we saw lights in here, and we thought maybe something was wrong."

Embarrassed because I was dressed for bed, I tried to explain. "This is my office," I told the police. "My son and I are staying here until we can find a place to live."

"What kind of office?" asked the other cop in a less cordial voice than the first officer.

"It's a newspaper," I explained. "See?" I gestured around the room at all the desks and computers and light table. "We're the *Buffalo Billboard*, and my name is Bridget Martin. And this is my son, Jason."

The policemen at once relaxed and turned off their flashlights. "Sorry to disturb you, ma'am," said the first cop. "We didn't know."

I smiled. "Of course."

After they left and the lights on their squad cars had been turned off, Jason and I sat at the small kitchen table for a few minutes to calm down. "Wow," said Jason.

"That was rather unexpected," I said with a sigh. I hoped we didn't have to deal with the local police force anymore. Little did I know at the time that we would see them again.

8

The next couple of weeks comprised so much activity that I was left exhausted at the end of each day. Peg, Rodney and Colleen were all selling ads. Classifieds, however, were few and far between, but at least there were some people calling in to place the free reader ads. I had taught Jason how to use the publishing software, and he excelled at creating exciting display ads for the upcoming paper. He had always had a flair for art, and his enthusiasm grew each day.

Everyone would go home at five o'clock, except Jason and me. Jason would either connect with some of his friends or just relax with his video games. I remained in the office, able to accomplish a lot more with my employees gone for those precious quiet hours. I would have to force myself to stop working and go to bed. Then I would lie awake, unable to get to sleep right away.

"What if" thoughts plagued me, at night especially. Had I created a monster? Was this paper really going to work? Would people in the Lower Valley enjoy it and eventually come to rely on it? What if I ran out of money? What if something happened beyond my control? I would have to dismiss those gruesome thoughts and focus on the positive outcome, hoping I hadn't made a terrible mistake. After all, the people involved were all counting on me to get things right.

Jason told me one day that one of his friends knew of a house we might be able to rent. But it turned out to be a dive, plus it was on the other side of the valley. I didn't want to be too far from Valle Viento. "Keep talking to your friends," I encouraged him. "Something's bound to come available that will work for us." We were both getting tired of living in the back of the office.

One day in late July, while Jason and I were designing a few display ads that Peg had brought in, a girl about 19 or 20 came into the office. Dressed in designer jeans, sandals and a sleeveless pink T-shirt, she had long blonde hair parted to one side and green eyes that were enhanced by heavy eye shadow and mascara. She spoke to Aspen first and then my receptionist summoned me on the intercom.

"Can you come out here please, B.J.?"

Jason watched with interest while he continued working on a half-page ad for a local car dealer. I got up and walked into the big room and met the pretty girl's broad smile. "Hi, how can I help you?" I asked.

The girl's smile was dazzling. "My name's Kelcie McKelvie," she said. "I was wondering if you are hiring." Her eyes darted toward the door to the inner office, where Jason now stood, staring out.

"Nice to meet you, Kelcie. I'm Bridget," I told her. "What is it you do?"

Aspen, who was tasked with creating an address database on her computer, looked up from her work.

"I can typeset," said Kelcie. "I can answer phones. I know how to lay out, and I've done distribution work." Her green eyes swept the office and she smiled. "Oh, you have light tables?"

"Yes," I replied, "but those are mostly for art work. We'll be laying the paper out on the computer and sending it electronically."

"Oh, cool," said Kelcie.

I turned to Aspen. "Get an application form and let Kelcie fill it out." I then started back into the inner office to continue what I was doing, but noticed Jason's fixed stare on the blonde girl.

"Mom," he said in a low voice after he returned to his desk. "Are you going to hire her?"

"I don't know," I told him. "Why?"

Jason went back to his task. "I hope you hire her," he said.

Glancing through the window into the main room, I watched as Kelcie took a seat at one of the tables and Aspen gave her the form and a pen. I smiled knowingly at my son and said, "We'll see."

Colleen stopped by the office a few minutes later, while Kelcie was still working on her application. Colleen had turned out to be quite the conversationalist. I found it was hard to get a word in edgewise with her. She had just interviewed her first subject for the articles she was writing for the *Billboard*. As her first assignment, she had chosen the proprietor of the gift shop in the back of our building, and she wanted to tell me all about it.

The phone rang while Colleen rattled on. I needed to concentrate on the work in front of me, but I didn't want to hurt her feelings. I was beginning to wish more than ever that my inner office had a door that I could close for privacy.

"And you should see the cute little pendants she has in her shop," Colleen was saying after giving me a description of half the items in the gift shop. "Most of the things are handmade, and ..."

Just then the intercom came on and Aspen's voice said, "B.J., the shop just called. The Black Beast is ready to be picked up."

"Thanks, Aspen." I felt relieved to have an excuse to get away from Colleen.

"Do you want me to go get the Suburban?" Jason asked, having overheard.

"Uh ... no. I think I'll go pick it up myself." The service station where we had taken the company vehicle for an oil change and an overall check-up was only three blocks away. Jason had dropped it off that morning.

Colleen laughed out loud. "That's so funny! The name of the company truck is the Black Beast!"

I stood up after saving my work. "I could use some fresh air," I said.

Colleen took the hint and went into the main room to find a computer so she could write up her article. I noticed that Kelcie was just finishing her application. She stood up and offered it to Aspen. I walked over and smiled at the girl. "I'll take that."

She handed it to me and I quickly scanned through it. I didn't have time to look it over too carefully, but it was obvious she had a lot of experience and had worked at *The Mountain Sentinel* as well as the college paper.

"So you have a degree from Blanca State?" I commented.

Kelcie nodded her head. "In Environmental Studies," she added.

"Hm." I wasn't quite sure how a degree in environmental studies related to journalism, but all I cared about at the moment was that she was qualified to work for me. I would give her a chance to prove herself. "I'm looking for someone who can multi-task," I told her.

"That's me," said Kelcie. "I'm very good at multi-tasking."

"Okay," I said. "How soon can you start?"

In the inner office, we all heard Jason call out, "Yes!" Both Aspen and Colleen giggled.

Kelcie shrugged and said, "How about right away?"

"Tomorrow morning is soon enough," I told her. I accompanied her to the door and revealed the days I wanted her to work and the pay I was offering, both of which she seemed fine with. She thanked me and then left and got into her car, which was parked just out front on the street. It was a small, teal-colored Smart Car.

I left the building and walked through downtown toward the service station, which was just off the highway. The fresh air revived me. I had been working really hard at the computer lately, getting templates made for ads and scheduling them, plus instructing Jason how to do them. It would be helpful to have someone with Kelcie's experience to help us get the paper off the ground. I could see already that I was going to be under a lot of pressure to coordinate everything, but at the same time I felt wonderful. My vision was becoming a reality.

"Here are your keys, Ms. Martin." The attendant behind the counter at the service station smiled as he gave me the Suburban's keys and had me sign the sales slip, saying all work had been completed to my satisfaction. "You're all set." He tore off the customer copy and handed it to me.

I headed for the door. Before I left, I sighed and turned around. "So everything's good with the truck?" I asked. "No problems?"

"You're good to go." The young man nodded, then grinned and said, "You have an impressive sound system. Top of the line."

I found the Black Beast parked outside the door and climbed in. Somehow the fact that the sound system was its most redeeming quality did not fill me with confidence. But I was glad we had gotten the SUV serviced before our first publication run. The Suburban was vital to our success. I drove it back to the office and parked it beside my Camry, then went inside.

Rodney was there with some new ads for me to schedule. I was pleased that he and Peg were actually competing with one another to see who could bring in the most revenue before our first issue. He was on the phone when I put the Suburban's keys in the drawer of Aspen's desk.

"The accountant called while you were gone," reported Aspen. She handed me a slip of paper with a phone number on it.

"Thanks, Aspen. Are you ready to type some classifieds?"

The girl sighed with relief. "Anything to take a break from this database."

I reached for the folder that had the classifieds that we had collected so far. There were several of them, but still not enough, in my opinion. I had Aspen call up a file and type in the first one. I wanted to be sure she remembered how to do it after I'd given her instructions a couple of days ago.

"Good," I told her with a smile. I went to the kitchen for a glass of tea and the phone rang.

"Good afternoon, *Buffalo Billboard,* this is Aspen … may I help you?" Aspen was always prompt at answering the phone.

Rodney strolled into the kitchen area. "How many more ads do we need for this issue?" he asked.

"We've got enough right now," I replied, "but you can sell as many as you want. We'll just expand the paper a bit." I smiled at him. "You guys are doing terrific, you know."

Rodney puffed up like a peacock with a broad smile. "The more I sell, the more I get paid."

"That's right." I opened the dorm fridge to get a couple of ice cubes.

Just then, the lights went out. The machines in the office went dead. Both Aspen and Colleen let out a cry. Jason popped his head out of the inner office and we all groaned in dismay.

"What happened?" asked Jason.

"Did we blow a fuse? A circuit?" asked Colleen.

Aspen pressed some buttons on the front desk telephone. "Phone still works," she said.

"Where is the circuit breaker box?" asked Rodney.

"Jason, do you know?" I called out. It was dark in the building, but there was some daylight coming in through the windows—enough that we could see our way around.

"No," he replied.

"Let's look around," suggested Rodney.

We all started looking at the walls, wondering where the breaker box was. All the logical places were not where it was. I finally directed Aspen to look up the number of the landlord, so I could call him.

"What's going on in here?" Peg had just come in from outside, carrying a briefcase. She set it down on one of the tables and joined us. "Did the power go off?"

"Yes," said Colleen. "Maybe it's out all over town?"

"No," said Peg. She went to the window and looked out from between the blinds. "I see lights on in other stores. Must be just us."

After searching without finding the breaker box, I called Otto Breitbart. Unfortunately, the cell phone connection was choppy at best. I could barely make out anything he said, plus it was hard to understand him anyway with his German accent. He kept saying, "What? What you say? I don't hear you."

"Look in the back room," I instructed Jason. "Maybe it's there."

Jason opened the door to our private quarters and Rodney and Peg followed him inside. Aspen had found a penlight in the desk drawer, which they needed because the back rooms had no windows.

"Can you come down here and help us?" I said into the phone. "We need to find the box."

Otto did not seem to comprehend, and his replies kept breaking up.

"We've got a bad connection," I told him. "I'm going to hang up and call you back."

But that didn't help either. After a couple more attempts to converse with the landlord, I gave up. Then I went into the private quarters, where the others were fumbling around. After another ten minutes, Jason called out, "I found it!"

We all congregated next to the closet room that was too narrow for me to use for my clothes. Jason and Rodney were both inside, and a moment later someone flipped a switch and the power came back on. Everyone cheered as Rodney and Jason squeezed back out of the cubicle.

"It was in there?" I was floored.

Peg looked around and then ushered everybody back out into the main part of the office. Always my protector and defender, she respected my privacy and closed the door as everyone went back to their business. When Otto called later, even though the connection was still choppy, I managed to tell him that we now knew where the breaker box was. He jabbered more language that I could not make out, so finally I thanked him—even though he'd been no help—said goodbye, and hung up.

It was dusk when I returned to the office after going to the gym to grab a shower. Jason had gone with one of his friends to a movie, so I sat in my inner office and went over some bookkeeping. Before I knew it, my eyes blurred and I decided to go to bed. Tomorrow the new girl was coming in to train.

Before turning in, I switched on my bedside lamp and stared at the door to the narrow closet. I found it strange that the breaker box was in such an inconspicuous place. I went over and opened the door. It was a long dark and narrow closet. The circuit breakers were on the inside wall to my left. With a sigh of frustration, I walked over to my small vanity and got my flashlight out of the drawer.

I had been too preoccupied to explore the closet when I had moved in. When I had moved my stuff into the back room, I had thought about using the closet for clothes, but it didn't even have a pole from which to hang anything, plus it was so narrow that it seemed useless except for a small stack of torn-down cardboard boxes I had saved. There were no shelves, and the walls were unfinished with some pink insulation torn loose in places.

I stepped inside and shone the flashlight into the depths. Then I walked farther inside, amazed that the little room was actually about 10 feet long. As I moved toward the other end, I noticed a loose board sticking out from floor to ceiling, and I thought, *how strange* ... Then, as I got closer and felt it with my hand, I realized it was loose and opened into another space. My flashlight revealed a second room—much to my astonishment.

Now curious, I found that I could push the loose board, which acted as a door or a panel, and I stepped into a skimpy passageway that connected to my narrow closet. I was not one to worry about spiders or other creatures in old buildings, but I nevertheless used caution and projected my flashlight beam in every corner before walking in. I saw light coming in from a couple of round holes in the wall of this enclosure and slowly moved toward them for a closer look.

There appeared to be a hallway on the other side, and I then discovered another narrow door panel, and this one had a latch that was in the closed position. Now even more curious, I lifted the latch and carefully pulled the door open, revealing a stark hallway that connected the *Billboard's* building with the other stores in the adjacent building behind us. I was in awe.

Stepping out into this corridor, I could see that there were three connecting stores or offices, and that their back doors were like mine. The light in the hallway was coming from a storage room to my left. I figured someone might be in there working, so I decided to not check it out. Otto had never mentioned this, and because it was latched, it probably meant the door was only there in case of an emergency.

I took a few steps to the right and saw some plumbing pipes coming from the bottom half of the wall. I realized that was where my office bathroom was located. Touching the plywood, I realized the wall to our bathroom was not very thick. There was plenty of dust and a musty odor. It gave me the creeps, so I decided to return the way I'd come.

Carefully, I latched the door to the hallway and wound my way through the two narrow rooms until I emerged again into my private quarters in the back room of the office. Then I closed the closet door and stood for a few moments, marveling at my discovery. This was intriguing, but it didn't make me feel very safe all of a sudden. As long as Jason was there with me, I felt somewhat secure … but now that I knew that there was an entryway into other parts of the complex, I began to worry.

I promised myself that the next day I would make an effort to find us a better place to live.

9

The next morning Kelcie McKelvie showed up promptly at nine o'clock to begin her new job at the *Buffalo Billboard*. All three salespeople were there for our morning meeting, which had become routine before they went out to sell ads. Aspen was at the front desk, talking on the telephone to a friend or a relative. Since the phone was never busy, I let her accept personal calls as long as they did not interfere with her duties. She was a good worker, but there just wasn't enough for her to do—yet.

Jason had stayed out late the night before and was now in the kitchen area, blending a smoothie for his breakfast. When he heard her come in, he shut off the blender and peeked around the corner to watch. Everyone else had stopped what they were doing to come and greet Kelcie, and I stepped out of my office with a smile.

"Good morning, Kelcie," I said. "Are you ready to show me what you can do?"

Peg walked up right away and was the first to introduce herself. "Hi, Kelcie. I'm Peg."

"Hi." Kelcie stared at everyone, wide eyed.

I took the cue and added, "Yes, let's introduce everybody first." The others surrounded us and introduced themselves, one by one, and explained what their jobs were.

"Want some coffee? There's some brewing in the kitchen," said Aspen.

Kelcie took a travel mug with a lid out of her backpack-purse. "I brought my own," she said. "I like my espresso first thing each day."

Jason stepped into the room with his glass of liquid fruit and greens. "Hi," he said to Kelcie.

"This is Jason," Peg told her.

"Oh ... what do you do here?" asked the blonde girl, regarding Jason with interest.

Jason took a sip from his smoothie and said in a small voice, "I'm distribution manager."

"He also composes ads," said Colleen, who was wearing her pair of purple jeans today.

"*Not* to mention," said Peg, placing her hands on her hips, "he's the boss's *son!*"

Kelcie stared at me with wide eyes. "Oh," she said with a smile.

"You mentioned you had worked in distribution," I reminded Kelcie. "Would you be interested in helping Jason with the papers?"

"Of course," she said, suddenly no longer shy. She smiled at him, then took a sip from her mug.

"Hey, you look kind of familiar," said Rodney, his brown hand gripping his chin. "I've seen you around, I think."

Kelcie shrugged. "I've lived in Blanca Hills for six years. Did you go to State?"

Rodney made a face and shook his head. "Nah ... not me."

"*I* attended Blanca State," proclaimed Jason.

"Well, I would have remembered seeing *you*," she said.

"It was a few years ago," he told her.

"Jason's a student at the University of Colorado now," said Peg. "Did you graduate yet?" She squinted her eyes at my son.

"Next semester," I replied.

"Maybe," Jason quipped.

"Cool." Kelcie kept smiling at him and it seemed Jason couldn't stop staring at her.

The phone rang right then and Aspen jumped on it. "Good morning. *Buffalo Billboard,* this is Aspen. How may I direct your call?"

"Good grief." Peg giggled as she slipped away to sort through some insertion orders.

The group broke up at that point, and I showed Kelcie where I wanted her to sit so that I could show her some things on the computer. Colleen and Rodney began talking about which businesses they were going to visit that day. Everything seemed very normal, for which I was thankful. Jason sauntered back into the inner office to do another display ad. I spent the next hour getting Kelcie familiar with the program for classifieds, and told her that later we'd train her on the publishing program.

The day passed swiftly. Once the salespeople had driven off, we could concentrate on our work. Aspen played some low-key music from her cell phone, and there were a few people who came off the street to inquire about running classifieds. Still, I was worried that we would have a very small amount for our first issue, which was now only twelve days away.

A week passed. We were so busy getting ready to put out our first issue of the *Buffalo Billboard* that Jason and I had absolutely no spare time to look for rentals—even if there were any.

Peg, Colleen and Aspen had gone out to the farmers' market every Saturday since they'd been hired, passing out literature and telling people about our paper. They did this on their own time, not because I had asked them to, but because Peg was so enthusiastic. They brought dozens of classified ads back to the office each Monday. We still didn't have enough, in my opinion, but we would fill the empty space one way or another.

Rodney had proven to be a go-getter. He had a natural talent for getting people to buy ads, and Peg was giving him pointers from her many years of experience. She had brought in the lion's share of ads for our first issue. Poor Colleen, I noticed, was struggling with her sales. She remained cheerful, committed to her little features she was writing, and continued to be overly talkative when I needed to concentrate on production.

Aspen was faithful, showing up on time each morning, even though I knew she had a small boy in day care. I found out she was not married. Her boyfriend, the trucker, was the father of her son. She was often on the phone with him during the long, monotonous afternoons with no one around. Aspen also loved gossip, and had filled me in on a lot of interesting tidbits of local information. As long as she performed the duties I required of her, I did not object to her telephone time. Whenever a business call came in, she would put her boyfriend on hold to take the incoming call.

Meanwhile, Jason and Kelcie had become friends. Jason loved answering the girl's questions and helping her when she needed to know something about an ad she was creating. In the background,

I often heard them speaking in low tones, laughing out loud, and kidding each other. I was happy to see Jason taking interest in a girl. He had been rather shy in high school, and even though he had gone on dates in college, he hadn't really connected with anyone. As his mother, that was perfectly fine with me.

That morning, Rebecca, the accountant I had hired, came to the office and dropped some notebooks off for me to examine. She was setting up the accounts at her office in Blanca Hills. I would be posting checks myself, but would leave payroll entirely in her hands. Rebecca was in her mid-40's, short with dyed red hair and glasses. She was all business, so I felt confident having her in charge of my financial obligations. Besides, Mr. Starkmore at the bank had recommended her.

I had been surprised one afternoon the week before, when the bank president had walked into my office to pay a visit. "Hi," I greeted him, wondering if something was wrong.

"Good morning, Ms. Martin," said Mr. Starkmore as he looked around. "Well, this does look impressive." He smiled at me. "I just wanted to see how you are doing."

"Well, so far we're selling ads," I told him with a grin. "Our first issue is coming out on the sixth."

"That's excellent," he said and turned to go out the door.

"Is there something you needed?" I asked him.

"Oh no, no ... just thought I'd come by and make sure you're really in business. We have to check things out when we give someone a business loan, you know." He laughed.

"I see."

"I'm looking forward to seeing your first issue," he added, and then left the building.

That afternoon a truck brought us fifteen brand new newspaper bins I had ordered from a supplier. Jason took charge while I continued working inside my office. He and Kelcie were going to load them into the Suburban and take them to the various locations we thought would be best for people to pick up papers on the street. Even though we were mailing out a copy of the paper to everyone in the Lower Valley, we wanted the shopper available outside certain high-traffic areas.

The man who had made the big aluminum sign for above our

storefront had also created the placards with our logo for the bins. Jason and Kelcie left on their mission while I started going through the accountant's notebooks.

After five o'clock, when Aspen and Colleen had gone home for the weekend, I fixed myself a sandwich and a salad in the kitchen area while working on the books. I came to the pages of employee data and something stood out as I glanced through it all. I noticed that Kelcie's entry gave her legal name as Kelcie McKelvie-Tucker.

"Hm ... that's strange," I muttered as I noted her address. She lived in an apartment in Blanca Hills on Greenwood Street. I smiled at the word "Greenwood," since Kelcie had her degree in environmental science. Then I wondered why she had not introduced herself with her full name that day she was hired. Had she been married? Why the hyphenated last name?

After my supper, I drove to the gym to work out on the exercise bike before taking my shower and coming back to the office. It was dark and I wondered where Jason was. I always felt a little nervous being there by myself after dark, especially after I had found the hidden door in the narrow closet that had led out into the back halls of the adjoining buildings. I had meant to call Otto and ask him about it, but shrugged it off because it was too hard to speak with the man with his accent and his bad cell phone connection.

Jason got in around eleven. I had gone to bed and was reading. He had to pass through my section of the living quarters and said, "Oh, you're still awake."

"Jason, thank goodness you're back. I was getting worried."

"Sorry, Mom." He smiled sheepishly. Then he perked up. "Guess what? There's a rental coming available at Kelcie's apartment complex."

"Really?" I sat up and put my book on the bedside table. "In Blanca Hills?"

"Yeah," he said. He sighed. "I know you wanted to find something closer to work, but it's a real cool area. It's on Greenwood, not far from the college. The apartment has two bedrooms and two baths, and it's affordable ... I hope."

"How much?" I asked, although I was desperate enough for housing that I didn't really care what the rent was at this point. He told me, and then I asked, "Were you over there?"

"Yeah," he admitted. "Kelcie showed me where she lives." He pulled a piece of paper out of his jeans pocket and handed it to me.

Looking at it, I saw he had scribbled a phone number. "And did you get all the bins set up?"

"Yup."

"We'll go look at the apartment tomorrow," I told him. "That's the best news I've heard all day."

"I'm as anxious as you are to get a place," said Jason.

"Your hair's wet. Did you stop at the gym?" I asked him.

"Nope. Kelcie's shower." He flashed a quick grin, then disappeared into his corner.

Uh-huh ... I knew it ... and I wasn't sure if it was a good thing, or a bad thing. But I couldn't help liking Kelcie. So far, she had proven to be a fast learner and was extremely likeable. I just prayed she would not end up hurting my one and only beloved son.

10

One afternoon the following week, the employees were conversing with each other in the main office area while I was busy at my computer, double-checking the parameters of the pages for layout I had designed. Rodney and Peg were laughing and joking with Aspen and Colleen. Jason had left earlier to run some errands, and Kelcie had taken the day off, having finished all the work I had given her.

"That's so funny!" Colleen burst through my doorway, interrupting me for about the twelfth time that day.

"What is?" I tried not to act annoyed.

"The man on the street column that Jason thought up." Colleen grinned at me, then peered over my shoulder at the screen. "Hey, that looks good, B.J."

More laughter burst out of the others in the main room.

"What are they laughing at?" I asked Colleen.

"Peg came up with the perfect name for the column," explained Colleen. "*Yak It Up!*"

The others were suddenly at my doorway, peering in. Rodney said, "Yeah ... and the graphic on the header is a *yak!*"

"A what?"

Peg whipped out a slip of paper. "A yak. You know ... the animal."

I took the paper and couldn't help but smile at the cartoon ungulate someone had found on line and printed out. "Yak it *up?*" I looked at the three of them. "Are you serious?"

"*The Mountain Sentinel* does something similar," explained Peg. "They interview people on the street about a subject ... and they call their column 'Sound Off.' "

"*Bor*-ing!" rang out Colleen.

"What do you think?" asked Peg, her eyes shining.

"Well ..."

"Aw, come on, B.J.," prodded Rodney. "People are gonna love it."

Everyone seemed to agree, and even though I wasn't quite sure, I said okay, we'd try it. When Jason got back, I'd have him draw up something similar that we could use for the art. Peg ushered the others out of my inner office and soon things quieted down.

After Rodney and Peg had left for the day, Colleen wandered back into my office and sat down at Jason's station. "B.J.," she said in a lowered voice. "Aspen told me something ..."

I glanced at her curiously. "What?"

Colleen lowered her voice a little. "Aspen said she found out that Kelcie's last name is really Tucker and not McKelvie."

I sighed. "Well, yes, I know already," I said with a smile.

Colleen went immediately into gossip mode. "B.J., we think Kelcie is a spy!"

"Wait a minute ..." I stopped what I was doing and buzzed Aspen to join us. A moment later, the girl stood at the doorway. "Aspen, did you tell Colleen that Kelcie's a spy?"

Aspen's brown eyes widened and she stepped all the way in. "No!"

"She didn't exactly say that she was," explained Colleen. "We just figured that it made sense."

"Why would you think that?" I was floored. I looked from one to the other.

"Because she's the daughter of Grant Tucker, the publisher at *The Mountain Sentinel*," Colleen explained to me.

"What!" Now I was surprised. I hadn't made that connection. I suddenly had a flash of an image of a good-looking man standing in the parking lot of *The Mountain Sentinel*, observing my car tire, after I'd come out from his building that day. I had forgotten the name Tucker. It hadn't seemed important to remember it.

"She's his daughter?"

"Yes!" cried Colleen and Aspen at the same time.

"The very fact that she hid that information from you means she must be here to check on the competition," said Colleen.

"Kelcie didn't give her real name because she didn't want you to know," suggested Aspen. "We think she is working undercover ... and she might do something to sabotage your business."

"Oh, surely not!" I blinked my eyes and looked around the room. "You can't be serious. A spy?"

"Why not?" Colleen shrugged. "Maybe she goes and reports everything she hears to her dad."

"Well …" I wasn't quite sure what to do at that point. I wasn't buying their idea, but I realized that it was true, she had given the name McKelvie on her application, not Tucker. But I had seen that the name McKelvie-Tucker had been on her W2 that Rebecca had brought over. Why would she not have disclosed that to me?

"Are you going to fire her?" asked Aspen, her eyes wide as she clung to the door frame of my office.

"No!" I told her. "So far, Kelcie's been a good worker. I don't think she's a spy either."

Colleen let out a big sigh. "I sure hope you're right, B.J."

"Yeah, we don't want you to fail," said Aspen. "I heard Peg and Rodney talking yesterday … and Rodney asked Peg, 'Do you think B.J. knows what she's doing?' and Peg kinda said, 'I have no idea.'"

"Hey, it's late," I said with a glance at the clock. "Let's just act as though we never had this conversation. If Kelcie's going to be a problem, I'll know soon enough."

"We just thought you should know," said Colleen, innocently batting her eyes as she stood up to leave.

"Yeah, I like Kelcie." Aspen flashed a quick smile, then returned to her desk.

For a long time I stared at my computer screen, fears beginning to take root. I couldn't believe that we had a spy among us. It was so out of character. I wondered if Jason knew anything about Kelcie's relationship with her parents, or if she had ever mentioned anything I should know about. Certainly he would have told me if he knew she was related to the owner of Blanca Hills' daily newspaper. I was finally able to finish my project after Aspen and Colleen went home.

When Jason got back, we went out to get some supper at the café up the street, and I asked him about Kelcie. "What's her family like?"

Jason wiped his mouth after swallowing part of his burrito. "I dunno," he told me. "She's never mentioned them."

"Really?" I stared at him. "Did she grow up in the valley?"

"I guess," he said.

"What do you two talk about when you're together?"

Jason squinted his eyes at me. "Mom ... why the third degree?"

I didn't want to reveal to Jason what Colleen and Aspen had told me. I took a sip from my iced tea and then said, "No reason. I'm just curious about her."

Then, in order to change the subject and hide my embarrassment, I asked, "What do you hear from your father?"

Jason said, "He keeps asking me when you're gonna give up."

"What!" I laughed. "We haven't even published our first issue yet."

"I know." Jason grinned. "I told him this job is the best I've ever had. Mom, I want to learn all the aspects of this business. Will you teach me how to do it?"

"Seriously?" I stabbed my fork into my chile relleno. "Well, Jason, I'm glad. I'll be happy to show you everything I know, but it's going to take time."

"Yeah, I know."

I went on. "I mean, at some point I might need to take some time off, and I'd need somebody who can take charge."

"Another thing," said Jason as he reached for his glass of cola. "They say that Avery wants to drop out of school."

"Oh?" This news startled me a little as I tried to envision the teenage stepsister who had spent most of her years in boarding schools out East.

"Yeah, I guess she's home in Utah for the summer at least."

"Will they make her go back to school in the fall?" I asked.

"I doubt it."

"You know, Avery is a real mystery, isn't she?" I dipped a tortilla chip into the dish of salsa.

"You can say that again," Jason smirked.

"What's she really like?" I asked.

Jason chewed, then swallowed and looked at me. "She knows how to put on an act, and she's stand-offish."

"How so?"

"Well," said Jason, "she's never acted friendly toward me, and she and Alicia are always fighting."

"What is her problem, I wonder?"

"Dad once said she might be autistic," Jason said in a guarded voice.

"Hm." I didn't comment.

"Also," Jason added a few moments later, "I've figured out that for some reason they don't seem to want her around."

"Do you think Avery senses that?" I asked.

Jason shrugged and continued eating his meal.

"It sounds like she's insecure," I mused. "What I don't understand is why they treat her like the red-haired stepchild."

"Her hair is kind of auburn colored," Jason remarked. "It's real dark like yours, but when I last saw her, she had streaked it with reddish dye."

"Your Aunt Liz used to do that." I smiled, thinking of my sister and what a problem child she had been. "She was a real piece of work."

Jason shook his head sadly. "I'm sorry, Mom. I'm still freaked out about her ... and Dad."

"That's all water under the bridge," I remarked. "Don't give it a second thought." We ate the rest of our meal in silence, both of us lost in our thoughts.

The next day was Saturday. I called the manager of the apartments on Greenwood and she eagerly offered to show us what she had available. Jason and I drove to Blanca Hills in my Camry. The housing complex was modern and appealing, a series of tastefully landscaped brick buildings near the center of town, yet away from congested downtown traffic.

A middle-aged woman with dark hair and a friendly smile met us outside after Jason announced our arrival with his cell phone. "Hi! I'm Maria Hernandez. So pleased to meet you."

We shook hands while introducing ourselves, and she beckoned us into the building that had the vacancy. The apartments were accessible from inside, not outside, and I was relieved that the one she was going to show us was on the main floor. We passed the wall of mailboxes and I noted with relief that the hallway looked swept and tidy.

"I hear you are doing a new paper," said Maria as she pulled out her keys after we stopped at a door that had the number "7" on it.

"Yes," I told her. "It's a shopper."

"That is wonderful," said Maria. "People are excited."

She pushed the door open and we entered a spacious living room with a kitchen off to the right and a nice sized picture window overlooking the quiet street with trees and some older stick-built homes on the other side. The drywall had been freshly painted in a pale shade of green and the drapes were dark olive. The beige carpet smelled fresh after just being shampooed.

"And in here we have two bedrooms," Maria directed us as we followed her into a short hallway off the main living quarters. The larger of the bedrooms was on the left, with a small half bath connected. The second bedroom was at the opposite side, next to a larger full bathroom that sported a clawfoot tub.

"Nice!" I proclaimed, stepping into the back room to explore the closet and window that faced the same view as from the living room.

"No pets," Maria told us.

"We have no animals," I reassured her. I looked at Jason, who grinned and nodded his head. "We'll take it," I said. "Is there a lease?"

"Yes," said Maria. "We can work all of this out in the office. Follow me."

"Can we move in right away?" asked Jason.

"After I run a background check and get the security deposit and first month's rent, you can move in." Maria smiled. "Welcome to the neighborhood."

I followed Maria and Jason out of the apartment, whispering as I went out the door, "Thank God." No more going to the gym for showers, and I would be making a trip to Dexter to get some things from my storage unit and arrange for a truck to bring the rest.

11

Jason and I drove over Buffalo Pass Saturday afternoon and arrived in Dexter around six. I had phoned Merle ahead of time to say we were coming. He was relieved that we had found a place to live and wanted to help us move the rest of my things out of storage.

It felt familiar and relaxing to arrive in Dexter after being gone for a few weeks. Now that it was near the end of July, Dexter was hot and dry, and the summer was in full swing. The community's annual festival, "Dexter Days," was happening that weekend, so there were lots of people in town. We marveled at the crowds and the music and carnival atmosphere as we drove past the town park.

"Hey, long time no see," Merle greeted us after we pulled into his driveway. I didn't see Janie's car and asked where she was.

Jason carried our overnight bags up the porch steps as Merle put his arm around me and we walked toward his house. After Jason went inside, Merle said, "Janie's on a business trip this weekend. She'll be back tomorrow night."

"Are things going well with you two?" I asked.

"Oh, yeah," Merle said in his usual matter-of-fact tone. "What about you? I want to hear all about the *Buffalo Billboard* and how it's progressing."

"As well as to be expected," I said with a sigh. "It's only a week till our first issue comes out."

"I know," he said.

Jason came out of the guest bedroom and pulled a pocket comb out of his jeans. Sliding it through his thick dark hair, he said to us, "I think I'll walk down to the park for a little while. I think I saw a few of my friends hanging out."

"Go ahead," I urged him.

"You don't mind?" Jason asked Merle.

Merle shrugged and gestured toward the door. "Knock yerself out."

"Don't stay too late," I said. "Remember, we have to pack up and leave early in the morning."

After Jason left, Merle invited me into the kitchen and made us each a roast beef sandwich. "How about a beer, Beej?"

"Oh, why not?" I collapsed on one of the counter stools while he went to the refrigerator to get us each a bottle.

"How's Jason liking it?" asked Merle.

"Oh, Jason's doing great. He's learning a lot and he's turning out some very creative work. Plus ... he has a thing for one of the girls I hired."

"A thing?" Merle scrunched up his face.

"Well, I don't know how serious it is," I explained. "But from what I can tell, Jason is infatuated. And she seems to enjoy his attention, at least."

"I've missed you, you know." Merle opened both bottles and handed me one, then took a seat beside me.

"Well, I've missed you too, Merle." I smiled and took a swig, then pushed some bangs out of my face. "Actually, I had no idea how much work I was going to make for myself." I began to tell him about some of the challenges I was facing and how worn out I was, working sixteen-hour days.

"But you're loving every moment of it, aren't you?" A smile curled the ends of his mouth.

I sighed. "Yeah." I lifted the bottle to my lips and took another sip.

Merle then started talking about the progress he was making with the *Billboard's* website, and we spent the next half hour brainstorming about it. Later, we sat in the living room and Merle turned on his favorite Saturday evening shows. I could hear some loud singing and band music coming from the park, just four blocks away, and hoped Jason was enjoying his friends.

Midway through the second hour, I yawned several times and Merle caught me nodding off. "Beej, you're beat. Why don't you go to bed? I'll wait up for the boy."

"He should be back pretty soon." I stood up and sighed. "Sorry. I'm not very good company tonight."

Merle stared at me and said in a serious tone, "Beej, you're always good company."

"Thanks, Merle. Good night."

"Night." He settled back in his recliner and focused on the television.

Sunday morning, the three of us had some of Merle's famous breakfast burritos. Then we all drove over to the storage shed to see what Jason and I could take back for the apartment. Merle agreed to rent the moving truck again and get someone to help him load the rest of my stuff. What wouldn't fit into the apartment, I would store in a unit somewhere in the valley. At some point, my plan was to buy a house again. But right now, that money that should have gone into a down payment on another house was being used as collateral for my business. I just prayed there would be something left when it came time to shop for real estate.

Before Jason and I left Dexter, we drove past my old house. We slowed when we got there and both of us were astounded that already the new owners were making improvements. The little house looked more inviting than it ever had, and I suddenly felt homesick for it.

"I wish we hadn't looked at it," Jason told me afterwards. He hung his head. "I miss the place."

"I know how you feel," I admitted. "Hey, I've got to stop at the grocery store for a couple of things."

"That's cool," said Jason. "I can gas up the Camry while you're there."

"Oh, that's a good idea," I said. "I'll probably be about twenty minutes."

Jason let me off at the local mercantile. I was in the produce aisle looking for some avocados when I heard my name called. Looking up, I saw Sally, my old boss from the *Dexter Chronicle*.

"Sally! Nice to see you." We hugged.

"Well, are you back in town?" she asked.

"Just picking up some things from the shed," I explained. "Jason's putting gas in the car and then we're heading back to Valle Viento."

"Well, darn," said Sally and folded her arms. "You know, we could really use you right now."

"I thought you hired a replacement."

"We did," said Sally, "but she's not ... well, never mind. She'll get better with time." Then she added, "I just thought maybe ... seeing you here and all ... you might have given up your paper already."

"Oh, no, quite the contrary," I said with a grin. "We're publishing in ten days."

"Everything's going well, then?"

"Yes," I reassured her.

Sally smiled and hugged me again. "I'm happy for you, Beej. But I must confess, Zach is really beside himself. The new guy ..." She just shook her head and clicked her tongue.

"What's wrong?" I asked.

"He's overwhelmed," said Sally. "He doesn't know what to do. I know they'd love it if you could even come in on weekends and ..."

"Sally, no way!" I examined a couple of hard avocados in the bin. "I can't possibly come to Dexter on weekends to work on the *Chronicle's* web site. Zach and his professional are on their own."

"Well ... okay ... great seeing you, though. Bye, Beej."

I smiled at her. "Good luck, Sally. You'll be fine."

"I know," she called whimsically as she floated away toward the dairy aisle.

I found everything I needed, then rolled my basket to the checkout aisle and was paying for it all when I glanced out the window and saw Jason pulling my car up to the curb. When I came out of the store, he jumped out and packed the sacks into the trunk. Then we headed south, back to the Lower Valley.

It was mid afternoon by the time we arrived at our new apartment in Blanca Hills. Jason helped unload the smaller items and boxes we had been able to cram into the back seat and trunk of the Camry. Merle would be bringing the truck filled with my remaining furniture and possessions on Monday afternoon.

As I was putting some items I'd purchased in Dexter into the cupboards, a knock sounded on the front door. Jason ran to answer it and I heard him exclaim, "Hey, Kelc!"

Peeking out from the kitchen area, I watched Kelcie stroll in, carrying a large house plant wrapped in cellophane. "Hi, Kelcie," I called out.

She grinned at me as she handed Jason the plant and he set it down next to the window. "I'm so excited that you got the place," she said.

I walked into the living room and admired Kelcie's gift. "Oh, how wonderful!" The new arrival had waxy green leaves and clusters of tiny star-shaped flowers.

"It's a hoya," said Kelcie. "I hope you'll like it."

"How nice of you." I bent over to smell one of the live bouquets. "It's so fragrant."

"They are fantastic plants," said Kelcie. "Just don't water it too much. And they don't like a whole lot of sun."

"Do you live in this building?" I asked the girl.

"No, I'm in the next building, on the first floor," said Kelcie.

"How long have you lived there?" I asked, wondering how I could quiz her about her family without sounding suspicious.

"Almost six months now," said Kelcie.

"Is your family living with you?"

Immediately, Jason shot me a warning look.

Kelcie hadn't noticed, however. "Nope. Just me," she said with a smile.

I had thought about asking her about her parents and siblings, but Jason cleared his throat and put his arm around Kelcie. "Hey, come on, I'll show you my room," he said.

Kelcie glanced at me, probably expecting me to disapprove, but I nodded my head. "Thanks for the hoya." Then, as they slipped down the hallway to the second bedroom, I returned to my kitchen task. After five minutes Kelcie came out again, popped her head around the corner to wave at me, then left.

That night Jason and I brought over more things from our living quarters in the back of the office. We didn't want to spend one more night in that place. Merle would be able to handle the heavier things, such as my bed, dresser and Jason's mattress.

In the morning, I made coffee in our new apartment, then left an hour early for the office. I liked being there before the others arrived, in order to get more done. Jason would drive over to clock in at nine. We were now just one week before our first deadline day.

At ten o'clock I needed a break, so I left the office to go to the post office, make a payment at the bank, and swing by the local hardware store for some light bulbs we needed at the apartment. When I returned to the office, Peg and Aspen were talking with Jason in the middle of the room and it was obvious that something was going on.

"Is everything okay?" I asked, looking around.

The girls glanced toward the kitchen area, then sighed. Jason took a seat near the window and stared outside, obviously displeased.

"Tell me what's going on," I demanded.

Aspen spoke up first. "Kelcie's in the bathroom ... crying."

Peg stood with her hands on her hips. "Rodney and Colleen were here a short while ago, and somebody said something ..."

"Who?" I asked.

"I'm not sure who started it," said Aspen. "I think it was Rodney."

"No, it was Colleen." Peg blinked her eyes. She turned to me and said, "They asked her if she was working for *The Mountain Sentinel*."

"They accused her of spying on us." Jason was angry.

I sighed and slowly shook my head. "And?"

"She denied it, of course," said Peg.

"But Rodney started badgering her," said Aspen. "You know how he is."

Jason stood up and walked across the room toward the kitchen.

"Really?" I took my things into the inner office, then came out again. I could hear Jason knocking on the bathroom door and coaxing Kelcie to come out.

"Rodney said he called *The Mountain Sentinel* this morning," Aspen blabbed. "He asked for Kelcie."

"Yeah, he wanted to know what they'd say ... if she was working there or not," added Peg.

"Anyway," Aspen continued, "whoever answered the phone put him on hold."

"That doesn't mean anything," Peg chided.

"Rodney said the girl came back on the phone and wanted to take a message," said Aspen.

"He thinks that means Kelcie's a spy," added Peg.

"Then Colleen heard what Rodney said, and when Kelcie walked in a little while ago, she confronted her," said Aspen.

"Well, that doesn't prove anything," I re-emphasized.

"We know," said Peg, shaking her head. "But it was too late. Kelcie got very upset."

The bathroom door opened and a moment later, Kelcie emerged slowly, her face red and her green eyes swollen from tears. She tried to look dignified as she joined us in the main room.

"We're sorry," Aspen told Kelcie.

"Rodney's a jerk," added Peg.

Kelcie refused to look at them. She dared to peek at me, then turned to Jason. "I'm not a spy." Her voice trembled and I could see she was about to burst into tears again.

"Come on into my office, Kelcie." I shot a glance at Peg, who understood my meaning and herded the others away. The blonde girl sullenly followed me into my office without the door. Maybe I could get Merle to fashion something to give me more privacy, I thought as I beckoned Kelcie into the seat opposite my desk.

"Are you going to fire me?" Kelcie sniffed, staring into her lap. "I didn't do anything."

"I want to ask you a few questions first," I told her. "Then I'll decide."

12

"I'm sorry they upset you," I told my employee, who was struggling to maintain her dignity. "I do not want to let you go, Kelcie. You've proven that you're a good worker and have skills we need."

"Honestly, B.J., I did not ask for this job in order to spy on you." She dabbed at her nose with a Kleenex.

"Well, maybe you can tell me then *why* you put the name McKelvie on your application," I said. "When Rebecca gave me the W2 reports, I discovered your last name is Tucker. Grant Tucker is your father, right? The publisher of *The Mountain Sentinel?*"

Kelcie nodded her head. "I've been using my mother's maiden name," she confessed. "My dad and I haven't exactly been friends this past year."

"May I ask why not?" I sat back in my chair and waited for her response.

"I don't want to go into that," she said. "I'm sure he knows by now that I'm working here. I'm sure he's upset about it. I really don't care if he knows now or not."

"I see." I waited during a long pause, then added, "Well, Kelcie ... I don't object to your working for me as long as you're being honest about it." Then I asked, "What about your mother?"

Kelcie slumped forward and lowered her eyes. "I lost my mother five years ago. She died of cancer."

"Oh ... I'm sorry."

"I'm an only child," she stated. "It happened when I was a junior in high school. It was kind of a bad time for us."

"I can understand," I said, smiling gently. "Jason may have told you that our family suffered a tragedy two years ago. Right here in the valley, as a matter of fact."

Kelcie nodded. "Yes, he said his aunt died. She was ... murdered?"

"I don't know what happened. It could have been suicide. She was a drug addict."

"It's hard on everybody when something like that happens," said Kelcie. "I just wish ... I wish ..." She turned away. "Well, never mind. If I still have a job, I'd better get back to my computer."

"Of course you still have a job, Kelcie. I'm glad we cleared this up."

"I hope the others believe me," she said emphatically. "I am not a spy."

Later that afternoon, Merle showed up with the rental truck. I left the office an hour early and had Jason meet us at the apartment when he got done with his shift. Merle followed me to Greenwood Street, and I helped unload boxes until Jason showed up to help Merle with the larger items.

"Thanks so much, Merle," I told him after the truck was unloaded. "You might as well stay the night."

"No, that's all right, Beej," he said. "Janie's expecting me back tonight. I'd better not disappoint her." He smiled sheepishly.

"Have you two set a date yet for the wedding?"

Merle scratched his head and pushed his spectacles up on his nose. "She's thinking December."

"Well, let's at least go get a bite to eat," I suggested. "I can't fix a meal because everything's scattered in my kitchen."

He agreed to that, and I asked Jason if he wanted to join us, but he declined. He and Kelcie had plans for the evening. Leaving the truck in the parking lot, I drove Merle over to a hamburger joint in downtown Blanca Hills. I could already feel my muscles starting to hurt from the physical lifting.

Merle's cell phone rang just as we sat down at a booth. The restaurant wasn't too crowded, but the classic rock music playing was rather loud. Merle answered his phone and said, "Hi, Janie."

A waitress brought us two menus and left. Merle listened a minute, then said, "I'm having a bite to eat and then I'm starting back over the pass." Finally, he said goodbye and hung up.

"Peg says the food here is really good," I commented, scanning the pages to see what I was hungry for. "She got them to advertise at least."

"Hmm." Merle studied his menu intensely, and when the waitress came back, we both ordered Angus burgers and fries.

"Janie's not wasting any time," I said with a smile. "Are you sure you're ready for marriage, Merle?"

He looked at me strangely, then sighed. "Seriously? I don't know, Beej."

"Does she want to start a family right away?" I asked.

"I don't know." He made a face. "I can't picture Janie with kids." Then he added, "Heck, I'm almost too old to be a dad."

"You're younger than I am," I protested. "Janie's still in her 30's, isn't she?"

Merle shook his head. "Nope. She's 40."

"Oh." I looked around and noticed a tall man who had just walked in and taken a seat at the counter. He had his back to me, but there was something familiar about the blondish-brown haircut and he was dressed in brown pants and a short-sleeved turquoise shirt. I noticed sideburns and kept staring.

Merle noticed my observance and swung around. "Somebody you know?" he asked.

I smiled and turned back to him. "Nope." Then the waitress brought our drinks and we started discussing the paper and the website and the progress Merle was making on setting up an order form for classifieds online.

People walked in and some left, but the man at the counter sat by himself, drinking coffee and eating a chef's salad. During the course of Merle's and my discussion, I couldn't help but notice that the man was glancing our way every so often. The light in the restaurant was dim, so it was hard for me to really see him. But I began to think he was listening to our conversation. Where had I seen him before?

Soon the hamburgers and fries arrived and we were busy eating. An Hispanic man walked to the counter and recognized the light-haired man in the turquoise shirt. "Hey, Grant! You get stood up or somethin'?"

Both men laughed and fell into a conversation I couldn't hear. But at the mention of the name, it clicked. The man eating at the counter was none other than Grant Tucker, publisher of *The Mountain Sentinel* and Kelcie's father. No wonder he had caught the drift of our conversation about the *Buffalo Billboard*. I was rather surprised that the owner of the *Sentinel* would come, by himself no less, to a diner for his dinner. I would expect such a man to be living in luxury, eating in fancy places or going home to ... *oh, that's right* ... Kelcie had said her mother had died five years ago. Grant Tucker might be a widower, unless he remarried. Maybe he was working late and had just come by, like us, for a bite of supper ...

"Where did you drift off to?" asked Merle, nudging my arm gently with his hand.

I blinked up at him and giggled. "Oh, sorry, Merle."

"You know, Beej. I'm a little concerned that you are so far away from Dexter."

"Why?" I asked, surprised.

"I mean, you have to be pretty brave doing this all by yourself. Don't you worry about ..."

"Merle," I chided him, "I'm a big girl. I can take care of myself. Besides, Jason's with me."

"Yeah, true," he said and took a sip from his coffee. "But what if Jason goes back to school at some point? I mean, he's only got another semester to get his bachelor's."

"He's taking a break," I replied. "I want him to finish. But he seems more interested in learning how to run a newspaper right now, and besides ... he's got a girlfriend."

Just before we finished our meal, I saw Grant Tucker and his friend get up and leave the diner. Merle was telling me something about stats and SEOs and I turned my head just in time to watch the two men at the cashier's counter, paying their tab. I caught Grant Tucker's gesture toward me and then the frown that appeared on the other man's face. I could only imagine what disparaging exchange had just taken place involving me and my business.

Merle thanked me for the meal and we parted company in the parking lot. He hadn't seemed too eager to get home to his fiancée, I noticed, and decided that Janie meant to keep Merle on a short leash.

As I drove the few short blocks back to the apartment, I wondered if Merle was having second thoughts about his relationship. When we had been together, I noticed that Merle wanted more than intimacy—he had hoped for a commitment. That had been something I simply couldn't give him. Since the bitter divorce from Dirk Martin seventeen years ago, I had avoided commitments and had no intention of making a similar mistake.

There had been a few men I'd dated over the years, but I had to be careful and not give Dirk the ammunition he craved to take Jason totally away from me. Most of the boyfriends I'd broken up with took it as rejection, but Merle was different. He understood. We remained friends and had the understanding that we would always be there for each other, no matter who else might come into our lives. Janie had appeared almost right away, it seemed. Even though Merle had explained our history to her and had reassured her that I was not competition, I often picked up on Janie's fear that Merle might change his mind.

When I parked the Camry in my spot at the apartment complex, I noticed a car parked across the street that had its parking lights on, just idling. It looked very much like a Porsche, even though it was dark and I couldn't tell the exact color. Not being that familiar with my new neighborhood, I felt naturally more cautious than usual. I waited a whole minute before deciding to get out of my vehicle. It wasn't until I had locked up and was walking to the main entrance of my building that the driver of the Porsche slowly moved on down the street.

As soon as I put the key in the door to Apartment 7, it hit me. Grant Tucker drove a Porsche. I remembered that day several weeks ago, when I had gone to *The Mountain Sentinel* to place the help wanted ads, and he had thought I was applying for his copy editor position. For a moment I entertained the thought that maybe he had followed me. Yet he had arrived before I had.

Jason came home shortly after I did. "How is Kelcie doing?" I asked as I closed the blinds in the living room windows. "Is she feeling better after this morning?"

"Oh yeah," said Jason, heading for the kitchen to get something out of the refrigerator.

"That's good," I said.

"Mom, there's no way Kelcie's involved in corporate espionage. We talked. She really hasn't seen or talked to her father in months."

I didn't say anything about that. But it did occur to me that possibly her father did know where his daughter lived, and perhaps that was the reason Grant Tucker was parked on our street. I realized I didn't have to worry about a stalker at this point. Maybe the man was just looking out for his child.

The rest of that week passed too quickly. Most of the logistics fell entirely on my shoulders, which included finalizing the bulk mail permit with the post office, and also working out how we would upload our paper to the printer in Shambleton, which was eighty miles north of Valle Viento.

The shop in Shambleton had a web press and had contracts with several of the papers in southern Colorado. Several references had assured me that they were the best bet for the *Buffalo Billboard*, which would be sent electronically over the Internet no later than four o'clock on Tuesday afternoon.

They would process the pages and print all the papers for us, wrapped in bundles that Jason would then pick up later that evening. He would then drive the Suburban, loaded with 19,000 newspapers, back to the office Tuesday night. We would then bag them up so he could haul them off to the post office first thing in the morning for the Wednesday mail delivery.

Everyone was excited about our first publication. I was a basket case and went home late each night, exhausted. Then I'd have to get up early, so I could hurry back to Valle Viento and get a couple of hours in before the crew showed up for work. It was the most productive time of my work day.

Jason, with Kelcie's help, had set up the bins in the specified areas we chose. They figured out which locations would be most convenient for people to get the free paper. They would also be delivering some papers to convenience stores and gas stations throughout the small towns in the valley. Wednesday would be nothing but delivery for the two of them. Some of the towns were twenty or thirty miles away, so there was a lot of driving to do. But Jason said he loved his job.

With Kelcie busy working for Jason, the office had settled down and no one had spoken further about the idea that Kelcie McKelvie-Tucker was a spy. I had plenty of last-minute display ads to set up with Rodney and Peg hard-selling on Friday and Monday. Colleen had not brought in many ads at all, but at least she had written a couple of features that we would use. I wrote up an editorial introducing our shopper and made sure the classifieds we had collected got proofed and were ready to be laid out on Monday night and Tuesday morning.

I was pleasantly surprised when I got a call from Zach at the *Dexter*

Chronicle, saying they were putting in a full-page ad, congratulating me and thanking me for all my years of dedication at the *Chronicle*. The ad came camera-ready and I felt humbled when I saw that the staff had all signed their names. "We wish you the best of luck with the *Buffalo Billboard*. The Lower Valley is lucky to get you!" At that moment, even though I felt exhausted and overwhelmed with all the stress I was under, the first hint of satisfaction came to the surface. My business was going to be a success. How could it not be?

13

"Here you go, B.J.!" Peg burst into my office five minutes after nine on Monday morning. She plopped down a wad of papers on my desk.

Surprised, I met her excited grin with a smile. Then I poked at the papers and saw that they were all classified ad forms that had been filled out. "Wow ... farmers' market again?"

"Yup." Suddenly, she scrunched up her face, then turned away and blew out a loud sneeze.

"Bless you."

"Thanks." Peg sniffed and whipped a handkerchief out of her pants pocket to blow her nose.

"You're not coming down with a cold, are you?" I asked.

"Maybe ..." Then she stuffed the hanky back in her pocket. "Oh, and at noon I'm stopping by the animal shelter. They want a quarter page ad. Will that be too late?"

"Nope," I assured her. "Deadline's at five today." Then I gathered up the papers and handed them back to her. "Take these to Aspen. Kelcie will be in at ten and she can help type."

The office was buzzing. Jason and I had plenty of designing to do, plus I wanted to start a run sheet and figure out the ad layout before we had to start worrying about building our first pages of the *Buffalo Billboard*.

When I walked into the kitchen area to get a mid-morning cup of coffee, I overheard Peg talking with Colleen in the main room, where Aspen and Kelcie were pecking away on their computers at the stack of classifieds Peg had brought us.

Peg was saying in a low voice, "My husband doesn't like me working weekends."

"Well, don't then," said Colleen.

"But I just felt I had to promote the paper," Peg continued. "The market's been a good place to let people know about the shopper."

"Well, naturally," said Colleen. "Especially when they can put their ads in for free."

Peg laughed. "Right ... though I always tell them that eventually we'll be charging for our classifieds, like the other papers in the valley."

"Yeah," agreed Colleen, "but it takes time to get people used to something new."

"Can you cover the farmers' market next weekend?" Peg asked.

Colleen sighed. "I can't, Peg. My kids ..."

"Yeah, well ... I won't be going back, at least for a while," said Peg. "My husband thinks I'm working way too hard on this job."

"That's probably why you caught the cold," said Colleen.

"I mean, the Saturday thing was my idea," Peg made clear. "B.J.'s not paying any of us to go. I just feel so ... dedicated."

I walked through the main room with my fresh cup of coffee and smiled at them. "You certainly are, Peg," I told her, "and I want you to know that I appreciate all that you guys have done to help us get to this point."

"You mean we're actually going to put out an issue on Wednesday?" Colleen grinned, watching for my reaction.

Peg jabbed the other woman playfully, then walked over to the table to organize her newest insertion orders while Colleen followed me into the inner office.

"I don't have time to chat, Colleen." I tried to sound polite as I set my coffee down on a coaster and got ready to tackle my next challenge on the computer.

"Oh, I won't bother you, B.J.," Colleen said as she hovered over my station. "I just wanted to know what you thought of my other article. Did you read it yet?"

I sighed in frustration. "Did you give it to Aspen to type?"

"No, I gave it to Kelcie."

"I haven't seen it," I told her. "Look, I'm really busy right now ... do you mind ..."

"Colleen, get your butt in here!" Peg ordered from her corner in the main room. "Let the boss get her work done."

Thank goodness for Peg, my right-hand assistant. What would I have done without her? She was my most valued employee and she had agreed to be the sales manager since she had brought in almost twice as many display ads as Rodney or Colleen. In fact, most people she called on thought she was the owner of the *Buffalo Billboard*. I had to smile ... because I almost believed it myself.

It was three o'clock when Rodney showed up with the rest of his ad orders. He couldn't believe that Peg had brought in the most revenue for this first issue, and I overheard her telling him that she liked to call on prospective customers that were willing to place the larger, more costly ads. "You're not gonna make any money selling those piddly little two-by-twos or Service Directory ads," she told him. "The car dealerships and the real estate people are who you need to call on."

When five o'clock came and everyone else left the office, I stayed to clear my head and see about starting on the layout. Jason had finished what he needed to do and had left at the same time as Kelcie. I locked the front door, closed the blinds, and went into the kitchen area to make myself a sandwich.

I was alone at last. Maybe some progress would be made. After all, it wasn't as though I had never done this before. Paste-up was old hat to me, and I at least understood the concepts when it came to putting the puzzle together on the computer screen.

Armed with my ham sandwich and some left-over macaroni salad, I sat at my desk and drew up the dummy on the grid sheets I had designed. Aspen had photocopied a number of them for future use. First, I decided where all of the large display ads would go, then found the spots for the smaller ones. I blocked out sections where the feature articles and filler would go. This was fun.

Finished with my meal, I sipped iced tea while I opened up the publishing software to get a head start on tomorrow's major task. The template I had already created popped in and I renamed it with the date.

Then it locked up on me. I couldn't draw in any text boxes or picture boxes. What was wrong? Had I forgotten what I had just recently learned? Why couldn't I get this thing started? Jason had played around with the program last week, so that he'd know how to use it as well. But I was suddenly dumbstruck. Fear began to seep in as

I played around for almost an hour, trying to get the software to work. As it grew later into the evening and darkness had set in, I grew more tired and more upset as the problem mushroomed.

Finally I had to quit. Tomorrow was a big day and I had to get some sleep. Surely Jason would be able to help me figure it out. It was doing me no good trying to make the layout program work when I was this tired and this stressed out. I finally shut down my computer and left the building after locking everything up.

All the way home from Valle Viento to our apartment in Blanca Hills, I worried. My mind was in a whirl. All of the "what ifs" started hammering in my brain. I dismissed them. I wasn't going to let anything stop me. Even if the worst should happen, and we couldn't get the new software to work, we had light tables and I had a hand waxer. I'd break out the box of Xacto knives and package of tabloid grid paper that was on a shelf in the storage room. If necessary, we would use primitive tools to put our paper together, and it was still possible to physically drive the pasted-up flats to Shambleton, provided we finished on time tomorrow.

"*Beej ... oh Beej!*" The distant, dream-like, taunting voice of my sister ran through my mind as I drove east on the highway. The image of her contorted, mocking face was laughing at me. "*It's a waste of time ... just a waste of time ... you'll see.*"

I shook my head to flick that image away. Why were these memories of her still haunting me? I hadn't had time to think about her with everything going on. At least the dreams about Liz that had bombarded me since summer began were now less frequent. Yet I had no one to talk to about them, and I certainly didn't want to resort to seeing a shrink. "Liz ... please go away and leave me alone," I said out loud. Then I picked up some speed to get through the intersection where the light had just turned yellow.

It seemed I barely slept at all that night. When I'd gotten home, I told Jason about the problem with the publishing software.

"Oh, Mom, we'll figure it out in the morning," he said. "And besides, maybe Kelcie knows something about it. She can help."

Nevertheless, I worried. I wondered what was going to happen if we did not get the paper laid out on the computer. I almost called Merle for some moral support, but it was too late. I did not want to have to bother him this late at night, and Janie certainly would not approve.

In the morning, despite my lack of a good night's sleep, I was up and rarin' to go. At seven-thirty I was out the door, cup of coffee in hand, and drove to Valle Viento, determined that this was going to be a good day. It was, after all, the birth of the *Buffalo Billboard*.

On the car radio I heard one of our commercials playing. The announcer was promoting our paper. "Your source for bargains and more ... the *Buffalo Billboard* ... a weekly shopper coming to you each Wednesday throughout the Lower Valley, starting this week. For a limited time, you can place classified ads for free. Call and place your ad today ..."

By the time I got to the office, my coffee was gone and I started some brewing before everyone else showed up for work. Jason and Kelcie got there just before nine, and Aspen hurried in a few minutes past the hour, apologizing for being late.

"Be sure to clear the voice mail," I reminded my receptionist.

Aspen got settled in behind her desk and the phone rang. I ducked into my office, where Jason was seated at his computer, checking his email first. I didn't wait to check mine, but went immediately to open the new software. I could hear Aspen on the phone in the main room, talking to someone. A moment later my intercom buzzed and she said, "B.J., is it too late for someone to get a classified in?"

"No, take it," I told her.

"When should we cut them off?" she wanted to know.

"Well, normally our deadline is Monday at five," I replied, "but we need all the classifieds we can get ... so I'll just let you know."

"Okay, B.J." She went back to her call.

"Jason, did you try calling up the software on your computer yet?" I asked him. Mine was just opening on my screen.

He grunted a little as he closed up his email window. After a few clicks from his keyboard, he had it opened. A few moments later he said, "It let me in, but I can't navigate on any of the pages."

"That's the trouble I was having," I told him.

"There's got to be a way," he commented. "Let me try a few things."

Jason knew more than I did about troubleshooting, so I tried to concentrate on my other tasks for the morning, praying that he would be able to figure out what was wrong and correct it. Meanwhile, the other employees had come to work and were busy getting their work done and conversing while the phone rang every now and then. Aspen took a few more ads that people had called in at the last minute. I paid little attention to the employee banter and laughter.

I summoned Kelcie into our room as soon as she arrived at work. "Do you know anything about this software?" I asked her.

Kelcie peered over Jason's shoulder as he puzzled over our problem. "No ... I don't," she replied with an apologetic smile. "That isn't the software they use at the *Sentinel* either. What's wrong?"

Jason began to explain it to her and I stood up and went to look out my window. This was not a good sign. We hadn't even started to lay out any pages and at three o'clock I had to upload the paper to the press in Shambleton. We were on the clock and my worries turned to dread.

Next, I picked up my cell phone and called Merle in Dexter. He didn't answer his cell, so I left a message for him to call me immediately.

Colleen popped her head in through my doorway. "B.J., is something wrong?" she asked. Both Jason and Kelcie were too engrossed in what was on the computer screen to even glance at her.

"I don't know yet," I replied, which was a lie because I knew we were in trouble.

Peg appeared then at the doorway, dabbing at the end of her nose with a handkerchief. "B.J., what happened?"

I let out a big sigh and walked out into the main office, where Aspen stopped typing to look at me with a worried expression on her young face. "The publishing software is not working properly," I told them. "I'm afraid we're going to have to do cut-and-paste on the light tables."

"For real?" Peg placed her hands on her hips.

"Yes. I'll print out all the display ads on that waxable paper in the storage room. I have some newspaper grids ... it's a good thing I thought to purchase some supplies in case something like this happened."

"What about all the classifieds?" asked Aspen.

"I'll print those out too." I glanced up at the clock. "Stop taking ads at eleven."

"But how are you going to send the pages?" asked Colleen.

"Jason and I will have to drive the flats to Shambleton," I explained. "It's critical that we get started right away. I can't wait for Merle to call ...

and I'm not sure he can resolve the problem with the new software anyway."

"Yeah, and he lives four hours away," added Peg. She blew her nose into her handkerchief.

"Are you sick?" I asked.

"Just a few sniffles," said Peg.

I went to the back room and found all of the items we would need. I told Kelcie to plug in the waxer so that it would heat up for us to use. Then I grabbed my dummy sketch I had done last night and started marking the tabloid grids with their page numbers.

"I can help you," offered Kelcie. "How many pages are we?"

"Sixteen," I told her. I handed her a light blue colored pencil. "Remember... one and sixteen, fifteen and two ..."

"I know what to do." Kelcie smiled at me, then began setting the flats onto the light table while the others hung around to watch her. "Go print out the galleys," she prompted me. "I'll get Colleen to help me wax them."

"Me? I've never done that before," squealed the talkative one.

"You've never done anything before," smirked Peg. "You said this was your first job."

Merle called me a few minutes later, while I was busy printing everything out that we needed to paste up, including headers and page numbers. "What's up, Beej?"

"Oh Merle, it's a disaster. Our publishing software has a glitch. Jason can't get it to work either!"

"Okay, calm down," he said in his soothing voice. "Tell me what's happening with it."

I explained how both Jason and I had worked successfully with the software over the course of the week, practicing how to do the pages, how to lay out Colleen's articles, getting used to it all. Then, suddenly, the program had just locked up on us.

"Hm," said Merle. "I don't have a clue."

"I was afraid you'd say that." I was close to tears.

"So what are you going to do?" he asked, clearing his throat. "I don't think I'd be much help even if I drove down there."

"No, I can't ask you to do that," I said. "I mean, we have deadline in just over five hours. Jason and I are going to have to drive up to Shambleton and wait for them to print the paper, then bring it back.

We're doing cut and paste."

"Yeah, I guess at this point you don't have much choice," said Merle.

After we ended our conversation, I finished printing out all the copy and had Peg proofread the classifieds that Aspen had typed that morning. Later, Jason and I joined Kelcie in the main room, where the light tables were located, and we put on a show of panic and frustration for the other employees.

When Rodney walked in at noon, he saw what we were doing and exclaimed, "Wow! It looks like a newspaper office."

Aspen quickly explained to him what was happening and he, too, joined the audience as the three of us labored to get our first issue put together.

I didn't take a lunch break. Neither did Jason, though Kelcie had an errand to run and left for half an hour. At that point, the sales people settled down at their desks and waited, looking a bit worried. When the phone rang around one o'clock, Aspen answered it, then called to me. "B.J., the press is on the line."

I took the call in the main room. They wanted to know if we were still on schedule for our first run. I practically burst into tears, but managed to stifle my emotions as much as I could and explained the situation to the manager at the press.

"Don't feel bad, Ms. Martin," he assured me. "We've worked with a lot of start-ups. You're not the first ones to be late with your first issue. Take your time. Call me and let me know how things are in another hour."

I hung up, relieved that they were so understanding. Yet I still felt like a fool. We should have been more prepared for something like this happening. We still had several pages to fill, and I put Peg and Colleen to work, proofing, as we moved on to the next flat. Progress was painstakingly slow, compared to how much easier it would have been doing it on the computer.

Kelcie came back from her break and we worked together while Jason ran to the store to get some snacks to see us through this ordeal. At three o'clock the press called again. I had been too absorbed to call and report on our progress the hour before. I told them I hoped we would be done in another hour, and they reassured me once again that they would be waiting for us, no matter how late it got.

Five o'clock came. Aspen had to leave to pick up her little boy, and the other three reluctantly left, worry written all over their faces.

"Are you going to be all right?" asked Peg before she left the building.

I tried to smile, but it wasn't convincing.

Peg gave me a hug. "B.J., it's okay. You're going to make it. You have to." Then she hurried out, and I went to lock the door.

14

It was six-thirty by the time Jason and I finished pasting up the issue. I called Shambleton and told the press we were on our way. That would make it eight o'clock or after. Kelcie had left at five-thirty to go to her yoga class. At that point we didn't need her any longer. Without further delay, Jason and I placed the flats into a portfolio box from the storage room, and I grabbed my purse, my cell phone and the company checkbook, and we headed out the door.

Jason drove the Suburban, which he had filled with gasoline the day before. As we drove north on the highway, I leaned back in the passenger seat and relaxed for the first time all day. A moment later, emotions took over and I burst into tears.

Alarmed, Jason turned to me and said, "Mom, what's wrong?"

I let out a sob. "Don't pay any attention to me," I told him. "I'm okay ... I've just had a very stressful day. I'm ... just so wound up." I continued to sniffle and cry and he just kept on driving. After a minute, Jason turned his music on and the SUV's superior sound system was actually a comfort to me. We had not eaten since a few munchies around three o'clock, but all I could focus on was getting to Shambleton and returning with 19,000 new papers—hopefully before midnight.

A while later, Jason brought up the subject of Liz. "Don't you wonder what happened to Aunt Liz in that motel room?" he asked.

I sat up straight in my seat and blinked my eyes. "What makes you ask that?" For one thing, it startled me that he would talk about my deceased sister right out of the blue.

"Well, I don't know why, but I think about her from time to time,"

Jason replied. "I know you said she was a drug addict and probably died of an overdose."

I let out a big sigh. "Jason, we don't know for sure that was the cause of death. I think the authorities just assumed it."

"Do you think it could have been something else?"

"Like what?" I opened my purse to pull out a tube of chapstick.

"Was she in trouble? Did somebody kill her?" he asked.

After moisturizing my lips, I dropped the tube back into my purse and stared ahead at the road. "Sometimes I wonder," I said. I then disclosed to my son that my sister had tried to contact me before she had lost her life. "And I guess I feel a little guilty because I ignored what could have been a cry for help."

"I remember you told me," Jason muttered. "It's really sad."

"Yes, especially if it could have saved her," I commented. "At the time I was afraid she just needed money. She hadn't come around begging for a long time. I chose to ignore her."

After a minute, Jason asked, "What do you think she was doing in Blanca Hills?"

That was another question I couldn't answer. "I don't know."

We drove a few more miles, and then Jason said, "I guess Avery's really not going back to school." He signaled to pass a slow pickup truck, then pulled into the passing lane. "I talked to Dad last night."

"I'll bet Alicia isn't happy about it," I remarked.

"Yeah, but Alicia couldn't control Avery. I don't think she ever liked her own child."

"Jason, that's a terrible thing to say ..."

"Well, Mom, it's true. At least from my perspective. I mean, when Avery was home, she and Alicia were always fighting. She seemed to get along with Dad okay, but he'd get uptight around her."

"I can imagine," I added.

We were getting close to the intersection of the adjoining highway that would take us another thirty miles to Shambleton. I sighed with relief, knowing that we were more than halfway there, and that there was still daylight.

Suddenly, there was a loud *bang*, followed by a huge puff of grayish-black smoke. The Suburban slowed and then Jason nudged the SUV over to the side of the road as the engine quit.

"What happened?" I exclaimed. "What's wrong?"

"I don't know!"

"Jason ... what's wrong with the Beast?"

We could see the intersecting highway ahead of us. Traffic was coming from the southeast on that road, headed up toward another mountain pass and our destination, Shambleton. "Oh no!" I cried.

Jason tried starting the engine several times, but the SUV would not turn over. We stared at one another, horrified. Jason opened the driver's door and stepped out to see if there was a flat tire. I climbed out and walked around the vehicle, inspecting every bit of it. The tires were not flat. The Beast had just quit! Jason got back in and tried the ignition several times, but there was nothing. Not even a grinding noise of the engine trying to start up.

"Oh, this is the end," I moaned, leaning against the side of the black Suburban. Tears filled my eyes once again and I began to sob. "This is the end ... the *Buffalo Billboard* is doomed ..."

Jason looked at me in pity, not knowing what to do or say. I could only stand there, defeated as tears clouded my vision. My son released a huge sigh, then strolled away from me, kicking a stone out of his way as he muttered some profanity.

I knew I had to call for help. Regretfully, I had not renewed my Triple A last spring. I went to the Suburban, opened the door and grabbed my purse. Pulling out my cell phone, I got ready to call for assistance when a dirty, beat-up old Volkswagen bus pulled to a stop on the opposite side of the highway. Both Jason and I watched as a thin, scraggly man in faded jeans and a long-sleeved ragged maroon shirt stepped out and waved to us. He wore rimless glasses, had long, stringy gray hair underneath a faded tan military cap, and a bristly looking attempt at a beard. After making sure the road was clear, he crossed the pavement toward us. I noticed the cuffs of his jeans were thready and he wore sandals.

"You folks need some help?" asked the stranger, sporting a smile as his gaze focused on me. Jason protectively rushed to my side. "Looks like you broke down," he added, this time directed at Jason.

I wiped the tears from my cheeks and responded. "Yes."

"Where are you headed?" he asked.

"Shambleton," Jason told him, still guarded.

"I'm headed there myself," said the man and grinned, revealing a missing tooth on top. "I live in Rockcrest. I decided to drive up to

Shambleton tonight and catch the movie."

"We're taking our newspaper to the printers," I said. "And we're already several hours late. Then our truck broke down."

"Newspaper?" He leaned over and looked inside, then grinned again. "I know the guys at the press. I used to put out a little rag myself. Hey, how about if I take you?"

"Oh, would you?" Hope began to seep back into my heart. But a part of me still wondered, could we trust this stranger?

Jason shot me a warning look, but I said to the stranger, "I'll pay you. We need to get our paper printed."

"Tell you what." The man held his chin a moment as he ran some ideas through his mind. "I don't want your money ... but if you fill my bus with gas after I deliver you and your papers to ... where are you from?"

"Valle Viento. The office is in Valle Viento," I said.

"Oh ... okay. That's fine. You fill me up with gas in Valle Viento after we get the papers, and I'll take you to Shambleton and back."

"But, Mom ... what about the Beast?" Jason reminded me.

"We'll deal with that later," I said. "Let's get our things and lock up the truck."

I took out the portfolio box and after Jason had everything secure, we followed the tall thin man across the highway to his VW. From what I could see as I climbed into the passenger seat, the back of the van was messy with all kinds of clothes and junk. I didn't see how we were going to fit 19,000 newspapers in there. We waited while he made some room in the back for Jason to sit comfortably, and then he climbed into the driver's seat and took off to the north.

We came to the stop sign, and he pointed out that he had been driving up to the intersection when he noticed us stranded and decided to stop. I considered it a lucky sign that possibly this unkempt individual, strange as he may seem, was our guardian angel. I asked what his name was.

"I'm known in Rockcrest simply as The Captain," he told us. Then he proceeded to tell us that he had been in the military for a number of years, had fought overseas and returned in one piece. He rattled on about his background while Jason and I just sat and listened, too tired and too leery to question him. He said he'd been married once and he was now a loner and really dug Rockcrest, which Jason and

I both knew was the Lower Valley's counter-culture community, set several miles off the main highway, hidden in the hills and cliffs, but remarkably beautiful as far as scenery went.

I was extremely relieved when the Volkswagen bus pulled into the parking lot of the press. Dusk was starting to settle in, and Jason grabbed the portfolio as we bailed out. The Captain made no move to leave us, but followed us into the building. It was our first time at the press. I had hoped to drive up to Shambleton and meet the printers before this, but there had been no time. At least The Captain seemed to know where to go, and he greeted certain employees as we made our way into the huge web press room. Machines were running and making a loud rattling noise.

"I'm so sorry," I said when we came face to face with the boss, whose name was Clark. I then told about the breakdown of our vehicle and how The Captain had come to our rescue.

Clark glanced knowingly at the tall hippie, then reassured me that everything was fine. "Come back in two hours," he said. "We'll have it ready for you."

"Really? Oh, that's wonderful." I sighed with relief.

"Well." The Captain shrugged. "I'm gonna go meet with some friends. There's a good place to eat just up the road ... within walking distance. I'll meet you back here at ..." He glanced at the watch he was wearing, then looked up and said, "Ten-thirty."

"Thank you." I smiled warmly at the man. He nodded, then turned to leave. Then I looked at Jason, who sighed. "What's wrong?" I asked him.

"Nothing." He shook his head and managed a smile. "I'm hungry."

"Me too. Come on." We headed for the door. I was so wound up, I wasn't sure I could eat anything ... but I knew Jason must be starved. So we walked a couple of blocks until we found the quaint little restaurant The Captain had mentioned.

After we ordered some food and caffeine, I walked outside to make a cell phone call to Merle. Fortunately, he answered after only two rings.

"Hey, Beej. What's up?"

"Oh Merle ..." I tried not to, but suddenly found myself growing emotional. He could tell I was fighting off tears.

"Beej, what is it? What's wrong?"

"The Suburban broke down."

"Where are you?"

I explained the situation to him and said that a man had stopped to help and was going to transport our papers back to Valle Viento. "I'll have the truck towed tomorrow," I added. "Can you believe all this? I think it's a miracle. I don't know what we would have done had he not been driving by."

Merle hesitated, then said firmly, "Don't let this guy fuck with you."

I had never heard Merle say *that word* before and had to stifle a laugh. "Don't worry," I said, "he's harmless."

"You don't know that. Bridget, watch yourself," Merle warned. I knew he meant it when he used my first name. "Call me in the morning. Or ... better yet ... I'm driving down there tomorrow."

In protest, I told him, "That's not necessary."

"I think it is."

"Merle, what for? I'll have the Beast towed to the service station and they'll fix the problem."

"How is Jason going to deliver all the papers?" he asked.

"We have cars," I reminded him. "I'll get my crew to help. We'll be fine." We talked a little longer and then I thanked Merle for offering to come and help, then hung up and returned to our table.

Jason was busy texting on his cell phone and the food arrived just after I got settled.

At ten-thirty Jason and I returned to the press building after wandering around some of Shambleton's streets after our meal. The Captain was not there yet, but I took care of the invoice and saw our 19,000 newspapers bundled in piles, tied with strings, on a couple of wooden pallets. There they were—our first edition—and now all we had to do was get them transported back to our office, 80 miles away. But what if our rescuer had abandoned us? I dreaded the thought of having to call Merle again.

"The Captain's here," Jason announced. I turned around and watched as the lanky bearded man with his military cap and worn-out jeans approached us, grinning as he caught sight of all the papers.

Five minutes later, the Volkswagen bus appeared at the dock entrance of the building. After our rescuer climbed out, one of the men working in the shop helped us load papers into the van. But when there were about twenty heavy bundles remaining on the cement floor, The

Captain held up his hand and said, "Stop."

"What's wrong?" I asked, staring up at him.

"I can't haul any more papers than what's in the bus right now," he explained. "I don't have room."

I peered into the back of his van and was astounded. He was right, there was no room left, except for a small space where Jason would sit.

"Even if I crammed a few more in," said The Captain, "I don't think my vehicle can take the extra weight. It's stressed enough already."

"Oh ..." I frowned as I eyed the papers on the floor of the shop. Clark walked over to see what was wrong. After we told him, he said, "Fine, that's no problem. You can leave them here and pick them up tomorrow."

"Jason?" I looked at my son questioningly.

"I think I can get the rest of them into my car," he said.

"But do we have enough to take to the post office?" Getting the shoppers to the post office first thing in the morning was critical.

"Yeah," he said. "It just means I'll have to deliver papers around the valley a little later. Kelcie can start without me. She knows where to go."

"I guess we have no choice," I told him. "But I don't want you to take time away from deliveries on our first run. I'll drive back up here tomorrow with the Camry."

"Okay, whatever," said Jason.

We crowded into The Captain's bus and started south for Valle Viento. It was already after eleven o'clock, which meant it would be way past midnight when we got to the *Billboard's* office. By now I was really starting to feel fatigue set in. I think Jason was dozing in the back, surrounded by all those papers. The Captain was in a talkative mood and continued telling me his entire life story. My mind wandered from time to time as I fought to stay awake and alert.

We pulled into an all-night gas station just outside of Valle Viento and I paid to fill up the Volkswagen with gas. Then I gave directions to The Captain to take us to our office. Jason was wide awake after his nap. We all went immediately to work, unloading the bundles of papers onto the floor of the main room. When we were finished, I once again thanked the man who had sacrificed his whole evening to help us.

"Always glad to be of service," he said as he shook my hand before leaving. Then he cocked his head sideways and added, "You know, if you're looking to hire more help, I might be of some use to you. As I said, I had a small publication several years ago. I know a thing or two about newspapers."

"You don't have a job now?" I asked.

"No. Actually … Well, let's put it this way … I am looking to be gainfully employed."

"Do you have a phone number?" I was growing very tired again as I looked around for a pen and some paper.

The Captain gave me his land line number, then smiled, tipped his cap, and went out the door. Jason had already started cutting open some of the bundles. He had picked up the mail bags from the post office the day before. We started stuffing the bags with the appropriate numbers and tagging them.

"You're not gonna hire him, are you?" Jason asked as we worked at our strenuous task.

"Probably not," I said. "Of course it depends."

We were too tired to talk about it. Before long, we had everything ready and Jason brought his car around. The Camry was parked right out front. We hauled all of the bags out to the two cars and loaded everything. It was going on two o'clock A.M. by the time we left the office and drove in tandem to the apartment in Blanca Hills.

I set the alarm for five-thirty. We had to get the mail bags delivered by six-thirty in the morning. I was so wound up, I didn't think I could sleep. There was a lot on my mind, including the abandoned Suburban fifty miles north of us. I needed to call the sheriff in the morning to let them know what had happened. Then I had to deal with getting the Beast towed to the garage.

"Good night, Mom," Jason called from his room.

"Night," I called back as his light went out. I lay in bed, hoping my pounding heart would settle down. Finally, exhaustion overcame me and I slipped quickly into oblivion.

15

I knew I was dreaming. Somebody was after me and they meant to harm me. I struggled and fought to escape, but could not move. A looming dark figure towered over me. I needed to wake up, but I couldn't. I wanted to scream, but no sound came out. I knew that my son was in the next room. I tried to call out his name. Gasping and frozen, I heard only my strained voice ... and as hard as I tried, I could not force the word "Jason!" to my lips.

Suddenly, I heard Jason's voice and felt him shaking me gently. "Mom! Mom, wake up ... you're having a bad dream."

I was slow to recover full consciousness, but then my eyes fluttered open and my breathing slowed to its normal pace after a few more gasps for air. My tongue felt like a parched obstruction in my mouth. "Oh ... no! ... *NO!!!*"

"Mom, it's okay," he said. "I heard you crying out."

"What time is it?" I managed to ask.

"Almost five," he said.

I sighed as my body relaxed. "The alarm goes off in half an hour." I rolled onto my side and pulled the sheet over my neck. "Go back to bed," I muttered.

Without a word, Jason left my room. I wanted to sleep some more. I needed to rest. But the assailant in my dream still felt very real. I shuddered and tried to wipe the memory out of my mind. As tired as I was after only three hours sleep, I could not relax. Instead, I lay on my side, scared to move ... scared that whatever had been after me in my dream would be there again. This dream had been worse than any of the others. This time I'd been afraid for my life.

When the alarm finally went off at five-thirty, I reluctantly dragged myself out of bed. Jason was already stirring in his room. The first thing I did was go into the kitchen and make coffee. I heard Jason using the shower and wished I would have had time to do likewise, but we had to get those mail bags with the papers to the dock at the post office.

As soon as I got to the office, I called the sheriff's office to report my abandoned vehicle. They had already tagged it. Next, I called the service station in Valle Viento and made arrangements for them to tow it back so they could fix whatever was wrong with it.

Jason and Kelcie had loaded into their two cars the rest of the bundles for delivery to stores and news bins, leaving one bundle at the office. When my employees came in, they were relieved to see that we had our first issue. Right away they each grabbed a copy and started paging through it, delighted with our efforts.

Peg came in a little later than Aspen, Colleen and Rodney. She was all stuffed up with a cold and looked miserable, but she, too, made a big fuss about how good the paper looked. "You did it, B.J.!"

After I explained the details of the truck breaking down and our rescue by The Captain from Rockcrest, everyone was flabbergasted. I apologized for my appearance. "I only got three hours sleep last night," I said.

"I need to talk to you," said Peg. She blew her nose into a fresh tissue.

"Sure. Come on into my office." She followed me through the doorway and took a seat at Jason's desk, sniffing and clearing her throat. "You should be home in bed," I told her.

She came right to the point. "B.J., I'm quitting," she said.

"What! Peg!" I stared at her, hoping this was just a joke.

It was not. Peg looked at me with sad eyes and I could see she had been crying. "My husband is making me quit the paper," she said in a low voice. She obviously didn't want the others to hear, but I knew there was no privacy in my inner office and they were probably hanging on every word.

"Why?" I asked.

"He's upset because of the time I've been putting in. He says I should quit and go back to substitute teaching."

"But, Peg ... this was our first issue. There was a lot of work we all put into getting this paper launched. I'm sure that after things settle down ..."

"Nope," she said firmly. "I agreed with him. I'll sell ads for next week ... and maybe the week after that ... but then I have to stop. I'm sorry, B.J. I really am."

"Oh, Peg ... what will I do without you?" This news was devastating. I counted on Peg more than any of my other employees.

"You'll do just fine," she insisted, attempting a smile.

"No, I won't." Panic began to rise in my voice. "The Beast is being towed to the repair shop. My publishing software isn't working. And now this!"

"Make Rodney the sales manager," said Peg. "He's aggressive. He'll bring in the ads for you. But you still have to hire more sales people."

I knew Peg was right, but I just didn't want to lose her. "Isn't there any way I can make this work so that you don't have to quit?"

Peg shook her head, blotting her nose. She stood up. "I'm so sorry ... I have no choice." Her voice was cracking as she left my office and gathered up her purse at her desk, along with a paper and her notebook, then left to go home.

As soon as she was out the door, Colleen and Rodney pounced and stood at the door to my office, gaping at me in surprise. Aspen stared across the room from the receptionist desk, equally enthralled by this turn of events. "Peg's quitting?" cried Colleen.

I didn't want to break down in front of my employees. Sucking in a deep breath, I grabbed my purse and keys and prepared to leave for Shambleton. "I'm afraid so," I said. "But right now I have to drive up to Shambleton and bring back the rest of our papers." I turned to Aspen and said, "Call me on my cell if you hear from the shop about the Beast."

"Drive safely," Colleen called after me as I left the building. Once in my car, heading north, I was able to calm down and think more clearly.

All sorts of scenarios played out in my mind. First and foremost was my desire to bail out. I was tired, I was stressed out, and there seemed no possible way I could continue this venture with all that had gone wrong. How comforting it would be just to abandon the *Billboard* and move back to cozy Dexter. I could probably go back to my old job at the *Chronicle*. Suddenly, all my little peevish complaints about that place dissolved in the light of this horrific monster I had created here in this valley.

When I passed the spot near the intersection of the highways where the SUV had quit, I saw that the Beast was still there on the side of the road. An orange flag had been tied to the antenna, indicating that a state trooper had paid a visit. I didn't stop, but kept on driving toward Shambleton.

Half an hour later I arrived at the press. Clark came out of his office to greet me and then instructed one of his crew to help load the remaining bundles of my shopper into the back of the Camry. It was a hot day and the sun was in its highest point. Before leaving to return to Valle Viento, I decided to go back inside the press and use the restroom. I needed to wash up. As I crossed the large room where the presses were running, I saw Clark standing outside his office, talking to a tall man with light-colored hair. As I passed them he waved at me and I smiled. Then I noticed the other man, who looked right at me and smiled. It was Grant Tucker from *The Mountain Sentinel*.

"Nice paper," Grant Tucker called out, then held up a copy of the *Buffalo Billboard*.

For a second, I was shocked and must have shown it. Unable to respond, I quickly darted into the ladies' room. No one else was in there. I saw myself in the mirror as I washed my hands. My face was a mess. My hair was awful and sweat was showing on the underarms of my top. *What a slob!* I dug for a comb in my purse and tried to remedy the situation, but to no avail. There had been no time that morning to fix my hair. My dark bangs hung like strings over my eyes and I stubbornly pushed them back, returned the comb to my purse and left.

The men were no longer standing there. I slunk out the back door and headed right for my car, pulling the keys out as I walked. As soon as I reached my car, Grant Tucker seemed to appear out of nowhere. He had been sitting in his car, the silver Porsche, not far from mine.

"Hello," he said. "We meet again. I'm glad I caught you before you left." He smiled and his green eyes were kind and captured me in the moment. I was instantly embarrassed by my unkempt appearance and quickly looked away.

"I really have to get back to my office," I said with a tremor in my voice.

"Yes, I heard about your bad luck," he said, edging a little closer. I then noticed that his shirt also was wet under his armpits from this heat. Still, I was uncomfortable. "Are you in a hurry to get back?" he asked, having noticed my discomfiture.

"I kind of am," I said, avoiding eye contact.

"I understand." He sighed. "Still, you probably could use some lunch. Would you consider my taking you to lunch? There's a cozy diner just down the street."

Now I was floored. The competition wanted to take me to lunch. "Really?" I almost laughed.

"Leave your car here," he said. "Come on. I promise, I don't bite." He smiled again.

With a sigh, I looked inside my car at all the stacks of papers taking up the back seat. "Well, I don't know. I'm not exactly dressed to go to a restaurant."

He studied me from head to toe and smirked. "You look just fine to me. This *is* Colorado, you know."

I was going to decline. I really did have to get back to the office, but I was also hungry, and I was something else … curious. This was my chance to find out if Kelcie was telling the truth, or if she might really be giving information to the *Sentinel* about my paper. I wanted to know more. My silence convinced him.

"This way." Grant Tucker beckoned me toward the Porsche and I followed him as if I had no resistance. He opened the passenger door for me and I climbed in, noticing the plush interior. I hoped I wasn't falling into a trap. I would have to be careful what I said.

16

G rant got in and started up the engine. Then he drove out of the press parking lot and into downtown Shambleton. We passed the restaurant where Jason and I had eaten last night, and he stopped in front of a small quaint diner called Ruby's.

After we got out and were walking up to the restaurant, I asked him, "What are you doing in Shambleton today?"

"The press is printing our fall visitors' guide," he informed me. "We publish special editions throughout the year. I wanted to get out of the office, so decided to drive up myself."

I didn't comment. I was sure Clark had told Grant about the failure of the *Buffalo Billboard* to send its first issue electronically. He probably also knew about our software failure. I followed behind him as the hostess led us to a small table in the corner next to a pot of ferns. After we sat down across from one another, she handed us each a menu, then left.

"At least it's a lot cooler in here," Grant remarked. He looked around. "Not very busy either."

I noticed about half the tables were occupied, then studied my menu, which comprised an assortment of sandwiches, salads and the usual array of burgers. Reading the menu helped me hide my face. I didn't know why I cared what he thought of me. I wasn't exactly sure why I had even allowed this to happen—*Grant Tucker* taking me to lunch—what if this little meeting got back to my office crew? I'd never hear the end of it.

The waitress appeared at our table, a blonde in her 30's, wearing rhinestone-studded jeans and a sleeveless white blouse. "Would you like something to drink before you order?" she asked.

"We're ready to order now," Grant told her. "Miss Martin, did you decide?"

Startled that he'd addressed me so formally, I blinked in surprise, then turned to the waitress and ordered a gyro with a glass of iced tea and extra lemon.

She wrote it down, then asked, "What do you want for your side?"

"Just give me the coleslaw," I said and handed her the menu.

Grant made no comment. After studying the menu again, he ordered a Reuben sandwich with a fruit cup, along with an iced tea. The waitress scribbled it on her pad, collected his menu and hurried off.

"A *yee*-ro?" He rested his forearms on the table and leaned toward me, a slow smile forming. Those cursed green eyes of his were just too hypnotizing. I stared, a little confused that he'd questioned my choice of sandwich.

"Yes," I said. "A *yee*-ro ... it's spelled G-Y-R-O. You know? Slices of lamb and beef, tomato, onion and yogurt on pita bread."

"Are they actually good to eat?"

I couldn't stop staring at those eyes. "Uh ... yeah," I said. "Delicious, as a matter of fact."

"Are you of Greek heritage?" he asked bluntly.

Startled, I averted his eyes and looked down at my lap, then swept a wayward strand of my greasy dark hair over my ear. "No, I'm part Italian," I said, suddenly feeling intimidated.

"Don't be embarrassed, Miss Martin," he said, his face edging even closer across the table. "You are a very nice-looking woman."

With a huge sigh, I shook my head and stared right at him. "I would much prefer it if you call me by my first name."

"Oh," he said. "Okay ... Bridget ..."

"Actually, no," I interrupted him. I sighed again, then said, "Everyone calls me B.J."

"B.J. Well ... okay, B.J." He took a sip from his water.

I was beginning to feel extremely irritated, not so much because of him, but because I felt conspicuous and unkempt in my appearance in front of an attractive man. The silence was too much for me, and I asked him, "Are you going to tell me why you asked me to lunch?"

Grant's expression did not change. Another endearing smile started curling on the left side of his mouth. "It seemed like the right thing to do at the moment," he replied. "Besides, we're both in the newspaper business. I thought it might be a good idea to talk to you ... to find out if you're planning to put *The Mountain Sentinel* out of business."

"What?"

I must have looked shocked because he chuckled, then diverted his eyes and slowly shook his head. "No, that is not the reason. I just wanted to take you to lunch."

I was suspicious and I knew it was showing. I nervously looked around the room and was relieved to see the waitress hurrying over with our drinks. As soon as I got mine, I opened my straw and took a few sips. I almost wanted to get up and run out the door right then, but he had driven far enough away from the press building that it would have taken too long to get back to the Camry.

"I'm sorry," he finally said, stirring his iced tea with his straw. "It wasn't my intention to make you uncomfortable, and I can see that I have."

He was right about that. I hoped the food was coming soon. I just wanted to eat and get out of there. This had been poor judgment on my part.

"You know, everyone at my paper thinks you won't last six months."

I perked up at once. "Oh?" I took another sip of my cold drink. Was he picking a fight?

"Yeah, well ... not just anybody can run a paper," he said.

"And how long have you had yours?" I asked boldly.

"I bought the paper six years ago," he said. "My wife and I bought it. The previous owner was getting old and we decided to give it a try."

"You had previous experience, I'm sure," I guessed.

"Not much," he revealed. "Actually, I didn't know a thing about putting out a newspaper. I had to learn as I went. It wasn't easy." He took a drink from his glass.

"What did you do before?" I asked, quite surprised that he'd admitted what he had.

"I was a teacher. High school math. Then I went into business for a company in Denver, but I didn't like the big city. My wife was originally from Blanca Hills and wanted to move back. Unfortunately, she died a year later from breast cancer."

"Oh ... I'm so sorry." Instinctively, I reached my hand out to comfort him, but grew embarrassed and withdrew it quickly. I reached for my drink and took a few sips of iced tea. I remembered that Jason had said Kelcie's mother had died a few years ago.

"It was a terrible time," said Grant. I could see the hurt still in his expression as he recalled it. "But ... everything heals with time."

"Maybe," I said, remembering that my sister's death still haunted me in dreams. But I wasn't going to disclose that to him.

"What about yourself?" Grant smiled at me again. "Married?"

I slowly shook my head. "No."

"Partner?" he asked.

I hesitated a moment, then said, "No. Just my son."

Grant nodded. "Are you close?"

I studied him, a little surprised at the question. Apparently he didn't know that Jason lived and worked with me. "Yes," I said without further comment.

"You must have prior experience in the newspaper business," he said. "Your paper is remarkably well done for a start-up."

"Thank you. I've worked for newspapers most my life," I told him.

"Well, I'm impressed," he said. "Congratulations."

"Why are you congratulating me?" I asked, still unable to trust him. There had to be a trap.

"Why shouldn't I?" he questioned.

"Because ... we're competitors ... aren't we?"

Grant chuckled. "I don't really see it that way, B.J."

I was thinking, *to heck you don't.* I wanted to ask him about his daughter. So far he had not given any clues to suggest he had sent her to me as a spy. Yet some of my employees still believed that.

"Your daughter ... Kelcie," I said. He looked at me in surprise, but I went on. "You do know that she's working for me at the *Buffalo Billboard.*"

The waitress brought the tray of food just then, so we waited until she had served us. Then Grant spoke up. "Yes, I know Kelcie's working for you."

"You two are close?" I smiled, playing the game of getting to know him better.

"We were," Grant disclosed, stabbing his fork into a strawberry.

"You mean ... you're not now?" I prompted.

"We haven't spoken to each other in a while," said Grant. "You could say we had a falling out."

So it was true. What Kelcie had told Jason about her father was not a lie. Yet I had seen Grant's Porsche parked outside the apartment building where Kelcie lived. "So she doesn't live with you?"

Grant shook his head. "No. She moved out some time ago. I thought she was going to move away from the valley after she graduated from college. But for some reason she stuck around. I think she has a boyfriend. At least I hope so." After a pause, he added, "No one should be alone."

Strange to hear a father speak that way about his only daughter. I wanted to tell him that my son was Kelcie's boyfriend. But I didn't dare, not knowing what kind of reaction I would get with that kind of news. The relationship between fathers and daughters could be complicated. I started into my gyro and Grant sat, eating in silence while we both got lost in our thoughts.

My cell phone rang halfway through the sandwich. I grabbed my napkin to wipe my mouth, then answered the call, which was from the office in Valle Viento.

"B.J., the mechanic called." It was Aspen on the other end.

"Oh, okay," I said. "What did they say?"

"You probably need to call. He wanted to discuss it with you," said Aspen. "Do you want me to give you the number?"

"No ... I have their number in my phone." Then I asked, "Everything going okay at your end?"

"Yes. When will you be back?"

"I'm still in Shambleton, but I'll be leaving shortly." I thanked Aspen for calling, then hung up.

Right away I dialed the service station and got Roberto. He started giving me a long, detailed report on all that was wrong with the Suburban. I couldn't concentrate on anything he was saying. I finally interrupted him and said, "Just give me the damages. I need it fixed ... and sooner than later."

When I hung up, I was numb. Fatigue was setting in from my lack of sleep last night, and all I cared about at the moment was having them fix our vehicle so that Jason would be able to drive it when he needed to pick up the papers next week. To his credit, Grant Tucker did not question me about the call. I would have had to tell him that it was none of his business.

"Why did you choose the Lower Valley for your paper?" Grant asked when he had finished his meal. I was still working on my coleslaw and once again reached for my napkin.

"I love the valley," I confessed. "Jason went to the college his first year. I drove down from Dexter several times to attend his art shows. He was also in a couple of plays at Blanca State."

Grant commented, "He must be very talented."

"Yes," I agreed, "but he needs to finish school. He has one semester left at Boulder, but he decided to take a year off to work for me."

"Is he as good-looking as his mother?"

Startled, I blushed and looked down at my plate. Suddenly I felt so tired ... I couldn't eat another bite and pushed my dishes away.

"I'm sorry, I didn't mean to sound so forward." Grant waved to the waitress for the check. "I know you need to get back to Valle Viento with the rest of your papers."

The cell phone rang a second time. I glanced down and saw that Merle was calling. I answered the call. "Merle?"

"Beej, are you okay?" he asked. "I called the office earlier and they said you'd driven back up to Shambleton to get the rest of the papers. Is everything all right?"

"Everything's fine," I lied. "I'm just really tired."

"Did the Suburban get towed?"

"Yes."

"Do you want me to come?"

"No," I told him. "I'm okay."

"Beej, you sounded so stressed out last night when you called. I'm worried about you."

"Merle, I'll be fine. You don't need to drive all the way down from Dexter."

"Did you figure out that software yet?"

"No." I didn't need to be reminded of that problem right now.

"I think I can get it working for you," he offered. "Janie thinks I should help you out."

I don't know how he finally got me to consent to letting him come, but after I ended the call, Grant was putting money on the table for the food plus a tip. I pulled the wallet out of my purse, but he put up his hand and frowned at me, shaking his head. Defeated, I dropped my wallet back into the purse and smiled at him.

"Thank you for lunch, Mr. Tucker."

"Hey, we're on a first name basis here." He smiled. "You're B.J. and I'm Grant."

"Okay ... Grant. Thanks." I smiled at him and got up from my seat. He stood up and walked me out of the restaurant to his parked car on the curb. After he got me safely into the passenger seat, he walked around, got in and started up the engine. Then he drove me back to the press building to my Camry. Again I thanked him.

"My pleasure," he said. I noticed he waited until I had unlocked my car and started up the engine. Then he took off in his Porsche and I was starting to leave the parking lot when my cell phone rang for the third time. I saw that it was Jason calling.

"Yeah, what's up?" I asked.

"Mom, we need more papers. I'm out."

"I know, sweetheart. I'm starting home now."

"Where've you been?" he asked. "I thought you'd be halfway back by now."

"I had lunch. I'll see you in an hour and a half."

After I hung up, I pulled down my sun shade to view myself in the little mirror. I looked hideous. I could only shake my head and grumble. Having lunch with Grant Tucker had drained me. Plus, he had seen me at my worst—sloppy, sweaty and dirty—yet he had been courteous, had demonstrated chivalry, and ... something else ... he had stirred something in me that had been dormant for way too many years.

17

After I returned to Valle Viento, the help unloaded the bundled papers from my car for me. I decided to go home and take a shower ... and possibly a nap. Jason and Kelcie were anxious to deliver the rest of the shoppers, so they could go home. Aspen said she was happy to handle things at the office for me.

I drove home to the apartment in Blanca Hills and was finally able to relax for the first time in what seemed weeks of pressure and never-ending tasks. After my shower, I dropped onto the couch in the living room, dressed in my lounging robe with a glass of rosé, and turned on the boob-tube just to have an excuse to let my mind drift off to anywhere except the *Buffalo Billboard*.

I had dozed off when I awoke to the sound of the door unlocking. Jason walked in a moment later. He greeted me, then sank into the nearest chair with a big sigh.

"Did you get done?" I asked.

"Whew ... yeah, what a day."

"Tell me about it." I sat up and stretched. "I sure hope things go easier from now on."

"Me too," he said, then studied me. "Mom, you're not gonna quit, are you?"

Startled, I stared at him. "No. Why? What makes you say that?"

"I dunno," he said. "Just ... you were so upset last night when the Beast broke down."

"I know."

"And I just want you to know. I don't want you to give this up."

He sighed. "I meant it when I said I want to learn everything about the business." Then he leaned back in the chair and crossed his legs, staring at the TV screen. I had turned the volume down so I could sleep. "Everyone's concerned because Peg is quitting."

"Well, it's true. I'm very disappointed to lose Peg," I admitted. "But that isn't going to stop me. I've had this dream for a long time, Jason. I'm not going to let a few stumbling blocks keep me from succeeding at something I think will make a difference."

"People I've talked to say they like the new paper," Jason told me.

"I hope that's true." I stood up. "Want me to fix some supper?"

Jason declined. "Kelcie and I grabbed a bite at the pizza place over by campus. I'm good."

The mention of Kelcie reminded me of my lunch in Shambleton with Kelcie's father. I decided not to say anything about meeting Grant or what we had discussed. It was unlikely I would see the man again as it was. I went to the kitchen and fixed myself a salad, thinking about Grant's enchanting green eyes peering into my mascara-stained blue ones, the sweat and the dirt and newspaper print on my skin. Yet he had called me an "attractive woman." What was it he really wanted from me?

The next morning I awoke feeling rested. From now on, Thursdays would be Jason's day off so that he could rest after his long day of deliveries. I drove to work feeling perkier and more relaxed than I had felt since before this venture began. It was another sweltering hot day in the Lower Valley. Even though we lived in an area that was above 7,000 feet in elevation, the August heat wave had arrived and there were no rain clouds in sight over the mountains.

The sales people were out selling ads, and Aspen had little to do in the office, so she talked on the phone with her boyfriend off and on throughout the day. I had plenty to do with bookkeeping and getting timecards turned in to my accountant for payroll. I had sent Aspen out on a couple of errands when the phone rang, and since I was the only one in the office at the moment, I answered it.

"*Buffalo Billboard*," I said, looking for a pen in case somebody wanted to place a classified.

"Is this the damsel in distress that I rescued the other night on the highway?" It was The Captain's voice. My pulse quickened. I had not expected to hear from this man again, yet I remembered he had mentioned that he needed a job.

"Uh...yes, this is B.J.," then added, "this must be The Captain."

"One and the same," he said.

"Well … thanks again for helping us."

"You said you might be able to use my expertise," he said. "I happen to be available tomorrow morning for an interview. Would you like me to drop by?"

"Uh … sure," I said. "What time would you like to come?"

"How about nine o'clock?"

"That's fine," I said. "See you then."

After I hung up, I had an uncomfortable feeling about this man. But I owed it to him to give him a chance to be interviewed. I wasn't quite sure what he could do for the paper, but he claimed he had newspaper experience. I just wasn't sure I could afford another employee at this point, and he didn't seem like the type that could sell ads.

Shortly after Aspen returned from errands, Merle showed up. I was surprised to see him because I had thought I had succeeded at convincing him he didn't need to come all the way from Dexter. "Merle! Hello."

"Beej, how's it going?" Merle smiled and pushed his wire-rimmed glasses up his straight nose.

I introduced Merle to Aspen, then beckoned him into my inner office. "You didn't have to drive all the way down here," I reminded him.

"Well, I'm here." He shrugged. "I can be of help. How's the apartment?"

"It's great," I said. "We still have plenty of boxes to unpack. How's Janie?"

Merle sniffed, then sat down at Jason's computer and turned it on. "Don't ask."

I frowned. "Merle? What's going on?"

He glanced at me, then sniffed again and worked his mouse. "She's so controlling."

I sighed. "Come on, Merle. Did you two have a fight?"

He grunted. "Let's not talk about it right now."

I nodded knowingly, then got up and stood over him as he opened the publishing program. I then explained to him why Jason and I were having problems. Merle went through everything, picking up knowledge as he went and applying his common sense that came with his being a computer guru. He soon pointed out what we had been doing wrong, and gave me a crash course in how to effectively paste up text and graphics, and how to adjust columns. Soon everything else that went with putting together a page became clear to me.

An hour later, I was at my own computer, doing a mock-up as Merle looked over my shoulder and instructed me until I felt comfortable with what I was doing. "Jason will be so pleased," I said as I finished. "This is going to be so much better than all that crazy cutting and pasting we did on Tuesday. Oh Merle, thank you! You're a godsend."

"I know." He looked at me sheepishly, then said, "Wanna go to lunch?"

I once again left Aspen in charge of the office while Merle and I walked up the street to the Mexican restaurant across from the bank. I explained to him while we ate how so much had gone wrong Tuesday. I hadn't heard back yet from the shop about the Suburban, but hopefully the problems would be fixed. Then I told Merle that The Captain had called and was coming for a job interview the next morning.

"You're not going to hire him, are you?" Merle's face puckered up as he dipped a corn chip into some guacamole.

"I don't see how I can," I told him. "Until I know what kind of profit margin we're going to have, I can't really hire anybody else."

"Don't you need another sales person with Peg leaving?"

"I do, that's true."

"Are you thinking of hiring him for the sales position?" asked Merle.

"No," I told him. "Colleen has a friend who's interested in the job. I'll see if we can hire her before I contact the Work Center. But I owe it to The Captain to at least interview him. I have to pick his brain and see what he knows."

"Be careful, B.J.," he warned. "You don't know anything about him."

"You have nothing to worry about," I promised, then took another bite of my burrito.

After we finished the meal, which Merle insisted on paying for, I reached over to pick up my napkin, which had fallen on the floor, and I caught a man seated in a booth by the window staring at me. He quickly turned away, but I glanced at him again. He looked very familiar, yet I wasn't sure where I had seen his face before. He was in his mid-50's and of Hispanic ethnicity, which was nothing unusual in the Lower Valley as the population was more than half Hispanic. The man was sitting by himself and was reading something on his cell phone while sipping a cold drink and apparently waiting for his food.

When Merle returned from the restroom, having also paid the bill, we got up and left the restaurant, and at the door I turned around one more time to look at the dark-haired man with gray in his hair, sitting in the booth. He was watching me again and quickly turned around. We left and I quickly dismissed it from my mind. We walked back up the street toward the office.

I invited Merle to stay overnight and suggested that he drive back to Dexter in the morning, possibly after sitting in on my interview with The Captain. But he decided it was best that he head home.

"Merle, you're welcome anytime," I reassured him with a smile.

For a moment, a look of hope flickered across his face, and I knew then that things must be falling apart with Janie. He was still hung up on me. I was afraid he was going to change his mind and stay. My face must have shown what I was thinking.

I quickly added, "Merle, you're right. You should go home tonight and straighten things out with Janie."

With a sigh of defeat, Merle reached over and squeezed my hand, then said, "Thanks, Beej." Then I watched him saunter off to his car in the office parking lot, his hands in his pockets, looking like he had just lost his best friend.

Back inside the office, Colleen was there, talking up a storm with Aspen. They were laughing and greeted me with wide smiles.

"I sold some ads today," Colleen announced.

"Well, good," I said.

"B.J., the shop called. The Beast is ready," said Aspen.

That was the best news I'd heard all day. I left right away to walk up to the highway and get our vehicle. As I passed the restaurant that Merle and I had just eaten in, I saw that man again. He was sitting in a sporty red car on the sidewalk, watching me. I pretended I hadn't noticed him.

When I crossed the highway at the stoplight, I noticed the red sports car waiting for the red light. I tried to shake off the funny feeling that someone was watching me. As I glanced back at him, I saw him pull out and make a right turn, heading east toward Blanca Hills. Yet it still bothered me because I knew I had seen that man before, some-where, and it brought back a feeling of disturbance for some reason.

The repair bill on the Suburban was substantial, and they gave me a list of everything that had been wrong with it. They promised me that it would run just fine now, and that I had nothing to worry about. After writing out the check, I climbed in and drove the Beast back to the office. It did seem to run better. Maybe everything was going to be all right with it. I had my publishing software working, my vehicle running, and I felt successful having put out our first issue. Hopefully, the friend of Colleen would work out and bring us in a bunch of ads, and more classifieds would come in as people learned about our paper.

I dismissed all fears and bad thoughts and concentrated on the *Buffalo Billboard* being a huge success. I was no longer chasing the dream, I was living it.

18

Friday morning we held our first official staff meeting. Everyone was present, including my three sales people, my receptionist Aspen, along with Jason and Kelcie. Peg was in better spirits, her cold having progressed from one miserable stage into the next. She had also developed a cough.

We discussed the feedback that was coming from our new readers in the valley. The sales people said their clients were happy with the paper so far. Aspen reported that there still weren't very many people calling in classified ads, but she and Colleen were going to come up with some ideas to promote the paper and let people know about placing ads for free the rest of the month.

I announced that I was promoting Rodney to sales manager after Peg left. He whooped out loud and Peg reached over and high-fived him. "Congratulations!" she said with a grin.

"Thank you, B.J.," said Rodney to me. "I won't let you down."

"Is your friend still interested in selling ads?" I asked Colleen.

"Yes, her name is Molly. I think she's coming in to meet you this afternoon."

"I wish you weren't leaving, Peg," said Aspen with a mournful look at the older woman.

I quickly changed the subject and we discussed how we needed to have all ads turned in on time, in order to avoid further chaos such as we'd seen earlier that week. "Merle drove over from Dexter and fixed the software. I think we're going to be able to send the paper electronically this week," I announced.

Kelcie grinned. I noticed that she had her father's smile.

"Any other things to discuss?" I asked.

There were a few other issues that were brought up, but the meeting was over by nine-thirty, and I wondered where The Captain was. Hadn't he said he was coming for his job interview at nine o'clock?

Jason went right to work on a stack of ads that Peg had brought in. I scheduled them first into the computer, and then gave Kelcie some tasks to perform. At nine-forty The Captain finally walked into the office.

He was dressed up, but his attire was a bit old-fashioned and, for all intents and purposes, he looked like the same Rockcrest hippie who had stopped to help us on the highway the other night.

"Good morning, everyone." The Captain smiled at my employees, who were at their desks, preparing for their day. He looked around the office and nodded. "Hey, I like your set-up. I couldn't really see it the other night when we dropped off the papers."

I introduced The Captain to everyone, and then we moved into the inner office where Jason continued to work on his first ad for next week. I sat down at my desk and The Captain pulled up a chair across from me.

"Let's start with your previous jobs," I said.

The Captain leaned back in his chair and rolled his eyes before answering. "What would you like to know?"

"How long has it been since you've held a job?" I asked.

"Oh ... now ..." He frowned as he tried to come up with an answer. "It's been a coupla years. I had my own newspaper, you know. You saw the guys at the press. They remember me." He grinned.

"What was this paper you published?" I asked, leaning forward a little.

"It was a weekly ... likes yours ... and it was small ... it was slightly political ... and a lot of people liked it." He crossed his arms. Then he added, "Oh, the name of it was *The Rockcrest Stoner*."

I heard a chuckle burst forth from Jason, who pretended to be busy working on his ad. With a deep sigh, I shook my head slowly and told The Captain, "You know ... I'm not sure I can afford to hire anybody else right now. When I heard you'd had experience, I thought maybe we might have a place for you here ... part-time ..."

"Oh, I don't want to work part-time," said The Captain, sitting up straighter. "I want full-time work. I need to be gainfully employed."

"What else have you done in your career?" I asked.

"This and that ... dishwasher, bag boy at the local market, garbage collector ... and artist." Then he added, "You could hire me to sell advertising," he suggested.

Jason shot me a warning look and I smiled at The Captain. "We do have an opening right now, but I have someone coming in later today. What experience do you have selling?"

"What experience do I need?" He sounded a bit on edge now. I could tell he was irritated with me. He had expected to march into my office and get hired on the spot, just because he had helped us out.

"Thank you for driving all this way from Rockcrest," I said with a smile. I stood up from my desk and reluctantly he did the same. "I'm sorry, but I don't think I can use you."

Now disgruntled, The Captain hung his head and trudged out of my office into the main room, where the other employees were chatting and joking. He turned to me one last time and put on a wide smile, which showed that blatant gap where his tooth was missing. "May I call you sometime?" he asked me in what he must have thought was an alluring pitch for a rendezvous.

That was absolutely the *last* thing I wanted to happen, but I put on my most appealing smile and walked him to the door. "I wouldn't waste my time if I were you, Captain. My boyfriend Merle is our web guy and ..." When we got to the door, I opened it and looked up and down the street. "I'm sure he'll be back from his errands anytime now."

Without another word, the tall hippie walked out the door and headed for his Volkswagen bus, parked on the street. I went back inside, and all of my employees cheered me and clapped their hands. Jason stood at the door to our office with a knowing smile on his face.

"You handled that like a pro." Peg ran up to me and gave me a hug, then turned away to cough.

"I didn't know your mom had a boyfriend." Kelcie looked at Jason in surprise.

"Have I met this Merle?" asked Rodney, scratching his head.

Colleen put her hands on her hips and chided him. "You were out selling when Merle was here yesterday."

"Merle is not my boyfriend," I disclosed to everyone. "We are just good friends."

"Who once lived together," Jason added.

Aspen giggled. "Still … it worked."

"It sure did," said Peg as she wandered back to her area.

"I'm glad you didn't hire The Captain," Colleen said with a sigh. "He's weird."

"You can say that again." Aspen sat down and started typing.

When things had settled down again, I went back to my desk to get some work done. Then I thought of Merle and how strange he had acted when we'd parted company yesterday. I had the feeling he hadn't been very happy with me. For one thing, he and Janie were obviously having problems. When I had offered for him to stay at the apartment overnight, I had seen that look of hope in his eyes and it had frightened me. I didn't want to go there again with Merle … seeing him suffer because I was a woman who wouldn't make a commitment. He needed to stick with Janie.

After lunch, Peg and Rodney left to go work on sales while Colleen sat down at a computer to write up her feature ad for next week's paper. Her friend Molly came in just after one, and I interviewed the girl, who was about 25—the same age as Colleen.

Molly was a tall and spindly girl with red hair and freckles. She had a personality like Colleen, meaning she was very talkative and interested in people and their affairs. When I hired her on the spot, I hoped I wasn't making a mistake and getting a clone of Colleen. I simply told Molly we would give her a chance to see what she could do, and she agreed. I then turned her over to Colleen, who would show her the ropes, even though Colleen had not brought in half the amount of advertising revenue that either Rodney or Peg had sold.

That night after I got home, I gave Merle a call. I felt I should touch base with him. He didn't pick up, so it went to voice mail and I left him a message to call me back.

Later, while I was preparing for bed, Merle called. "Beej, is anything wrong?" he asked.

"No, Merle, I'm fine," I told him. "I was just concerned about you."

"I'm good." He did sound a lot happier, which was a relief.

"I didn't hire The Captain," I said to reassure him.

"Good girl."

"Are things good between you and Janie?" I asked.

"Oh, yeah," he said.

"Is she there?" I pried.

"She's watching television," he disclosed. "I'm actually on the back porch." He chuckled.

"Oh," I said. "Well, it sounded kind of like you two were having a spat."

"You could say that," he said with a sigh. "She tries to run my life sometimes." Then he seemed to want to quickly change the subject. "Hey, Beej, you're getting more hits on your new website." He then started giving me a report on the *Billboard's* stats, which didn't interest me that much.

After a minute or two, I couldn't help but yawn. "I'm sorry, Merle," I said. "I'm tired."

"I'm sure you are," he said. "You get some rest. And Beej ... thanks for the call."

I hung up my cell phone and then heard Jason coming in the front door. He had been out with Kelcie. He popped his head into my bedroom to say hi.

"You're back early." I glanced at my clock, which said it was only a few minutes past eleven. "It's Friday night. I thought you'd be out all hours."

"Kelcie was tired," said Jason. "We're going to the Sand Dunes tomorrow."

"Oh, fun," I said. "Make sure to take some sun screen and plenty of water. It's going to be hot again."

"I will. Good night, Mom."

"Good night, Jason."

I smiled as he left and I reached for the book I was reading. It was good to see my son happy. It was good to see that there was a young lady he liked, even if she was my competitor's daughter. That still bothered me at times, but I had to believe what I had finally convinced myself must be the truth—that Kelcie McKelvie-Tucker was somehow estranged from her father, owner of *The Mountain Sentinel*.

19

The next several weeks passed quickly. We were leaving summer behind in the Lower Valley as the mountainsides turned golden from the changing aspens. The nights and mornings were noticeably colder. Jason's 21st birthday had come and gone. Peg had been away for two months now and I still missed her.

Rodney had stepped up to the plate and was now the top salesman at the *Billboard*. Colleen was doing a little better at selling ads, but only a fraction of what my male employee was bringing in. Molly, however, was proving to be a good saleswoman and we were getting by because of her. At least Colleen was good at giving me filler articles and features to fill the space as our classifieds were still not as prolific as I had hoped they would be by now.

Back-to-school events, local elections and getting ready for the cold winter months had become the focus of our advertising promotions. I had been able to solicit a few flier inserts from some local merchants. The big ones had already been contracted out to *The Mountain Sentinel*. I knew that inserts were a huge source of revenue and there was little I could do to get them.

Just when I thought my work life was going to settle into a comfortable pattern, I was alarmed when I walked into the office to a horrific shouting match one morning in mid-October. Rodney, Colleen and Molly were yelling and swearing at each other. More accurately, the girls were quarreling with the sales manager, who was shouting profanities at them.

"Stop it!" I commanded as they all turned and noticed me standing at the door. "What are you doing?"

Poor Aspen cowered behind her computer screen, peeking out at me in fear.

"Rodney is stealing my clients!" Colleen was red in the face.

"He's been calling on my advertisers too," said Molly. "I walked into Natalie's dress shop yesterday and she got mad at me because someone had already come by earlier. Rodney sold her an ad."

Rodney frowned, shaking his head. "Neither of you would go see her, so I did!"

"But it's not your territory!" cried Colleen.

"That doesn't matter," replied Rodney. "You failed to call on them. I had to step in and do it."

"But that's not fair," argued Molly. "I was planning to get an ad from Natalie today. You had no right ..."

"*I'm* the sales manager!" Rodney was livid. "When you're too lazy to visit a customer ..."

"Shut *up!*" Colleen screamed at him. "You had no right taking Molly's client." She turned to me, angry and upset. "B.J., we have our territories. When Rodney goes out of bounds, like he's been doing ... it just makes all our advertisers mad."

"Then they're not going to want to advertise with us," whined Molly.

All three of them started yelling at each other once again, and I shouted for them to stop and listen to me, but it was no use. Being so absorbed in their fight, they ignored me completely. My voice could not rise above theirs. Finally, I retreated into my inner office and prayed the fight would end soon. Confrontations like this left me unbalanced and frustrated. Never, in any of the places I had worked before, had there been open warfare between sales people like what was going on here.

The quarreling finally quieted when Rodney marched into the bathroom and slammed the door. The two girls ran into my office, tears in their eyes. "That man is horrible," said Colleen.

Molly was still shaking. "I can't believe what he did."

"Let's just calm down," I said. I was shaking, myself, but I didn't want them to see that. "I'll have a talk with Rodney," I told them. "Just ... carry on ... please."

"We're sorry, B.J.," said Molly as they went out.

I didn't get a chance to talk to Rodney. The phone rang and it was Rebecca, my accountant, praising me for all the checks that were coming in at a steady pace. While we were discussing quarterlies, I watched Rodney come out of the restroom and stomp out of the building, carrying his briefcase.

After I got off the phone, Aspen buzzed my intercom. "Sorry about all that ruckus, B.J."

"No, *I'm* sorry," I told her. "Any messages for me?"

"Nope. But it sure would help if you could get some aerosol spray for that bathroom," she told me. "After Rodney uses it in the morning ... *whew!*"

I chuckled. "If that were the only thing we had to worry about, I'd be happy."

Things settled down somewhat after that first blow-up with the sales team. But the next week, when I came in one morning, Aspen confronted me with some startling news.

"B.J., did you know that Rodney was in jail?"

I let out a gasp. "What? He's in jail?"

She shook her head. "No, this was some time ago. Rodney stole some money from the convenience store he was working at."

"For real?"

"Yes. He served his time and got out."

Immediately I regretted the stupidity of hiring the man without checking into his background. Actually, I hadn't done background checks on any of my employees. I didn't bother asking Aspen how she'd found out about this. She went back to whatever task she was performing, and I sat at my desk and pondered this disturbing information for quite a while before delving into posting checks into QuickBooks.

With being able to submit our galleys of the paper electronically, Jason would leave in the Suburban by three-thirty in the afternoon on Tuesdays, pick up the 19,000 bundled shoppers from the press and return to the office by eight o'clock. He and I would unload and start filling the sacks for him to take to the post office the next morning. Sometimes Kelcie helped us. She and Jason distributed another large portion of the papers to bins and pick-up points throughout the valley.

More and more, people were phoning in their classifieds, which we were now charging for at twenty cents per word. Some people mailed them in with payments. The *Buffalo Billboard* had acquired a nickname ... the "valley's little paper." As our brand became more familiar, new advertisers who had been dubious when we began publishing, now wanted to try us out.

Unfortunately, the ongoing battle of the sales people intensified during the week of Halloween. I had made it clear to my staff that there would be absolutely no yelling and screaming inside our office. So what did they do? My employees took their fight outside into the parking lot, where the town could hear it. I was mortified.

One of the business owners from our building came in and warned me that if the disturbances did not stop, she would be forced to call the police.

"You've got to fire Rodney," Colleen begged me. "He's going to take us all down."

I sighed with regret. Rodney was still bringing in the majority of revenue. Yet I couldn't let him trample over everybody else. So I called Rodney into my office that morning and told him that the shouting storms had to end or I would have to terminate his employment.

A scowl the likes of which I had never seen on a man turned its vengeance on me, and it made me break out in a cold sweat. To make things worse, Jason had just arrived and was witnessing everything being said.

"I dare you!" fired Rodney. "You just try firing me. I'll have my attorney sue you for every penny, for racial discrimination."

"What!" I cried in alarm. "Are you calling me a racist?"

"Yes, you *are*," Rodney ranted. "You and your whole crew ... even your preppie son." He shot a venomous glance at Jason, who shook his head in denial. "You're all racists! I've felt it from Day One. You're against Muslims!"

I could not believe what was happening. I had never felt so humiliated in my life. Finally, I took a deep breath and said in a calm voice, "You're wrong. I have nothing against your religion. I really don't want to fire you, Rodney." My voice was shaking. "But I can't have you dominating the other women who are trying to sell ads. We're all in this together."

The anger continued to seethe in his black flashing eyes, and I waited patiently for him to calm down. I realized that without Rodney, the *Buffalo Billboard* would sink quicker than a quack in quagmire.

Almost a whole minute passed. I finally noticed that he was cooling down. He finally nodded his head and said in a calmer tone, "Okay ... I'll do my best. I won't interfere in the women's areas. I'll concentrate on finding new and better clients ... whether anyone likes it or not." And with that, he hurried out of my office and went to his chair to recover.

Jason settled down to get some computer time in, and the rest of the office had become strangely silent. Molly left, and within minutes Colleen also got up and went out. I couldn't concentrate on what I was doing, so I grabbed my purse and told Aspen I had to run to the bank, then left the building.

Outside the cool fresh air revived me. I decided to go for a walk after tending to my bank business, and strolled some of the back streets of Valle Viento. I didn't feel ready to return to work and the cloud of negativity that hovered over my business. My mind kept playing over and over the scene where Rodney had screamed at me, calling me a racist. I could not believe he had succeeded at intimidating me in such a way. I was not used to people treating me like that, and I surely would have fired him on the spot—regardless of his threat—had I not been afraid of coming up short on ads to support us.

Despite the fact that it was a sunny day, a chill was in the air. The leaves had pretty much been stripped off all the trees and swirled around in little piles on the pavement. I wrapped the collar of my jacket tighter around my neck and picked up my pace, heading for a small city park on the west end of town. I just needed time to regain my composure before returning to the office.

It wasn't until I sat down at one of the shiny dark green park benches that I noticed the red sports car pulled up against the curb. Two people sat in the front seat, obviously having a conversation. But I noticed the man was the same one I had seen several weeks ago in the Mexican restaurant across from the bank. I hadn't yet figured out where I remembered seeing him before, but it was definitely him. I was careful not to give away the fact that I had spotted him. As a cover, I pulled out my cell phone and pretended to call someone. Without looking straight in their direction, I could still see the red car's occupants, and now they were focused on me. There was no doubt I was being watched.

I wondered if they would dare to step out of the vehicle and try to approach me. What could they possibly want from me? As far as I knew, I had no enemies. I had no reason to feel paranoid, except now I was feeling a little afraid of the fact that my sales manager, Rodney, was an ex-convict. Was the man in the red sports car somehow connected to my belligerent employee?

After a few minutes, I put my cell phone away and was relieved to see that now there were other people in the park besides me. An older man and his little terrier dog were strolling across the lawn, and a couple of young boys ran to the swing set. An Hispanic woman pushing a stroller with a curly-haired toddler called to the boys to be careful and stopped next to the jungle-gym to watch them.

I stood up, suddenly filled with conviction, and nonchalantly began walking purposefully in the direction of the sports car. If they continued to observe me, I was going to challenge them. At first I pretended not to notice the car's occupants, but as I got within ten feet of them, I peered directly into the front seat. For a moment they appeared startled at my brave approach, but I actually gasped and stopped in my tracks when I saw the face of the young woman sitting in the passenger seat.

Before I could react, however, the man driving the car hit the accelerator, and with a screech of tires, the sports car peeled off in a burst of speed toward the highway, just four blocks away. I stood there in the park, unable to believe what I had seen ... or what I had thought I had seen.

For a moment or two I felt disoriented. I wondered if I was caught in one of my dreams. I swore the passenger in that red car had been my sister, Liz ... only she looked the way she had when she'd been a teenager. It was bad enough having ghosts appear in my dreams at night, but now ... in the light of day ... and a couple of days before Halloween?

20

Halloween was the Friday following the publication of our thirteenth issue of the *Buffalo Billboard*. Colleen and Aspen joked about the number "13" as being unlucky.

For the most part, we had settled into a more comfortable routine, although flare-ups surrounding Rodney and the sales girls continued. Aspen's little boy was sick with an ear infection and she had to stay home with him for a couple of days. Colleen and Molly helped me run the front office.

There was a definite change in the weather and talk of snow coming to the Lower Valley. Dexter winters had been mild in comparison. I braced myself for more severe winter driving conditions than I was used to. We checked to make sure the Suburban's tires would handle icy roads.

Since the startling enigma in the park earlier that week, I had been forced to think more about my sister. I could not get the image out of my mind of the young woman seated next to the Hispanic man behind the wheel of the red sports car. She had looked a lot like Liz as I'd watched the idling vehicle take off after I'd approached it. Of course, I knew there was no way it could have been her.

Liz invaded my thoughts, night and day. She continued to step in and out of dreams at night, sometimes in a fleeting way, but more often than not, pleading with me about something. Why couldn't I stop being haunted by her?

The afternoon of Halloween night I stayed late at the office to work on some end-of-the-month reports that Rebecca had requested.

It was dark much earlier now and past the time for trick-or-treaters to roam the streets. It must have been around nine-thirty when the office phone rang.

Ordinarily I would have let the voice mail answer the call, but I reached over and picked up the receiver. *"Buffalo Billboard,"* I said into the mouthpiece.

No one replied.

I repeated, *"Buffalo Billboard.* Hello? Is anybody there?" Again ... only silence. I waited another half a minute, then heard a click at the other end. Whoever was calling had hung up.

A shiver darted across my shoulder blades and I looked around inside my inner office. For a second, I felt frightened. Then I relaxed and shook it off. I was sure it had just been somebody who may have dialed a wrong number. Still, I realized I was here all by myself, and for the first time I felt vulnerable.

Finally, I shut down my computer and decided it was time to leave. I'd have to come in tomorrow morning. There was enough work left to do on the reports, plus I liked to come in on weekends and get a head start on the next week's issue. Without the distraction of my employees, I could get more done.

Jason was out partying with Kelcie and some friends. For some reason I felt uneasy going directly home and decided instead to stop at a sub shop in Blanca Hills. I hadn't eaten any supper and needed some food, even though it was kind of late.

The bars in town were busy. Adults in costumes were out having a good time. The younger trick-or-treaters were already home and in bed. After receiving and paying for my meal, I carried my sandwich and drink to an isolated corner table and sat down to eat.

Halfway through my meal, a man's voice behind me said, "B.J.?"

I glanced over my shoulder to find Grant Tucker holding a tray of food. He was dressed casually in jeans and a gray zippered sweatshirt with a hood over the back. His smile and the twinkle in his green eyes caused my heart to race.

"Oh, hello," I said with a cautious smile.

"Mind if I join you?" he asked.

"No, please do," I said and wiped my mouth with a napkin, in case some of the mustard had dribbled. As he sat down across from me, I asked, "What are you doing out and about so late in the evening?"

"I could ask you the same thing," he retorted. "It is Halloween, after all."

"I hope you aren't implying that I'm a witch," I replied.

Grant laughed. "As long as you don't think I'm a vampire." He cleared his throat when he saw my flicker of concern. "Seriously … how are you?"

I took a sip from my drink and glanced at him. He appeared sincere, but I didn't trust him. "Things are … good." I had to divert my eyes. His kind smile had a way of throwing me off balance. I grappled for words to keep from showing my distress at seeing him again. "We have a nickname now … the Valley's Little Paper."

"I've heard," he commented, opening his napkin and stretching it across his lap.

"And you?" I asked without skipping a beat. "How've you been?"

"Thank you for asking," he said warmly, peering into my eyes. "I've been better. It's been a rough fall. But I'll survive."

I couldn't help wondering what he meant about having a "rough fall." Was he referring to *The Mountain Sentinel* or his personal life? I didn't want to probe, so I just ate my sandwich.

After he started into his meal, he paused to ask, "How's Kelcie doing?"

"She's fabulous," I said truthfully. I noticed he was suddenly nervous. I sighed and then asked, "Do you mean to say you two still are not talking?"

Grant's troubled face confirmed what I'd suspected. I knew he had to be concerned for his only child. I recalled the night Merle had moved my furniture into the apartment and I had spotted Grant's silver Porsche parked outside the building. I was sure he was checking on his daughter.

"Whatever happened between the two of you, you should try to resolve it," I told him bluntly. "Too often, things that should have been said don't ever get said … and then you lose someone and realize you should have taken the chance." I was thinking of Liz.

Grant cocked his head and stared at me in a thoughtful way. "It sounds like you've had some experience with this kind of thing."

I reached for my drink, took a sip, then set the glass down on the table. "I once had a sister who was a drug addict," I said. "I could have reached out to her when she asked for help. I didn't. Then … she lost her life. I never got the chance to talk with her. Maybe if I had, things would have been different."

Grant sighed, then pierced a slice of pickle with his fork and ate it. "Were you close?" he asked.

"You mean ... with my sister?"

"Right."

"No," I confessed. "We couldn't stand each other."

"Tell me about her," he prompted.

My guard was down. I had always succeeded at holding back the dam, but now I was haunted by the girl in the red sports car who had reminded me of Liz. I didn't mean to release everything to this man ... this *stranger* ... but for some reason I felt compelled to tell him the story, believing he might understand. After all, hadn't he lost his wife?

"Growing up, she was the wild one," I said. "We were always competing for our parents' love. She just needed attention more than she needed their approval. Liz was a free spirit and could not be controlled. She used people ... she used *me!* She betrayed me by having an affair with my husband. I came too close to losing my son. She never apologized, she never cared a damn about my feelings or my life ... until the end, when she was desperate." I began to sniffle as tears filled my eyes.

"I'm sorry," said Grant. He reached his hand out and placed it over my wrist as silent sobs erupted. I felt warm energy flow where his skin touched mine and at that point I burst into tears.

Embarrassed and humiliated, I tore away from his grasp and rushed off to the ladies' room, leaving him sitting there alone. The crying stopped after a minute or two, and I washed my face and returned to the dining room, expecting him to be gone.

Instead, he sat at the table, slowly eating his meal, and waited until I had sat back down. "May I ask you one more thing, and then I'll leave you in peace," he said in a compassionate voice.

"I'm so sorry about my outburst," I said. "I don't know where that came from." I tried to chuckle, but it wasn't convincing. I stared at my half-eaten sub.

"Your sister ... she died here in Blanca Hills?"

"Yes, as a matter of fact."

"Two years ago?"

"Yes," I said. "At the Blue Heron Motel."

"Was her name by any chance ... Elizabeth Russo?"

I stared at him. "That's right. You must have heard about it. You probably ran the story in your paper."

"We did," he admitted. "We actually did some investigative reporting on it."

"Then you already know the death was deemed accidental overdose," I said.

Grant looked around the room, then leaned over in a low voice and said, "I never believed that." He then gathered up his tray of soiled wrappings, napkins and paper cup, and stood up. "I didn't realize she was your sister. I'd like to talk about this some more another time. Would that be all right?"

I looked up into Grant's compassionate green eyes and managed a smile. "Uh ... sure."

"Good." He reached over and put a warm hand on my shoulder. "And do keep an eye on my Kelcie. Would you do that for me?"

"Of course."

Grant smiled once more, then went to dump his trash before walking out the door. I had lost all interest in my food, but lingered in the restaurant another five minutes, absorbing what had transpired between us in the course of just ten minutes. The man had seemed so unlike the newspaper publisher I had first met in the parking lot of *The Mountain Sentinel* five months ago, or the man who had whisked me off to the diner in Shambleton, hoping to win me over because we were professional rivals.

I finally gathered my wits and left, heading home to the safety of the apartment.

Jason must have gotten home late. He was asleep in his room when I got up Saturday morning to make coffee. I did not disturb him. After my shower and a quick breakfast, I drove to Valle Viento to work. The first day of November was gray, cold and dismal with a strong breeze.

When I unlocked the front door to the office, a shudder rippled through me and I wondered why it was cold in the office. I remembered that in my haste to leave last night, I had forgotten to turn the heat down to conserve costs. It should have been comfortably warm. Last night I'd been too worried about the late phone call with nobody on the other end. I hoped we didn't have a problem with the furnace, especially now with winter coming on.

I set my things down on the front desk and removed my jacket. One of the desk drawers was open a couple of inches, so I instinctively closed it. Then, I caught sight of two quarters on the carpet, underneath Aspen's chair. That seemed odd to me, but I didn't give it a second thought … until later.

Before buckling down to work in my inner office, I went to the kitchen to make some coffee. While it was brewing, I walked into the restroom. When I switched on the light, I cried out in alarm. There was a large gaping hole in the wall at the rear of the bathroom, and I now understood where the cold was coming from. What had happened? Why was there a hole? I stared at it as the most likely possibility came to mind. Someone had broken into the office!

From my exploration of the passageway that had led from that closet storage room, I knew that there were connecting units on the other side of our building. My heart began to pound as I retreated through the kitchen into the front room of our office and headed directly for the telephone.

I dialed the Valle Viento Police Department and got the dispatcher. "There's been a break-in at our office," I said. "Somebody busted their way into our bathroom!"

"Okay, ma'am, calm down," said the female dispatcher. "First, give me your address and your name, if you would."

"226 Willow Street," I said. "My name is Bridget Martin. I'm the publisher of the *Buffalo Billboard*."

"When did this break-in occur?" asked the woman.

"I don't know." I looked around, then opened the drawer that I had closed earlier. The metal money box that we kept for cash was gone. I had stashed a dozen or so checks in the box after stamping them for deposit. "I think we've been robbed!" I then explained that I had worked late last night, and I mentioned that there had been a caller late in the evening, but no one had been on the line.

"I'm sending an officer over," the dispatcher told me. "Just to be safe, ma'am, I'd like you to leave the building."

"Oh, I don't think anyone is still here," I protested. Then I thought, *how would I know?*

"Ma'am, just to be safe."

"Okay," I agreed. "I'll wait out in my car."

I called Jason on my cell phone after I climbed into the Camry. I was shaking and concerned. I couldn't remember how much cash had been in the money box and I regretted our carelessness in not locking it up. We had become complacent and having to punch in the code each time we needed to get cash had been a hassle. I wasn't going to blame Aspen or anyone else because I had been just as guilty.

"Mom, what's up?" Jason sounded half asleep when he answered.

"We've been ... robbed." I was on the verge of tears.

"What? Where are you?"

"I'm at work. I came in and found that somebody had pushed in a huge hole in the bathroom. They got in and stole our cash box."

"Oh, no, did you call the police?"

I explained that they were on their way. Jason then asked if any computers or equipment had been taken. I told him that it didn't look like anything else was missing, but I would check more carefully after the police arrived.

"Do you want me to come?" he asked.

"I don't see the point."

"Call me after you've talked to the police."

I said okay and hung up.

Within fifteen minutes a squad car arrived and a single officer got out. I stepped out of my Camry and identified myself, then followed him into the building. I showed him the bathroom and waited while he crawled through the opening the intruder had made in the wall. When I stuck my head through, I saw him exploring the outer hallway with his flashlight beam.

His radio crackled and then I heard a voice say, "A break-in was reported at Naft's Jewelry Store. What is your location?"

The officer replied, "I'm at the location. The shopper office backs up to several stores and the jewelry store is one of them." I waited until the man in uniform had wandered farther away, then climbed through the opening and looked around. It was chilly and there was not much light, but right away I saw on the concrete floor what looked like a metal box. I stooped down and picked up our cash box, which was open and empty. Apparently the thief had grabbed what he could and discarded the box.

The policeman had disappeared around the corner. I started back toward the opening when I noticed several pieces of paper scattered on the floor in the hallway. I knelt down and found them to be checks. Quickly I gathered up all I could, then carried the checks and the empty cash box back through the opening into our office.

To my surprise, Colleen had showed up. "B.J., my husband heard about the break-in on his scanner. Were we robbed?"

I set the cash box and the fistful of checks on top of Aspen's desk. "Yes," I said. "Somebody pushed in the bathroom wall and got away with our cash."

Colleen stared, open-eyed at the checks. "They didn't take the checks, at least."

I sighed. "That's because they're all endorsed and stamped, ready for the bank."

"Oh, so no way could they cash them," she reasoned. "When did this happen?"

"I'm not sure," I told her, then repeated what I'd told the police and explained about the phone call last night when I had been working late.

"Oh, how creepy!" Colleen looked around. "Maybe we should see if anything else was taken."

The two of us wandered throughout the office and the storage room, but could find nothing amiss. By this time, the police officer had returned and I showed him the empty cash box. He made note of everything, then took my name and phone number and said he'd get back with me.

"Apparently the other stores were robbed as well," the officer told us. "Do you have any clue who may have done this?"

"Why, no," I said.

He nodded his head, then left the building. I sat down at the desk and held my head in my hands. I felt numb and violated. "I'll have to call Otto about that wall."

Colleen stood with her hands on her hips. She was wearing her purple designer jeans again today. She shook her head and said, "It seems very odd that whoever did this knew exactly where we keep the cash."

I looked up at her, startled by her comment. "What are you suggesting?"

"Maybe it was an inside job?"

I sighed. "Colleen ... certainly you're not thinking ..."

"Rodney," she said bluntly.

"I'm not going there." I stood up, put all the checks into my purse, then closed and locked the cash box and returned it to the drawer in Aspen's desk.

"I couldn't help it," she replied. "He infuriates me."

"It would be foolish for him to try something like this," I continued. "I mean ..."

"Well," said Colleen, "maybe he has friends?"

I looked at her a moment, then shrugged. "Ask him if you want," I told her.

Colleen laughed. "I wouldn't dare!"

"Well, as long as I'm here, I'm going to get some work done." I carried my coat and purse into the inner office.

"Want me to stay awhile?" asked Colleen.

I smiled and nodded. "You'd do that? You don't mind?"

"B.J., I don't want you to be here alone right now. At least not until we find out who did this."

"Thank you, Colleen."

"I have my article to write anyway," she said cheerfully. "Oh, would you like me to call Mr. Breitbart about the bathroom wall?"

"No, that's okay. I'll do it right now." I reached for the telephone.

It was around noon when I finished what I wanted to do. Colleen had some errands to run, so I told her to go ahead, that I was leaving soon anyway. Besides, I felt a lot calmer. Otto Breitbart had listened sympathetically to my news about the bathroom wall. He promised to come out the next day, even though it was Sunday, and get the damage repaired. Before he had hung up, he said, "I want you to be careful, Bridget. I hope the cops get whoever did this."

I was ready to go home when I remembered to check the supply room to see if I needed to order more toner for our laser printer. I thought we had a spare, but wasn't sure Jason had used it already. The ink quality was starting to fade and I preferred to keep on top of such situations.

When I opened the door to the storage closet, a chill tingled my spine as I recalled the day I had discovered the hallway that led to the outside—the same area in which the thief had tossed our cash box onto the concrete in his haste to escape. Apparently he hadn't discovered that entryway.

As a precaution, I walked the narrow passageway to make sure nothing had been tampered with. It made me uneasy to think that during the time I had been living in this back room —before Jason and I got our apartment—someone could easily have entered through this passageway and confronted us. I was relieved to see that the door was latched and secure from the inside.

Colleen had left when I came out of the storage room. I gathered up my things and pulled the keys out of my purse as I headed for the front door. It was still gray and windy outside. I closed the door behind me and was locking up when somebody behind me said, "Excuse me."

I jerked up in surprise. An adolescent girl, almost as tall as I was, stood six feet away, dressed in a long black coat and black boots with pointy toes. She had long dark hair, hazel eyes, and a narrow nose. She didn't smile. She stared at me in a strange way—looking almost desperate. But what took my breath away was her resemblance to my sister. My heart raced as I realized this was the young woman I had seen in the red sports car at the town park yesterday.

21

Startled, I froze, keys in hand. The girl's hazel eyes widened and she stuffed her gloved hands into her coat pockets.

"I'm looking for Jason Martin," she said with a tremble in her voice. "I was told he works here."

I relaxed and dropped the keys into my purse. "Jason isn't working this weekend," I told her, immediately suspicious ... but not knowing why.

She sighed and stared at the cement. "I really need to see him."

"Who are you?" I asked. When she hesitated, I quickly explained. "Aren't you the girl who was in the red car at the town park a few days ago?"

She looked flustered and her eyes darted from side to side. I guessed she was probably about 17 years old. "I don't know what you mean," she said with a quiver in her voice.

"A man was in the car with you," I added.

The girl cleared her throat and blinked her eyes with their long lashes. "I need to talk to my brother."

"You're Avery!" I cried out.

She was the one to look startled now. "Uh ... yes, how did you know my name?"

"I'm Bridget Martin, Jason's mother."

"Oh!" Avery managed an attempt at a smile, but I detected nervousness. It made me wonder what kind of a monster Dirk and Alicia had made me out to be in her eyes.

"Did you try calling him?" I asked.

"N-no." Then she quickly added, "I wanted to ... surprise him."

"Where are you staying?"

"Uh ... here and there."

"Where's your vehicle?" I looked around the parking lot, but only my Camry was present.

She turned her head around and mumbled, "Oh ... uh ... it's ... it's a block or two away."

I knew she was lying. She didn't have a car. She looked lost to me, yet I hesitated about inviting her to come to the apartment with me. Something about her frightened me, and I couldn't forget that the man who had been in the car with her that day had been spying on and following me.

Finally, I made up my mind. "Avery, come home with me. You can talk to Jason if he's there."

Again the girl looked around as if she was afraid of being watched. "That's okay ... I've got to go now. I'll come by the office another time to see Jason."

"Are you sure?" One part of me was relieved, but the other part of me was curious about this stepsister of my son whom he hardly knew.

"Yes. Goodbye." She flashed a quick smile and then turned around and walked quickly away, the heels of her pointed boots tapping against the concrete.

I stared after her in amazement. Now that I'd seen her up close, the resemblance to my sister faded a little. She had similar features was all. She didn't even look a thing like her mother, Alicia. All I could think about was driving home and hoping Jason was there, so I could tell him what had just transpired.

On my way home, troubled thoughts ran through my mind. What was Avery doing in Valle Viento? Why did she desperately need to talk to Jason, and why had she seemed so scared?

My cell phone rang and I was tempted to answer it, but I was now in heavy traffic and decided to let it go to voice mail. After I pulled into my parking spot at our apartment, I glanced at the phone and recognized The Captain's number. He hadn't left a message and I had no intention of calling to see what he wanted.

I climbed out of my car and hurried into the apartment, where I found Jason barefoot, dressed in jeans and a sleeveless white undershirt, his hair wet from the shower, playing a video game on the TV screen. "Hey, Mom." Right away he put away his joystick and asked,

"What did the police say?"

"Well, whoever did it also broke into some of the other businesses around us," I told him.

"Did they catch them?"

"No." I removed my coat and set down my purse.

"What was stolen? Any of our computers?"

"No, Jason, just some cash out of the cash box."

"That's bizarre," said Jason. "How much cash did they get away with?"

"I'm not sure. Maybe seventy or eighty dollars." Then I looked Jason straight in the face. "Tell me, when was the last time you spoke to Avery?"

Jason's face scrunched up. "Avery? What has she got to do with anything? Mom, you were just robbed!"

"Avery showed up in front of the office," I said.

The look of surprise on my son's face was of genuine innocence. "What? Really?"

I took a seat beside Jason and explained. "She was looking for you," I said. "She didn't know who I was at first. She said she needed to talk to her brother."

"Mom ... breathe." Jason studied me and then said, "You've had a traumatic day. Are you sure it was Avery who asked for me? What would she be doing in the valley? She can't stand me!"

"That's who she said she was," I told him. "Plus ... I saw her last week, sitting in a red car at the park ... only I had no idea who she was then." I purposely didn't reveal how she had reminded me of my sister Liz. I was beginning to believe I might have some weird obsession regarding my sister.

There was a knock on the door and I startled a little. Jason put his hand on my shoulder to calm me down. "It's okay, Mom. It's just Kelcie. She said she was dropping over." He went to the door and opened it, and I was relieved to see that it really was Kelcie.

Kelcie's sea green eyes were wide as she noticed my emotional state. "I heard about the break-in," she said. "What happened?"

I filled both of them in on the break-in. We didn't discuss Avery further. The kids had planned to catch a movie and grab some dinner out. I decided to soak in the bath tub after they left. I needed to recover from my unnerving day. By the time I had dried my hair after the long indulgence and had given myself a decent manicure, it was growing dusk.

For the first time in months, I had the urge to call Merle. But I convinced myself not to. It wasn't fair to dangle him along on a string just because I was feeling blue and a bit insecure. Plus there was Janie. Still, it would have been comforting right then to hear the sound of Merle's voice.

As if on cue, my cell phone rang just as I was standing in my kitchen, contemplating which frozen entrée to prepare in the microwave for this evening's meal. For a frantic moment, I was afraid it might be The Captain calling me again. I did not want to talk to him. Then I noticed a number I didn't recognize.

A little fearful that it could be Avery, I hesitated as I reached for the phone. After I punched it, I asked timidly, "Yes?"

"B.J.?" I knew the deep voice, but was uncertain who it was at the moment.

"Yes? Who is this?"

"It's Grant Tucker."

Relief flooded through me just then. "Oh… Grant… thank heaven."

"B.J., you sound a little distraught. Is everything all right?"

I immediately composed myself. "Yes, of course." I needed to cover up my insecurity. "Grant, I'm surprised you called."

"I hope this isn't a bad time," he said.

"Not at all," I assured him.

"Have you had your dinner yet?" he asked.

"I was just picking something out of my freezer," I said.

He laughed. "How about if you put it back in your freezer? Have you ever had a steak from The Bandito House?"

"Bandito?" I asked. "No … what's that?"

"Only the finest steakhouse in Blanca Hills," said Grant. "And I'd like to have you join me for dinner tonight." When at first I hesitated, he quickly put in, "Oh, I know … it's rather abrupt, asking you out at the last minute. But I would be very honored to take you to dinner tonight."

I had been caught off guard … *again* by Grant Tucker. "Well …" I realized he seemed harmless enough. We were on a comfortable peer basis, though I wasn't sure I wanted to take any steps that might go beyond casual friendship. On the other hand, I was fresh out of the bath tub and the idea of spending an evening away from this lonely apartment appealed to me, especially after such an upsetting Saturday.

"Okay," I finally said. "Where is this Bandito House?"

"I'll be by in half an hour to pick you up," said Grant.

"Wait ... do you know where I live?"

"Yes, I believe you moved into the same apartment complex my daughter lives in ... on Greenwood."

"Yes, but ..."

"See you in half an hour," Grant interrupted. He then hung up before I could protest.

My heart was beating rapidly as I left the kitchen and went to my bedroom to pick out something to wear. A date with Grant Tucker? Was I nuts? The competition? What would people say?

I finally calmed down when I realized this was an opportunity for me to find out from Grant what he knew about Liz's death. He had mentioned the fact that he hoped to discuss the case with me, and that his paper had done some investigative reporting into the tragedy two years ago. So this wasn't really a date ... it was a chance for me to learn something about the horrible ending of the sister who continued to haunt me in my dreams ... and even in my waking hours.

22

Just as I finished brushing my hair and applying a fresh coat of dark lipstick, the cell phone rang again. It was Grant. "I'm outside Building A," he told me. "I forgot to ask you which apartment you're in."

"Building C, number seven," I told him. "But I'm ready. I'm heading out the door now." I hung up, grabbed my coat and turned off a few lights before heading out the front door with my purse. Grant's Porsche was parked right in front, and as soon as he saw me, he got out to open up the passenger door for me.

The first thing I said after I'd gotten into the car was, "So you learned from Kelcie where I live." I smiled at Grant, my eyes bright. "You two talked!"

"Yes," said Grant. "Actually, I owe it to you."

"Why?"

"Because you convinced me," he said. "Life is too short." Then he pulled out of the parking lot and we headed toward downtown.

"Was your daughter happy that you called her?" I asked, gazing at the traffic as we crossed town.

"Surprised, actually," he replied. "We still have some things to work out between us, but it was a start. And, by the way, I was sorry to hear that your office had a break-in last night."

"Oh, she told you about that," I commented. "Well, it's been a rough day for me. Luckily, the thief or thieves only got away with some petty cash." I didn't want him to know that eighty dollars was more than petty cash, in my opinion.

When we arrived at the Bandito Steakhouse, I saw that it was a large restaurant on the edge of town and there were quite a number of cars already in the parking lot. Grant drove his Porsche into an available space and turned to smile at me. "It's always busy on weekends, but it's worth the wait."

In a flash he was out of the car, making his way around the front to let me out. I felt very capable of letting myself out of the car, but I had to admit, it was a treat to have a man show some concern. He took my hand as I stepped out and then closed and locked the car and we wandered toward the front door. A chilly wind reminded me that winter was soon upon us here in the Lower Valley.

Grant had made reservations, so we didn't have to wait for our table, which was located in a remote corner in a more isolated dining room. The lighting was dimmer and the small table had a candle burning inside a glass bowl. As the hostess seated us, Grant summoned a wine menu while I removed my coat and made myself comfortable. Soft piano background music played and this section of the restaurant was not as noisy as the larger room we had walked through to get here.

"Do you mind if I order a bottle to go with our steak?" Grant peered at me over the top of the wine menu.

"Not at all."

"What do you prefer?" he asked. "Merlot? A Cabernet ... or perhaps some Beaujolais?"

"As long as it's red."

He laughed and put the menu down on the table. The waiter appeared right away and Grant whispered his choice, then the waiter left. "I'm not a wine snob," he confessed.

"Neither am I," I told him. "I really don't drink that much. A bottle of Coors once in a while."

"You're right, wine is for special occasions." He leaned forward and his gaze made my heart quicken. "And tonight is an occasion."

I must have looked surprised. I stared down into my lap, then back at his face. "I didn't expect to hear from you this quickly," I said.

"B.J., I don't know what you might think."

I tilted my head questioningly and smiled.

He went on. "I lost my wife five years ago. I've told you the story ..."

I was thinking, *No, you haven't*. I wanted to hear more about it, but said nothing.

"I could have been remarried by now," he said. "At least a lot of people who know me think that. After Samantha died, it was a difficult time, both for me and for Kelcie. There were several women who tried to push their way into my life. I just ..." He sighed.

"Grant, you don't need to make excuses," I told him gently.

He cleared his throat, then said, "I'd much rather spend time talking about you. Tell me about yourself. You have a son?"

"Jason," I said. "He is my right hand."

"Well, tell me more," he encouraged. "Where did you grow up? Where did you learn how to put a newspaper together? I'm fairly impressed with how the *Buffalo Billboard* looks."

Was he really? I wondered. If my little shopper was anything to brag about, shouldn't he be concerned about revenue and losing advertising customers? Was this a game he was playing with me?

I wasn't sure I wanted to share a lot of personal information with this man. Even though I felt he was kind and he appeared to be understanding and gentle, I had to remain cautious. Besides, I was feeling unusually attracted to him all of a sudden. I wasn't sure it was wise for me to reveal a lot about my past.

"I've worked in every department." I felt I needed to back up my claim, so told him about my first job in Denver as a reporter fresh out of journalism school. "That was back when writers actually investigated their stories and checked all the facts." I saw that I had his full attention, so I continued. "Soon I was learning the other aspects of the business. I've worked in not only editorial, but in distribution and advertising. My favorite has always been in production."

"Most people would say that's where you get your hands dirty," he joked.

"To me, how a publication looks to its readers is very important," I added.

He smiled and nodded his head. "Things changed when we became so addicted to the Internet."

"That's right," I agreed. "Now, anybody can be an author ... with the click of a mouse." I saw that I still had his complete attention, so I continued. "When I was a little girl, I dreamed about being a writer one day. I had lots of ideas for stories. But now ... well, as I said, anybody and everybody seems to be an author and the glamour is not there anymore." I was on a rant. "All you have to do is type up a bunch of words and turn it into a book on line. I'm appalled when I read books that are full of typos, bad sentence structure, messy layout ... so I gave up wanting to write books and stuck with periodicals."

"I wish I could have hired you for my copy editor," he replied as the waiter appeared at our table with a bottle of Beaujolais Villages in a bucket of ice and two tall wineglasses.

We waited while he opened the wine and poured some into our glasses. Grant took a quick sip and nodded at the waiter. As soon as the young man left, a curly blonde waitress dropped two menus onto our table and said, "If you'd like a few minutes, I'll come back."

"No, we'll order right away," said Grant.

I opened my menu and made up my mind quickly that this was a night for a T-bone, medium rare, with a baked potato and tossed salad. Grant ordered a sirloin, medium well, and then we lifted our wineglasses after the waitress left with our orders.

"To new beginnings," said Grant with a warm smile.

"And happy endings," I added as we touched our glasses together. His eyebrows lifted in response.

The wine was excellent, but quite potent. Our conversation continued as he prompted me to give him more of my background. The waitress brought us our salads, but I was too busy talking to eat mine. I had intended to keep the dialogue focused on work-related topics, but as my glass of wine slowly emptied, I developed a more relaxed attitude about everything in my life and drifted into the failure of my marriage to Dirk Martin.

The dialogue naturally entered into the unsavory events involving Liz. He listened to every word as I relived in my mind the agony of betrayal and the unfair influence of the Martin family's money in which they were able to keep me from prospering in the divorce and had almost succeeded at placing the guilt on me, the injured party.

"But you raised your son," said Grant. The waitress came and took his empty salad bowl. I decided I needed to start on mine and picked up my fork.

"Yes," I replied. "Dirk soon discovered it was an inconvenience to care for a toddler. We settled on joint custody at that point."

"It sounds like you've struggled over the years. Was there never another man?"

I stared at him and found his quizzical look amusing. "I had some flings," I admitted as I took a bite of salad.

"You didn't remarry, then?"

"No." I wiped my lip with my napkin. "Dirk had me watched. I knew he was looking for any excuse to take Jason away from me, so when I had boyfriends ... I had to be discreet."

"I see." Dirk reached for the wine bottle and poured more wine into our glasses. "Anyone in your life now?"

I smiled in amusement, then took another sip of wine. "No," I said. There was nothing to gain by explaining about Merle, so I sat and finished my salad, aware of his green eyes observing me.

"It's your turn," I told him as I pushed the empty salad bowl away from me. "Now that I've shared my story ... I'd love to hear about yours."

Grant sighed, then gave me bits and pieces. "I grew up in Wheat Ridge. Samantha and I met in college. She was originally from Blanca Hills. That's what brought us here. *The Mountain Sentinel* was up for sale, and she wanted to move back. Kelcie was still in high school and resented having to leave her friends."

"Weren't you a teacher?" I smiled, studying him closer. "And you bought a paper?"

"I became a business man after I left teaching," he reminded me.

I nodded, now remembering.

"Samantha had a good business mind," he revealed. "It was really her idea, and she hired the right people to get things done. She basically ran the business herself ... until she became ill."

"I'm so sorry," I said in sympathy. The waitress appeared at the table then with a large tray of food. We waited as she set all of the dishes down in front of us. The steaks were still bubbling on their metal trays and the baked potatoes were garnished with sour cream, butter and chives. I felt my mouth begin to water.

After the waitress left, Grant picked up his steak knife and fork. "If this isn't the best steak you've ever eaten, I'll take out a full page ad in your shopper," he joked and began slicing some meat.

I laughed and followed suit. The first hot mouthful sent my taste buds exploding with pleasure as the salty juices from my steak caused my eyes to expand. I chewed and was surprised at how tender it was. Usually, tough meat irritated me and I'd stop eating a serving if it annoyed me. "Mmmmm... this is scrumptious," I told him and began to carve another small chunk.

As we ate our meal, Grant disclosed to me that his wife had basically run the *Sentinel* at first, and Kelcie had started working part-time while she was enrolled at Blanca State University. They had kept a lot of the old employees, but as Samantha's illness progressed, they had hired a general manager to oversee all operations. "Without Javier, we'd fall apart," said Grant. "I don't make a decision without consulting him."

"Javier?" I echoed, amused by the sound of his name.

"Javier Gallegos," said Grant. "His family has deep roots in this valley."

I wondered if Javier Gallegos was the Hispanic man I had seen with Grant that evening at the counter in the diner when I'd sat with Merle. Now, as I remembered back to that time, a sudden recognition hit me when I recalled how Grant had pointed at me as the two men were leaving, and the Hispanic man had frowned. Then I suddenly gasped.

"B.J., are you all right?" Grant stared at me with concern.

I reached for my glass of water and took a quick sip, then smiled. "Fine," I said. But I wasn't really. I had just remembered who that man was in the red sports car, whom I suspected was spying on me. I hadn't made the connection before, but just now I recalled that the Hispanic man in the car, who had sat with Avery in the town park, was this man, Javier, that Grant said was his colleague at the *Sentinel*.

I occupied myself with finishing my meal as fear began to seep in. Grant was busy eating and we didn't talk again until we were through. All the time I was thinking, this is not what it seems. Grant is not here because he's attracted to me. It's all a scam. He's probably invited me to dinner to find out all about me so that he can plot and plan to sabotage my business. How could I have been so foolish as to think I might be falling for this man?

"Let me pour you another glass of wine," said Grant after I pushed my plate away. He had finished as well and reached for the bottle, which was only one-third full.

I waited until he filled both our glasses. The waitress came over and carried away our dishes. Then, with a straight face, I asked Grant, "Why did you ask me here tonight?"

Startled, he looked at me with squinty eyes, then took a sip from his glass. "B.J., why would you ask me that? I just ... want to get to know you."

I folded my lip in and looked at him, trying not to appear emotional. It wasn't working, however. "Why are you so interested in the *Buffalo Billboard*, anyway?" I demanded. "I mean ... are you trying to butter me up so that you can maybe buy me out at some point?"

Grant looked startled. He glanced around at the room, then turned back to me. "No!" He tried to keep his voice low. "It never entered my mind ... B.J., what happened? We were having a great time."

"That's what happens to small town papers, you know," I blabbed. "The big sharks come in and buy out all the little guys. Soon all you have are conglomerates ... syndicates! I won't let that happen to my little paper. People love the *Billboard*, and I aim to hang onto it."

I expected Grant to fold, to admit the game he was playing, and then condescend toward me. Instead, he just stared, unable to believe what I had just told him. He just sat there, confused and alarmed.

After a couple of agonizing minutes of silence, I shrank back in my seat and turned away, completely embarrassed. Then I slowly shook my head and dared to look at him. This time tears were in my eyes. "I'm sorry," I said, fighting sobs. "I don't know where that came from ... please forgive me."

The waitress appeared at our table. "Would you like to see our dessert tray?" she asked cheerfully.

Grant looked questioningly at me, but I shook my head and reached for my napkin to dab at my eyes. He dismissed the waitress, then reached across the table and gently touched my wrist. "B.J. ... no matter what you think about me, I would never ... I can't even conceive of ... hurting you in any way ... nor your business. I admire you."

His words sounded sincere. When I looked into his eyes, I saw no deception. I decided to give him a pass. I almost wanted to bring up the subject of his colleague, Javier, allegedly following me. Something told me to hold off. I would continue to be on my guard, however, and play along for now. Maybe he truly was oblivious to my being watched, and truly unaware of what Javier was doing. Or ... maybe he had arranged it and was very good at hiding the fact.

For the time being, I knew it was better if I didn't tell him my suspicions. I could find out a lot more by being observant and aware. From now on I would be careful what I said to Grant. As much as I wanted to get to know him better and was attracted to him, I had to remain reserved. I could not let my guard down and trust him in any way. I knew what that had felt like in the past.

Grant asked for the bill, then continued to hold my hand and gaze at me in sympathy. "You have my word. I will never hurt you," he said.

I took some deep breaths and managed a smile.

"Do you believe me?" Grant asked.

I nodded my head and relaxed. "Okay."

"Would you like to leave now?" he asked.

I perked up. "After I finish my glass of wine."

"Okay," he said cheerfully. He let go of my hand and reached in his pocket for his wallet. "Then where should we go? Your place or mine?"

My head was foggy, but I laughed. "I think this is all moving too fast for me."

This time he laughed. "Don't you worry. I'm not asking for anything you're not ready for." He winked at me. "I just want to talk some more. Just talk."

The way he looked me in the eyes convinced me that I was probably wrong to have jumped to conclusions earlier. Aside from Merle, he was the most sincere man I had ever gone out on a date with. Besides, I was curious to learn more about the paper's investigation of my sister Liz. So I nodded my head in agreement and drank up the rest of my glass of wine.

23

Grant drove me to his home, which was in a prestigious upper-class neighborhood on the north side of Blanca Hills, not far from the university campus. Of course I couldn't see anything because it was dark, plus I was feeling the effects of the wine and felt drowsy. The soft buzz had relaxed me and the quiet music playing on Grant's sound system in the Porsche made me feel satisfied just to be where I was, in this man's company.

Within ten minutes he had pulled into a long driveway that led up to a triple-door garage. One of the lift doors opened and Grant drove the Porsche inside. "Sleepy?" he asked, having noticed that my head was bobbing a little.

I smiled at him. "I'm all right."

After he parked and shut off the engine, the garage door came slowly and quietly down as Grant got out of the car and came around to help me out. I had never seen such a spacious garage and one that was not cluttered with a lot of junk and useless storage. There was an ATV two-seater and a riding lawn tractor parked on one side, and a pegboard on the far wall with plenty of tools hanging above a bare workbench. Grant was obviously someone who valued order and kept his possessions where he could find them when he needed them.

We entered the home through a door in the garage that led into a hallway. Grant flicked on a light switch and I saw what must have been a laundry room to my left, beside a small half bath. Storage closets lined a wall on the right, and we moved on into another hallway that had a massive kitchen on one side and the great room on the other. Grant flicked another switch and a couple of decorative lamps came on, revealing a tastefully furnished living area with a gorgeous stone fireplace along the far wall, massive picture windows which had their blinds drawn, and a long comfortable looking blue couch with built-in recliners and a set of matching stuffed chairs. I loved the knotty pine woodwork and the tongue-and-groove cathedral ceilings.

"Grant, you have a beautiful home," I exclaimed in admiration.

"It seems a little too big at the moment," he commented, removing his coat and waiting to take mine as I wiggled out of it. "Would you like something? A drink, perhaps?"

"Oh no," I told him quickly. "I'm afraid the wine has given me a little bit of a headache. Red wine does that to me now and then."

"I'll put on some coffee then," he offered.

"That would be fine," I said with a smile as I sat down in one of the comfy chairs.

While he was in the kitchen, I gazed around at the beautiful decorations and paintings in his house. There were many *objets d'art* displayed on shelves and hutches, and I admired the pictures on various walls and finally stood up to go have a look at a few. Grant found me staring at a large portrait of himself, his wife Samantha, and a much younger Kelcie, who was probably about 10 or 12 at the time.

"That was painted by Samantha's uncle who does portraits for a living," Grant explained as he stood beside me.

"Wow, it's impressive," I breathed. Samantha had been a gorgeous lady with long, flowing thick blonde hair and soft, alluring blue eyes. I could see that Kelcie resembled her mother quite a bit.

A couple of long beeps came from the kitchen. Grant put his hand on my shoulder and said, "Coffee's ready. I'll get us a cup." Then he returned to the kitchen. I wandered around, admiring other paintings in the great room, then sat down again—this time on the big couch—as Grant handed me a small porcelain mug. "I think you'll like this, B.J. It's a dessert coffee … a bit of chocolate and some mint. Would you like some cream or sugar for it?"

I took a small sip from the hot drink and looked at him. "It's good … just the way it is. Thank you."

He reached for his mug, which he had set down on the large polished coffee table in front of us, then gently eased himself beside me on the couch. I was quite aware that he was watching me closely, studying me without wanting me to notice.

After a few sips of our coffee, he finally leaned back on the couch with his left arm resting on the back, and asked in a soft voice, "What do you do when you're not working?"

"Hmm." I turned to look at him. "That's a good question." I took another sip of the chocolate treat and frowned. "It seems all I ever do is work."

"Any hobbies? Interests? Sports?"

"Actually ..." I let out a sigh. "I'm afraid I'm fairly mundane." I wanted to steer the conversation away from me, so I asked him, "What about you? What do you do for fun?"

"I like sunsets," he said.

I stared at him. "Sunsets? You mean, watching them? At the end of the day?"

He nodded. "I've always been captivated by the colors and the beauty of the sky at that time of day."

"Really?" I smiled. "Are you an artist?"

"No, but I take pictures," he revealed. "Photography was my passion ever since high school." Then he added, "Of course now it's like being an author ... photographers today are a dime a dozen. Everyone seems to be able to take mind-blowing pictures with their cell phones."

"Guilty," I said with a giggle.

"I have a collection of old fancy cameras," Grant explained, "but nobody wants them."

"I'd love to see some of your work sometime," I said.

"Well, I'll be happy to show you," he told me, then said, "but right now, I'm curious to know what you can tell me about your sister."

I hadn't expected the conversation to suddenly shift to a heavy subject. I remembered that I had agreed to talk to him about Liz, and actually I was anxious to know what he had found out during his investigation of her death. But I wasn't sure I was in the right mood.

Grant appeared to sense my apprehension. "That is ... if it doesn't make you uncomfortable."

I couldn't help but notice that Grant possessed genuine compassion and it showed in those green eyes of his. I could have declined at that point and asked him to take me home, but instead I said, "No, I *do* want to hear about it." I didn't tell him that I'd been experiencing terrible dreams about Liz. But I knew that even as unappealing as the subject was, I had a need to know what really happened.

"I don't believe anyone really knows what occurred," Grant confessed. "I was interested in the case because things didn't seem right. The police concluded death by overdose with hardly any investigation at the scene. When the *Sentinel* reporter investigated, he discovered conflicting stories and his questions only resulted in dead ends."

"Why are you so interested in my sister's death?" I asked.

"Because there may have been foul play," said Grant.

"Did you ever meet Liz?" I asked.

Grant looked shocked that I would ask. "No!"

"What makes you think there was foul play?"

"One of my reporters received an anonymous tip," Grant told me. "If it hadn't been for that, we wouldn't have investigated. Then, when we started getting more questions than answers, our lead reporter received a death threat."

I was appalled. I took another sip of my still-warm coffee, then said, "My sister was involved with some unscrupulous characters at times. She had gotten into something over her head. She hung out with drug dealers and thugs, for heaven's sake."

"How was your relationship as sisters?" he asked me.

"What do you think?" I looked him in the eye. "I already told you what happened between Liz and my ex-husband. She was living under our roof at the time, and Jason was just a toddler, for God's sake." I could feel myself growing emotional.

"B.J., the last thing I want to do is upset you," said Grant. He took the coffee mug gently away and set it on the table in front of us, and then he moved toward me and drew me close to him in an embrace. I had been on the verge of tears and now they erupted and I sank against him, welcoming the comfort of his arms and aware of the rousing male aroma of aftershave. I continued to sniffle with a sob or two breaking in, but as he held me and stroked strands of dark hair off my forehead, my eyes closed and I basked in a soothing pool of solace.

Ten, maybe fifteen minutes passed and we continued to sit together, just relaxing. I let my sandals drop to the carpet and snuggled into a ball. It felt so good just to curl up against Grant as he stroked my face with his gentle fingers, and I felt safe and warm ... and also felt something I hadn't felt in a long time, contented.

From the other room Grant's cell phone buzzed suddenly and we straightened up on the couch. With a loud sigh, he got up and walked into the kitchen, where he'd left it. "Excuse me a moment, B.J."

"Of course." I sat and fluffed my hair a little, recovering from the spell I had been under. I heard Grant answer his phone.

"Hello." There was a pause, then he said, "Isn't it kind of late, Javier?"

After another silence, Grant sounded impatient with his colleague. "Can't you deal with this?" Another pause, and then I heard, "I suggest using your own judgment. I really don't know why you called me about this, Javier. You know how to handle these problems."

I couldn't help wondering what the problem was, and I was sobering up fast because I knew that Javier, Grant's right-hand man, had called him late on Saturday night. Finally, Grant's voice rose in pitch and he said, "Deal with it. I'll see you Monday morning."

A moment later Grant walked back into the living room, shaking his head. "So sorry. I have no idea why Javier had to call me this late."

"Is there a problem?" I asked.

"No. Not really," said Grant, smiling but looking annoyed. "Just an employee matter." He sat back down on the couch beside me and seemed to have dismissed the phone call from his mind as he turned to me with a smile. "Are you feeling better?"

"What time is it?" I looked around for a clock. "I probably should be getting home."

Grant put his hand on my thigh. "Why don't you stay with me tonight?" he invited. There was a twinkle in his eye.

Surprised, but not exactly shocked, I drew in a quick breath and stared at him with wide eyes. "Why, Mr. Tucker, we hardly know each other."

His expression changed to embarrassment. "I'm sorry ... I didn't mean to ... uh ... I'm not trying to take advantage of you, B.J. I just thought ..."

I laughed. "Grant!"

He glanced at me, uncertain. "What?"

"I'm messing with you." Smiling, I edged closer to him and leaned into his face. Then as our lips touched, it developed into a sudden, passionate embrace. Our mouths locked together in a long, drawn-out kiss that left me reeling when he finally released me.

It had been months since I'd been with a man—namely Merle. I had been swept up in my business and had smothered all bodily urges, but now my hormones were literally screaming for action. He planted the next delicious kiss and I let him cradle me in his arms as we stretched out on the couch, exploring kisses and tempting our tongues. He was deliberate without being demanding, and I was satisfied just to kiss and let him slip a hand down between my breasts.

The pleasure that surfaced was overpowering and I groaned and gasped. His caresses felt wonderful and brought warm, thrilling sensations that rippled to every part of my being. It wasn't long before I stopped myself for fear of going too far. I gently raised his wrist from inside my bra and sat up.

"B.J., is anything wrong?" he asked.

"I'm okay. I need some air," I said, panting.

"You're a beautiful woman," said Grant. "I'm surprised you aren't with someone already."

"I've been too preoccupied," I said. "I haven't had time for a new relationship." Then I looked at him curiously. "How come you don't have a girlfriend? Or ... do you?"

"Not for a while now," he confessed, still caressing my neck and shoulder. "I'm not exactly a man on the prowl like some women think. I haven't asked anyone out on a date for ... well, months."

I found that news to be almost unbelievable. A man as gorgeous and appealing—not to mention rich—as Grant Tucker surely had women stalking him. Was he telling me the truth, or giving me a line?

Grant moved his finger up my ankle toward my knee as we continued to cuddle. "I saw you with a man in the Main Street diner a few weeks ago," he said softly.

I remembered that time well, especially how Grant's colleague, Javier, had frowned at me while they were paying their bill and leaving the restaurant. "Oh, that was my friend, Merle Franklin, who lives in Dexter," I explained.

"Is he ... special?"

I looked into Grant's green eyes and smiled. "How perceptive you are, Mr. Tucker. Yes, Merle and I were involved for a couple of years. About a year ago, we broke off our relationship. He has since become engaged to a mutual friend of ours, Janie Sanders. Merle is also my web master."

Grant nodded his head. "How come you let him go? Or did he dump *you?*"

I shook my head slowly. "He wanted a commitment. I couldn't do it." I smiled.

"Hmm." Grant continued to stroke my leg and I loved it. I rested my cheek against his chest.

"I want you to know," I told him softly, "I'm not promiscuous, by any means. I just get turned off when a guy wants to make things permanent."

"And why is that?" he murmured, now twisting a lock of my dark hair in his fingers.

"I don't know," I said truthfully. "Ever since Dirk ..."

"Well, I will never cause you harm," he said.

I almost commented and wanted to say, "That's what they all say," but instead I stayed silent and let him continue his caresses. Several minutes passed. Grant's touch and the sound of our breathing was lulling me into a relaxing stupor. He then removed his shirt and gently pulled me up into a sitting position.

"B.J., stay here tonight," he urged.

My heart began to pound with anticipation and the sight of his well structured bare chest, with only a slight patch of light-colored hairs, thrilled me and I felt a gush of desire ripple through me. My lips opened as he placed a firm kiss on my mouth and pulled me close against him, where I could feel his heart beating rapidly.

The kisses were irresistible and I wanted so much to be possessed by this man—right now—no matter what the consequences. The feelings overpowered me in ways I didn't understand. No man in my past had made me feel such an urgent need for fulfillment.

Yet I once again came to my senses as Grant helped me to my feet and gently took my hand. He started leading me out of the great room toward the master bedroom suite. I stopped suddenly and held up my hand. "Wait!"

24

"What's wrong?" Grant demanded, surprised by my sudden reprimand.

"I can't stay," I told him, even though my heart was racing with desire and I would have loved to wake up tomorrow morning in Grant Tucker's bed.

"Why not?" he asked, baffled.

"My son," I said. "Jason doesn't even know that I went somewhere tonight."

"Well, text him," Grant suggested. "Leave him a message."

For a second or two I was tempted to fling caution to the wind and take him up on his suggestion. Then I sighed and said, "What will be think? I mean, I usually don't sleep with a man on the first date."

Grant smiled and held me in an embrace. "B.J., it's not really a first date," he teased. "After all, we've shared two meals together before tonight ... lunch in Shambleton, and meeting at the sub shop last night."

"True," I said, "but both those times weren't exactly dates." I shook my head. "I'm just concerned about Jason finding out I'm dating Kelcie's father."

"Why should it matter?" he asked. "What does Kelcie have to do with any of this?"

I looked directly into Grant's eyes. "She didn't tell you?"

"What?" Grant's eyebrows shot up.

"Jason and Kelcie have been dating for a couple of months now." Then I said, "They went out tonight, as a matter of fact... to a movie and... whatever."

"Kelcie is going out with your son?" Grant looked truly surprised.

"Yes, is that a problem?"

"B.J., how come you didn't tell me this?"

"Grant, I thought she told you. You said the two of you talked."

He looked befuddled and turned around in a circle. "No. I knew she was seeing someone, but ... no, she didn't bring it up. I guess she didn't want me to know."

"I'm sorry," I told him. "I should have said something earlier."

"It's not your fault." Grant managed a smile.

"Your daughter is such a nice person," I told him. "She's an excellent worker and gets along with everyone at the office." I didn't mention about the crew once suspecting Kelcie of being a spy for his paper. "I really like Kelcie ... and naturally, so does Jason."

"Wow ..." Grant continued to pace and rub his chin. Then he shrugged and sat back down on the couch, patting the cushion beside him. Obediently, I sat down next to him.

"In fact," I went on to say, "it was Kelcie who told Jason and me about the apartment opening up in her complex. Before that, the two of us were living in the back of our office in Valle Viento."

"You didn't have a place to live?" Grant stared at me.

"No, I'd just sold my home in Dexter," I explained. "I didn't know if my business was going to work out or not. So we camped out in the back rooms of the office."

"B.J., I'm sorry." Grant took both of my hands and gazed into my eyes. "I had no idea."

"It was a blessing moving into the apartment," I continued. "If we hadn't, there's no telling what would have happened when that thief tore the bathroom wall apart to break into our office last night. I still shudder when I think about it."

Grant pulled me closer to him. "I'm glad you're safe," he murmured in my ear and nuzzled me with his lips. "I am just surprised Kelcie kept that news from me," he said.

We were silent for a few moments, and then I asked a daring question. "What caused you and your daughter to drift apart? Why do you think she applied for work at the *Billboard?*"

Grant released another big sigh.

I then asked him, "Do you have any idea why she gave her name as Kelcie *McKelvie* on the job application?"

When Grant didn't answer right away, I felt fear begin to rise within me. Perhaps he *had* known. Perhaps he was playing a game with me right now. Had he been responsible for sending her to work at the shopper, just as my employees suspected? I didn't want to think he was capable of such a thing. Yet he didn't answer me. I moved away from him and stood up.

"I think you should take me home now," I said. I was feeling insecure and frustrated. Grant was not answering my questions, and now I was sorry I had asked them. Obviously, there was something going on with him that he didn't want me to know. And, of course, I could only think the worst.

Grant slowly sauntered into his bedroom as he put his shirt back on. I waited only a couple of minutes and then he came out with my coat and purse and handed them to me. Then he helped me on with my coat. Neither of us said anything.

I followed him out into the garage, where he slowly helped me into the Porsche. He looked so sad, but I was concerned about the possibility that I was being set up ... but for what? Why did I think the worst?

Soon Grant was in the driver's seat and started up the car. We left the garage and I watched as the big door slowly came down after we'd backed out. Not a word was said as Grant drove me home. I stared out the side window the whole time, blaming myself for ruining what had started out to be a beautiful ending to our first date.

When Grant dropped me off at the apartment fifteen minutes later, I put my hand on his arm to stop him from getting out. "I can let myself out. Thank you for dinner, Grant ... and thank you for taking me to your home."

He glanced at me and his look reminded me of a puppy that knew it had misbehaved, but didn't understand exactly what it had done. It tugged at my heart. I continued to stare at him, wishing he'd just say something ... *any*thing that would make these doubts I had disappear. Then he hung his head in despair and said, "Another day ... another sunset."

Puzzled, I patted his arm, then opened the door and climbed out. After I closed it behind me, I expected him to drive off and get as far away from me as he could. But the Porsche just idled. I then realized he was waiting to be sure I got safely inside, so I waved at him, then hurried to the entrance and went inside.

When I got into my apartment and turned on the light, I looked out the living room window and saw Grant's Porsche leaving. He was truly a gentleman, and I felt like a fool! I suddenly realized that I'd finally found a decent man I was really attracted to, yet I had insulted him and made him feel rejected. Why had I behaved this way?

Jason hadn't come home yet. After my traumatic day, starting with the break-in at the office, then coming face to face with Alicia's daughter, Avery, and finally the dynamic evening with Grant, which had ended in disappointment for both of us, I was exhausted and went straight to bed.

That night I didn't hear Jason return. I had fallen into a deep slumber when I started dreaming again about my sister. Liz and I were young girls in my dream. We were at a park near the home where we had grown up, and there were lots of shade trees, green grass, playground equipment and a large sandbox. She was about nine and I was eleven years old.

I was baby-sitting a toddler, whose hand I was holding as the three of us headed toward a big slide. Liz was frolicking and dancing around, laughing and sucking on a red Tootsie Roll pop. When we reached the slide, I lifted the little boy who was in my care to the top of the slide. He had thick dark hair and I saw that he was actually my son, Jason. Startled by this, I was unaware that Liz had climbed up the ladder to the top of the slide and grabbed Jason, pulling him up against her.

"Be careful, Liz!" I warned her.

"Watch out, Beej, we're coming down!" Liz laughed and I backed away just as she and my baby boy went down the slide together. Jason laughed and cried out, "Again! Again!"

The next thing I knew, I had placed Jason at the top of the slide again and Liz climbed the ladder once more. They slid down together, laughing, until they reached the bottom. Then Jason began to howl and scream.

"Jason! What happened? Liz, what did you do?" I shouted. My little sister turned her dark head, still laughing, and I saw an evil look on her face that frightened me. Jason, the toddler, continued to cry, so I immediately rushed over to grab him away from her.

As I picked him up, he was Jason no longer. Liz continued to laugh sarcastically as I set down a little toddler girl with dark hair and curls.

Tears streamed down the little face, but there were also mascara stains on her cheeks. I could only stare, puzzled at first and then terrified. I found myself staring into the face of Jason's stepsister, *Avery*.

The dream caused me to wake up. Since I couldn't go back to sleep right away, I reached over and turned on my bedside lamp. Then I got up to use the bathroom and strolled into the hallway to see if Jason had gotten home. His bedroom door was closed, so I knew he had returned.

After going to the kitchen for some painkiller to ease my wine headache, I went back to bed, but lay awake for quite a while, disturbed by the events of the previous day and particularly troubled by how my evening had ended with Grant.

Sunday was quiet. I stayed home and tried to catch up on some chores. Jason got up around noon and took a shower. When he was fixing himself something to eat afterwards, I asked him how his date with Kelcie had gone.

"Great," he commented, pouring himself a glass of orange juice. "The movie was excellent and we hung out at a bar downtown where she knew some people from college." He didn't ask me about my evening and I didn't volunteer the fact that Kelcie's father had taken me to dinner. I figured it was best not to even mention the fact I had been meeting with him. In fact, it disturbed me that I had let myself get as close to the man as I had. It was unlike me to open my heart like that. I had to be more careful.

Later that afternoon my cell phone rang. I was afraid to look and see who was calling. I wasn't sure I wanted to have a conversation with Grant, and yet I really wanted it to be him calling me. But when I picked up, I saw that it was Peg Espinoza, my former sales employee, on the other end.

"Hello?"

"B.J.! It's Peg."

"Well, hello. How are you?" I wondered if she had changed her mind and wanted to come back to work for me at the *Billboard*.

"I'm doing just fine," Peg said. "I've been meaning to catch up with you. How is it going at the *Buffalo Billboard* these days?"

"Never a dull moment," I told her, taking a seat on the couch. "How's substitute teaching?"

"Always dull," she grumbled. "No, really ... it's okay. I was a bit ... concerned about you."

"Oh," I said, "you must have heard about the break-in."

"No!" Peg's voice rose. "Break-in! When?"

I gave her a quick summary of what had happened Friday night and also mentioned that I had received a strange phone call before leaving the office with no one on the other end.

"Oh, B.J., that's awful," she sympathized. "Did the police find out who did it?"

"Not yet," I said.

"How are you holding up?" she asked. "Is everything going smoothly at the office?"

"Well, it's funny you should ask," I said. "Ever since you left, we have these screaming matches going on at the office about once a week."

"What!"

"Sometimes I think I've lost control of my crew," I confessed. "Rodney and Colleen and the new girl ... Molly ... get into these yelling fights about their territories. Ever since I made Rodney head of sales, he thinks he owns those women."

"Probably 'cuz he's a Muslim," Peg commented.

"That's not funny, Peg," I murmured.

"Oh, I'm sorry." But I could tell she wasn't. "Say, the reason I called is because I saw you in the Bandito Steakhouse last night. My husband and I were there eating, and who should walk in but my old boss from the *Billboard* with the publisher of *The Mountain Sentinel* ... namely Grant Tucker. B.J., what's *that* about? Are you two an item?" She giggled.

I looked around the room to be sure Jason wasn't within hearing range. Then I took my cell phone into my bedroom and closed the door ... just in case. "He asked me to dinner," I told her bluntly. "What surprises me the most is ... I agreed."

"Oh, B.J., he's a real catch." I couldn't tell if Peg was being sarcastic or if she meant it.

"He's really very nice," I confessed.

"And?" She waited.

"And no ... we're not an item," I told her.

Peg giggled. "He lost his wife, didn't he? Some years back?"

"Yes." I sighed. There was a long silence. I was hesitant to volunteer any information.

Finally, Peg said, "I think it would be a good idea if you and I sit down over a cup of coffee someday soon."

I was about to protest, but the small voice in my head that belonged to Liz was saying, *Peg wants to be your friend ... let her!* So I gave in. "I'd like that, Peg. Maybe it would help to have a chat so I can sort things out."

We left it at that. She told me she would call me next week. She had to fill in for a teacher this coming week, but as soon as she was free, we'd get together. I thanked her and we hung up.

"Going in to work this afternoon?" Jason asked me later that day. He knew that I often liked to work in the peace and quiet of a Sunday afternoon.

"No, I think I'll stay here today," I replied. Then I asked him, "Are you seeing Kelcie today?"

"Probably." He cocked his head at me. "Why?"

"No reason." I smiled.

"Mom, is everything okay?" Jason stared at me. "You seem awful quiet."

I sighed. "There's just been a lot that's happened lately."

"Don't let it get to you," he said. "Everything's going to be all right."

The next day at the office, Otto Breitbart came in and repaired the bathroom wall. The sales people were out getting their last-minute ads for this week's paper, and Kelcie and Aspen were typing up classifieds while Jason and I worked in the inner room. I kept expecting Avery to walk in. Jason seemed to have momentarily forgotten that his stepsister had shown up in town Saturday.

My mind was preoccupied with Grant Tucker. I tried to push him out of my thoughts as I concentrated on my work. But it wasn't working. I was confused and was having trouble sorting out my emotions. I had seen a glimpse of a man who was exciting and different from any other man I'd known. When he had said he enjoyed sunsets, that had triggered me. Even though I didn't understand exactly why, something inside of me leaped for joy because he found beauty in nature and had a sentimental part of him that appealed to me. He was also a gentleman, and most attractive.

I had envisioned Grant Tucker as the powerful businessman who ran *The Mountain Sentinel* and had accumulated wealth because of his successful paper. I had considered him the competition and therefore my enemy. Even though I hadn't wanted to believe that his daughter was working for me only to give her father inside information on the *Billboard,* so he could use it against me, I realized that line of thinking just didn't make sense. Grant did not fit the paradigm. He seemed to genuinely care for me.

So then why had he reacted the way he had when I had asked him about Kelcie? She seemed to be his Achilles heel. I realized I'd probably had no business asking him why he and his daughter had differences. I had just been trying to convince myself that Grant had not sent her over to me to be a spy. And he had not even denied it. That's what had me so confused. He could easily have said to me, "B.J., what are you talking about? I didn't send Kelcie over to work for you." But he hadn't. There had been silence.

Aspen buzzed me on the intercom. I hadn't even been aware the phone had rung. "Rebecca's on Line One," Aspen said.

I thanked her, then pressed the line. "Hi, Rebecca."

"B.J., I just finished some reports for you. I'll bring them over later."

"Okay, fine," I said.

"And there's something else," she said, then cleared her throat.

"What is it?" I prompted.

"Have you checked your bank balance lately?"

"Actually, no, I haven't. Is anything wrong?"

"No ... perhaps not," she said. "But I noticed the checks have not been coming in like before. I'm a little concerned about next week's payroll."

"Oh ... that." I sighed. "Well, I guess I'll have to pull some more money out of my savings."

"How many times have you done that?" asked Rebecca.

I thought about it, then told her, "Twice now."

"B.J., hopefully holidays ad sales will perk you up."

I remembered that Christmas and the holidays were usually one of the busiest times of the year for newspapers because the advertisers always ran bigger and more frequent ads this time of year. "I think we'll be fine," I told my accountant. "And yes, I'll transfer some money over this afternoon."

We hung up and then I went back to work, forcing myself to forget about Grant for the rest of the day. There would be plenty of time to worry about him later, or maybe it was just a waste of time to be thinking about him. Yet I couldn't seem to shake him. Somehow he had hooked me.

25

I went ahead and moved more money into the *Billboard's* bank account that afternoon. I had hoped I wouldn't have to subsidize it with my savings after already boosting it twice since the business had started. It was beginning to worry me. But at least I knew I had the holiday season ahead. Surely there would be an abundance of ads to see us through the traditional January and February slump that most newspapers suffered.

We had a healthy issue, ad wise, and my mood had improved by the end of the day. There had been no sign of Avery showing up at the office. Even though I was very curious to know what she wanted, Jason didn't bring up the subject of his stepsister. But I had a feeling she would make an appearance again, probably at the most inconvenient occasion.

That evening I sat at home, dwelling once again on Grant and trying to convince myself that I had been mistaken about my fears. I remembered the phone call he'd gotten Saturday night while we'd been on the couch. I had overheard enough to know that Javier, his general manager, had called him about some problem. I recalled how Grant had been annoyed with the call, telling him to handle the situation himself, then giving me the excuse that it was an "employee matter."

When my cell phone did ring around eight o'clock, I quickly reached for it, hoping it was Grant. Instead, Merle's name lit up on the front of my phone and I accepted the call. "Hey, Merle."

"Beej, how's it going?"

"Good. What's up?"

"Janie and I want you to join us for Thanksgiving. Are you coming home to Dexter for the holiday?"

I hesitated. "Well ... I hadn't thought that far ahead," I confessed. "Actually, it might be good to get away for that weekend. A lot has happened." I then explained to him how we'd experienced a break-in and had cash stolen from the office. I didn't tell Merle that I'd been working late on Halloween night and had gotten a phone call with no one on the other end.

"Geez, Beej ... did the police catch them?"

"Not that I've heard." I sighed. "But at least Mr. Breitbart repaired the damage right away."

"What else has been happening?" he asked, and I could tell he was genuinely concerned.

"Oh, just the usual." I didn't mention Avery showing up on Saturday morning, and I certainly wasn't going to talk about having dinner with Grant Tucker Saturday night. "How's Janie?" I asked.

We fell into a conversation that lasted a few more minutes. Then he seemed eager to end the call, so I agreed that Jason and I would drive to Dexter for Thanksgiving. Merle seemed pleased.

I was getting ready for bed when the phone rang again. Since Jason hadn't gotten home from Kelcie's yet, I thought perhaps he was calling to let me know he'd be spending the night with her. Instead, to my surprise it was Grant.

"Hello, B.J.," he said. "I hope I'm not calling too late."

"Hi, Grant. I was just getting ready for bed."

"I wanted to call and apologize for the other night," he said.

"Why?" I asked. "Grant, I'm the one who should apologize."

There was a pause, and then he said, "I somehow made you angry."

I sat down on my bed and leaned back against my pillows. "No, Grant," I assured him. "I didn't get angry. I was just embarrassed that I'd asked you something I had no business asking."

"Oh." Another pause, and then, "B.J., I'd like to see you again. And maybe then we can talk about it. There are some things, too, I think you should know about me."

A flag went up, but I was intrigued. "Sure, Grant." My heart began to beat a little faster.

"How about getting together Friday night? Are you free?"

I laughed. "No, I'm a slave to my job." Then I added, "Yes, I'm available Friday."

"Good," he said, sounding relieved. "I'll pick you up around seven then."

"Okay."

"Good night, B.J."

"Good night, Grant," I said. "Thanks for the call."

After I hung up, I relaxed in bed with a smile on my face and reached over to turn off my touch lamp. Suddenly my world had perked up and I was grateful that I was going to get a second chance with Grant Tucker. I also wondered what it was he wanted to reveal to me about himself. Right at the moment, I didn't care what it was. I had to get some sleep. Tomorrow was production day, and I had heard that there might be snow in the forecast. It never seemed to fail ... when you had to travel somewhere, it snowed ... and Jason would be driving to Shambleton late tomorrow afternoon to get the papers.

We were busy the next morning. Kelcie was now helping me lay out pages on the computer, which made everything less frantic on production day. The weather was cloudy and the forecast did call for snow that afternoon. However, Jason reassured me that he felt confident driving north to the printers. He left promptly at three o'clock and flurries were coming down.

I noticed there hadn't been any major yelling sessions with my sales people in the past week. So far, the girls were tolerating Rodney, who enjoyed bossing them around now and then. That afternoon, Aspen and I were the only ones in the office. It was rather quiet and I was busy, posting a pile of checks, when Aspen came to my doorway and smiled.

"B.J., can I talk to you a minute?" She appeared a bit nervous.

"Sure. Come on in."

Aspen walked in, but didn't sit down. "B.J., I was wondering ... well, I feel funny asking ... but would you give me an advance? I have a huge bill I have to pay. If I don't pay it off, they're going to come for my car."

I didn't answer right away. Then I asked, "How much of an advance do you need?"

"Six hundred dollars," she told me.

"Oh," I said. "Well ..." This was awkward. I wasn't sure what to tell her.

"B.J., if you can't, I'll understand," said Aspen. "I'll just have to come up with the money another way."

After considering her request for another minute, I said, "I think I can help. Then perhaps I can take so much out of your next few paychecks. Would that work?"

A big grin crossed my receptionist's face and she came over to give me a hug. "Oh, thank you, B.J. This really means a lot to me. I promise you, I will pay it all back." Then she added, "I wouldn't ask you except that it's important."

I reached into my desk drawer for the company checkbook and wrote out the full amount for her. The phone rang just then, and Aspen hurried into the main office to answer it. I tore the check out of the notebook and took it in to Aspen and overheard her on the phone.

"No, Jason's not here now," she said. After a pause, she asked, "Can I leave a message for him?" Another pause and then Aspen hung up. "Oh, thank you again, B.J.," she said as I handed her the check.

"Who was calling for Jason?" I asked.

"I don't know," she said. "Some woman. She didn't want to leave a message."

Immediately Avery came to mind. I wondered if it had been her on the phone.

"Well, if she calls for him again, would you put her on hold and I'll talk to her?"

"Of course," said Aspen.

I had finished posting checks and had moved onto my next task later that afternoon when an officer from the Valle Viento police force called to talk to me.

"Ms. Martin, this is Sergeant Baca, how are you doing?"

"Just fine," I said. "Do you have some news for me?"

"Indeed I do. We have caught the suspect of the robbery last weekend."

"That's good news," I said.

"We believe he acted alone," said the sergeant. "I can't reveal all of the details at the moment, but he did confess to the crime. His name is José Sanchez. I'll need you to fill out a form so that we can set up a schedule for him to pay restitution when he receives his sentencing." Then he added, "The other businesses that were robbed have to do the same thing. Just remember, it may take a while before you see your money."

I told him I understood and then, after we hung up, I went to tell Aspen the good news. She shook her head sadly. "A lot of us thought Rodney was involved," she admitted. "I'm relieved he wasn't."

I nodded and smiled. Looking out the front windows, I saw that snowflakes were coming down hard. The winter storm had arrived. I silently murmured a prayer that Jason would be safe driving back to town with the papers.

When five o'clock came, Aspen left after giving me another hug. "See you in the morning, B.J."

"Okay, Aspen." I watched her go out the door and knew she was one employee I didn't have to worry about. I wasn't so sure about my head salesman. I was relieved, at least, that they had caught the burglar and that it hadn't been Rodney. But it still puzzled me how the thief seemed to know exactly where the money box was kept and had gone right to it.

Peg called me on my cell phone while I was waiting for Jason to arrive. "Hey, B.J., I'm going to be in town next week. Want to meet for lunch at the Mexican café up the street?"

"What day?"

"You tell me," she prompted. "I have Monday free for sure because it's a teacher work day at school. Any other day I might get called in to sub."

"Monday works," I told her. "Just give me a call and let me know the time." Then I remembered to tell her about the thief that was in custody.

"Oh, I'm so relieved," said Peg. "And I can't wait to see you. We have lots to talk about."

Shortly after we hung up and it was already getting dark outside, headlights appeared as Jason drove the truck into the parking lot. Snow was coming down hard now, but I sighed with relief that he had made it, safe and sound. I grabbed my coat to go out and help him unload the bundles.

"How were the roads?" I asked.

"Not too good," he said, looking worried. "I feel like a nervous wreck."

He did look shaken. "Why?" I asked.

He opened the back and grabbed the first couple of bundles. I grabbed one and then hurried to open the front door. While I was finding the rock we used to prop open the door, Jason said, "We need to get the Beast checked, I think. It doesn't do it all the time, but the accelerator sticks a little. It might be just the wet weather."

"That certainly doesn't sound good," I said. "I'll make an appointment. How urgent is it?"

"It's off and on," he said. "I know money is tight, Mom. You can probably hold off for a couple of weeks, anyway."

I realized that I had just let six hundred dollars go when that money could have been used in case the Suburban needed something. I would have to rely on Jason's judgment about the Beast. Of course, if the problem grew worse, we would take it in right away. Later, I would regret my procrastination.

26

By the time Friday came around, I was stressed out. Our first snow-storm blanketed the valley with a foot of snow, and I didn't feel ready for cold weather this soon. Jason and Rodney shoveled the office parking lot. Those who had lived in the Lower Valley for years seemed to think this was not a big deal. Coming from lower altitude Dexter, I didn't like it.

Part of my insecurity stemmed from fears of running out of money. I had plenty of funds in my personal savings account, but I hadn't planned on dipping into it because I wanted to use those funds for a down payment on another house in the future, when my loan was paid off.

Aspen's little boy was sick again. She took Thursday and Friday off to stay home with him and get him to the doctor. Kelcie and I took up the slack with the phone customers and we managed.

My second date with Grant was that evening, and I was nervous. As much as I was looking forward to being with him again, I dreaded what he wanted to talk to me about. Certainly if he no longer wanted to be friends, or had lost interest in me, he simply would not have bothered to call. I had not been able to dismiss him from my mind, nor had I mentioned to Jason that I was seeing Kelcie's father.

"How about pizza tonight, Mom?" Jason asked as we were locking up the office after the others had left for the weekend. I had made it a habit now of taking all the cash and endorsed checks from the front desk home with me each night, keeping them safe in my bank pouch.

"Oh," I said, double checking the door. "You mean, you're not getting together with Kelcie this evening? It's Friday night."

"She's coming down with something," said Jason. "She said she needed to stay home and rest. I'll call her later and see if she needs anything."

"Chicken soup therapy?"

"It probably wouldn't hurt if you whip up a batch of your famous chicken soup this weekend, Mom."

"Well, if you decide on pizza," I said, "just get a small one for yourself. I've got a commitment tonight."

Jason stared at me. "What kind of commitment? A club meeting of some kind?"

"No. It's personal."

Jason grinned at me. "Mom, do you have a date?"

"Does that surprise you?" I asked. "Am I too old to be out on a date?"

"At 42? No!" He shook his head. "I'm sorry, Mom. I didn't mean to … I'm just a bit surprised." Suddenly, he looked worried. "Oh no … it's not The Captain, is it? Mom, please tell me it's not him."

I had to laugh. "No, Jason, it's not The Captain."

"Whew …" He wiped his forehead in a mock gesture, then asked, "Okay, then … who is he?"

I figured I might as well not hide it from him any longer. "Grant Tucker is coming to pick me up at seven."

Jason's look of surprise left him speechless at first, and then as we were walking to our vehicles, both of which he had cleared of snow earlier, he asked. "You mean, Kelcie's dad?"

"Yes," I said.

"The owner of *The Mountain Sentinel*, our *rival* paper?"

"Exactly," I said, digging for my keys.

"And Kelcie doesn't know either?" he asked.

I got the door open and stopped before getting inside. "That I don't know. You'll have to ask her."

"I think she would have said something if she knew her dad's dating my mom. Oh wow, she is gonna be blown away." He grinned as I climbed into my Camry. "See you at home," he added, then carefully closed my car door as I reached for my seatbelt and started up the engine.

On the way home I had the flutters. Kelcie, if she knew, hadn't told

Jason. I had to assume she was innocent and really didn't know her father was taking me out. I was sorry to hear that Kelcie wasn't feeling well. I might just decide to purchase a whole chicken at the grocery store tomorrow and cook up a batch of my therapeutic soup.

When seven o'clock came, I was dressed in black slacks and a multi-colored sweater with aqua and soft browns. I had chosen a blue Amazonite pendant on a silver chain and put on turquoise earrings. The doorbell rang while I was applying my lipstick. From the living room I heard Jason say, "I'll get it, Mom."

I fluffed my hair one more time, then entered the hallway just as Jason opened the door to Grant. His light-colored, almost blond hair was combed back and he wore a brown leather coat. He smiled as soon as he saw me, then turned to my son. "You must be Jason."

"Pleased to meet you, sir." Jason extended his hand and Grant shook it, smiling.

I opened the closet to grab my coat and gloves, then picked my purse up off the coffee table. "Hello, Grant." I smiled at him. Then I turned to Jason and asked, "Did you find everything you need in the medicine cabinet?"

He picked up a small backpack. "Right in here. Hey, next time you go to the store, we need some more throat lozenges."

"How about cough syrup?"

"I got it," he said, tapping his pack.

"Is somebody ill?" asked Grant.

"Jason's taking over some cold remedies to Kelcie," I explained.

Grant blinked in surprise. "What's wrong with her?"

"She's coming down with the crud," explained Jason.

"I'm afraid it's going around," I added.

Grant rubbed his chin. "Maybe I should drop in on her." He looked at me for a response, and I turned to Jason. "Should we go see her before we leave?"

"Well, if you want to." Jason sounded dubious. "I mean ... I don't think she feels like having company right now. But I said I'd take her some relief."

Grant shook his head. "Uh ... never mind. You go ... take care of her," he told Jason. "And tell Kelcie I'll give her a call tomorrow."

Jason smiled. "Sure. I'll tell her." He looked over at me. "Bye, Mom."

I rushed over and gave Jason a quick hug. He then nodded at Grant and hurried out the door.

Before we left, Grant looked around at the apartment while I stepped into the kitchen to turn out the lights. "I like this," he said. "It's cozy."

"Well, I still have boxes to unpack yet."

"If Kelcie's apartment is as nice as yours, then that makes me feel better." Grant smiled as we left and made our way down the hallway to the building's entrance. He took my arm as we stepped outside onto the icy walkway that led to the parking lot. The air was frigid. The Lower Valley was known for having some of the coldest temperatures in Colorado during the winter. I decided not to comment on the fact that Grant had not yet seen his daughter's living quarters. Like before, he helped me into the Porsche and then we cruised toward downtown.

"I thought I'd treat you to some Italian tonight," Grant said with a smile.

"Considering the fact that I'm ... of Italian heritage?" I asked, raising an eyebrow.

Grant grew embarrassed right away. "Oh ... well ... I didn't mean ..."

"I'm flattered," I said, amused at his sensitivities.

"Did you have a good week?" he asked, obviously eager to change the subject.

"It wasn't too bad. The snow was kind of a surprise."

"This won't last," he said. "It's only the first week in November. It's supposed to warm up before we get another storm."

"Oh, is there going to be another storm?" I blinked.

"B.J., this is the Lower Valley," he mocked. "You mean to tell me you didn't get snow storms in Dexter?"

"Well ... mild ones ... maybe."

We arrived at the restaurant several minutes later. I noticed right away that the place was not as elegant or as popular as the Bandito Steakhouse, where we had eaten last weekend. There were only a few customers and the atmosphere was not as welcoming. I found the lighting to be too bright and there was no background music or candles at the tables. We were seated at a booth and I wondered why there were not more diners on a Friday night. Most likely it was the cold weather, I told myself as we opened the menus the host had given us.

I ordered the eggplant parmigiana and Grant ordered lasagna, along with a bottle of Cabernet. Somehow my mood had changed. Earlier I had been looking forward to being out with him again, but now I had this strange feeling of anxiety. I must have been fidgeting with my napkin and silverware because I suddenly caught Grant watching me and I asked him, "What? Is something wrong?"

"You're nervous," he said quietly. "Tell me what's on your mind." He continued to watch me with those mesmerizing green eyes of his.

I sighed. "I'm sorry. I'm a little curious about what it is you wanted to discuss with me."

He continued to gaze at me, then reached for his glass of water and said, "The other night, at my place, you brought up a sore subject. I wasn't prepared to talk about it then. I can't blame you for wanting to leave. I apologize." He took a sip of water, then set it down.

"Oh." I nervously pulled the napkin onto my lap, then said, "Well, what subject was that?" I recalled that we had been discussing a number of things. I could guess what it was and his answer proved me right.

"Kelcie." Grant looked at his hands. "You brought up Kelcie."

I waited patiently, not daring to say anything. Before he could continue, the waiter showed up at the table with the wine and opened the bottle for us, set two glasses down, and left. Unlike the service at the steakhouse, we were expected to pour our own wine. Grant reached over to do that.

After he filled our goblets, he continued. "My daughter was very close to her mother. When Samantha became ill, Kelcie did everything she could to help her mother. Sam had excellent business sense and it was because of her that *The Mountain Sentinel* flourished. I've done well only because my wife laid the foundation, plus I've hired competent people to manage the business for me." He took a sip of his wine, then said, "Samantha was offered the chance to go to a foreign country and receive treatments for her cancer. These treatments were expensive and controversial, and not allowed in the U.S. She didn't see the point of going. She was terminally ill and had pretty much given up fighting."

"Oh, Grant, that's so sad," I mumbled.

"Kelcie argued with her mother. She insisted that Sam go and get cured. She wouldn't do it. I knew for a long time how useless it was to try to get my wife to do something against her will. Yet Kelcie tried so hard to convince her to go."

"Was it the money?" I asked.

Grant shook his head. "No. I would have paid anything to give Samantha that chance. But she made the decision in the end. She wanted to die at home. Kelcie blames me now. She says I didn't work hard enough to get her mother to seek alternative treatment. At that point I was tired ... and indifferent ... I respected Samantha's decision, even if it tore me up inside to lose her."

I could see that Grant was still bothered by the loss of his wife, even after five years. "Is this the sole reason Kelcie feels the way she does?" I asked gently.

"She went to college right here in Blanca Hills," he explained, "and she could have lived at home and saved a fortune. But she wanted to live on campus, and soon she had her friends and her activities. I saw less and less of her, though she did continue to work part-time in production at the paper."

"It sounds like Kelcie has a streak of her mother's will in her," I ventured to comment.

Grant smiled, then sighed. "She's a fine young woman. I'm glad she's applying her skills for you at the *Buffalo Billboard.*"

"And how do you feel about her dating my son?" He saw my raised eyebrow and smiled.

"Naturally, I'm concerned, but there's little I can do about any young men Kelcie might take up with," said Grant. "She has a mind of her own and she's broken more than a few hearts in this town."

It wasn't long before the food arrived, at the same time as our salads, which I found a little unconventional. Grant and I broke away from the discussion about Kelcie and her mother and we ate our food. I didn't want to say anything to make Grant feel uncomfortable, but my parmigiana was not very good. When I looked over at his plate, he was picking at a burnt pasta crust on one side of his plate.

"How's the lasagna?" I asked.

Grant shrugged, then popped another forkful into his mouth, noncommittal.

"Tell you what," I said, pushing my plate away and reaching for the salad. "I'm going to cook you up a *real* Italian dinner sometime soon."

Grant's light-colored eyebrows shot up in surprise. "Just how Italian are you?" he asked.

"Enough," I said.

"Well, I can see why there aren't a lot of patrons," he said, looking around at the many empty tables. "And sure ... I'd love to have you cook an Italian meal."

"My place or yours?" I asked in a teasing fashion.

"That depends," he said, giving me another one of his irresistible looks.

We turned down dessert and left the restaurant after Grant paid the bill. Grant drove me over to his home in the ritzy subdivision near campus. The stars were very bright with a clear sky. The air was icy cold with a very slight wind. He pulled into his large garage and I realized it was heated when we got out of the Porsche.

Inside, Grant turned on his natural gas fireplace. I noticed the logs looked real, and if I hadn't known better, I would have mistaken it for a real wood-burning fireplace. He fixed us both some coffee and brought me my cup as I lounged on the big blue couch.

"Jason wants to know why I'm dating you," I said leisurely as Grant sat down next to me.

"Dating me?"

"He thinks it's rather weird that I'm going out with my rival publisher." I took a sip of the hot drink and recognized a touch of Amaretto.

"Oh, that." He chuckled. "I hope we're not rivals, Bridget."

I turned to him, startled. "People only call me Bridget when they're serious," I remarked.

"Then why do you want them to call you B.J.?" he asked. "You don't want people to take you seriously?" I knew he was kidding me.

I sighed. "I've been B.J. since I was a little girl. Though my closest friends call me Beej."

Grant made a face. "Beej," he said in low voice, then in a falsetto, "*Beeeej...*"

I laughed. "Stop it, you sound like one of those birds that flies around at dusk, catching insects."

"Bridget," he said. "I like Bridget. I like the way it sounds." He was serious again.

I stared at him, then relaxed. "You know what? I do too." I took another sip of my coffee. "I think I like it better when you call me that."

We chatted for several minutes and then Grant wanted to show me some of his photographs. He brought out a portfolio and opened it on the coffee table. We spent the next half hour looking through his collection, many of which were remarkable, outstanding, colorful portraits of sunsets and also a few sunrises. Some were local, but many were from distant places—at the ocean, on a mountain, in the forest, in a city.

"You have such talent," I remarked as he closed up the portfolio. I pulled my knees up on the couch after setting my empty coffee cup down on an end table. "Grant, you're an excellent photographer."

"That's good of you to say," he replied modestly. "I have lots more, but I won't bore you."

"I mean, you should put on an art show. I'm serious."

"Really?"

"Grant, you're talented. Maybe you could publish a book, even."

Just then his cell phone rang. He got up to go see who was calling. Then he returned with a frown. "I don't understand why my manager calls me in the evenings just when you're here."

"Are you going to answer it?" I asked.

"No." He sat back down. "Let it go to voice mail. Javier has such a knack for annoying me lately."

"Is Javier the man you were with in the diner last summer? Remember? When I was there eating with Merle, and you were at the counter."

"Yes," said Grant. "Why?"

I ran a hand through my bangs, wondering if I should bring it up. Then I said, "Does he drive a red sports car?"

Grant wrinkled his forehead. "Yes, as a matter of fact he does. How did you know?"

I popped up on the couch and faced him. "Javier has been keeping an eye on me."

Grant chuckled and shook his head. "Javier? Why would he do that?"

"Okay, let me explain." I sniffed, then told Grant about the first time I had seen Javier watching me, while I was eating with Jason in the little Mexican café just up the street from our office. Then I told him about the time I had walked to the service station on the highway and had seen Javier's red sports car and how it had seemed to be following me.

"Then, about two weeks ago," I continued, "Javier was in his red car at the town park in Valle Viento, where I had gone for a walk to get away from the office."

"Why would Javier spend time doing such a thing?" Grant shook his head. "He's a busy man. You say he was in Valle Viento all those times?"

"Yes," I insisted.

"Are you sure it wasn't just a coincidence?" asked Grant.

"But it gets even weirder," I said, my eyes growing larger. "There was a young woman in the car with him. A young woman with dark hair. I know who that young lady was. She was Jason's stepsister from Salt Lake City." I was growing excited now. "At the time I didn't know who she was. But then, last Saturday, after the robbery at my office, that young woman showed up in front of the *Buffalo Billboard* asking for Jason."

Grant was truly baffled, I could tell. He didn't know what to say at first. "Hmmm ... that is bizarre."

"And when I walked up to the car, as if I wanted to talk to him, Javier took off like a fiend." I didn't mention that the incident had shaken me up, especially because at first I thought I was seeing a ghost—the likeness of my dead sister.

"Bridget," he said, leaning closer. "I have no idea what's going on with Javier."

"Has he been acting kind of strange lately?" I asked.

Grant shook his head slowly, then stopped and put a finger up. "You know, now that you mention it, he has been acting kind of nervous."

"I don't want to ask you this," I said carefully, "but why do you think your employee would be spying on me? I mean, I'm absolutely positive that's what he was doing. There were too many coincidences. And then ... with Avery in that car with him ... I can't make head nor tails of it."

Grant got up and went for his cell phone.

"What are you going to do?" I asked, afraid that he was going to call Javier.

Grant walked back to the couch with his phone and checked his voice mail. After a minute, he shut it off and blinked his eyes at me.

"What's wrong?" I asked.

"He didn't leave a message," said Grant. "That's not like him. If it was something urgent, he'd leave a message. I'm going to have to figure this out."

"Are you going to confront him?" I asked.

"I might."

I stood up. "Grant, maybe you should wait. I want to see if he tries anything else. And if he really is following me, we need to know why." Then I cocked my head and asked, "Do you have any idea?"

"No, Bridget." He moved closer to me and took me into his arms. "But this has me very concerned. Let's not say anything to anyone further about this, until I can check out a few things."

"Grant, I hope I'm not acting paranoid," I said, comforted to be once more in his arms as his hands massaged my back and slowly found their way up the inside of my sweater.

"I was going to ask you to spend the night with me," he disclosed as his lips brushed over my left ear. "But this discussion has caused me quite a bit of concern."

I ordinarily would have melted in his arms at this point, but I, too, was stricken with uncertainty and dire possibilities. Could Javier's motivation be corporate espionage? If so, there was no indication that Grant knew about it. I really didn't believe that Grant Tucker was behind it—if that was what was happening with Javier, his general manager. "Okay, Grant," I whispered back. "I'll stay with you another time," and then I succumbed to a deep, delicious kiss that was prolonged and sent my head reeling and my heart thumping.

"Another night, Bridget," he told me softly. "Another sunrise." He smiled.

27

Saturday morning I drove to the market and bought some groceries, including a large organic whole chicken. When I got home, I cut up some vegetables and added broth to the chicken in my largest stockpot. Then I let it simmer for a few hours on the stove, filling the apartment with its comforting aroma. Jason was pleased that I'd picked up on his idea to make the soup, not only to help Kelcie, but to keep the two of us from catching whatever was going around.

Grant checked in with me later that morning. We chatted briefly. We both had weekend tasks and I planned on driving to the office Sunday, to get in a couple of constructive hours while there was peace and quiet. While working, my thoughts drifted to Friday evening and the time spent with Grant. My feelings for him were growing stronger, yet I was concerned about what I had revealed to him about Javier, his general manager.

As much as I wanted to believe that Grant knew nothing about Javier's activities in regard to appearing in places unexpectedly and my assumption that I was being watched, I could not let go of the possibility that I was being set up. What if Grant had asked me out only to deceive me? He didn't seem to be concerned that the valley's new "little paper" was a threat to his daily *Mountain Sentinel,* which had been around for decades. I wondered how much my paper was affecting his advertising revenue.

I also puzzled over the fact that Avery had not come back to the office, asking for Jason. My son seemed to shrug it off as if there was nothing unusual about a younger stepsister showing up out of the blue once, then vanishing again. It didn't make sense. What had Avery wanted to see Jason about? And why—assuming it was her—had she been riding in the passenger seat of Javier's red sports car in late October?

That night I had another disturbing dream, this time about Avery. She looked just as she had that Saturday afternoon outside the shopper office, wearing her black trench coat and pointed boots, her pale face even paler, with a frightened expression on her young face. In the dream she was beckoning me to go somewhere with her, but I was preoccupied. I was busy making chicken soup in the office kitchen during production day. My employees were buzzing around, hurrying to get their tasks completed. But I had to cook and try to get the paper put together at the same time. Avery was a major distraction.

Then, in the dream, just before I woke up to my alarm, Dirk and Alicia had come into the office, looking for Avery. I had seen the girl slip into the storage room to get away from them. The dream ended with the three of us going into the back room, which was completely dark, and then heading into the storage closet. Somehow I knew Avery had escaped through the secret hallway that led to the outside where the other stores had their enclosed alleyway.

The last thing I remembered from the dream was Alicia refusing to follow Dirk and me into the closet, bursting into tears and shouting, "I never signed up for this. Let her go!"

Jason had showered and was brewing coffee when I walked into the kitchen to gather my morning smoothie ingredients. "Hi, Mom," he said.

"Jason, do you know if Kelcie is going to work this morning?"

"Probably," he said, pouring water into the machine. "She felt a lot better last night, thanks to eating your chicken soup all weekend."

I started peeling my banana over the sink. "Hey, did Avery ever call you?"

"No. Why?"

"She never bothered to come back. I'm just wondering why she didn't call you."

Jason closed up the top of the coffee machine, then turned on the switch. "I have no idea why she wanted to see me," he said. "She never wanted anything to do with me. So why would she now?"

"Did anything happen the last time you were at your dad's?" I asked.

"Like what?"

"Well, you told me that Avery decided not to go back to school."

"Yeah, well, the parents pitched a major bitch about that." He chuckled. Then he added, "I really have no idea what's going on with her. It's almost like she really isn't a part of the family. Avery never seemed to fit in. I mean, I never really felt like I fit in with Dad and Alicia either. They just liked to control me."

His words struck a pang of guilt. "I'm sorry, Jason," I said as he left the kitchen.

That morning the sun was out and the temperature had warmed up. The snow was melting and my mood had improved as I drove to work. I remembered that Peg was going to come by at noon, so we could go to lunch together. I had something to look forward to. I missed Peg a lot.

Aspen was back at the front desk, busy taking ads over the phone. Colleen and Molly were still out, gathering their ads, and Kelcie came in shortly after Jason's arrival. She reassured me that she was a lot better, although she had a loose cough and was blowing her nose a lot.

I was busy with my email when Rodney showed up to work. As was his habit, he went to the coffee pot first thing, then headed for the bathroom. Later, when he came out, he popped his head into my inner office.

"Good morning, B.J."

"Hi, Rodney." I glanced up, but continued typing.

"Hey." He stepped in and scratched his head. "I was wondering ... did the police ever get back to you about ... I mean, did they ever figure out who stole the money?"

I continued to type without looking over at him. Obviously, he hadn't heard that the police had captured the thief named José who had broken into the office on Halloween night. "They have a suspect," I said.

There was a short silence and then Rodney sighed. "Well, that's good." Then he turned around and left to go about his business.

If it hadn't been for the fact that I knew Rodney had a rap sheet and had been to prison, the conversation wouldn't have bothered me. But I just couldn't help wondering if, as some of the others in the office suspected, Rodney had been part of an "inside job." I had to presume he was innocent of such a thing and not worry about it. Yet the idea still lingered in my mind. At least there hadn't been any really big blow-outs among the sales people since the time of the break-in.

Peg showed up promptly at noon. Everyone cheered when they saw her, and Aspen came over to give Peg a hug. "We miss you."

"I miss you, too." Peg looked around. "Yup. Still the same."

I laughed as I came out of the office to greet her. "Did you expect anything different?"

"Hi, B.J." Peg walked over to hug me. "Well," she said, looking around, "I don't want to disrupt everyone on deadline day. Let's go to lunch!"

"Back in an hour," I called out to Aspen, who was getting her sack lunch out of the kitchen.

After grabbing my purse and pulling on my winter jacket, Peg and I walked the two blocks up Willow Street to the Mexican café, which was filling up fast with lunch clientele. The blue sky and bright sun contrasted with the snow, which was now crusty and starting to melt.

After we ordered, Peg's sparkling blue eyes gazed at me. "B.J., first and foremost, I want the goods on your relationship with Grant Tucker. Spill, girl."

I took a sip of the water the waitress had left. "It's not a relationship. We've just gone out for dinner a couple of times," I said.

"He's a catch," Peg remarked. "How did you meet?"

I ended up telling her the story, how I'd met Grant Tucker in the parking lot of *The Mountain Sentinel* and he'd asked me if I had come to apply for a job. Then I told her how he'd taken me to lunch in Shambleton on that very hot day in August, when I had made the extra trip in my car to bring back the remaining papers that hadn't fit into The Captain's van.

The waitress brought our chimichangas, and Peg told me what she knew about Grant. "He's obviously good-looking, successful in business, and lives comfortably," she said, dipping a tortilla chip into the bowl of salsa. "And he's been a widower for a number of years ..."

"Five years," I added, opening my napkin.

"A lot of women admire him," Peg continued, "and yet he has proven to be discriminating in his tastes. I know of some women who have tried to win him, and he might take them out one time ... but rarely does he ask a woman out a second time. So, B.J. ... it appears that you have captured his interest."

"He is calm … and quite the gentleman," I replied. "But I'm wondering if he has befriended me because of something else."

Peg stared at me. "Oh, you mean because you started up the *Billboard*? Do you think he's concerned that your paper might be too much of a rival?"

"No, it's not that." I picked up my fork and examined the chimichanga, trying to decide how to start eating it.

"What then?" asked Peg. She picked hers up with her hands and took a big bite out of it.

"Do you remember a couple of years ago, when a woman was found dead at the Blue Heron Motel in Blanca Hills?" I asked.

"Oh yeah," Peg said right away, still chewing. She swallowed, then said, "The police came to the conclusion that the woman had overdosed. I believe they ruled it a suicide."

"Grant's reporters covered the story," I said. "For some reason, Grant took a special interest in the case and had his people do some deeper investigation."

"Hmm," said Peg and reached for her napkin to dab at some sauce on her lip. "And?" she asked.

"Peg, that woman who died was my sister."

"What!" Peg's voice rose and other patrons in the café glanced our way.

I lowered my voice. "My sister, Liz, was the victim. Grant thinks there was foul play and that it wasn't just a drug overdose … even though my sister was an addict for many years."

"Oh, B.J., I'm so sorry," said Peg, reaching for her drink. "I had no idea."

"There's no reason why you would have made the connection," I said with a smile.

"Well, did Grant bring this up to you? How did he know you were sisters?"

"No, I brought it up," I told her. "I told Grant that my sister and I hadn't seen each other in years. I was trying to make a point because he and his daughter weren't getting along. I told him my story, and he remembered. In fact, he was really interested in what I knew. He told me that one of his reporters received a death threat."

"From who?"

"I don't know. He must have told the reporter to bow out, but somehow Grant believes there's a story ... and when he found out Liz was my sister, I think it made him want to look into it further."

"Who would make a death threat like that?" asked Peg.

"That isn't all," I said. "Peg, two weeks before she died, Liz reached out to me. She left a message on my voice mail, begging me to get in touch with her. She sounded desperate."

"And did you?"

"No," I confessed. "I ignored it. You see, my sister and I were at odds most of our growing-up years, but she really blew it when she had an affair with my husband, right under our roof after we took her in."

Peg shook her head in dismay, then picked up her chimichanga again and took a bite.

I continued. "So, I was still angry and hurt. I didn't believe she was in danger. I didn't want anything to do with Liz at that point. She would call me every so often, trying to get me to help her out with one thing or another. I always refused. It always brought up old pain. Can you understand?"

Peg nodded her head as she chewed. "What else?"

"Since Grant learned about my relationship with her, maybe he just wants to see if I can shed any light on a cold case."

We were silent for a few moments as I finally started eating my lunch. Then, Peg spoke up. "You know, B.J., I can definitely see why you would think Grant may be using you to get information. But personally, I think it's more of a concern that he's your competitor."

"Yeah, that's what I thought at first," I confessed.

"Tell me what he's like. What he's really like." She grinned.

I smiled, remembering how good it felt being in Grant's arms. "Okay. Did you know he's a fantastic photographer?" The conversation then evolved into art and sunsets, and then veered off into what Peg had been doing with her life since quitting the *Buffalo Billboard*.

It was after one o'clock when we returned to the office. Peg visited briefly with the others while I helped Jason with some questions he had on a full-page ad he was designing for an upcoming arts and crafts show. Peg stuck her head through my doorway to tell me goodbye, then added, "We'll have lunch again real soon." I smiled and said I was looking forward to it, and she left.

"Did you edit those photos before importing them onto the page?" I asked Jason as I studied his work over his shoulder. "That holiday table display looks kind of grainy."

"It's what they gave us," replied Jason.

"It's awful," I said. "The resolution is too low, and remember you've got to change the color to CMYK. Why don't you look on the Internet and see if you can find some art that's more suitable?"

The phone rang in the front office.

"I'll call the advertiser first and see if they have a better shot," said Jason. "If not, I'll find something that works."

"You're actually turning into a decent graphic designer, you know that?" I said as I returned to my desk. Colleen's latest article featuring the business person of the week was waiting on top of my piles.

"Thanks, Mom," Jason said.

The intercom buzzed and Aspen's voice said, "B.J., Grant Tucker's on the line."

I heard giggles from the girls out front as I reached for my phone. Apparently my employees had been properly informed of the fact that the publisher of *The Mountain Sentinel* was in my life. "Hello, Grant," I said in a low voice. My heartbeat had picked up.

In Jason's corner I heard the soft clicking of his keyboard.

"Hello, Bridget," Grant said, "sorry I didn't call yesterday. I meant to."

"That's okay," I told him. "How are you?"

"Not bad, and you?"

"I'm good."

"Bridget, how's Kelcie feeling?"

I rose from my desk and craned my neck to see through the window into the main room. "She's plugging away at her computer," I told him.

"She's better then."

"Chicken soup," I quipped.

"I tried calling her yesterday afternoon, but she didn't pick up. She was probably napping and I didn't want to disturb her." He cleared his throat. "I have some meetings lined up in the Denver area and I have to go out of town for a week or two."

"Okay," I said. "When are you leaving?"

"Wednesday morning." Then he added, "I was rather looking forward to your home-cooked Italian meal. Now I have to wait. By the way, do you have Thanksgiving plans?"

I glanced at my desk calendar and saw that the holiday was coming up in just two weeks.

"Oh, darn," I told him. "I already accepted an invitation from Merle and his fiancée to have Thanksgiving with them in Dexter."

"Merle ... the ex-boyfriend," he murmured.

"*Very* ex." After a pause, I said, "Well, I could call and cancel ..."

"Bridget," he interrupted, "I understand." He sighed, then said, "Listen, I don't have time to get into it now. I don't want to discuss this over the phone, but I might have some intel to share with you."

"What intel?"

He said, "I pulled some old files from two years ago. You know what I'm talking about ... right?"

I could tell he was purposely being secretive. Possibly his office had big ears, like mine did at times. "Yes," I replied, quite sure he was referring to Liz's death at the Blue Heron Motel.

"After we both get back, let's get together and discuss it."

For a moment my heart sank. It sounded as if Grant was more interested in the unsolved case of my sister's demise than the romantic dinner I was planning to make him.

When I didn't answer right away, Grant said softly into the phone, "I'm going to miss you, Bridget. I wish there was some way I could take you to Denver with me."

Exactly what I needed to hear. I smiled and told him, "That's sweet ... but you know I've got responsibilities ... we have some big papers coming up."

"How well I understand," he remarked. Then he said, "Have a good trip to Dexter. And drive safely."

"You be careful yourself."

"I will. Bridget ... another sunset," he said in a soft voice. Then the phone clicked as the call ended before I could respond. I had to smile as I placed the phone down. It was rather eccentric how Grant always referred to sunsets and sunrises instead of saying goodbye.

At the same time, my heart sank because I suddenly realized that I wouldn't get to see Grant now for almost three weeks. Suddenly, that seemed like an eternity.

28

That week was passive. Things actually went smoothly, for a change. There were no sales people yelling at each other outside the office doors. The weather grew warmer, melting most all of the snow. When Jason returned in the Suburban with the load of papers on Tuesday night, I asked him how the SUV had handled the roads.

"No problem," said Jason. "The accelerator is a little sticky at times, but I didn't have any trouble."

"Good." I sighed with relief, but inwardly I realized that I needed to spend money to get the vehicle serviced again. Even though it might have been a fluke, the accelerator doing what it had a week ago, I couldn't risk a potential accident, especially with my son behind the wheel. But I chose not to spend money right now. Payroll was continuously taking chunks out of the *Billboard's* revenue. I was counting on holiday advertising to see us through the end of the year.

The Thanksgiving week paper turned out to be a big one for us, with plenty of ads from businesses. The sales people were happy with their larger than usual commission checks. Jason decided not to ride with me to Dexter to have Thanksgiving with Merle and Janie. He wanted to stay in Blanca Hills and keep Kelcie company. I told him I understood.

I was tired after Wednesday, but I didn't let it stop me from baking the traditional dinner rolls, a recipe that had been in my family for decades. The kitchen was filled with the sweet, yeasty aroma of my great-grandmother's rolls in the oven. I had also managed to bake some apple pies to take along with me to Dexter in the morning. The pies were cooling on the counter when Jason walked in later.

"What are you and Kelcie going to do for Thanksgiving?" I asked as I filled a glass with cold water from the refrigerator.

"We're getting together with some friends of hers," he said. "One of them is gonna try to roast a turkey."

"Well, good," I said. "You can take this extra pie I baked."

"Thanks, Mom. Man, it smells fantastic in here. Did you make Grandma Russo's rolls?"

"I did."

"Can I take a few of them along as well?"

"I don't see why not," I said, then took a long drink of cold water.

Peg Espinoza called me that evening to wish me a happy Thanksgiving. She also told me that she had been doing some research when she had the time, trying to dig up some helpful information on the police case surrounding the event of my sister's death two summers ago.

"Peg, why are you doing this?" I asked, surprised at first. Then I remembered how Peg was just one of those people who put herself completely into a project once she got involved.

"My husband's brother is a deputy sheriff," she told me. "I picked his brain the other night when he was over having a beer."

"Oh? What did he have to say?" I asked.

"Not too much," she said with a sigh. "But he did mention that there was some funny business at the time."

"Funny business? What does that mean?"

"I don't know, B.J. But I'm going to see what I can dig up over the long weekend. I'll go online and see what I can find out."

I told Peg I appreciated her interest, but I really didn't want her to waste time digging into something that might just be a dead end. It had seemed strange that Liz had landed in the Lower Valley, when she was used to big cities and lots of action. I began to wonder just what she had been doing in this town. Then again, what good was it now to find out why Liz had been in Blanca Hills?

"I'll call you next week," said Peg. "You're driving over Buffalo Pass tomorrow, aren't you?"

"Yes," I said. "I'll be in Dexter until Sunday morning."

"Be careful, B.J. This time of year, it can snow at the drop of a hat."

"I will," I promised. "Peg, you have a happy Thanksgiving. Talk to you soon."

After we hung up, I was getting ready to step into the shower when my cell phone rang. Grant was calling, so I picked it up. "Hello."

"Bridget, good evening. You haven't left for Dexter yet?"

"No, Grant. I'm just getting into the shower."

He laughed. "Well, I won't keep you. I just wanted to hear your voice. How was your week?"

"Good," I told him. "Do you have plans in Denver for Thanksgiving dinner?" I asked.

"A colleague invited me to his home. His wife is cooking and they're having a bunch of people over. Not really my cup of tea ... but I said I'd join them."

"I'll be thinking of you," I told him.

"The same here," he said with a sigh. "But I'll be back home Sunday night. I'll call you then."

We talked only a short time. I was getting cold, having removed my clothes before he called. After we said our goodnights, I turned on the water and stepped into the bath tub. Grant's call had filled me with peace of mind and I basked in the memory of his voice. In just four nights he would be back. I was looking forward to seeing him again. Suddenly, it seemed like my life was finally settling down into something I had only dreamed about in the past. I believed I had a wonderful future ahead.

It was usually a four-hour drive over the pass to Dexter, in good weather. I left early Thursday morning with blue skies, just as the sun was coming up. I had loaded my baked goods and was looking forward to the getaway. It had been awhile since I'd traveled to Dexter. I marveled at the beauty of Colorado this time of year. Snow was in the mountains after that last storm and the highway was icy only in spots, but it grew worse as I approached Buffalo Pass.

There were more than the usual amount of travelers on the road, headed to their own Thanksgiving destinations. I took my time and played my music, enjoying the solitude. I felt thankful for everything in my life right now.

"Your life is far from perfect." The disdainful voice of my sister sounded in my head, and I tried to ignore it, but she continued to chastise me as I drove. *"B.J., you'll never succeed with your enterprise. You are wasting money and time. Can't you see that?"*

"Liz, leave me alone," I said out loud, annoyed that I was thinking of her when I had been in such a good mood starting out on my journey. I was driving toward the summit of the pass, wanting to enjoy the splendor of the snow-covered pines against a vivid blue sky. "My paper is a success. The people of the Lower Valley love the *Billboard*. You are the one who failed in life."

Her wicked laughter filled my head. Why did she continue to haunt me? I tried to focus on my surroundings, but she wouldn't leave me alone. *"You think you've found a real prize in Grant Tucker,"* she taunted. *"Well, I predict you'll go crawling back to Merle before long. After all, he's the one who really deserves you. Grant is too good for you, plus ... he's playing you for a fool."*

"You're wrong, Liz," I snapped. "Just like always, you don't know what you're talking about."

"I think I do," her whiny voice continued. *"Tell me, what do you see in him?"*

I sighed. I had been drawn into her little game. "Grant is different from other men in my life ... especially Dirk."

"He's rich like Dirk," she reminded me. *"Rich men play by another set of rules."*

"He doesn't act that way at all," I defended. "Grant is kind and considerate. He is a gentleman, and ... and ... he hasn't forced himself on me."

Liz cackled. *"Oh, you fool. Don't you know the reason for that?"*

I didn't want to hear what else she had to say. "Please, Liz, just go away and let me enjoy all this beauty in peace."

"No, I want you to hear what I have to say," she continued. *"The truth is, you are just not good enough for a man as respected and admired as Grant Tucker. He's biding his time. He knows you will fail."*

I was growing angry. "Liz, stop it!"

"Eventually, you will use up all of your savings," she said. *"You think your paper is going to sustain itself. How much of it have you lost already? How many thousands of your own money have you used to bail yourself out?"*

"What does Grant have to do with any of this?" I demanded.

Again, the laughter. *"You're going to find out! Oh, dear **older** sister ..."* She had always enjoyed mocking the fact that she was my junior. *"Grant is a younger man. You did know that certainly."*

I couldn't believe she had brought up age. Actually, I had not considered that Grant might be younger than I. But even if he was, what difference did it make?

"He loved his wife," Liz said. *"He still loves her. He can't forget how beautiful she was."* When I didn't comment, she went on. *"Here on the Other Side, she is glowing like an angel."* Liz laughed. *"And she watches the two of you ... cuddling together on her couch ... kissing!"*

I had heard enough. "Liz, leave! Now!" I demanded. "I doubt that on the Other Side—if that is where you are now—Samantha is harboring jealousy. Certainly not if she is an angel, as you claim. And I honestly can't imagine you on *that* Other Side. I think you're stuck in a very dark place."

There was sudden silence from Liz. In the next moment, a deer pranced into the road in front of me. I slammed on my brakes, which caused me to swerve on the ice to the side of the highway. Brakes were screeching as the animal bumped against the left side of my car. It wasn't a direct hit, but the deer stood—dazed—behind me as I came to a stop. The event had certainly thrown me off balance, but at least I had not gone too far off the road.

My heart was racing. Out the rear-view mirror, I watched the doe recover from being stunned and wobble down the snowy embankment. It had been a very close call. It took me a couple of minutes to sit there and gather my nerve to continue on. I did get out of the car to see if any damage had occurred. There was a dent on the left side, but it wasn't a big deal. I returned to the car and continued on toward Dexter, now alert and focused on only the road ahead of me. Liz's precarious presence had vanished.

It was shortly after the noon hour when I pulled into Merle's driveway. There had been no snow in Dexter from that latest storm. I considered myself fortunate that the roads had been good the rest of the way, even though traffic had been busy. The deer incident had shaken me considerably, and Merle picked up on it as soon as he came out the front door and saw me get out of my car.

"Hey, Beej," he called with a grin, which flipped into a look of alarm. He walked toward me and stared at the dent in the Camry. "What happened?"

I must have been trembling and was definitely trying to hold back tears. "A deer," I said.

Janie stepped onto the porch and shaded her eyes from the sun. "Hello, B.J." she called to me.

Before I could answer her, Merle rushed over to me and put his arms around me. At that point I broke down and sobbed. "You're all right, though," he said in a soft voice. "You're safe."

"Merle, it was so sudden." I pulled away and sniffed, wiping my nose with my hand.

"Well, go on inside. I'll get your bags," Merle told me.

"The pies are on the floor in the back seat," I said.

Janie sighed as I climbed the stoop. She smiled and gave me a quick hug. "Hello, stranger," she said. "Why are you crying?" She frowned as she led me inside the warm house. I smelled turkey roasting.

"A deer decided to run out in front of my car when I was on Buffalo Pass," I explained as I started taking off my jacket.

Janie gasped. "Oh, B.J., that's terrible. But you're not hurt?"

I shook my head and attempted to make light of it. "It... it just popped out of nowhere."

"They do that," she said. "Come sit down. I'll pour you a glass of wine."

"Thank you."

A couple of moments later, Merle brought in my overnight bag and the box with my laptop and the two apple pies I'd baked. The rolls were also packed inside the box, and he set my bag down and carried the box into the kitchen.

"What's this?" I heard Janie ask him.

"Beej made her famous apple pies," he said, "and her scrumptious dinner rolls that her grandmother used to make."

"*Great*-grandmother ..." I called out, but they didn't hear me.

"*I* made rolls," Janie said. "B.J. didn't have to. And I made pies too."

"I'm sorry," I heard Merle say in a low voice, and then they were whispering, but I couldn't hear it. Finally, Merle left the kitchen with two glasses of wine and brought one of them to me on the couch. "Here you go, girl. This ought to help calm you down." Then he let out a big sigh and sat down beside me.

We could hear Janie making lots of noise in the kitchen. It sounded like she was doing dishes with all the banging around of pots, pans and glassware. "Janie, do you need some help in there?" I called out.

Merle stopped me from standing up and made a face. "Shhh! She doesn't need you in there," he said in a low voice. I saw that it was a warning, and he was telling me not to interfere.

So I relaxed and took a sip of the wine, which was sweeter and whiter than I liked, but I didn't say anything. It was just good to have finally arrived in Dexter, in a familiar house, with friends and the whole weekend away from my life in the Lower Valley.

"How's everything here in Dexter?" I asked Merle. "Has anything changed?"

"Nothing ever changes in Dexter," Merle joked. He drank some wine, then glanced at the kitchen, then back at me. "Nothing's changed."

I took that to mean that he and Janie were still at odds with each other. Here I had assumed all was well and that I would be hearing about their wedding plans. I decided it was best not to bring up that subject. On the other hand, I wasn't going to be comfortable staying in their house if I had caused a rift.

"How's the *Buffalo Billboard?* Do you like what you've started?" Merle asked. He leaned back on the couch and crossed a leg over his knee.

"Yes," I replied. "The paper's off to a good start, I think. Jason loves the work, and he's doing a great job."

"Any more fighting among your employees?" asked Merle.

"Once in a while Rodney stirs up trouble."

"Rodney's the one from the Middle East? What is he, an Arab?"

"No." I smiled. "Rodney's American born. And I'm not sure what country his family emigrated from, but it doesn't matter to me. He thinks it does, however."

"What do you mean?" asked Merle.

"Oh ... he accused me of being prejudiced."

"Really ..." Merle had that look.

"I'm not prejudiced," I insisted. "Am I?"

"No, Beej, you like everybody. But it sounds like this employee could be trouble."

"That's not all," I disclosed. "He's been in prison."

Merle's eyes shot up and his round glasses slid to the end of his nose. "Prison?"

"I didn't find out about it until after I hired him, of course. But he went to jail for stealing some money at a store where he used to work."

Merle just shook his head and sighed. "Maybe you should get rid of him."

"No, Merle, I can't," I replied. "So far he's my bread and butter. He sells the most ads for the paper, and even though Colleen and Molly bring in a share of the ads, it's Rodney who has been supporting the revenue. I can't fire him ... though sometimes I'd like to." I took a sip of wine.

Things had grown quieter in the kitchen. Merle picked up on that last thought and asked me, "Now what makes you say that?"

"Well." I paused, then went on. "Halloween night we had a break-in. Somebody tore through our bathroom wall from the enclosed alley in back. They went right to our cash box, in Aspen's desk, and left with it."

"You didn't tell me you were robbed." Merle was astounded.

"The thief was caught," I said. "He took about eighty dollars in cash, and dumped all the checks in the alley way. I retrieved those, thankfully."

"Who was it?"

"Some man," I said. "The police said he'd be making restitution, but who knows when we'll see it? Other stores in back were also robbed and he had taken a lot more from them."

"Whoa." Merle leaned back on the couch to think. "That's scary, Beej."

"I know," I said, and told him about working late on Halloween, then getting a phone call where nobody was on the other end. I hinted that maybe the thief had called first, to be sure the building was clear. "I got scared and left shortly after that," I said. "I never thought about taking the cash box with me. But I pack up those checks and petty cash every day now and take it home with me."

"Good girl," said Merle. "Do you think Rodney had anything to do with the break-in?"

"I kind of doubt it," I said.

"Hmm." Merle sipped some of his wine and Janie walked into the living room to join us. She sat down in the recliner with her glass of wine, leaned back, crossed her legs and smiled at me.

"Someone broke into your business?" She had obviously overheard our conversation.

"Let's change the subject," said Merle. "Beej has been through enough today already."

I didn't miss the shudder of envy that flashed on Janie's face, but she covered up right away and began talking about her job and what had been going on in Dexter over the last several months. The wine was relaxing me and I was starting to get hungry. I hoped the turkey was almost done. Janie's talk was mundane and there wasn't much to say in response except nod our heads and agree every other sentence.

Finally, a timer went off in the kitchen. Merle popped up and carried his empty wine glass into the kitchen. "It's time for me to get to work," he announced. "The turkey's done."

"Want some help, dear?" Janie called out to him.

"Nope. It's a man's job." He turned and winked at me before escaping into the kitchen.

I set my empty glass on the coffee table. "I think I'll go put my bag in the guest room," I told Janie. "I also need to wash up before dinner."

"Oh, be my guest," said Janie with a grin. "You know where everything is."

I thanked her, then retreated down the hallway, grateful to have a few minutes to gather my thoughts and sober up a little from that very potent wine. I could feel the tension in the air as soon as I had arrived. Things were not right between Merle and his fiancée. Was I the cause? Maybe I shouldn't stay the whole weekend. I wasn't sure I could tolerate Janie's jealousy. If she had ever felt I was a threat before, I hadn't noticed. I wasn't exactly sure Merle wanted to go through with a marriage to her. I suspected he still had feelings for me.

As I washed up in the restroom, I decided it was time to make it clear, once and for all, that I had no holds on Merle Franklin.

29

"That was a wonderful meal." I smiled at Janie as I set my napkin down next to my empty plate. "You are an excellent cook."

"Why, thank you, B.J." Janie's grin showed her sparkling white teeth as she reached for another one of my great-grandmother's dinner rolls. "And these ... are simply delightful."

Merle nodded and mumbled, "I told you so."

"Your biscuits are good too, Janie," I reassured her. I noticed Merle roll his eyes. Thankfully, Janie was too busy slicing some butter to notice him. "I can't eat another bite, or I'd have another helping of potatoes and gravy."

"What's Jason doing today?" asked Merle.

I had almost forgotten my son. "Oh! He's spending Thanksgiving with his girlfriend."

Janie looked surprised. "Wow, Jason has a girlfriend?"

"About time," commented Merle.

"Who is she?" asked Janie.

I sat back in my seat and sighed. "Her name is Kelcie McKelvie, and she works for us."

"Oh, so she's dating the boss's son," Merle remarked with a chuckle.

"She's also our neighbor," I added. I stared at Merle. "I thought you met Kelcie when you brought the truck load of our stuff."

"Yeah, now I remember," he said. "Cute blonde."

Janie giggled and jostled her head. "Blondes have more fun, you know."

"So they say," said Merle. If his remark had meant to agitate Janie, she didn't pay any attention.

"Well, I'm glad Jason is dating someone," Janie went on to say. "Does he plan to return to the university next semester?"

I watched her butter the roll. "I have no idea what his plans are. I think he should go back and finish. He only has one semester to get his degree."

"He could go to Blanca State," suggested Merle. "Can't he transfer his credits back?"

"That's right, Merle said he started out at Blanca State University," said Janie. "What's Jason majoring in again?"

"Art with a minor in business," I said. "His dad owns an insurance company and had hopes of bringing him into the firm."

"That would mean Jason would have to move to Salt Lake City," said Merle.

"I don't think Jason is going to do any such thing," I told them. "He has discovered himself and wants to learn all about the newspaper business."

Janie started eating her roll. She studied me from across the table, then asked, "B.J., have you met any eligible men in the Lower Valley?"

I caught the look of interest on Merle's face and hesitated before answering. "Well ... maybe ..."

Janie perked up right away and cried out, "You have! Okay, who is he? I want to hear all about him."

Merle crossed his arms and sighed as he leaned back in his chair.

"I happen to be dating Kelcie's father," I disclosed, then waited for their reactions.

As predicted, Merle was the first one to express surprise. "Whoa ... the neighbor man?"

"Not exactly," I replied. "Kelcie lives by herself."

Janie wiped her mouth, then said, "Come on, B.J., don't keep us in suspense. What's his name? How did the two of you meet? Is it serious?" Her eyes were twinkling.

Right then, the doorbell rang. Merle stood up. "I'll go see who it is."

"It's probably the O'Rileys," said Janie. "I invited them over for dessert." Then, as Merle headed out into the living room to greet their guests, Janie said, "They're friends from work. I hope you don't mind. They won't stay long."

I didn't mind at all, though it was something unexpected. My mention of dating someone in the Lower Valley had already eased the tension between Janie and myself, but I really wasn't ready to get into the details of my budding relationship with Grant. So—much relieved—I got up from the table with Janie and went into the living room to socialize.

Later, after their friends had left and it was already dark outside, I declined Merle and Janie's invitation to watch a movie with them on their satellite TV. I was quite tired and ready to retire for the night.

"So early?" asked Janie.

"I've been up since before dawn," I told her. "Besides, the L-Tryptophan got to me."

Baffled, Janie turned to Merle, who smiled and said, "She means the turkey."

"Oh." Janie continued to puzzle over my excuse.

"Good night," I said with a smile.

"Good night, Beej," Merle called after me.

I soon settled into the guest room, dressed in my nightgown, thinking that I probably should have shown the courtesy of joining them in watching their movie. But I felt drained after several hours of conversation between Janie and her colleagues, Joe and Patty O'Riley. They were pleasant enough, but I felt a bit uncomfortable and not that interested in their small talk, most of which centered around their work place. Even Merle had appeared somewhat bored.

I had brought along a novel to read and hadn't gotten too far into it when my cell phone rang. I reached for it eagerly, hoping it was Grant calling. Instead, it was Peg Espinoza.

"Hello, Peg," I said after picking up. "What a surprise."

"B.J., I'm sorry to interrupt your holiday," said my former employee. "But I just found out some pertinent information on the Blue Heron." Peg sounded excited, but also a little buzzed.

"Really?" I leaned back against the pillows on the guest bed. "It must be something hot if you're calling on the night of Thanksgiving."

She giggled, then let out a sigh. "Oh, B.J. I'm sorry. I forgot you went to Dexter for the weekend. How was your Thanksgiving?"

"Nice," I replied. "Yours?"

"As you can tell, I've had a few piña coladas. Juan's brother, the deputy, was here for dinner, and he remembered some other things about the motel where your sister was found."

"What things did he mean?"

"Well," said Peg, "For one thing, the motel owner had ties with the local cartel."

"What local cartel?" I asked, closing the book on my lap as I sat up in bed.

"There's a drug cartel in our valley," Peg disclosed. "According to rumor, there were ties to the Blue Heron Motel, and Rudy, my brother-in-law, thinks it's likely that Liz, your sister, was somehow involved with the cartel."

"What!" Even though the idea didn't seem far-fetched, I didn't want to think of Liz being part of a smuggling group. Until there was proof or evidence, I couldn't accept rumors.

"Listen," said Peg, suddenly lowering her voice. "I can't talk right now. Let me see what else I can find out, and I'll call you after you get home. When is that again?"

"Peg, I want you just to relax," I said. "I don't want you obsessing over this, especially over the holidays. Besides, what good is it to learn all this now? What difference does it make?"

"I have to go. Call you soon." Peg hung up on me.

After I hung up, I pondered Peg's words. How could Liz have been involved in a drug cartel in Blanca Hills? What other information did Peg have to share with me after picking her brother-in-law's brain?

I returned to reading my novel just so that I didn't have to think about it anymore. Inwardly, I kept hoping Grant would call me, but he didn't. After I heard the TV go off in the living room, I closed my book, turned off the reading lamp, and went to sleep.

The next day Janie insisted on driving me to Junction for Black Friday. She loved to shop and had been looking forward to all the sales and activities in the larger town. I wasn't planning to do much shopping, but I went along so as not to hurt her feelings. Also, I didn't want to stay behind with Merle, who had no interest in Black Friday.

For the most part, I welcomed the change of scenery, the decorated stores and excitement on the faces of the people looking forward to the upcoming holiday season. I was even looking forward to Christmas this year and my thoughts drifted to gift ideas. I wondered if Grant would be part of my Christmas this year, and what kind of future was in store for us in the new year.

Over lunch at the mall, Janie and I chatted like we were old friends. She steered the conversation away from her relationship with Merle and I was cautious not to bring up wedding plans. I noticed she wasn't wearing an engagement ring and knew it was best not to press her on it. She seemed to have forgotten our interrupted conversation yesterday and did not ask me anything more about Grant.

By four o'clock we'd had enough of shopping. Exhausted and laden with our purchases, Janie drove us back to Dexter before it got dark. Leftovers from yesterday's feast awaited us, and I consented to watch a movie with Merle and Janie that evening.

Before it was time to begin, I went to my room and called Grant's cell phone. He did not pick up, so I got his voice mail.

"This is Grant. Leave your message and I will get back with you," the recording said.

"Hi …" I said after the beep. "It's Bridget. Give me a call when you can."

All during the movie, I expected my cell phone to ring. It didn't. When the movie ended, I checked my phone to see if there were any messages, in case it simply hadn't rung. No one had called. With a sigh, I thanked Merle and Janie for the delicious meal and the movie, then said good night. They were heading for bed as well. Janie was more tired than I was.

As I got ready, I wondered why Grant had not returned my call. Maybe he was busy with his friends. I wasn't sure why he was in Denver, but at least he had said he would see me on Sunday. There was no reason for me to be concerned. Too tired to read tonight, I snuggled against my pillow after the light went off, and fell instantly to sleep.

Sometime later, the nightmare gripped me. It was a mixed-up dream, but Grant was in it, and so was Liz. It was violent. I was running from some evil men dressed in black, carrying weapons and shouting, "Kill her!" I couldn't see where I was going, and whenever I turned a corner and found myself in another alley, some other villain would jump out at me, threatening me and laughing.

"Help me!" I was shouting, but I was half awake and my voice was straining. I couldn't get the words out. How could anyone hear me? I knew that Grant was nearby because he had been ahead of me, walking and unaware that I was behind him. "Grant!" I croaked. "*Grant!*"

Then I saw Liz's face peering at me from around the corner. She had a gleam in her eyes and she started laughing at me. "B.J., what's wrong with you?" she cried.

I knew that if I didn't get Grant's attention, I would perish. "They're ... coming!" My voice continued to strain. My vocal cords just wouldn't work right. "Grant ... *help* ... me..."

The men had reached us. Liz was with them! *"Grant isn't going to help you,"* Liz said in scorn.

They were coming at me, and I recalled that I was in bed, but they were there, and Liz started laughing again, an evil laugh that sent chills up my spine. And then Grant appeared, looking around but not seeing me. He didn't see the others either.

I knew I only needed to get his attention. He was my only hope. "*Grrr ... aaa... nnnn..tt!*" I began gasping as the men descended upon me. "No! No! *Nooooo!!*"

30

"Beej! Beej! Wake up!"

My reading lamp suddenly lit up the guest room. Merle stood over me, dressed in his pajamas. Janie stood at the doorway, wrapped in her red bathrobe, her eyes wide. "Is she all right?"

I was still half asleep, the nightmare gripping me until Merle stroked my face gently with his hand. I broke loose, but was still gasping. My heart was racing as I struggled to regain my composure. "My God!"

"It's all right. You were dreaming," said Merle. Janie crept closer, her eyes still wide.

"B.J.?" she asked fearfully.

I blinked my eyes, then let Merle help me up into a sitting position. "I'm so sorry I woke you up." My voice was cracking with emotion. "I had a really awful dream."

"You scared us," Janie commented, to which Merle shot her a dirty look.

"Maybe you should get up for a while," suggested Merle. "How about a shot of brandy?"

I started to calm down and pulled the sheet up around me, shaking my head, "No, that's all right. I'll be fine ... in a few minutes." But I didn't believe it. I was shaken from fear and emotion, not to mention embarrassed.

"I'm getting it anyway." Janie hurried out of the room.

Merle sat down on the bed beside me. His compassionate face comforted me and I let him pull me closer to him until we heard Janie coming from the kitchen with a small glass of brandy.

"What was the dream about?" asked Janie. Merle shook his head in disapproval, but she ignored him and handed me the drink, which I sipped slowly.

"I've been having a few nightmares lately," I confessed. "But this time ... it was the worst one. I ... I can't talk about it."

"Maybe you should see a shrink," said Janie.

"No," I said, shaking my head. "I'll be all right." I felt really stupid and embarrassed having them there, while I sipped brandy in their guest room as I tried to recover from the terror I had felt that had not left me. I kept remembering Grant's face in the dream, and how he had been oblivious to my presence. Was the dream trying to tell me something about Grant? And why was Liz a portrayal of evil? Maybe it was because Peg had told me on the phone how she thought my sister might have been involved in the drug cartel.

After I finished the brandy, I handed the glass back to Janie, who managed a smile. Merle suggested I get up and watch television for a while, but I simply shook my head and once again apologized for waking them.

"Maybe you should sleep with the lamp on," suggested Janie.

I considered it, actually. After they left and returned to their bedroom, I grabbed my novel and started reading the next chapter. After ten minutes, my eyes grew heavy and I bookmarked the page, turned out the lamp, and slipped back into slumber. No further nightmares plagued me that night, and I slept later than usual the next morning.

Over a late breakfast, Merle discussed some web ideas he had come up with to promote the paper through our on-line presence. I praised him for keeping things running smoothly, and being responsive to customers who had issues with the process of placing ads or comments on the site.

"How are people responding to your shopper?" asked Janie as she brought the coffee pot to the table to refill our mugs. "Are you getting enough ads?"

"The web stats are improving a little," said Merle.

"We have ads," I commented, "but I don't think we have enough yet. I have to come up with filler material every week. However, the next three weeks should be really good because of the holidays."

"That's right," Janie said with a smile. "Our local shopper is huge this time of year."

"You're a success," Merle added, then winked at me as he lifted his mug to his mouth.

"Did you sleep okay after your nightmare?" Janie asked.

"Yes."

"No more dreams?" asked Merle.

"Nope." I reached for my cell phone to check for messages I might have missed. Grant still had not gotten back to me.

Later, after I'd settled down on the living room couch while Merle and Janie busied themselves with household chores, I punched Jason's name on my phone. He answered after four rings.

"Hey, Mom," he said.

"Jason, did you have a good Thanksgiving?"

"We did." He briefly told me about his and Kelcie's day at her friend's, and how everything was okay at home. "How about you?" he asked.

"It was good." Then I asked, "Has Kelcie talked to her father this weekend?"

"She didn't say anything about him," he replied. "Why?"

I paused, then said, "No reason."

"He's still out of town, I think," said Jason.

"Yes, I know."

We kept our conversation brief and hung up shortly after. I wanted to try calling Grant again, but I hesitated. I was certain that he would get back to me when it was convenient for him. He had told me he would be returning to Blanca Hills tomorrow. I felt the pull to want to go home today. Something was urging me to return early. It was probably just my own insecurity.

A while later, Merle turned on the television and switched to the weather channel. I noticed that a storm was headed our way. We both stared at the screen and paid attention to the time line.

"Looks like snow is coming again," said Merle.

"I see that." I stood up. "Maybe I should head for the Lower Valley before it gets too bad."

"Today?" Merle looked at me. "You want to leave today?"

"Why not?" I stared at him. "I was planning to leave in the morning, but if a storm is moving in, I think maybe I should leave this afternoon."

Janie, who had been working in the kitchen, stepped into the living room. "B.J., are you going home today?"

"I think so."

She frowned. "Ohhh ... I was planning on having Merle put the Christmas tree up."

"It's not Christmas yet," Merle grumbled.

"I thought you might want to help me decorate," said Janie, completely ignoring him.

I wasn't much for holiday decorating to begin with, and certainly not as early as the weekend of Thanksgiving. But I knew some people preferred it that way. Over the years, the holidays had not been my favorite time of year, mostly because I was by myself, with Dirk insisting that Jason spend his time off from school in Utah. Yet, from what I understood, Avery rarely came home for Christmas.

"It's coming down already," said Merle. He stood up and walked to the big window, where heavy flakes were falling. The sky to the east was dark and ominous. "The weather map shows the storm is already hitting the Lower Valley," he added. "It's best you wait, Beej."

My heart sank. I let out a sigh. I did not have any desire to confront Buffalo Pass nor the lonely highway between there and the nearest valley town in this kind of weather.

"There's no hurry for you to return home, is there?" asked Janie.

"Well ..." I sat back down on the couch. "I guess not."

"Good!" Janie clapped her hands. "Oh, I love snow, especially this time of year."

"It will be gone by morning," Merle predicted. "This is Dexter, after all." He offered a smile of sympathy.

It was actually a good thing that I stayed because the storm continued to dump snow. I helped Janie and Merle set up their tree and string the colored lights, half listening to Janie's chatter as she insisted on telling me about every little memory associated with every little trinket she hung on the branches of their artificial, ceiling-high Christmas tree. My thoughts wandered every now and then to how nice it would have been to sleep in my own bed tonight, and how I probably wouldn't have time to go to the office tomorrow afternoon to get a little work in before Monday.

Merle braved the weather and drove into town to get us a pepperoni pizza that night for supper. He and Janie had decided that perhaps

I did not want to eat turkey leftovers again. Even though I would have gladly indulged in another meal of the delicious leftovers, pizza sounded pretty good. When Merle returned, darkness had arrived and we sat at the kitchen table while Janie got out plates and napkins.

"Thanks for helping with the Christmas decorating," Janie told me after we were on our second slices. "Now you can put the tree up at your apartment."

I chewed, then swallowed before answering her. "I'm embarrassed to admit this, but I don't have a fake tree that I put up every year." Then I added, "No offense ... I just usually never bothered."

Merle enjoyed the startled look on Janie's face, then said, "Beej bought a real tree last year and had it set up in her living room here in Dexter."

"Jason spent Christmas with me last year," I explained. "Usually, he'd go to his dad's every year. I never felt like celebrating without him there."

Janie sighed and her cheeks sagged a little. "Oh, B.J. ... that's so sad."

"It was a condition they had when she and Dirk got divorced," Merle explained.

"So are you going to get a tree this year too?" asked Janie, reaching for her Coke.

"I'm sure we will." I smiled to cheer her up.

Merle wanted to view his Saturday evening television shows, so I helped Janie clean up in the kitchen, and then she asked if I wanted to see a movie with them later. I told her I had to get ready to leave first thing in the morning, and that I'd be going to bed early to get a good night's sleep.

I was in the guest room, organizing my stuff, and the television was going in the living room when my cell phone rang. When I reached to pick it up, I saw that Grant was on the other end. I eagerly answered it and sat down on the bed.

"Grant? Hello!"

"Bridget, I apologize for not calling you earlier. I've been tied up at this end with one thing or another. I just now had time to give you a call."

"That's fine," I said, so relieved that he was all right. "How was your weekend?"

"Busy." He cleared his throat. "Are you still in Dexter?"

"I am. I was going to leave this afternoon, but that winter storm moved in."

"Denver got hit with it," said Grant. "Probably the valley got a good amount of snow as well." Then he asked, "How are you? Did you have a good Thanksgiving?"

I leaned back against the pillows on the bed. "It was very nice," I said.

"Is everything all right, Bridget? You sound kind of ... anxious."

I paused, then said, "Actually, I've been a bit of a basket case."

"Why?"

"Well, for one thing, I hit a deer at Buffalo Pass on Thursday morning."

"No! Are you all right? Is your car okay?" He sounded alarmed.

"Everything's fine. The car has a dent, but other than that ..."

"Bridget, I'm relieved you're okay."

"Thanks, Grant. I haven't really thought that much about hitting the deer. But I did have a terrible dream last night. That really shook me up."

"A dream? What kind of dream?"

"Oh, it's nothing unusual." I tried to make light of it. "I happen to have a lot of those dreams lately."

"Nightmares?"

"Uh-huh." I laughed to cover up the serious tone that had crept into his voice. "Unfortunately, it woke up Merle and Janie."

There was silence at the other end.

Finally, I said, "Grant ... are you still there?"

"Uh, yes. Yes!" He chuckled, then said, "I find that interesting. You see, I have nightmares myself."

"You do? Seriously?"

"Yup." He sighed. "At least once a week."

"Me too!"

"Well ... we'll have to talk about it sometime," he said. "Listen, when I get back to Blanca Hills, let's get together."

"All right." I loved how his voice had suddenly softened. "I'm looking forward to it."

"Me too. I miss you, Bridget."

"I miss you too, Grant."

We said our goodnights, and then I got ready for bed, satisfied that he had called and basking in the memory of his voice and his soothing words. It didn't matter that he had waited two whole days to call me. When I returned home, I had something to look forward to besides the paper and my job. Was this a romance in bloom? Had I finally found a man who could understand me? That night as I turned out the light and let myself drift off to sleep, I prayed that I had found the right man at last.

31

The next morning I left after an early breakfast with Merle and Janie, who sacrificed their Sunday morning's sleep to get up and fix waffles and sausages. The storm had passed and there were blue skies over Dexter. I wasn't sure what I'd find once I reached the pass. The snowplows had cleared the roads, but I wanted to get a head start from all the holiday traffic with people returning to their homes.

This time I played my car stereo to stay alert, and was extra vigilant at Buffalo Pass. Traffic was actually light until I reached the upper end of the valley. I had topped off my gas before leaving Dexter, and the drive home was long but uneventful. Thoughts of Grant and the memory of the sound of his voice over the phone drove away any intruding thoughts about my sister and the mess she may have gotten herself into which led to her death. I wasn't going to let those disturbing thoughts ruin the sweet anticipation of seeing Grant again.

By two-thirty I pulled the Camry into its parking space at the apartments on Greenwood. I didn't see Jason's car. He was absent from the apartment when I walked in. Most likely, he was with Kelcie. I had just finished putting away my clothes and cosmetics when my cell phone rang. It was my son.

"Mom, did you get home yet?" he asked.

"I've been home about forty minutes. Where are you?"

"Kelcie and I are at the office. We decided to come in this afternoon and catch up with some of the ads. I hope you don't mind."

"Oh, Jason, that's just fine." I laughed. "I really am too tired to drive over to Valle Viento this afternoon and work."

"That was the whole idea," he said.

"Is there a lot?" I asked.

"Nope. Not much at all."

"Hm," I commented.

"We'll probably get slammed tomorrow," said Jason. "The sales people probably didn't do much over the weekend."

"I'm sure you're right."

After we ended the conversation, I grabbed a snack from the kitchen and collapsed into my recliner, wondering if I should find something to watch on TV or go get the book I was reading. I reached for the TV remote when the phone rang. It was Grant.

"Hello, Grant."

"Bridget, are you on the road?"

"No, I'm home. You?"

"I'll be in Blanca Hills in about an hour." After a pause, he said, "I know you're tired. I am, too. But I'd sure like to see you."

I smiled. "Why don't you come over?"

"I have a better idea. I'll pick you up and bring you to my place. We can stop at the sub shop and pick up something to take home. I'll be hungry by then. How about you?"

"That sounds fine." Then I quickly added, "I can't stay too late, though. I have to..."

"I know," Grant interrupted with a chuckle. "We both have to go back to work tomorrow. I've been away from the *Sentinel* more than a week. No telling what shenanigans have been going on in my absence ..." His voice was breaking up a little.

"Grant, I'll see you later," I said, but there was only garble at the other end. "Grant?"

After some static, I heard him say, "Gotta go ... bad reception ..." Then he was gone.

So much for my relaxation time. Leaving the TV remote on the coffee table, I got up and headed for the shower, satisfied that Grant had called and that he cared enough to invite me over.

It was still light out when Grant arrived in his silver Porsche and came to the door. I felt fresh and clean, having dried and curled my hair as I answered the doorbell and met his grin with my own. He stepped in and wrapped his arms around me, and I let him pull me close, basking in the warmth and security of his embrace. It felt so right.

"Mm, your hair ... it smells good," said Grant. He nuzzled my bangs with his chin, then placed a light kiss on my lips. Then he looked around. "Where's your son?"

"He's working. So's your daughter."

Grant nodded his head. "Kelcie is dedicated. You're lucky to have her."

"I know." I grabbed my coat from the closet, scooped up my purse and cell phone, and then we headed out the door to the parking lot, where the motor was still running in the Porsche. Grant helped me in. He stopped after he closed the door and shielded his eyes as he gazed out at the west. The sky had turned an awesome pink. Still staring, he made his way to the driver's side and climbed in.

"It's a gorgeous sky," I commented.

"Incredible," said Grant. "The sunsets are phenomenal this time of year. I especially admire Christmas sunsets."

"Christmas is still three and a half weeks away," I reminded him as he put on his seatbelt.

"I want to take you to the Sand Dunes sometime," he told me. "I've seen some truly remarkable sunsets there." He looked into my eyes and my heart began to melt.

"I've heard it's a special place," I told him, unable to take my eyes off him. "Kelcie took Jason there not long ago. They did some hiking."

Grant nodded, still smiling, and then he turned away to shift and drive out of the lot into the street. "I should have been an artist," he mumbled.

"You are an artist," I replied. "I've seen some of your photography."

We drove to the sub shop and I waited in the warm car while Grant went inside to get our supper. When he came out, he handed me the sandwich bag and then we drove over to his home north of campus. By now it was dusk and the western sky was crimson. He pulled into the long driveway and triggered the garage door opener. I felt a prickle of anticipation and was glad to be in this man's company, happy that he had invited me into his beautiful home, even after his extended business trip. I knew he must be tired, and yet he wanted me to be with him. More than that, I wanted to be with him right now.

While he unloaded his luggage and briefcase out of the car, I went ahead and made myself at home in his roomy, modern kitchen. I loved all the space and the stone countertops, recessed lighting above, a center island with an extra sink, and the tiled floor. Everything was modern and spotless. I found the plates and glasses, then opened the oversized refrigerator to get out condiments, in case we needed them. Even the refrigerator was organized and neat. This man seemed to have it together. There wasn't one dirty dish or utensil in his sink.

"Want some wine?" asked Grant as he came out of the bedroom after putting away his bags. "I'll get a bottle out of the wine cellar in the basement."

"Why not?" I grinned at him as I carried plates and napkins into the dining room.

He disappeared around the corner and I heard him open a door and walk down some steps. By the time I had brought everything else onto the table, Grant showed up, wiping off a bottle of dark, fruity wine in an unmarked green bottle. He went into the kitchen and returned with the opener.

"Is that homemade wine?" I asked.

"As a matter of fact, it is," he said. "Plum wine. 2008 Tucker vintage."

"You made the wine?"

"A little side hobby of mine," he said, and he popped off the cork.

I took a seat at the table and Grant set an empty glass in front of me and poured a small amount. "Try it first," he said. "If you don't like it, I'll get something else."

I sipped the wine and looked up at him. "Hmm ... it's sweet ... it has a mellow flavor ... very good."

"More?"

I smiled. "Please."

We ate the submarines, along with some dill pickles and a few potato chips. I had to admit, after eating heavily for three days, this was a treat and so simple. The wine was fairly potent and I felt myself getting groggy. He asked me about my trip to Dexter and I related the events, ending with having to help Janie decorate their house for the holidays.

"It sounds like you enjoyed yourself," Grant commented.

"It was good to get away from work," I said. "How about you?"

Grant sighed. "My trip wasn't exactly a break from work." He smiled at me. "But I won't get into that. I'm much more interested in finding out about these nightmares you were telling me about."

"Oh." I sat back in my chair and picked up my half-empty wine glass. "I can't really remember when they started, but it seems I've been having bad dreams for several months now."

"And? What are they about?"

I hesitated a moment, then said, "Usually they involve my sister ... Liz."

"Go on," he urged.

"It varies. Sometimes she appears innocent, like when we were kids. But in most of the dreams, she's angry at me. She resents me for working hard and making something of my life, if that's what I'm doing ... and the nightmare part of my dream is running away from danger ... men or monsters trying to kill me. I try to escape. I scream ... and I wake myself up half way ... only I usually can't escape the dream. When I finally do wake up, I've been yelling out loud ... and I'm shaken." I sipped the wine.

Grant pushed his chair back and got up from the table to take our plates and paper waste to the sink. "Why do you think your sister keeps appearing in your dreams?" he asked me.

"It's like I told you ... she reached out to me two weeks before her death. I didn't respond. Maybe I have a guilty conscience."

He returned to the table and pulled his chair closer to mine. "I've had nightmares off and on ever since Samantha passed away," he told me. "But she isn't in the dreams. It's kind of hard for me to explain."

My cell phone rang just then and I got up to get it out of my purse in the living room. "Sorry," I called back to Grant. Jason was on the other end. "Mom?"

"Oh hi, Jason."

"I just got home. Where are you?"

"I'm over at Grant's. Is everything okay?"

"Yeah." I heard someone giggle in the background.

"Well, don't worry about me," I told him. "Is Kelcie there with you?"

"I'm here," said Kelcie.

"Are you staying there tonight?" Jason asked me. This time Kelcie giggled louder.

Embarrassed, I turned and saw Grant standing in the doorway to the kitchen. Since I had my cell on speaker phone, he had heard every word we had said. I felt my face turning red and didn't know what to say.

"Mom?"

Grant quickly stepped closer and spoke close to the phone. "Your mother's staying here tonight. She's had some wine is all. Kelcie, are you feeling any better?"

It was obvious that the girl on the other end hadn't expected her father to be listening in on the conversation I was having with Jason. She suddenly burst out laughing and Jason chuckled.

"Hi, Dad," said Kelcie, obviously trying to keep her cool. "Yeah ... I'm over it now."

"Thank heaven," said Grant. "Why didn't you return any of my calls?"

There was a silence, and finally a loud sigh from the girl on the other end. "Oh, Dad ... I've just been busy. I'm sorry."

Grant glanced at me and rolled his eyes. "Let's talk soon," he told her. "Okay?"

"Okay," said Kelcie.

"I gotta go now," said Jason. "Mom, I'll see you at work in the morning."

"I'll see both of you," I said, and then he hung up. When I looked up at Grant, we both burst into laughter and then he embraced me. "I'm not drunk," I protested in a joking manner.

"I know," said Grant. He planted a light kiss on my forehead, then led me over to the couch, where we sat down. "But you are welcome to spend the night."

"I don't know." I suddenly felt shy and uncertain. "You just got back from your business trip. We both have to get up in the morning."

"Bridget ..." He gazed into my eyes and I saw that he had not just been playing around when he'd told Jason that. "I want you to stay tonight. Will you?"

"Well, I ... I ..." My heart was beating fast. "Grant, I didn't bring a toothbrush."

He shook his head and leaned forward to give me a deep, luscious kiss on the lips. Then he said, "I have spares." He blinked at my surprised look, then laughed and said, "I also have an alarm clock. I'll get you home on time ... or I'll drive you to Valle Viento myself, if you'd like."

"No, no, no ... that's not necessary." Then I looked deep into his green eyes. "Are we ... I mean, are you ... do you actually want to ..."

"Bridget, we have unfinished business." Then he took me into his arms again and kissed me some more. I was unable to think rationally beyond that point. The wave of desire he aroused in me was so strong, and not just because of the wine he'd given me, but my feelings toward him. I didn't want to think about anything else. I didn't want to think about the complications of our children being involved with each other, nor the fact that we were both publishers of rival papers in the Lower Valley. All I could think about was giving in to this desirable, gentle, extremely attractive man who had brought me into his life.

Our session on the couch could only lead to one thing, and after a while Grant excused himself to turn on some soft background music and check the locks on his doors. I sat up and straightened my hair, feeling slightly disoriented but still very aroused. He then walked over and took me by the hand and led me through the arched doorway into the master bedroom, which I had barely glimpsed the last time I was at his home.

I made my way into the master bathroom, which was another pleasant surprise. It was a large room with double sinks, an enclosed glass shower stall against one wall, and an attractive garden tub beneath a window that was closed with wooden blinds. Everything in this bathroom was elegant and inviting. After I refreshed myself, I returned to the bedroom. Grant had turned out the lights except for a couple of small glows from candle lamps on either side of his king size bed. The beautiful soft music was filtering in from the living room.

He lay on one side of the bed, naked except for his underwear, his hands resting underneath his neck as he watched me approach. A smile curled my face as I began to remove each item of clothing on my way to his side. As tired as I was after my long day of travel and the effects of the plum wine, my body was on fire with the need for this man's touch. I slowly climbed onto the bed and kicked my maroon panties that had dropped to my ankles onto the floor. I saw his eyes fall approvingly over my exposed breasts and furry mound. I could smell the masculinity of his skin as he rolled onto his side and reached out to draw me toward him.

How comforting it was to lie in this gigantic bed, caught up in the magic of being possessed by Grant Tucker, who was quickly becoming the main focus of my life. All weekend, while in Dexter, my thoughts had strayed so often, worried that he wouldn't call me ... and then he had. Suddenly, everything in my world seemed right. For the first time in my life, I felt a man wanting to love me without any conditions or restrictions. What was most important to me was that I could not hold back, even had I wanted to. In all my past relationships, I had gone through the motions of sex without really experiencing the feelings. Now —making love to Grant—I felt such a release and a total giving over of my very self to him ... a self I had kept hidden all these years, for fear of being hurt like I had with Dirk.

The love-making was passionate and enduring. This had not been a "quickie" as I'd known in the past. Grant had taken his time with me, getting to know my body, letting me explore his. It had been the most beautiful experience of my life so far. The fulfillment of the climax had been riveting, sending me out into the outer limits of my mind. He had waited for my sensations to peak before allowing himself any satisfaction. And then we lay afterwards, intertwined against each other's bodies, blissful and slightly exhausted. I only remember Grant reaching over to turn out the candle lamps, and then gently pulling the sheet over the two of us. I drifted off ...

32

Morning came too soon as the buzz of the alarm brought me out of a deep, restful sleep. I remembered where I was ... in the large, soft bed that belonged to Grant Tucker ... and I heard him reach over and shut off the noise. Then he lay back and I snuggled against his warm nakedness, not ready to open my eyes. There had been no disturbing dreams and I longed just to linger in the darkness of the dawn a while longer.

Grant apparently had the same longing. We both fell back to sleep until quite a while later I opened my eyes to the early morning sunlight hitting the window next to his bed.

I sprang up and startled Grant, whose eyes popped open in surprise. "What time is it?" I asked. Then I saw the clock above the large dresser across the room and exclaimed, "It's almost seven-thirty! I'm going to be late to work."

He sat up in bed, his light-colored hair ruffled, while I trotted off naked to the bathroom. When I came out, Grant was almost completely dressed and he smiled sheepishly. "I don't usually fall back to sleep when the alarm goes off," he admitted.

I gathered up yesterday's clothes and began getting into them. "Do you have time to run me home?"

He sauntered over and put his arms around me. "We could both call in sick."

"No, we can't. We're the bosses." Then I saw that he was only kidding and I laughed.

"I'll be glad to run you home," he said and planted a kiss on my cheek as he ruffled my messed-up dark hair. "But I'd love to have an encore first."

Momentarily startled, I looked into his eyes filled with desire for me, and almost gave in as I succumbed to a long, hungry kiss. But then I gently pulled away. "I'll take a rain check instead."

With a sigh of disappointment, he let me go, and I finished getting dressed. "At least let me make us some coffee."

"Oh, absolutely," I told him.

"Some breakfast?" he queried.

"Just some toast," I replied.

"How about a bagel?"

"Better yet." I smiled as he disappeared into the hallway, headed for the kitchen.

A short time later, competing with campus traffic, Grant drove me to my apartment and dropped me off. He promised to call me later. We kissed each other again before I got out and hurried inside to finally brush my teeth. Jason had already left for Valle Viento. I changed my clothes and washed up, then realized I had not charged my cell phone overnight. But I had a cord in my car and would plug it in after I got to the office.

It was going on ten o'clock by the time I walked into the *Buffalo Billboard*, ready to confront my employees with excuses for being late. But they only glanced my way, then continued working as if it was nothing to be concerned about that this was the first time I'd ever showed up late to work.

"Good morning. Sorry to be running late," I called out.

Aspen smiled from her desk and said, "Good morning, B.J.," then continued typing.

Colleen and Molly were busy at their desks, writing up their insertion orders for their ad clients. Kelcie was busy in her corner, building an ad on her screen, but she shot me a quick smile, then engrossed herself in her task. I noticed the bathroom door was closed and I assumed Rodney was inside.

"Hi, Mom," Jason greeted me as I entered the inner room.

"Hello, Jason." I set my purse down and removed my coat. I was waiting for him to comment on my lateness, or even inquire about my spending the night with Grant Tucker, but he just kept working. Since there was a pile of things to do on my desk—more than usual because of the extended holiday weekend—I decided to just buckle down and do my part.

The day passed quickly without any outstanding incidents. I stayed late and caught up on posting checks and catching up with some accounting after everyone else went home. It was dark by the time I closed up and headed for my car. The dent from the deer reminded me that I probably should call my insurance company, but I had more important things on my mind at the moment.

Then, as I was unlocking my car door, I noticed the red sports car parked on the opposite side of the street. Without making it obvious that I was interested, I slowly climbed into the Camry and adjusted the mirror after starting up the engine. I could see that Javier, Grant's general manager at the *Sentinel*, was watching me. He was alone. It made me shudder to think that I was being spied upon. I made up my mind to bring it up with Grant when he called me, which he'd promised to do.

Meanwhile, I headed back to Blanca Hills and stopped at the grocery store on the way home.

"B.J.?"

I spun around after picking through the bin of onions in the produce section to find Peg Espinoza pushing a grocery cart. "Peg!" I responded with a surprised grin.

She immediately stepped over to give me a hug. "I've been meaning to call you," she said excitedly. "I stumbled across some bizarre information you should know about." She told me she had planned on phoning me today, but had been called in to substitute teach at the middle school. "But maybe we can meet for lunch after the paper goes to press," she suggested. "It has to do with your sister and what went on at the Blue Heron Motel."

I looked around us, afraid that we might be overheard. I had been quite sure that Javier had not followed my car to this store, but I was feeling a bit paranoid. "Peg, we shouldn't discuss this in the open," I said in a lowered voice.

"You're probably right," she agreed, then changed the subject. "How's everything going at the *Billboard*?"

"Busy," I said. "I'm expecting big papers up through Christmas."

"Way to go!" Then Peg put her hands on her hips. "How are things with Grant?"

"Good," I said. "That's why I'm here. I'm picking up items I need to make him an Italian dinner."

"Whoa! You go, girl." Peg grinned and would have said something more, but her cell phone rang. "Talk to ya later," she told me and answered her phone while she wheeled her cart toward the meat section.

I was able to finish shopping for the special meal I planned to make without further interruptions. But as I was checking out with the cashier, I happened to see a glimpse of Javier in the store. He was standing over at the customer service counter, speaking with a clerk about something. I didn't want him to see me or know that I had noticed him in his red car, parked across the street from my office in Valle Viento. I already suspected he had followed me here. I hoped he had not been within earshot when I had talked to Peg.

After I loaded my groceries into the back of the Camry, I drove home, worried. Grant had not called and I needed to talk to him about Javier. Even though I had mentioned once to him that I had seen Javier watching me from his car, it appeared that Grant had not thought much about it. Lights were on in the apartment, and before I had even gotten out of the car, Jason came outside to meet me and help me carry in my bags.

"Mom, I was starting to get worried," said Jason.

"Seriously?" I joked.

"Were you really drunk at Grant's house?" he asked.

"No!" I laughed. "I had one glass of plum wine. I wasn't drunk."

"Well, it sounded like you were too wasted to leave his house."

I knew my son was messing with me. "Do you really want to know why I spent the night? All the mushy details?"

"No, Mom ... spare me."

"He practically lives in a mansion," I continued. "You should see that place. I can't believe Kelcie doesn't want to live there with her dad. There's so much room!"

Jason chuckled and opened the door for me. "Kelcie likes her space."

"Don't we all?" I walked in and put my bags down on the kitchen counter. "How are you two getting along, anyway?"

"Super," said Jason. "And speaking of Kelcie ... I promised I'd go over and help her with some project she's doing for the bird count."

"What bird count? What are you talking about?" I asked.

"Kelcie's into all kinds of environmental activities," he replied. "She's an Audubon member and is helping to organize the Christmas Bird Count. It's an annual outing here in the Lower Valley."

"Cool. See you later?"

"Sure, Mom. Don't wait up for me." He smiled, then went out the door.

I put away my groceries, then made myself a sandwich and opened a bottle of beer. I felt I needed to unwind from work, from my evening with Grant, and now with the concern about Javier spying on me. I dialed Grant's cell as I settled onto the living room sofa and pulled an afghan over my knees.

After three rings, Grant answered. "Bridget. I was just getting ready to call you. How was your day?"

"Hectic," I said. "What about yours?"

"The same. Want to come over again tonight?" he asked.

Of course I wanted to, but I declined. "I'm really tired. And tomorrow is production day. We have another big paper this week."

He was quiet, then spoke. "I understand. And just so you know ... I loved having you here with me."

My heart swelled and my voice faltered a bit. "That's sweet of you." Then I pushed sentiment aside and asked, "Did you know that your general manager, Javier, has been following me again?"

Immediately, Grant grew defensive. "What? Javier? Why would he do that?"

"You tell me," I said. "His red sports car was parked across the street from my office when I left work this evening."

"What time was that?"

"Oh, probably going on seven." I went on to disclose that Javier had been inside the grocery store in Blanca Hills, and that I had seen him when I was checking out the groceries I'd purchased.

"Bridget, it's most likely a coincidence," said Grant. "Why would Javier want to follow you?"

"I think you should ask *him* that," I said. "This was not the first time."

"Yeah, I remember you mentioned it before. I'm definitely going to confront him with this."

"Thanks." After a long pause, I said, "I'm cooking Italian Wednesday night."

Immediately the tenseness that had been in his voice a moment ago dissipated. "Oh?"

"That's why I stopped at the grocery store. Are you free?"

Grant laughed, then said, "I've got a better idea. Why don't you bring everything over here and cook? I have the larger kitchen." Then he added, "I'm quite sure I am free that evening."

"Both papers will be out," I added. "And if you don't mind, would you pick out the wine?"

Our conversation thus ended on a more relaxed note. We chatted awhile longer and then said our goodnights. When I hung up, I had good feelings again. I decided to put Javier and his red sports car out of my mind as I reached for my beer and my sandwich. The only thing I felt like doing right then was finding a decent chick-flick on TV.

Jason came home before too long. He had a big day ahead of him and reported to me that it looked like another winter storm might be headed for the valley. I hoped it wouldn't amount to much. The worst part about being a mother was having to worry about Jason driving to Shambleton and back with all those papers to deliver the next day. As soon as the movie went off, I put my dishes into the sink and went to bed.

When we awoke the next morning, fresh snow had fallen in the night, but it wasn't as bad as the weekend storm. At the office, everyone worked hard to get the issue ready in time for our scheduled upload to the press. I complimented my three sales people on the good job they had done, getting plenty of ads for this week's paper. Then I announced that we were going to have a Christmas party in three weeks at one of the valley's restaurants.

Colleen was excited and asked, "Are we going to draw names and exchange gifts?"

"Oh, please, let's do it," cried Aspen. "It'll be so fun."

"Well, sure," I agreed. "I guess we could do that."

Rodney grumbled to himself and stood at the windows, looking out with his hands in his pockets.

Colleen leaned toward me and murmured, "Rodney probably doesn't celebrate Christmas."

Molly and Aspen exchanged looks and I just shrugged. "Rodney, do you have a problem with an office party?" I called out.

My male salesman spun around and sighed, then smiled. "No, it's cool," he said. "I don't have a problem at all."

"Do you even celebrate Christmas?" Molly asked.

Rodney looked annoyed, then replied, "Of course I celebrate Christmas. I'm an American!" Then he stomped off into his corner and pretended to be busy, sorting through papers.

Jason was getting ready to leave for Shambleton and Kelcie came out of the kitchen with a fresh cup of herb tea. "Where's the party going to be?" she asked.

"I'm going to figure that out today," I said. "Jason, let me get the check for the press." I dodged into my office to make sure he would have everything he needed, then cautioned him once again to be careful. Kelcie followed him outside and I saw her give him a kiss before he climbed into The Beast. After the engine started roaring as he warmed up the truck, she came running inside, hugging herself.

"It's cold out there!"

"Thanks, everyone," I called to the crew.

"I'll write everyone's name on a slip of paper and we'll draw for the gift exchange on Thursday," said Aspen as she returned to her desk and began sorting piles of proofed ad galleys.

"Let's have two more weeks of ad sales like we just had," I told my sales people before they left. Things quieted down half an hour later. Everyone had left, except myself and Aspen, and she spent most the afternoon on the telephone, talking to her boyfriend because things were slow.

My mind was occupied with Grant and the menu I was preparing for Wednesday evening's special meal at his home. I had more book work to do, but it was hard to concentrate. I kept glancing outside, where the snow had started up again. I told myself that I had better get used to it, this was winter in the Lower Valley, and snow—lots of it—was the norm.

Aspen left at five. Shortly afterwards, Kelcie came back to the office, ready to work with us to bag up papers for the post office. The snow was still falling, but every now and then it would let up, then start again. "Jason called me an hour ago," she told me. "He should be here anytime now."

We both sat down in the front office to wait. I was glad to have an opportunity to converse with Kelcie about a couple of things. "I'm glad you're over that virus," I said.

"Me too," she said. "It was your chicken soup that did it, you know."

"How are you and your father getting along?" If my abrupt question took her by surprise, Kelcie didn't show it.

She smiled briefly, then grew serious. "Before I say anything, I want you to know, B.J., that I think you and my dad getting together is the best thing to happen to him. He's had a hard time of it since Mom died."

I flickered a smile before she continued.

"I'm sure you've wondered what it is that happened between me and Dad. Well, it's not that easy to explain."

"It must have been very hard on him, losing your mother," I said.

Kelcie nodded, then turned her dark-lashed green eyes up at me. "More than you'll ever know," she said. "But she really wanted to die. I've accepted that now."

After a short pause, I asked, "Okay ... so why do you still want to blame your father?"

Kelcie sniffed and swallowed. "It's not that," she said, her voice wavering a little. "In fact, I really shouldn't be talking to you about it."

"But maybe it will help," I tried to convince her. "Kelcie, your dad loves you very much."

"Did he say that?"

"Well ... he didn't have to. I know that he does."

"I just don't understand him," she grumbled.

Now I felt we were getting somewhere. Kelcie was starting to open up. "Why?" I prodded.

"He lets other people walk all over him," she said.

I shook my head in disbelief. "I don't understand what you mean. He's the owner of the valley's biggest newspaper."

"The people who work for him ..." Her eyes squinted at me. "They are the ones in charge, not him."

"What do you mean?"

"I ... I really can't talk about this now," said Kelcie with a tremble in her voice. "In fact, I shouldn't have said what I said." She turned to me with a pleading face. "Please don't tell Dad I talked about it."

"Kelcie, I think *you* should talk to him about this. He needs to know why you resent him."

She shook her head slowly. I reached over and drew her close for a hug. Just at that moment we heard a loud crash. Both of us jumped up in surprise.

"Oh, no! Jason!" Kelcie shouted.

Outside the office, we saw the Suburban had plowed into the back of my Camry, which I had parked next to the door. My blue sedan had been rammed up onto the sidewalk, the big black Beast slowly sliding backward, then jerking to a halt. Jason stepped out of the driver's door, cursing up a storm as Kelcie and I ran out the door, horrified.

"What happened?" I cried. "Jason, are you all right?"

Kelcie ran over to him, but stopped because he was angry and still spouting cuss words.

"The accelerator was stuck, damn it!" Jason yelled. He turned to me and his anger turned to despair. "Mom, I'm sorry about your car. I couldn't get it to stop in time."

My Camry's rear end had been bashed in and sported a worthy companion dent for the smaller one on the side where I'd hit the deer. But I was more concerned about my son. "Come inside," I told the two of them.

"We've got to get the papers out of the back," Jason protested.

"Later," I insisted. "Let's go in where it's warm."

While Kelcie was making a fresh pot of coffee, Jason told us that even though the accelerator had been a little touchy, he had made it to Shambleton without any trouble. Then, about halfway back to Valle Viento, the accelerator started sticking. The vehicle would speed up and he couldn't get the accelerator to release, so he had to put his foot on the brake at the same time.

"It was dangerous driving down that highway," he told us. "I thought I was going to run into somebody. Fortunately, there wasn't very much traffic, but the roads were getting slippery."

When he got into town, he made the turn into our parking lot and couldn't control the accelerator. My car was the buffer that kept the Suburban from crashing through the front office.

I shuddered and was in shock. I accepted the cup of coffee Kelcie handed me while she and Jason braved the weather and went out to the parking lot to bring in all the bundles of newspapers. That Beast had been nothing but a problem since I'd bought it. It could have cost my son his life. And now my car was damaged and undriveable. I sat and trembled while the two of them finished their work.

"Mom, are you going to be all right?" Jason asked an hour later, when everything was bagged up and he and Kelcie were getting ready to load the Suburban.

"You're not driving that thing in the morning, are you?" I cried.

Jason nodded, letting out a big sigh. "We have no choice. How else are we going to deliver the papers?"

"But, Jason ... it's dangerous."

"I'll take that chance," he said. "Mom, I'll drop the Suburban off at the service station when I'm through tomorrow afternoon."

"You're not taking that vehicle back to them," I told him. "They told me it was in good shape."

"They don't know what they're talking about," put in Kelcie. "Your mom's right, Jason. Maybe my dad knows of somebody who isn't out to rip you off."

"Thank you, Kelcie," I said. "But please ... please be careful."

"We will," promised Jason.

"What about your car?" asked Kelcie, looking at me.

I shook my head. "I'll call the insurance company in the morning."

"You should do it now," said Jason. "They have a 24-hour emergency number, I'm sure."

At that moment I was so grateful to have a level-headed son working for me. While I was in the inner office, reporting the accident to my insurance company, Kelcie and Jason waited in the main room. Then, fifteen minutes later, as I was gathering up my coat and purse to take home, Grant walked in with a worried look on his face.

"Bridget," he called to me. He shot a quick smile at Kelcie and Jason, then came over to embrace me.

"Grant, what are you doing here?"

"Kelcie called me." He turned to the two kids. "It's all right. I'll take her home."

I held it together until after the two young people went out the door, then broke down in Grant's arms and had a good cry.

33

G rant drove me home. I was spent and he was sympathetic to my needs. Since we both had to get up and go to work again in the morning, he stayed only a short time, to be sure I had calmed down. He was heading out the door when Jason returned from Kelcie's. My son went right to bed, knowing he had to get up before dawn to get the load of papers to the post office on time.

"Listen, if you'd rather ... we can forego that Italian dinner tomorrow night at my house," Grant said gently.

"I wouldn't hear of it!" I told him. "Of course I'm cooking for you tomorrow. I usually finish up by mid afternoon on Wednesdays, so I'll come over early."

"You might need this." Grant reached into his pants pocket and produced a house key with a ring on it that also held a golden trinket resembling a miniature disk. I took it in my hand and examined it more closely. It was a caricature of a sun with a face and eight rays.

"You're giving me a key?"

"That way, if I'm not home, you can let yourself in."

"Are you sure about this? I'm not sure this is a good idea. I mean ..."

He clasped his warm hand over mine and closed my fingers over the key. "It's yours." Then he leaned over and planted a kiss on my lips. "I'll see you tomorrow evening," he said with a smile as he turned and walked out the door.

That night I slept fitfully, tossing around in bed, worried about a lot of things. The Suburban had given us trouble since its first run, when Jason and I had gone to Shambleton to print the premier issue back in August. With what had happened this afternoon, and Jason barely able to control the Beast, I needed to find a competent, dependable mechanic. My son could have been killed, along with other innocent people. I had been negligent in not getting the truck checked out when Jason had first complained about it.

I also worried about finances. The *Buffalo Billboard* was barely breaking even. I knew that most new start-ups can't expect to turn a profit right away. My business class in Dexter had taught me to not plan on making any money for at least a year, and maybe two or more. My concern was how I was going to keep the business going for that long. I had already dipped into my house money, and unless we had a good sales month before the end of the year, I'd be going into the next year having to make some changes in staff, or find other ways to cut costs in order to survive.

I heard Jason get up before daylight. I had barely slept. I prayed that the Beast would hold out long enough for Jason and Kelcie to deliver the papers today and fill the racks in the Lower Valley. It would take most of the day.

Jason had left me the keys to his car so I could drive myself to the office. The tow truck arrived shortly after I got there. My Camry was towed to a garage in town, where the mechanic would hold it until the insurance appraiser had seen it.

My employees were alarmed to learn what had happened. Rodney, Colleen and Molly all offered to pitch in and help deliver some papers, so I called Jason on his cell phone.

"We're okay, Mom," he told me. "The Beast hasn't acted up like it did yesterday. Kelcie took a bunch of papers to the southern towns in her car. I should be finishing up in about an hour."

The others appeared relieved that they didn't have to help with distribution, and I made sure to thank them for offering to help. The sales people left for the day and I received a phone call from the insurance company, telling me that the Camry was totaled. A check would be sent out to me the next day. They asked if I needed to arrange for a car rental. I said no. I could ride back and forth to work with Jason until I figured out what to do about my car.

"B.J., Peg called while you were on the other line," Aspen told me after I hung up with the insurance company. "She wants you to call her."

A few minutes later I dialed Peg's cell phone on my office line. She answered right away. "B.J., Aspen told me about what happened."

"I know, it was frightening," I commented.

Peg released a sigh. "I'm glad you're all right. Hey, we need to talk. Do you have time?"

"Not on the phone," I warned her.

"Let's meet somewhere," she said. "Are you free later this afternoon?"

"Actually," I said, "I'm going over to Grant's house to cook dinner."

"Oh, that's right, the Italian meal." She laughed. Then she became serious. "B.J., I really need to talk to you about what I found out from Rudy, my brother-in-law."

"Okay, how about tomorrow for lunch?" I offered.

"I have to work tomorrow," she replied. "but I'll be free after four o'clock."

"Why don't you come over to my house after you're done at school," I said. "I live in those apartments on Greenwood Street. Building C, Apartment 7."

After Peg agreed, we hung up. Aspen walked into the inner office with the mail, most of which she had already opened. She smiled at me. "I heard you are seeing Kelcie's father."

I stared at her, not really surprised that she knew. "Yes, I am," I admitted.

"The owner of *The Mountain Sentinel?*"

"Yes, actually," I replied.

Aspen surprised me and came over to give me a quick hug. "I'm happy for you, B.J."

I didn't know what to say as she left the room. I reached for the mail on my desk and started looking through it all. I was sure everyone in the office now knew about Grant and me.

Aspen peeked in at me one more time and said, "At least he isn't The Captain."

I couldn't help but laugh as she disappeared once again.

At two o'clock that afternoon I drove home in Jason's car. I hadn't driven a stick shift in several years, but I hadn't forgotten how to drive using a clutch. When I got home, I showered, then gathered up the food and spices I planned to use for dinner at Grant's house. Then I loaded up the car and drove across town to the upscale neighborhood north of campus. I presumed it was home to a lot of the university professors, bankers and other prominent citizens of Blanca Hills. At least it wasn't a gated community. I pulled up into his driveway and parked outside the garage.

I rang the doorbell first, just in case he was already home. When no one answered after a minute, I used the key Grant had given me and let myself in through the front door. The spacious living room with vaulted ceilings welcomed me and seemed even bigger to me in daylight.

I set my load down in the kitchen, then went back out to the car to bring in the rest. For the first time since yesterday's crisis with the Suburban, I felt at ease and was excited as I made myself comfortable in Grant's big modern kitchen. Preparing dinner for the two of us eased my worries and I even found myself humming along to the tunes on the satellite radio I'd turned on.

As dusk settled over the valley and the cacciatore was ready to pop into the oven, I checked the timer and saw that the cake would be done in four minutes. I had already started working on the Parmesan asparagus side dish, and would start prepping my mixed greens for salad once the main dishes were baking.

Wondering if Jason had made it home safely, I picked up my cell phone and called him. It went directly to voice mail, so I left him a brief message. "Jason, I'm at Grant's house. Just checking in to see how deliveries went. I'll be home tonight. See you then. Love you."

Around six o'clock, while I was setting the dining room table for the two of us, I saw headlights through the big picture windows as Grant's car pulled into the driveway. A few seconds later, I heard the subtle grinding sound of the garage door opening, and my pulse quickened in my eagerness to greet him.

"Whatever you're conjuring up in here smells fantastic," said Grant as he entered the kitchen. I was at the sink, washing some dishes, and turned to smile up at him.

"Hello, Grant. I hope you're hungry."

"Famished!" He set his briefcase down beside the door and made his way over to me to wrap me in his arms.

I welcomed his deep kiss, which arose passions in me until I had to gently push him away to get my breath.

"What did you make us?" he asked, peering around at the cluttered countertops filled with evidence of my cooking.

"Chicken cacciatore, zucchini Italiano, asparagus, mixed salad greens ... and rolls," I said. "And for dessert, Italian cream cheese cake." I showed him the beautiful layer cake on top of the counter, decorated with white frosting, coconut flakes and pecan pieces.

"Bridget, I'm blown away by all this," he said. His green eyes twinkled as he added, "And I didn't forget the wine." He went to the refrigerator and pulled out a bottle of Beaujolais. As he busied himself getting out wine glasses and the bottle opener, I finished what I was doing in the sink, then dried my hands and quickly checked the oven window.

"Ready in about ten minutes," I commented.

A soft pop meant that he'd removed the cork. He filled our two glasses, then handed me one of them. We stood together, smiling, and at the same time took sips. Then he beckoned me to have a seat at the dining room table. "Sit down and rest, please."

"Okay."

"I must say, it feels really nice coming home to a delicious meal cooked by a beautiful woman," said Grant.

I felt embarrassed and diverted my eyes. "Please ..."

"What's wrong?" he asked. "You don't think you're beautiful?"

"Well ..."

"Bridget." He set his wine glass down on the table and reached for my hand. "Look at me."

I obeyed and stared into his mesmerizing eyes. I felt even more embarrassed. I thought about Liz's voice chiding me on Buffalo Pass, just before the deer hit my car. I wondered really how much younger he was than I.

"You are a very beautiful woman," he said. "And apparently a wonderful cook as well."

"We'll see about that." I laughed and took another sip of wine.

"What's bothering you?" he asked gently.

"Oh ... it's ridiculous." I shook my head, then sighed and looked right at him. "Grant, I'm 42 years old. I think you're younger than I am. Are you?"

Grant laughed out loud. "Is that all you're worried about?" He shook his head, then said, "Bridget, I'm actually older than you. I'm 43." Then he smiled. "But if I was in my 30's, would it matter?"

"Oh, probably not. It's so silly." I was thinking, *Merle is in his 30's.* I wanted to wring Liz's neck, but I knew it really hadn't been her criticizing me on the pass while I'd been driving. It had just been my own consciousness, questioning my confidence and not believing that I could be attractive enough or appealing enough to be with a man such as Grant Tucker.

He then wanted to know what I'd found out about my car, so I explained about the insurance company's verdict and we chatted about my options until the timer went off in the kitchen. Then I got up to get the food out of the oven while Grant went to change clothes and wash up for dinner.

We then sat down and enjoyed our fabulous dinner. Grant insisted, afterwards, that I relax in the living room while he put away the food and loaded the dishwasher. I had thought about turning on the TV to catch some of the evening news, but my cell phone rang. It was Jason.

"Hello."

"Mom," he said.

"Did you just get home?" I asked.

"I've been back awhile," he said. "When are you coming home?"

"We just finished eating," I told him. "Probably soon. Is anything wrong?"

"I'm not sure."

"Jason, did you have any more trouble with the truck?"

"No, but it's still doing its thing."

"Well, we're taking it in tomorrow," I said. "What else is going on?" I knew he had something on his mind. "Come on, Jason. I can tell when you're holding back."

He sighed, then said, "I saw Avery."

I perked right up. "Where?"

"Well, I was delivering papers at the convenience store on the highway east of town. Avery walked in and bought something while I was putting papers on the shelf."

"Did you talk to her?" I asked.

"No."

"Did she see you?"

"If she did, she didn't want to talk to me. Before I could approach her, she ran out."

"Are you sure it was Avery?"

"Yes, it was definitely her."

"Did you run after her?"

Jason explained that he had hurried out the store after his stepsister, but he couldn't see where she had gone. "I have a feeling she didn't want to be seen by me," he added.

"Was there anything about her that appeared strange?" I asked. "Was she scared?"

"I don't know. There were a lot of cars at the pumps, getting gas, but I looked and I didn't see her."

"Did you happen to see a red sports car, by any chance?"

"Mmm... no."

By then, Grant had finished in the kitchen and had walked in to join me. He could hear our conversation, since I had my speaker phone on. I thanked Jason for calling, then told him I'd be home within the hour. We ended our conversation, and Grant sat down beside me on the couch.

"Another glass of wine?" he offered.

"I'd better not," I told him. "I have to drive home in a while."

"Not staying the night?" A smile curled on his lips.

I smiled. "Not tonight." I pushed my bangs aside, then looked him in the eye. "Grant, did you have a chance to talk to Javier yet?"

"Actually, I did," said Grant.

"What did he say?" I asked.

"Well," said Grant. "I mentioned to him that you were complaining about him following you."

"And?"

Grant looked uncomfortable. "It was just like I expected. He denied it."

I leaned back against the couch and sighed. "He has been watching me. I'm not being paranoid. I'm not making this up." I turned to face Grant. "Can you tell me why he would do this?"

Grant folded his arms and his forehead wrinkled as he contemplated my question. "Bridget, if what you say is true, then all I can tell you is I have no idea why Javier would do such a thing. He's worked for me ever since I took over as publisher. He's my right-hand man. I don't know what I'd do without him."

"You mean he runs the paper?" I asked.

"No, I run the paper," Grant said. "Javier is my general manager. He does a good job and I trust him."

"Okay," I said, deciding not to press him further. "You heard Jason telling me on the phone that he saw his stepsister at the gas station today."

"Yes, what's that all about?" asked Grant.

"I don't know. But I did see her in Javier's car that day ... the week of Halloween."

"Yes, I remember," mumbled Grant, rubbing his chin.

"Grant, you need to ask Javier about that."

He sighed. "I was going to, but then you told me to wait."

He was right, I had convinced him not to confront Javier about the girl in his car until I knew more. And I still didn't know enough.

"Because maybe it wasn't her," Grant suggested.

I realized that I was pitting Grant against his right-hand man and that it did sound paranoid. But it wasn't a comfortable feeling to think someone was watching me. I decided to change the subject. "Grant, you said you had come across some information relating to the death of my sister at the Blue Heron Motel. Your paper covered the investigation. What did you find out?"

"Enough to decide not to touch it," said Grant. "I already told you there was a death threat and I made the decision not to endanger my reporter."

"So do you think there really was foul play? Was my sister murdered?"

"The cause of death was suicide, according to the coroner," said Grant. "Suicide by overdose."

"Who else was involved? Do you know anything else?" I asked. "Do you know if anyone had been staying with Liz at the time?"

Grant shook his head. "We were onto something ... two years ago ... but after the death threat, my reporter quit and he destroyed all his files."

"That's unfortunate," I commented. I wanted to bring up Peg's theory that a drug cartel was involved, but I decided I should talk to Peg again before letting Grant in on that kind of information.

He had fallen into deep thought and I felt responsible for once again ruining our intimate evening with accusations involving Javier. Bringing up Avery and also Liz's death had just made things worse. To compensate, I reached over and caressed his arm. He blinked, then looked me in the eye. "I'm suddenly tired," he said. "It's been a long day."

I took that as my cue to leave, but now I felt rejected. Embarrassed, I stood up and headed over to gather up my things. I didn't want Grant to see how disappointed I felt. He finally stood up and approached me after I had put on my coat and was heading for the front door.

"Bridget."

I turned to look at him. He walked over and put his hands around my waist.

"Thank you for the meal. You're terrific." He leaned over and gave me a peck on the cheek.

I wanted more, but he backed off. For a moment we stood, staring at one another. Then my lip trembled and my voice cracked. "Grant ... I'm sorry ... I didn't mean to bombard you with all those questions about my sister ..."

Before I could finish my sentence, he grabbed me and kissed me, hard this time, hungrily, desperately. I felt his need, but I also knew it was time to go. I had ventured a little too far in questioning him tonight. He needed some space, some time to think. His number one man, whom he depended upon, was in question and I could tell he wanted to believe I was making all of this up. He finally released me, gently, with a smile and love in his green eyes. "Good night, Bridget. I'll call you tomorrow."

I left, relieved yet bewildered, upset with myself for breaking our romantic mood. At least he had kissed me good night. At least he had said he would call me. Why was I so emotionally fragile? I had been with other men since my divorce from Dirk. Merle had been the closest to being a real friend to me, yet I had kept from giving him my heart. So now, why was I allowing my heart to be given away to Grant Tucker? I had already stepped out of my emotional comfort zone. I knew so because I was vulnerable and I didn't want to lose Grant. He was special. My tears in Jason's car, on the way home, confirmed it.

34

Thursday morning, after Jason and I got to the office, we took the Suburban to the new garage in Blanca Hills. I followed in Jason's car, and after arranging everything, we returned to the office.

I decided to rent a car for a week or two. I didn't want to have to keep driving Jason's stick shift, and it wasn't fair to make him wait for me or hang around the office on his day off.

Aspen came into the inner office when I got back with the rental car. She handed me another hundred dollars. "I should be able to pay off the loan by the end of January," she said. "Thank you again, B.J., for letting me borrow the money."

"You're welcome, Aspen. Did the Desperado get back with you about our Christmas party?"

"She's supposed to call today," said Aspen and returned to her desk in the front office.

Grant called me a little after noon. "I was hoping for a little getaway on Saturday," he said. "Are you up for a trip to the Sand Dunes?"

"The Sand Dunes? At this time of year?" I replied. "There's snow on the ground."

"The perfect time to see nature at its best," replied Grant. "I want to take my camera and get some shots. We can still walk around. The snow isn't that deep yet. Plus ... it's a good time of year to go with not so many tourists."

I told him I'd love to see the Sand Dunes with him, and then he had to take another call, so we said goodbye. The sales people were out that afternoon and things quieted down. I left at three-thirty so that I could meet Peg, who was coming to my apartment at four o'clock.

Jason had left to spend the day with Kelcie right after we had come back from dealing with the truck. I drove the rental car home.

Peg was prompt. I had just put the tea kettle on the stove when the doorbell rang. I let her in and we exchanged hugs, and then I beckoned her to sit down in the living room. We chatted until the tea kettle blew its whistle, and when I brought us each a cup of herb tea, she grew serious.

"I hope what I tell you isn't going to upset you too much," said Peg. "As I said, my brother-in-law, Rudy, was one of the deputies who responded to the call at the Blue Heron two years ago."

"When they found Liz?" I asked quietly.

She nodded. "You probably already know the details. The house-keeper found your sister on the floor in the room she shared with a man whose name was Harvey Franken."

I absorbed everything she said. I had not heard—nor had I cared to know—the gory details right after it had happened. I had been consumed with guilt for not responding to Liz's call for help.

"Harvey Franken was a drug pusher who worked this valley and other parts of southern Colorado. He was part of the drug cartel I was telling you about."

"Where is he now?"

Peg sniffed. "Prison."

"What else did Rudy tell you?" I asked.

"He doesn't know a whole lot else," she said. "The police did talk to a relative of Harvey's, an aunt I believe ... she was frightened that they would come after her, so she went into a witness protection program, then died last spring. Rudy said that Harvey had killed a man, an old Hispanic, who was going to rat him out. According to the interview with the aunt, your sister did not know about the cartel until the old man was murdered. She probably freaked out and was going to tell the police."

"How long was it after the Hispanic man died and Liz..."

"About two weeks, Rudy said," Peg told me.

I nodded my head, staring into my lap. "She tried to reach out to me two weeks before her death."

"She was no doubt scared for her life."

"How extensive is this cartel?" I asked.

"Extensive," said Peg. "Rudy believes there are cops who have been bought off. I wouldn't be surprised if there were moles in some of the local businesses around here. No one can defeat the cartel."

"You'd think someone would try to stop them," I protested.

"You don't know the people in this valley the way I do," said Peg. "I've lived here most my life. There are mobsters who will protect certain businesses in exchange for their silence. Anyone who doesn't go along with them is subject to break-ins, accidents, sabotage ... or worse."

A shudder went up my spine and I broke into a cold sweat.

Peg put her hand on my wrist. "There's nothing we can do, B.J. I just thought you should know."

"I've had a break-in," I cried, "and weird accidents!" Then I looked at her in fear. "And someone has been following me."

Peg's eyes grew large. "I'm so sorry, B.J."

"Grant said one of his reporters had a death threat when the *Sentinel* was investigating the story. Do you suppose ..."

"It's common knowledge that the newspaper has been infiltrated," she remarked. "But it's been that way for many years. Certainly before Grant Tucker and his wife bought the business." She gulped down the rest of her tea, then grabbed her purse and stood up. "I've got to run. Juan will be home soon. I have to make his dinner."

"Peg, thanks for coming over," I said, still shaken.

She sighed, then gave me a hug once again. "I know you're upset, B.J. But I thought you should know. By the way, how are things going at the *Billboard?*"

"I wish you were still working there," I told her. "Sales were good Thanksgiving week. But so far we don't have as many now as I expected we would ... I mean, with the holidays here ..."

"Rodney's behaving himself?" she asked.

"The usual." I smiled.

"Don't you worry. You'll get through all this. Things will get better ... I hope." She started for the door, then turned around and added, "If I should learn anything else, I'll call you."

"Okay." I walked her to the door, then shut it slowly after her. The news had not been uplifting. My sister had probably been murdered—silenced—and I shuddered to think about what Peg had said about police being paid off and moles working in some of the local businesses. I had a bad feeling about Grant's manager, Javier Gallegos. But what troubled me most was seeing Avery in the car with that man.

That night, after Jason came home from Kelcie's, I asked him to call his father in Salt Lake City. I asked him if he would mind putting his phone on speaker so that I could hear the conversation. I asked Jason if he would ask about his stepsister and find out what they knew. I was worried about what she might have become involved in.

"Uh ... sure, Mom," Jason said hesitantly.

"If it makes you uncomfortable, don't do it," I said. "Just give me your dad's number and I'll call him myself."

"No, that's okay, Mom. It's cool. Let's call him right now. I'm a little worried about Avery too."

We sat next to each other on the couch in the living room while Jason punched in his Dad's number. After it rang four times, I heard Dirk's deep voice through the speaker. "Hello, Jason."

"Hi, Dad. How's it going?"

Dirk chatted for a minute about how things were kind of slow right now at his business. He mentioned that he and Alicia were thinking about early retirement and moving to their condo in Hawaii.

"Sounds cool, Dad." Jason caught my look and he rolled his eyes, then said, "Hey, Dad, I was wondering ... how's Avery doing?"

There was silence for a few seconds, and then Dirk sighed deeply. "I suppose she's doing all right," he finally said. "Why?"

"Do you know where she is?" asked Jason.

In the background we both heard Alicia's voice, but we couldn't make out the words. She sounded angry.

Dirk said, "Uh ... we haven't seen Avery for a couple of months. I meant to tell you."

"Tell me what?" asked Jason.

"Avery didn't return to school," he admitted. "She ... she left home and we don't know where she is."

Alicia's voice rose and this time we could hear a couple of angry words. "Spoiled brat!" and then "ungrateful child."

"Dad," said Jason. "Avery's here in Colorado. She's in the Lower Valley."

"What!" Dirk's voice rose in alarm. "Where? Is she with you?"

Now Alicia's yelling grew louder. "Dirk, I'm warning you!"

Dirk must have put his hand over the phone to muffle his voice, but we heard him say, "Stay out of this. You've caused enough trouble!"

Then he got back on and said to Jason, "I'm sorry, son. Where is Avery?"

"I don't know, Dad. But I did see her today in a convenience store."

"In Blanca Hills?"

"Yeah. She ran out and I didn't get a chance to talk to her."

"What is she doing in Blanca Hills?" demanded Dirk. We could hear Alicia in the background and I couldn't tell if she was swearing at Dirk or crying.

"I don't know," said Jason. "And Mom saw her a month ago. She showed up at Mom's paper and said she was looking for me."

"Jason, I think you should come home." Dirk had that authoritative voice that made me cringe, remembering twenty years back. "I don't think Blanca Hills is the right place for you."

"Dad, I can't leave. I have a full-time job that I like a lot, and ..."

"What about your degree?" he cried. "Why didn't you return to Boulder to finish up?"

"Come on, Dad, we talked about this. I just needed a break. I plan to finish ..."

"Come home, Jason. We want you home for Christmas."

"But, Dad ... you're changing the subject. I called you because of Avery. What is going on with her? I want to know why she left and why she showed up here in the valley."

Alicia must have grabbed the phone from Dirk at that point because her voice came through, strong and emotional. "Jason, we'll explain everything to you if you'll just come home. Your dad is right. School is much more important than that sleazy job working for your Mom's pitiful shopper."

Dirk was on the phone again and we clearly heard a smack, and then a whimper in the background. I shuddered as Dirk's voice came through, unmistakably troubled. "Your stepmother didn't mean that. She's just upset because Avery isn't here. I'm more upset than she is, actually. But you should get away from the valley. If you come home right away, I'll fork out the full amount of your tuition so that you get your college degree. But you can't put it off. This proposal is only good until Christmas."

I had heard enough and now spoke. "*Dirk.* Dirk, don't you dare try to bribe my son!"

We could tell that he was shocked that he was on speaker phone. "What ... you didn't tell me your mother was there with you!"

"Dirk, Alicia's daughter might be in trouble. What do you know about all this?" I demanded.

"I'm ... I'm sorry," said Dirk, backing off. "Jason ... th-thanks for letting us know about Avery. I... I really don't have any explanation for her behavior. Just ... just please watch out for yourself. And ... and do think about coming home for Christmas. I love you, son."

We heard the click of the phone as Dirk hung up. Jason turned to me and made a face. "Typical," he commented. "Those two are wacky." He shook his head. "Now do you see why I never like to go to Salt Lake?" He rose from the couch, but I stopped him.

"Jason, wait. What do you think he was talking about? Why do you think he said you should get away from the valley?"

"Come on, Mom ... Dad is warped. And Alicia ... more so. Nothing's changed with them."

I felt sorry for Jason. Like always, I wanted to blame myself for the divorce and the fact that my son had to straddle through life with two homes. "Well, I'm sorry I made you call him."

Jason pocketed his cell phone and managed a smile. "Don't give it another thought, Mom. At least now they know Avery's here."

"What do you think they'll do about it?" I asked. "She's not 18 yet."

"Probably nothing," said Jason. "They never seemed to care before. Why should they now?"

35

Friday morning I called a meeting at work when my employees came in. We sat in a circle in the main room. Aspen stayed near the phone, in case someone called or needed to place a classified.

"How are ad sales going for next week?" I asked.

Rodney, Colleen and Molly didn't answer right away. They glanced at one another. Jason and Kelcie sat together in the far corner. Finally, Rodney crossed his arms and spoke up.

"We're trying. Our clients all say the same thing." He stopped there.

"And that is?" I looked at all three of my sales people, who fidgeted and appeared nervous.

Colleen finally told me. "Because it's so close to the end of the year, they don't have any money left to advertise with us."

"Explain," I prompted.

Molly then said, "The *Sentinel* has all the advertisers on a contract. They committed their holiday ad revenue at the beginning of the year. So they have nothing left to buy ads from us."

"But there are still a few of our loyal advertisers who want to place ads in December," said Rodney.

I felt right then as though I'd been sucker punched. "Contracts?"

They all nodded. I turned to Kelcie. "You worked at the *Sentinel*. Is this correct? Is there some kind of non-competing clause with their advertisers?"

Kelcie shrugged. "I don't know anything about advertising sales," she said meekly. "But I suppose you could ask my dad."

Colleen erupted with a giggle, which she quickly smothered and everyone frowned at her. "I'm sorry, B.J.," she said.

"Well, I still want you all to go out there and try to get some ads for the next three weeks," I told them. "It's vital. If we don't get that revenue flowing, I'm afraid we're going to be in deep trouble. Do you understand what I'm saying?"

At that point I stood up and walked into my inner office, wishing more than ever that there was a door I could close. My heart rate was up and that sinking feeling in my stomach conjured up fear, anger and despair.

The sales people either got on the phones or began texting their clients. Jason wandered into our room and slunk into his chair. "What's going to happen if we don't get any ads?" he asked.

"We'll get ads," I assured him with a smile that I knew was not convincing. "Some obituaries just came in. Here. Why don't you work on these for a while?" I handed him the printouts I had gotten off email before the meeting. "And don't worry ... we're going to get through this." I only wished I had the confidence to believe my own words.

At the moment I was tempted to call Grant and confront him with the startling news I had just been given. I began to wonder if I had been played for a fool. Yet I could not believe that Grant had issued a policy that prevented my shopper from obtaining its needed ad revenue. But if he had ... what a dirty, sneaky, humiliating act of betrayal!

The office quieted down when the sales staff went out to call on their customers—probably to no avail, if what they said was true. Jason had gone home early since we ran out of ads for him to do. I told Aspen she could leave early too, if she wanted. At four o'clock I was alone, which was a welcome relief. I walked through the rooms with a sinking feeling. How much longer would I last? What if I had to lay off some of my people? I couldn't bear the thought.

I wandered into the storage room and took a peek into the storage closet, where the door to the enclosed alley was. I checked it and was glad that it was latched tightly. I had not heard anything more from the local police. It was unlikely the cash that had been stolen would ever be repaid to me. But things could have been worse.

It was starting to get dark and I went to the front office to close the blinds. Outside was a rosy sky and I thought of Grant and his infatuation with sunsets. Tomorrow I was going with him to spend the day at the Sand Dunes. I had been looking forward to the adventure and spending time with Grant until I'd been bombarded with the bad news this morning at our staff meeting.

After locking the front door and taking down the "Open" sign, I returned to my inner office and punched Merle's name on my cell phone's contact list. It rang a few times before he answered.

"Beej, how are you? Are you in Dexter?"

"Hi, Merle. No, I'm still at the office. How've you been?"

He cleared his throat and shuffled around a bit. I figured I had caught him at a bad time. Maybe he had been driving and had to pull over. "Uh ... not bad," he finally said.

"Did I interrupt you from something?" I asked.

"No," said Merle. "No, Beej. I stepped outside."

"What's going on?" I asked. "How's Janie?"

Merle cleared his throat. "Actually, Janie and I are at a crossroads."

"Oh, Merle ... I'm sorry."

"Well, it's certainly not your fault," he chuckled. "But hey, why'd you call? Is everything okay?"

I sighed. "No."

"Oh," he replied.

"Merle, I just found out today that *The Mountain Sentinel* makes its advertisers sign a contract so that they won't have money left at the end of the year to advertise in other papers." A sob escaped and I quickly added, "If we don't get that ad revenue this month of December, I'm ... I'm not going to make it, Merle."

"Beej ... that's ... awful."

I sniffed and reached for a tissue on my desk. "I don't know what I'm going to do."

He was very consoling and sympathetic as I told him my tale of woe and spouted off about compete clauses and coercing customers to be faithful to only one publication. I didn't mention any names. As far as I knew, Merle did not know that I had been dating the publisher of *The Mountain Sentinel*. At Thanksgiving we had not discussed any of those details.

"Well, of course the decision is up to you," he said, "but you know you're always welcome to come back to Dexter. I can't tell you how much I miss you, Beej." Merle's familiar voice was a comfort to me at that moment and I felt relief wash over me.

There was always that escape route—a return to Dexter and the comfort of Merle's companionship—possibly even being able to get my old job back at the *Chronicle*. Suddenly that job didn't seem so distasteful to me anymore. It was tempting to think of not having to worry anymore about meeting payroll, or having to come up with money for all the taxes owed to the state and federal governments, not to mention workman's comp insurance.

Getting a regular paycheck for a thirty-five hour work week in production, or any other department, and not having to worry about every little thing, was suddenly like a drug I had once been addicted to and was now craving. Merle may not have ever been that exciting or appealing to me, but he had always been comfortable. If what he said was true, and he and Janie were at a crossroads, where did I fit in?

"Think about it, Beej," said Merle before we ended our conversation. "I know you can't make up your mind without weighing the checks and balances. But I'm here for you ... always."

I sighed and dabbed at my eyes. "Thanks, Merle. I can't think clearly at the moment."

"I know. If you want, I can drive down."

That woke me up. "No, that's not necessary." I glanced up at the clock. "Thanks for offering, Merle, but I'm fine ... really."

"Then I'll call you Sunday. Deal?"

I agreed to touch base with him after the weekend, and we hung up. Then I gathered my things and put on my coat to leave. I felt like a huge burden had been lifted, but at the same time I saw my life dissolving into fragments of failure, disappointment, the burden of debt, not to mention the lowering of my self esteem. In the last few weeks I had been riding high, getting to know Grant. But now I felt he was no longer my friend. Somehow he had sucked me into his world, only to watch me fail. Why had I let that happen?

I drove home in the dark, not proud of myself for pouring my troubles out to Merle. The poor guy. I wondered why Janie had dumped him—assuming she had? Maybe he had decided he didn't like her. I already assumed that Merle had never really gotten over me. He was a decent man and I had been in a relationship with him, but I had never committed myself to him. He wanted more than I had to give him. Would that change now that I was the one in need?

Leftovers were on the stove, cooking, when Grant called me. "Did you see the sunset?" he asked.

"Actually, I did. I saw it from my office window."

"How was your day?" he asked.

I stirred a saucepan of left-over chicken soup. "Oh, so-so ..." I didn't want to bring up anything negative at the moment.

"Why don't you spend tonight with me?" Grant proposed. "That way we can enjoy the full day together tomorrow." Then he added in a soft voice, "I enjoy waking up with you."

Mixed emotions surged within me. My heart pounded. As much as I wanted to fling caution aside and say yes, I held back and was silent.

"What's the matter, Bridget? Don't you want to come over tonight?"

Of course I wanted to, but instead my overly cautious common sense took over for me. "Actually, I have a lot of things I planned to get done in the apartment tonight, Grant. But I'll tell you what ... tomorrow night might be better."

It worked. Grant graciously replied, "I understand. I have a few things I need to attend to as well. But we're still on for the Sand Dunes tomorrow, aren't we?"

I relaxed. "Of course. I'm so looking forward to it."

"Good. How about if I pick you up around eleven and we stop at the sub shop for a carry-out?"

"Sure," I said.

We talked a little longer and then ended our call.

It was difficult to calm my mind that night. The week's events played over and over in my mind, and even though I didn't have to get up early, insomnia gripped me. Jason's frightening experience with the company truck had scared me so much, and then listening to Peg's report about what her deputy brother-in-law had revealed about Liz and the drug cartel ... that shook me up, too.

But learning this morning about the *Sentinel's* policy for their advertisers at this most crucial time of year made me livid. I knew I had to find a way to confront Grant with it tomorrow at the Sand Dunes. Oh, and then there was Merle ... why had I called him, anyway?

Yes, I had needed a friend to confide in after a depressing day, but the news about himself and Janie was a surprise, even though I should have expected it after observing how prickly things had been between the two of them at Thanksgiving.

Sleep finally took over, but I started dreaming again about my sister. This time, Kelcie was in the dream, and so was Jason, only they were both toddlers, and Liz was baby-sitting the two of them in a big warehouse that was crawling with decrepit individuals who appeared to be destitute and dirty looking. Nonetheless, the children, Kelcie and Jason, played on the concrete floor with little plastic action figures, laughing while all these strange people wandered around them.

Liz was not very attentive, I noticed, sitting in a short skirt with her legs crossed, wearing nylons and bright red sandals. She puffed on a cigarette, looking around at the men.

"What are you doing?" I cried. "Liz, get the children out of here. They don't belong in a place like this."

My sister didn't smile, nor did she speak. She lifted her arm and pointed across the large, windowless room. I looked over and saw Grant sitting in a corner on the floor, dressed in hobo clothes, his blondish hair messed up and greasy. His face was dirty and unshaved. He stared vacantly ahead with drooping eyelids.

I gasped and started walking toward him, but suddenly a dark-haired man in a trench coat blocked my way and stopped me. I looked up into Javier's face as he grinned wickedly. "You can't help him now," he taunted me in a gruff voice.

I began fighting Javier, who grabbed my wrists and laughed. Then, suddenly, someone intervened. A lanky man stepped in front of us and pulled me away from Javier. "Come on, B.J., you can do better than that." It was Merle's voice. "Let me take you back to my place. We'll stop at the Sand Dunes first."

"What about Jason? My baby! And Kelcie..."

The man grabbed me and held me, and when I looked into his face, I saw it was The Captain from Rockcrest! I recognized his long, grayish hair hanging in a ponytail, his hippie glasses and wooden beads that he wore around his neck. "I'm your knight in shining armor," he mocked, then turned to the crowd and shouted, "Meet my damsel in distress! I'm taking her home!" The crowd cheered.

Suddenly, the toddler Jason saw me and called out, "Mommy! Mommy, don't leave me!"

Then Kelcie was no longer the blonde-headed, green-eyed little girl playing on the cement floor with my son. She was now a dark-haired, hazel-eyed Avery! "Stay, Jace," she told her stepbrother. "You can't go with her. That lady's *bad* ... Mommy said she's *bad!*"

I struggled to free myself from The Captain's strong grip. My little boy was bawling and reaching his short arms out for me, but I was trapped and couldn't move. I tried to call to him. I strained to make my voice work. It was like in all the other dreams ... I was unable to move, unable to speak. "*Jaaaa-sooon...*"

My head was throbbing when I slowly came out of the dream. It still felt like I was there, but I now knew I was safe in my own bedroom. It had only been another nightmare, yet it had left me sobbing and struggling to regain control. After half a minute, I was able to reach over and turn on my bedside lamp. The light flooded the darkness and I breathed a prayer of relief. A glance at the clock told me it was only 1:26 A.M. I didn't want to fall right back to sleep and risk getting thrown right back where I was.

So I got up and went to the kitchen to get some painkiller and a glass of juice. Jason's bedroom door was closed, so he must have gotten home after I'd fallen asleep. I sat at the kitchen table and took the medicine, then sipped the juice while clearing my head. That one had been horrible. Most of them were. I began to wonder when these dreams were going to stop.

"*My LIFE was a nightmare,*" said the voice in my head. Liz, I presumed.

"Why do you torment me?" I moaned.

"*I'll stop when you've learned the truth.*"

"And when will that be?" I asked.

Silence.

I began to grow drowsy, so I finished the glass and went back to bed.

36

Grant arrived promptly at eleven the next morning. I was groggy and tired, but hoped the outing on this sunny early December morning would perk up my spirits.

"Good morning, beautiful." Grant smiled at me as he met me on the walkway and escorted me to the Porsche.

I tried my best to hide the fact that I'd not had enough quality sleep or that so much was weighing on my mind right then. For Grant's sake, I wanted this to be a pleasant day for us.

We stopped and picked up our lunch at the sub shop to take along, then headed up the highway that went toward Rockcrest. The Sand Dunes came into view as soon as we left Blanca Hills. The mountains as a backdrop threw shadows over the mysterious dunes and made sparkly patterns with the snow from the latest storm.

"You've really never been here before?" Grant seemed amazed that I'd never taken time to enjoy this monument.

"No," I admitted. "Do you come here often?"

"When Samantha was alive, we would come here a lot with Kelcie. We used to do a lot of hiking in those days." He seemed to drift off into his memories. I just sat and gazed out the window, relaxed by the hum of the vehicle which helped calm my mind, along with the soft music he had turned on.

When we pulled into the parking area, there were only a few other vehicles parked. Grant turned to me and asked, "Are you hungry?"

"Not really," I said.

"Then let's walk first," he suggested. He reached into the back seat to grab his bag with his camera and equipment, and I unbuckled my seatbelt and opened the car door to step out. Cool, refreshing air invigorated me and I could feel the sun's warm rays on my face.

After Grant locked up the car with my purse hidden under the seat, we started out on the nearest path. Grant slung his gear over his left shoulder and took my hand as we started walking, side by side. It wasn't long before I relaxed even more and really started to enjoy the exercise and the clear blue sky and nippy air. The sun had warmed us and every so often Grant stopped to take out his camera and take pictures. The sand dunes were fascinatingly beautiful and colorful, even with the traces of snow.

After close to an hour of walking, we turned back and went to the car to get our picnic lunch. We ate on one of the park picnic tables. There was just a handful of people we could see walking around on the dunes in the distance. The ham and cheese sandwich I had chosen tasted especially good to me after the exercise, and Grant had brought a thermos of hot coffee to go along with the chips and two huge peanut butter cookies we had purchased with our subs.

Grant was in a good mood and his good nature lifted a lot of the weight I had been carrying around. Our conversation stayed light, focused mainly on current events in the news, memories of trips we had both taken, how our kids had behaved when they were younger, and I enjoyed learning more about this man who was quickly becoming important in my life. I was relieved that we were pretty much in sync about politics and religion. He didn't focus hard on his former wife either, or dwell on the tragedy of her illness and death.

"Let's drive around some more," Grant suggested after we'd cleaned up after the meal. "I want to explore more areas. Do you mind?"

"Not at all," I said. "I'm enjoying myself."

"I'm glad." As we stood up, he pulled me close to him and kissed me on the lips. I succumbed. Then he murmured, "Thank you, Bridget."

"Thank me? For what?" I replied softly.

"For coming with me on this day," he said and gazed lovingly into my eyes. "I want to share the sunset with you. Do you mind?" He looked at his watch, then added, "That will be in just about two and a half hours from now."

"Really?" I smiled. "Are we staying here that long?"

"We don't have to, if you don't want to," he said. "Are you cold?"

"A little," I admitted and pulled the collar of my jacket tighter.

"The wind is coming up," said Grant. "We should leave soon, but I'd like to drive around to another section where I always get some good shots when the light is right."

So we drove some more and I was content just to ride, listening to the music and satisfied after the lunch we'd eaten.

An hour or so later, we headed back to town. The sun was getting lower in the west. "How about we swing by your place and pick up what you might need at my house?" Grant asked casually.

I looked at him. "Oh ... you mean to spend the night?"

"Do you want to?" He glanced at me, surprised that I had even asked such a question.

"Uh ... sure," I said and stared at the road ahead.

After a few seconds, Grant released a deep sigh. "Bridget," he finally said, "I know that something's bugging you. I wish you'd tell me about it."

I was thinking, *should I? or shouldn't I?* I could hear Liz's voice in my head, pressing me. "*Tell him*," she prompted. "*Don't chicken out. Give it to him.*"

I stared into my lap, afraid to say something. Then, almost as if I didn't have any control, I turned to Grant and I asked the question that had been on my mind since yesterday. "Why do you have an exclusion clause for holiday advertising?"

He was silent for a few seconds, then let out another sigh. "Explain to me what you mean," he said.

"Grant, my sales people told me that they can't get anybody to advertise with the *Billboard* until after the Christmas holiday. What's that all about?" Mentally I heard Liz's voice say, "*Thatta girl.*"

Grant shook his head, then said, "Okay, I know what you're inferring. Bridget, that clause has been in our advertising contracts since before I became CEO of the company. The *Sentinel* has been fair with its advertisers for decades."

"Fair? What do you mean?" I asked.

"Well ... we give them breaks now and then ... discounts ..."

"Grant, I'm not getting any ads in my December papers," I told him. "That isn't fair."

"I'm sorry," he said. "It's been our policy since ..."

"How can you do this?" I was feeling rebellious all of a sudden. "I mean ... why is that clause still in force? Why didn't you do away with it when you became publisher?"

Grant sighed again. "The previous owners set it in place and my general manager believed we should continue offering it. It has worked very well for us. We never have to worry about losing revenue."

"But Grant ... did you even hear what I said? I'm not getting display ads for my next three issues of the shopper. Nobody is advertising in my paper!"

He dared to look at me and I think my angry face startled him. "It's out of my hands," he said. "I can't do anything about it ... at least for now." Then he asked, "What do you expect me to do?"

I sighed and relaxed, my lower lip trembling with emotion. "If I don't get any ad revenue by the end of the year, the *Buffalo Billboard* is going under."

Grant looked over his shoulder, pushed his turn signal indicator and pulled off to the side of the highway. We had not yet reached Blanca Hills. He put the Porsche into park and turned towards me, sympathy on his face. "Bridget ... I'm sorry ... I don't really know what to say at this point."

"Are you?" I challenged. "Are you really? I don't think you care about me at all. In fact, I think you've used me. I feel you've ... betrayed me." I tried to hold back tears, but I couldn't. I let out a sob.

Grant hung his head. He said nothing to defend his position further. "Don't cry ... please ..."

I let loose and the tears poured from my eyes. I grabbed my purse and dug out a tissue. "I just don't understand," I said between sobs. "Grant ... don't you see what's happening? I was doing so well ... we were starting to be liked in the valley. People refer to us as the 'little paper.' Now, all of a sudden ..." I fell apart at that point and cried harder.

He reached over and tried to pull me toward him for an embrace, but I resisted. I had stiffened and my frustration, fears and anger gushed forth. His apology had not been enough. He couldn't offer me a way out of my predicament or lend a hand to help my business. But then, after all, he was the competition. The *Sentinel* had the upper hand and he must have known what would happen in December from the beginning. My world was crumbling and there was nothing to hang onto.

"Okay," he finally said stiffly and clutched the steering wheel. He took the car out of park, signaled, and resumed driving while I sat and sniffled, dabbing at my eyes and feeling worse than I had felt in a long, long time. Why had I spoiled such a beautiful day with Grant in a place that he cherished? Had Liz's voice in my head caused me to lose it and lash out at this man who had been so kind to me? Suddenly I regretted everything, but it was too late. I could see it by the way Grant accelerated and kept his eyes on the road, saying nothing as he drove me back to my apartment.

The rest of my weekend was depressing. Somehow I succeeded at hiding my emotions from Jason, who was focused on Kelcie anyway and barely noticed my state of mind. Merle called as promised Sunday morning and we talked a long time.

"Beej, maybe you should just come home," he encouraged once again. "You're obviously very upset and you gave the shopper all you had. I hate to see you sock more of your savings into it."

Something in my core rebelled, but I heard myself say meekly, "Maybe so, Merle. Maybe I should make a decision and let everyone know." I was thinking of how the news would affect Grant. Would he feel even sorrier for being the cause of it all? Or would he feel he had succeeded at putting me out of business? It was hard to tell. Since he had dropped me off, I had not heard from him.

"Want me to come down and be with you?" he asked.

"Not yet," I said quickly. "I mean ... it's not necessary, Merle. I'm going to try to get through the next three weeks ... and then we'll see. I'll make the decision then."

"Why not make the decision now and get it over with?" he asked.

"I can't do that to my employees," I replied. "It's Christmas. I just ... I just need to see if there's still a chance I can work this out. I've put too many hours and too much money into this paper."

Merle relented and we talked a while longer. I found out that Janie was planning to move out of his house by the first of January. He appeared indifferent toward her now. After we hung up, I decided to head to Valle Viento and spend the afternoon at the office. There probably were not many ads to compose, but I would have to get on line and see about finding some filler for our remaining issues. I thought I would give Peg a call to see if she had any ideas about holiday material to replace the ads.

"Hi!" Peg responded when I phoned. "How is your romance going?"

"Fine." I didn't want to clue her in on the fact that Grant and I had argued. "Hey, Peg, I'm calling to see if you have access to any filler articles we might be able to use over the holidays?"

"Let me think ..." It turned out that Peg knew another teacher who edited the school employees' monthly newsletter, and she would ask her friend to share some of it with me to use in the shopper. Before we hung up, Peg told me she had some new information about "Blue Heron," which she had adopted as her code name for Liz's alleged murder. She lowered her voice. "Of course I can't discuss this over the phone," she told me, "but I think you'll be blown away when I tell you what I found out."

Thinking of Grant and the fact that Peg had mentioned the *Sentinel* had probably been infiltrated by people involved with the cartel, this was not news I was eager to hear, but I told her we could meet later in the week, after I got the paper out, and she agreed to call me on Wednesday.

I settled into my work, worried now about what Peg had discovered and concerned that Grant might be involved somehow in the illegal mafia-like shenanigans in which Liz may have found herself. I was typing on the computer later that afternoon when I heard noises in the building. I stopped typing and listened. It sounded like somebody was in the office with me, yet I had not seen nor heard anyone come through the front door.

When, after a couple of minutes, nothing else was heard, I decided the noises must have come from outside and went back to work. Then, about ten minutes later, I heard more noises. There was definitely somebody inside the building and I grew frightened. Fearing that another thief was trying to get in, I got up and grabbed my cell phone, my coat and my purse, and walked into the main room, careful not to make a lot of noise. Perhaps the intruder had no idea someone was present in the office.

I waited near the front door, listening for further sounds. When I heard nothing more and another ten minutes had passed, I calmed down and reassured myself that the noise must have come from outside, yet it had sounded like it was coming from the back room. I set my things down on one of the desks and slowly made my way to the kitchen and then to the door to the big storage room, where Jason and I had slept before we had moved into the apartment.

First, I checked the bathroom. Nothing was different. The repaired wall had not changed or been damaged in any way. I then moved toward the storage room and stood a minute, listening. When I heard no further sound, I decided to go inside. Slowly I turned the doorknob and was met with the darkness. I quickly flicked on the light switch and flooded the room with light from the ceiling fixtures. There was no one there. Everything was quiet, just as it had been the last time I'd been in that room. Still, I cautiously moved in and looked around at the shelves and cabinets, then turned to the narrow closet where I knew there was that passageway and door into the enclosed alley. My heart began to beat faster. I hesitated before stepping in. What if someone was hiding? Waiting for me?

"Hello?" I called out. "Is anyone in here?"

After no answer, I bravely took a deep breath and stepped inside and looked around. It was hard to tell if anyone had been hiding in that closet because boxes and supplies were strewn and I hadn't brought a flashlight with me. Finally, I felt confident that the noises I'd heard had to have come from somewhere else, and I left. I went back to my inner office and continued working without further incident.

Just before I left the office to return home, I was slipping on my coat when my eye caught a fleeting shadow of movement from the front windows. Had someone been looking in at me? It was just starting to get dark. On edge, my heart began to race. I quickly made my way to the front room and looked out the window just in time to see a figure in a long black coat disappear around the side of the building. I had not been quick enough to see if it was a man or a woman, and suddenly I was too afraid to step outside and try to chase the person.

My cell phone rang just then and startled me further. I hurried back inside to answer it. Grant was calling, so I picked up. "Hello?"

"Bridget ... are you still at work?"

"Yes."

"I need to see you. I want to apologize for yesterday."

I set my purse and coat down and took a seat at one of the desks in the front room. "Grant, I'm a nervous wreck right now. I need to get home."

"What's wrong?" he asked.

"I'm not sure. I think someone was spying on me."

"Get out of there," he ordered. "Now."

"I was just getting ready to leave," I told him.

"Bridget, your safety is my main concern."

Was it? I wondered. But I believed him. "I'll be okay." I continued to talk with him while I turned out the light and locked up the office, then walked to my car parked in front. "I'm getting into my car now. Nobody's around. Everything's all right."

"Good," he said with a relieved sigh. "Why don't you come over?"

I glanced at my watch. I was torn. Finally I said, "Okay. Just for a short while."

"Good. I'll see you soon."

We hung up and I started up the engine. As I backed out of the parking space and turned my steering wheel to get onto the street, I saw a young lady in a long black coat walking down the sidewalk away from me. She was walking in a hurry, but glanced back at me briefly and then turned into an alley and disappeared.

I stopped and blinked. I wasn't sure because she had been far enough away … but I wondered … had it been Avery?

37

The sun was going down when I arrived at Grant's house. Even in my confusion and turmoil, I couldn't help but notice what a gorgeous sky was in the west. The rosy colors and shades of orange, pink and lavender prompted me to pause before getting out of the rental car. I gazed in awe for several seconds. Living in Dexter, sunsets had never appeared this spectacular. Suddenly, my heart sank at the thought of giving up my paper and leaving the Lower Valley.

"Come in, Bridget." Grant was at the door as I hurried up his front steps. The concern on his face was genuine as he pulled me to him and embraced me, even before I had a chance to set down my purse or remove my jacket. It felt good to be in his arms and to feel his strength. He gently released me and looked into my eyes. "You're trembling. Take off your coat and join me on the couch, where we can talk."

He helped me out of my wraps and laid my jacket across the parlor table in the foyer. Then he took my hand and led me into his vast living room, where soft gas flames flickered in the fireplace. We sat and I fidgeted, not knowing where to begin.

"First let me tell you how sorry I am about the other day," said Grant. "Please believe me when I tell you that it had not crossed my mind that your advertisers were restricted from placing their ads in your paper. As I mentioned, that clause was put in a long time ago. I knew about it, but I didn't think about what it would do to you. I feel terrible about it, Bridget."

I looked down into my lap, not knowing what to say. "You said there's nothing you can do."

"Not at this point," he admitted. "The ad space has already been committed for the remaining weeks of this fiscal year. If I could change that, I would. I'm sorry, Bridget."

I forced a smile and saw that he appeared totally sincere. Still, I felt like a fool. His apology did not change the fact that I would not be able to meet payroll, or that the *Buffalo Billboard* would most likely be forced to quit publishing right after Christmas. I had already decided that the next day I would call Rebecca, my accountant, and set up an appointment to talk to her about my options.

"Was someone really spying on you today?" Grant asked me.

I told him what I had observed, but didn't mention the fact that I thought I had seen Avery. I mentioned the noises I had heard earlier and how I had checked out the other rooms in the office, but had found nothing.

"I don't think it's a good idea for you to be there on weekends by yourself," said Grant.

"Well, you're probably right about that," I replied. "Sometimes Jason's with me on Sunday."

"Bridget, something has come to my attention regarding my general manager, Javier Gallegos."

I perked up when I heard the man's name.

Grant continued. "As you know, Javier is very good at overseeing all the departments at the *Sentinel*. He has been there many years and worked his way up the corporate ladder. When you told me you thought he was following you ... or at least watching you ... I couldn't believe it." He sighed. "Honestly, I didn't want to believe it. I've put my 100 percent trust in that man since I bought the *Sentinel* six years ago. He never gave me any trouble, although I'd heard some complaints from disgruntled employees now and then. But that seems to be true in any business."

I nodded, then waited for him to say the rest.

"I spoke to Javier last night," said Grant. "I called him and I confronted him about what you had told me."

I sat up straighter on the couch and folded my hands in my lap. "And?"

"Well," said Grant, "I was expecting him to deny it. I mean, he had denied it the last time I talked to him, after you told me about seeing him ... well, last night he confessed that he felt he needed to check out your business, to be sure you were not a threat to us."

"How can a small weekly shopper be a threat to a big daily

newspaper?" I asked.

"I think your little paper is an asset to the valley," Grant admitted with a smile. "At first, I admit I was a little concerned about the competition for advertising. But later on, I ran the numbers and it seemed as though there was plenty of ad revenue to keep both of us in business for a long time."

"And Javier thinks I'm a threat?" I asked.

"No." Grant folded his arms and leaned back against the couch. "There's more to it. But I can't get into that right now. Besides, I have to check out a few things before I'm certain. More information has surfaced about the reporter who quit two years ago after the death threat connected to the Blue Heron murder."

I gasped and stared at Grant. "I learned more about that too," I disclosed. "One of my former employees has been investigating on her own my sister's death, and she learned that Liz was most likely murdered, and that it wasn't a suicidal overdose after all."

Grant nodded, studying me. "I know. I wasn't sure how much you knew."

"Grant, is it possible that Javier is mixed up in this?"

"Javier?" Grant shook his head. "I hope not." He looked me in the eye. "Why would you think he had anything to do with it?"

I wasn't sure I should talk about everything Peg had told me. Plus, I knew she had something even bigger she had wanted to tell me about the crime. Javier's name had never come up, and I suddenly realized that it was wrong of me to suggest that Grant's trusted manager could be implicated in any way. So far I had heard nothing about his involvement ... yet I still harbored suspicions about him, especially after seeing him in the town park with Avery sitting in the front seat of his red sports car.

"Bridget ... what are you holding back about Javier?"

"Okay," I said, looking again at my lap. "Do you remember how I told you that I saw Javier sitting in his red car last fall at the town park?"

"I remember you said you had walked to the park and that you saw Javier's red car."

"Yes, and I told you I saw a young woman in the car with him. Remember?"

"Vaguely," Grant replied.

"That girl was Jason's stepsister, Avery. She was sitting in the car beside Javier."

"Jason's stepsister? Are you sure it was her?"

"I didn't know who it was at first," I disclosed. "I had never met Avery. But she showed up at my office a few days later—the day after Halloween, in fact. That's when I recognized her as the girl I'd seen in the car. It was the weekend of the break-in. She asked for Jason. At the time I didn't know she was Avery."

He looked astounded. "Go on ..."

"When I asked why she wanted to see Jason, she said she was his stepsister."

"Why hadn't you met her before?" asked Grant.

I sighed. "Dirk and Alicia sent her off to boarding schools. Even Jason rarely saw her. Then she shows up, out of the blue, asking for Jason ... and then disappears again. So you can imagine how shocked I was when I recognized her as the girl in Javier's car."

Grant slowly nodded his head, taking it all in. "Bridget, somehow I believe you. I'm sorry I doubted you. I think Javier has a lot of explaining to do."

"Are you going to talk to him about this?" I asked.

"I have to. He has no business stalking you." Grant's anger began to rise in his voice. "If I find out he's been lying ... and the girl ..."

"Avery," I repeated.

"Yes, Avery," he said. "I don't want to alarm you, but I've heard rumors."

"What kind of rumors?"

"Human trafficking."

"Oh, Grant!" I was instantly afraid for poor Avery. "You mean ... Javier?"

"I don't want to believe it," he said, "but something's going on. I've been oblivious to it ... and it's not just at the paper. I've heard from other business owners ..." He stood up and went to stand by the fireplace.

"Grant, I'm scared." I stood up. But just then, my cell phone rang. I reached into my purse to answer it. "Jason?"

"Hey, Mom, are you coming home? I was getting worried about you."

"Oh, yeah ... sure," I told him. "I stopped over at Grant's for a few minutes. I'm leaving shortly."

"Okay," he said. "I cooked up some chili and we saved some for you."

"We?"

"Yeah, Kelcie's here. Hey, Mom, is it okay with you if Kelc spends the night?"

Since I was on speaker phone, Grant had heard the conversation and frowned in disapproval.

"Why would she want to spend the night, Jason?" I asked.

"Uh ... something happened."

"Huh? Come on, Jason, is Kelcie all right?"

"She saw a prowler is all." He chuckled. In the background we heard Kelcie's voice yell out, "It's not a joke, Jason."

"I'll be home in twenty minutes," I told him. "We'll talk about it first." Then I hung up.

Grant right away asked, "What happened to my daughter?"

"Jason said she saw a prowler, so she wants to stay at our apartment tonight."

"Who's room is she sleeping in?" His fatherly look of concern almost made me smile.

"I don't know yet," I said, feeling flustered. I already suspected that Jason and Kelcie were sleeping together, at least at her apartment. Why should Grant be surprised? Our kids were both 21.

Grant relaxed and smiled. "I'm not criticizing." He took me in his arms then and kissed me. "After all ..." Then he sighed and rubbed his chin. "A prowler? That kind of worries me."

"I'm sure it's nothing," I said, but I felt nervous myself at the thought of a prowler in our neighborhood. There were too many strange occurrences happening in my life. "Anyway, I'd better get home." I went over to put on my coat.

"Okay," he said, following me to the door. "Please call me if there's any trouble."

I assured him I would, then quickly left to drive home in the dark. Everything was becoming more mystifying, I realized, but at least now Grant had acknowledged that his right-hand man, Javier Gallegos, had been lying to him. I knew there was more to all of this than Grant was letting me know, and even though it bothered me, I had enough to worry about without more involvements. Hopefully, when I met with Peg Espinoza on Wednesday, I'd know a lot more. I would be sure to fill

Grant in on that.

When I returned to the apartment, Jason and Kelcie were eating chili and left-over dinner rolls that had been in the freezer since Thanksgiving. They were laughing and did not appear apprehensive.

"These are the best rolls I've ever eaten," Kelcie complimented me as I dished up my own bowl of Jason's chili at the stove. "Jason said you made them."

"Thank you, Kelcie." After I was seated, I asked, "Did you really see a prowler?"

"Somebody was lurking outside my bedroom window," she disclosed. "It startled me and I called Jason."

"Did you call the police?"

"No," said Kelcie. "I don't think it was necessary. Actually, I'm over it." She dug into her bowl for another spoonful of chili. "I'll go back to my apartment tonight."

"You don't have to," Jason protested.

I shot Jason a warning look. He merely shrugged and reached for another dinner roll.

A t work the next morning, I called Rebecca, my accountant, and asked if I could schedule some time to talk to her. She sounded a little reluctant, but finally said I could come that afternoon between two and two-thirty. The sales people were all out, trying desperately to gather ads for that week's paper. Aspen had plenty of classifieds to type and had come back from the post office with a huge pile of mail, which perked my spirits after having sent the invoices out last week from the Thanksgiving issue.

Our Christmas party was happening in two weeks. Colleen and Molly had gotten everyone in the office to draw names for gift giving. I had pulled Kelcie's name. If circumstances had been optimal, I would have been looking forward to the party for my employees. Unfortunately, it looked like the *Buffalo Billboard* might be on the rocks as far as the new year was concerned.

Right at two, I arrived at Rebecca's accounting office, which was in Blanca Hills. She called me into her private office and closed the door, and I sat down across from her and began to explain my reason for the visit.

"I need your advice," I said. "I'm worried about my business."

Rebecca's look of surprise took me off guard. "But, B.J., your newspaper is off to a great start. You have advertisers and they are *paying* you ... what is the problem?"

I sighed. "I'm losing money."

"How much are you paying your*self?*" she asked.

"Enough to pay my rent and keep food on the table," I said. "That's all."

"So what's your problem?" Rebecca folded her arms and leaned back in her chair. I got the feeling I was taking up her time with my trivial problems.

That's when I broke down. The tears gushed forth and I didn't hold them back. "We're not getting many ads for December," I sobbed. "It's ... it's ... awful!"

"And why is that?" Rebecca asked with a frown.

I then told her, between sobs and sniffles, about *The Mountain Sentinel's* contract with all of the valley's advertisers, and how they made them abstain from advertising anywhere else during the vital Christmas season.

"Ah," said Rebecca, "the exclusivity clause." She shook her head sadly. "I'm sorry, B.J. But I see no reason why you should think about quitting right now. You've only been publishing for five months."

"I know," I said, then cleared my throat and reached for a tissue in the box on her desk. "But that's not all." I then told her about all of the obstacles that had happened since I had begun this venture, starting with the thief who had broken into the building and stolen cash. Then I told her about the problems we'd had with the truck, especially on our first run when Jason and I had taken the paper to Shambleton and were rescued by The Captain, as well as Jason's very dangerous drive almost two weeks ago, when he'd been unable to control the accelerator and had rammed into my Camry and totaled it.

"I lost my top sales person after the first week," I lamented. "Peg decided to go back to substitute teaching."

"Why?" pressed Rebecca.

"She became obsessed with promoting the shopper," I explained. "On her own time, she'd spend weekends at farmers' markets and in front of shopping centers, trying to get people interested in us and offering free classified ads. Her husband made her quit."

Then I poured out the problems I was having with Rodney, my sales manager, who provoked shouting matches and was accused by the ladies of stealing their ad customers. "And when I told them I would not tolerate any screaming and fighting inside the office, what do they do? They go outside in front of the building and start screaming ..."

Rebecca shook her head in a condescending way. "Well, it sounds like you have been through a lot. Did you ever consider going out and soliciting ads yourself?"

"No, I am not good at sales," I confessed. I didn't tell her that I had once tried to be in sales at one of the papers I'd worked at, but had found it not to my liking. Production and management had been where my expertise lay, and yet as I looked at the last few months, I realized my management skills were not much greater than my ability to sell.

"Why did you come to see me?" asked Rebecca.

"I figured you might be able to give me some advice," I said meekly.

With a glance at her watch, Rebecca stood up and paced the floor in front of me. "B.J., if I were you ... I'd want to quit too. But, you know, starting your own business is not a piece of cake. It is a lot of hard work, long hours, and it's costly. You have to believe in yourself, and believe that you're going to succeed. A lot of people who do start-ups quit during their first year. Are you going to be another statistic?"

Her coaching, I realized, was not helping me any. I didn't want to hear it. I had expected to come in and be able to cry on her shoulder. Instead, she was acting as though my failure was totally my own fault. I rose and picked up my purse and said to her, "Thanks for your time." Then I walked out.

38

The *Billboard* put out a smaller paper that week. Nobody at work appeared bothered or complained about being able to go home early. Quite the opposite, they were all excited about the Christmas party we were having at the Desperado Mexican restaurant right after we finished our last issue of the year, the Wednesday before Christmas.

Due to an influx of checks from late November, there was money for payroll and the sales people—Rodney, in particular—were happy with larger than normal commission checks. I restrained myself from expressing my despair. Maybe a miracle would happen and I would be able to keep going.

On Wednesday afternoon, after I got home, Peg called me and said she was sick and wasn't coming over as planned to talk to me about further developments related to the Blue Heron case. She had a loose cough and her head was stuffed up, but she hoped she'd be well enough to attend the shopper's Christmas party, now just two weeks away. Everyone had been happy that I had included Peg. After all, even though she had quit her position selling ads, we still considered her one of us.

That evening Grant called. I was tired and thought I might be coming down with some kind of virus.

"I'm sorry you're not feeling well," he said. "You should stay home and get some rest."

"I will," I told him. "I think I still have a little of my homemade chicken soup in the freezer."

"Well, I called to tell you I need to go out of town again."

"Oh ... more business?"

"Not this time," he replied with a sigh. "My mother's health has been failing for quite some time now. It's reached the point where she can't live on her own anymore."

"I'm sorry to hear that, Grant."

He went on. "My sister has been looking in on her since her illness revealed itself about six months ago. Cindy has sacrificed a lot during this time and she called me this week to ask if I could come and be with Mom through the holidays. She and her partner, Gail, want to fly to Oregon to visit some friends."

"Where does your mother live?" I asked.

"Florida."

"Wow ... Grant, what's wrong with your mother, if you don't mind my asking?"

"She has dementia," he murmured, followed by a deeper sigh.

"How old is she?" I asked.

"She's in her early 70's." Then he added, "She had my sister first, and then I came along about nine years later."

I did not envy him. I had lost both my parents eight years ago, when they had died from complications following an auto accident in California. My own father had been showing signs of forgetfulness and sometimes not remembering where he was, which had worried my mother.

"I'm really sorry, Grant. It must be hard. Isn't there anyone else in your family who can share this burden with you?"

"No," he replied. "Cindy and I are Mom's only remaining relatives. I decided I'd better go and see about arrangements for her to go into a facility. Cindy can't convince her to cooperate and was on the verge of having a nervous breakdown herself. So I'm going to go and give my sister a much needed vacation."

I found out Grant was planning to leave the next morning. I wondered if I should plan to go visit him tonight as it might be the last time I could be with him for a while. But I did not want to pass any germs on to Grant which he could pass onto his ailing mother.

We talked awhile longer and I wished him well. He said he would see me when he got back from Florida. "I'm just not sure when that will be," he said. "I'll call you from time to time."

That weekend I suffered through sneezing and a runny nose. I didn't go into work on Sunday, but there really weren't enough ads to prepare anyway. In spite of that fact, my sales people remained in high spirits and felt assured that things would pick up again in January. Rodney had even bought a better used car for himself. I was not at all convinced that our situation would improve when the new year was here. Experience told me that January and February were traditionally slow months for advertising. I wasn't sure I could make it through the next couple of months.

The next two weeks passed slowly. Grant had phoned only twice, the first time just to let me know he had arrived in Orlando. He called again on Wednesday night to check in on me. His mother was fighting him on going to an assisted living-care facility. He had his hands full dealing with her and trying to run his newspaper business from a distance. To me, he sounded exhausted.

"Don't worry about me," I told him cheerfully. "Just focus on getting your mother the care she needs … and take care of yourself, too."

The last shopper of the year came out two days before Christmas. We held our employee party that evening at the Desperado in Blanca Hills. Everyone was in good spirits and enjoyed the meal. We laughed and talked, and then exchanged presents after the waitress had cleared the table.

I had bought Kelcie an enclosed glass diamond-shaped planter with a succulent growing inside. I knew that she liked plants, and she was tickled to receive this gift. Rodney had drawn my name and he nervously watched as I unwrapped the rather large flat box in front of me with a big red bow.

"Wow! Look at this …" I uncovered the box and asked Rodney, "Is this really what it says it is?"

He nodded his head, smiling.

"Oh, it's a marble laptop case," called out Colleen.

I got the cardboard box open finally, and slid out the light-colored marble case for a laptop computer. Then I turned to Rodney and smiled. "I like it. It's beautiful, Rodney. I'll use it with my MacBook."

Peg, who was sitting next to Rodney, slapped him gently on the back. "Well done!"

Then, after everyone had opened their presents from their coworkers, I handed out envelopes to all of my employees except Peg. They were the fifty-dollar bonus checks I had asked Rebecca to prepare for me. I could tell they were surprised and pleased to receive bonuses, and each one of them thanked me.

Our office closed early that week. Aspen came in to tie up some loose ends on Thursday morning, and I thanked her for being such a good assistant to me. She gave me a hug before leaving at noon.

At last I was alone in the office. The solitude comforted me as I wandered around and looked at everything and grew sad because it was still very likely the *Buffalo Billboard* had just produced its last paper.

I had been discussing my dilemma over the phone with Merle a few times in the past two weeks. He was a good listener and it had been helpful to tell someone my problems. He said he didn't want to sway me one way or the other, that I had to make the decision myself whether to stay the course or quit and come back where I could take a long break and then decide what direction to take in my life.

Grant had not called me since the week before and I understood that he must be overwhelmed with his mother's problems. Naturally, I had not discussed the closing of my business with him. Not even Jason had a clue what was about to happen. Jason and Kelcie were two happy young people in love, and I couldn't bear to burst their bubble.

Before I went home that afternoon, I noticed that Aspen had placed a pile of opened mail on the corner of my desk that I hadn't dealt with. I fingered through the envelopes and saw that there were no checks, but there was an invoice from my accountant. She had sent her bill early instead of the last day of the month as usual.

I decided to open it, and when I did I was annoyed to see that Rebecca had charged an extra fifty dollars for "consultation." She actually had the nerve to make me pay for the time I'd gone in to get her advice on what I should do about my financial state.

No one was around, so I let out my anger by shouting out a curse word. Then I fell into Aspen's chair at the front desk and buried my head in my arms and sobbed.

The telephone ringing interrupted my pity party. I was tempted to let the answering machine take it, since it was the office phone, but something prompted me to pick it up. "Thank you for calling the *Bargain Billboard*," I managed to say.

"B.J.? You're answering the phone now?" It was Peg and she laughed. "Did everyone go home?"

I sniffed and wiped my nose, then said in a muffled voice, "Well, yeah ... it is Christmas Eve."

"B.J., I'm sorry I didn't get a chance to talk to you. First I was sick, then you ... then I had to work."

"Peg, it's okay," I said.

"Hey, have you been crying or something?"

"Uh ... I'm all right." I perked up. "Can you tell me what it is over the phone?"

"I'd rather we talked in person," said Peg, "but I don't want to bother you on Christmas Eve."

"It's okay," I said with a sigh.

"Hey, has Grant said anything to you?" Peg asked.

"He's out of town," I told her. "And what do you mean?"

"How long has he been gone?"

"A couple of weeks now," I said. "He's helping his mother in Orlando, who has dementia."

"Oh, that sucks," said Peg. "Do you know when he's coming back?"

"Soon, I hope."

"Listen, B.J. I've dreaded telling you this ... but you really need to watch out for Grant."

I perked up at the sudden change in her voice. "Why? Peg, what's wrong?"

"I really can't explain without seeing you in person."

"Peg ..."

"Grant Tucker is dangerous!" she blurted.

I thought she was joking and laughed. "Oh, come on ... really?"

"He's part of the mob that's trying to destroy you and your paper," Peg told me. "I think the best thing you could do is pack up and leave town before something disastrous happens."

"You can't be serious," I said, but there was a tremble in my voice.

"His own daughter doesn't want anything to do with him," Peg reminded me. "Ask Kelcie if you don't believe me."

I wanted to tell Peg that I had talked with Kelcie about her father, and that they were at least on speaking terms now. What was Peg insinuating? And where was she getting this information? But before I could ask any further questions, she interrupted me. "Whoops, I have to hang up now." And with that, the connection ended.

I placed the phone back in its cradle and stared at the wall across the room, suddenly feeling confused and unable to accept what Peg had said. How could I possibly believe such a thing, that Grant Tucker was part of the organized crime that plagued the Lower Valley? Who could have told her that? Was it just Peg jumping to conclusions with her obsession about the mystery surrounding Liz's death? Was her brother-in-law, Rudy Espinoza, her source of this outrageous claim?

Then I remembered the time I had talked with Kelcie, right here in this office, and how she had clammed up over the subject of her father. Grant had once told me that his daughter was angry with him because he had let her mother die when she refused further treatments. Yet I remembered that Kelcie had told me she had accepted and respected her mother's decision, even though it disturbed her. So that apparently was not the reason for their estrangement. I wondered if Kelcie knew anything about the cartel, and if she would open up to me.

I left the office shortly after Peg's phone call, making sure everything was locked and the computers were turned off. My employees were expecting to come back after their week of vacation. I didn't want to think about the decision that lay ahead of me in respect to the *Buffalo Billboard*. It certainly had put a damper on my Christmas, on top of Grant being in Florida with his mother, and now this terrible burden of news Peg had delivered to me on this Christmas Eve.

Snow had started to fall during the drive home. I knew a lot of people in the valley would be happy to have Christmas snow. I was not at all in the spirit. The only gifts I had purchased had been the ones at Thanksgiving, when Janie and I had shopped the mall in Junction on Black Friday. This was my worst Christmas since I had just gotten the divorce from Dirk Martin. All I could think about was the idea of Grant betraying me, stringing me along while getting ready to stab me in the back. My heart ached with the pain of having come so close to totally loving someone. I was more than attracted to Grant. He had made me feel alive and happy when we were together.

"*Unless you were arguing!*" The voice in my head was Liz, once again chastising me. "*Admit it, Bridget. You just couldn't keep your mouth shut, could you?*"

"Liz, what are you talking about?" I sighed. "What did I do to deserve this treatment?"

Her laugh echoed in my head. "*Oh, big sister, I tried to warn you. You kept pushing him closer to the edge, accusing him of trying to put you out of business.*"

"But was he?" I asked. "Maybe Peg doesn't know what she's talking about."

"*You pushed him away ... far away this time ... he's enjoying beautiful Florida!*"

"Liz, were you murdered?" I demanded in a firm voice. "Or did you commit suicide?"

There was momentary silence, and then her voice began to fade. "*I ... think you ... will ... know that ... answer ... sooooon.*"

"What does that mean?" I shouted. "Liz! Liz, tell me!"

At that moment the car ahead of me swerved dangerously into my lane. I slammed on my brakes to avoid hitting them and my brakes screeched. Ahead of me the derelict car was sliding right and left, trying to stay on the road. I managed to keep back from it and watched other vehicles ahead of me trying to avoid what must have been a drunk driver. A few of them went off the side of the road into the ditch.

Then, behind me I saw flashing red and blue lights. The police were in the chase. I had control of my car and slowly pulled to the side of the road to let the squad car pass. My heart was racing and as I came to a halt, I put the car in park and leaned over the steering wheel to close my eyes and gather my wits. It didn't look like anyone had been in an accident, but the police siren continued down the highway in pursuit. I said a prayer of thanks, and after a couple of minutes to recover from the shock, I signaled to pull out and drove the rest of the way home.

I was in for a surprise when I got there. The front window of my apartment was lit up with a Christmas tree and colored lights. When I walked in, Jason and Kelcie grinned at me like two little kids expecting Santa.

"Merry Christmas, B.J.!" Kelcie shouted.

Jason put his arm around her shoulder and echoed, "Merry Christmas, Mom."

I gave them each a hug, then began to sniffle. Without giving them an explanation, I went to the closet and hung up my coat, then hurried into my bedroom to change clothes and to compose myself. Holiday music was playing on Jason's stereo in the living room, but the two of them were quiet. When I finally came out, they watched me solemnly. They were too polite to ask why I was sad.

"I almost was in an accident coming home," I told them. "A drunk driver was weaving and causing a lot of people to go into the ditch."

"Crap," said Jason.

"That's awful," said Kelcie, then added, "We're cooking supper. It should be ready soon."

It was growing dark outside. I walked over to admire the decorated tree. There were even little gifts under the tree already. I hadn't had time to wrap mine yet.

"Mom, there's something you should know," said Jason. His face was filled with worry and it caused me to grow shaky once again. Kelcie stood behind him and rolled her eyes, knowing what he was going to tell me. "There's a surprise waiting for you ... in my room." His eyes shifted toward the hallway.

"Jason, what?" I couldn't possibly imagine what kind of surprise he had for me in his bedroom. The kids were not acting as though it were anything too pleasant. "It's not a puppy, is it?"

Kelcie burst out laughing, then covered her mouth. Jason just shrugged and smiled.

With a loud sigh, I walked into the hallway, saying, "Jason, you know we can't have pets in this apartment. For heaven's sake ..."

When I opened the door, I heard breathing. The room was dark, so I hit the light switch, and there on the bed lay a man, fully clothed, asleep! I released a loud gasp and then I saw that it was Merle taking a nap in Jason's room. He woke up immediately and sat up in the bed.

"Merle!" I cried.

"Oh hi, Beej." He scratched his red hair and smiled sheepishly. "A little Christmas surprise for you."

"I can't believe you're here," I said, astounded. "Why didn't you tell me you were coming?"

"I dunno." He reached for his glasses, then stood up and walked over to me for a hug. "I just decided at the last minute to drive down and spend Christmas with you and Jason."

I must have looked shocked. Too much had happened in the last hour, starting with Peg's call. I began to whimper and leaned on Merle's shoulder ... a shoulder that had comforted me many a time.

"It's okay," said Merle, patting my back as he held me. I was aware of the kids watching at the door and didn't want to make a spectacle of myself, but my emotions were out of control. "It's going to be all right, Beej. I'm here now. I'm going to help you pack up and come home to Dexter."

Startled, I looked up just in time to see Jason's face staring at me in disbelief. Then he turned and walked back toward the living room.

"Wait .... Jason ..." I called after him.

"Jason!" I heard Kelcie shouting at him, and the next sound was the front door slamming.

39

Merle and I left the bedroom and watched as Kelcie gathered up her things and grabbed Jason's jacket out of the closet, then hurried out the door after him. I could only stand there, frozen with emotion. I sank into the nearest chair and hung my head.

"I'm sorry I caused an upset," said Merle. "I take it you didn't tell Jason yet."

I cleared my throat and reached for a tissue on the end table beside me. "No, Merle. I haven't told anyone." I sniffed, then blew my nose.

We sat silently for a couple of minutes. When I glanced over at him, Merle was fidgeting and uneasy. Finally, he jumped up and went into the kitchen, where he opened the refrigerator and took out a beer. "There's something in the oven," he called out to me.

I remembered that the kids were cooking supper. But before I could reply, my cell phone rang. I quickly got up and went to my purse to retrieve it. When I saw that it was Grant who was calling, I hesitated, but then hurried into my bedroom with the phone and closed my door. "Hello?" I said softly.

"Bridget? Merry Christmas."

It was all I could do to keep from sobbing. I took a few seconds to compose myself , then sniffed and said, "Hello, Grant. How are things going?"

"Bridget, it's so good to hear your voice," he crooned. "I've really missed you."

My lip trembled. Words I had longed to hear were now tainted from words Peg had given me.

When I didn't answer right away, Grant asked, "Is everything all right? You sound funny."

"I just got over that cold," I managed to reply. "I'm okay." Then I asked, "How is your mother?"

"She is getting settled into her new apartment, where she receives care. It was a bit costly ... but we'll manage somehow. I talked to my sister and Cindy and Gail will be returning after the weekend. I will be flying home early next week. I can't wait to see you again, Bridget, and to give you your Christmas present."

My heart started to pound. I didn't know what to say to Grant. While I was thinking, Merle knocked softly on my bedroom door. "Beej, is everything all right in there?"

I quickly put my phone on mute and went to open the door a crack. "I'm on the phone. I'll be out in a minute or two." I smiled at Merle to reassure him, and he nodded as I closed the door again.

"Bridget? Bridget, is everything okay?"

I took the phone off mute and spoke to him. "Yes ... and no," I said, "but I can't really talk right now, Grant. I'm sorry."

There was a silence at the other end. Then Grant mumbled, "Well ... okay then ... I'll leave you alone. I just wanted to wish you a merry Christmas."

"Merry Christmas to *you too*, Grant," I said with feeling. "We need to talk when you get back."

This seemed to put him on the defense. "Oh? What's up? Can't we talk now?"

"No ... not now. We have company."

Grant let out a sigh, then said, "Now I understand. Okay, Bridget, I'm expecting Cindy's return Saturday. I'll probably be home Sunday evening. I'll give you a call then." He hung up quickly, which was a clue to me that I had upset him.

When I came out of the bedroom, Merle was watching TV and drinking his beer. I went to see what was baking in the oven. It was a casserole the kids had concocted. I wondered where they had gone and if they were going to return. I joined Merle and saw that he was still feeling remorseful.

"I shouldn't have surprised you," he said, staring at the TV, which was on low volume. "I think I upset your son."

He was right, but I knew Merle was genuinely apologetic. I thought this might be a good time for us to clear the air. I had not told Merle about my relationship with Grant, and he deserved to know the truth, especially since Kelcie was around and the subject would inevitably come up at some point. Then again, I had mixed feelings at the moment. What Peg Espinoza had told me on the phone that afternoon had thrown me for a loop. How could I believe that Grant was part of the cartel? How could that possibly be true? And yet, part of me suspected that he knew not having ad revenue during the holidays could totally destroy my efforts to succeed with the shopper. He hadn't made an effort to fix the problem with those advertising contracts. How could it be out of his hands when he was the boss?

"Merle ... there's something I think you should know," I started to tell him.

Just then, the front door opened and Jason and Kelcie came bouncing in, all smiles. Surprised, I stood up and stared at them. They each carried a pile of gifts wrapped in fancy paper and bows.

"You're back!" I exclaimed and couldn't help but grin.

Jason led Kelcie over to the tree they had put up and they started stacking the gifts underneath. "It smells like the casserole is getting done," said my son.

"I'll take it out of the oven." Kelcie danced into the kitchen area and grabbed the potholders.

Merle and I both stood, amazed at what the kids had done. "Jason, I'm sorry," I said.

My son looked up at me with a smile. "For what, Mom?" He glanced at Merle, then shrugged. "Let's just enjoy Christmas."

I walked over and my son stood up and gave me a hug. "Thank you, Jason." Then I turned toward the kitchen and said, "Thank you too, Kelcie. Supper smells delicious."

"Wait until you see what she conjured up for dessert," said Jason.

I looked up at Merle and smiled. "It's nice that you're here," I told him warmly and squeezed his hand. "And now I'm going to go wash up for supper."

"Put on some more of your Christmas music, Jason," Kelcie called from her duties in the kitchen.

"Right on," he called back.

We sat down at the small dining table and enjoyed the supper the kids had prepared. Jason and Kelcie were in good spirits, and I couldn't help but wonder if I had just imagined that he had appeared upset when Merle had spoken about packing me up to take me home to Dexter. Either Jason hadn't understood it, or he was somehow in denial. I also wondered what part Kelcie had played in getting my son back on track so that we could all enjoy a peaceful Christmas Eve.

After dinner Kelcie took a non-dairy cherry cheesecake out of the freezer that she had prepared that afternoon. While we were enjoying dessert, the conversation centered around safe subjects outside of work. I did notice that Kelcie would glance at Merle a lot and I wondered what Jason had disclosed to her about him, and what she thought about him with respect to me.

I asked Kelcie what her Christmases had been like in her younger years. She opened up and told about her happiest memories as a little girl, but steered away from the subject of her mother's illness. Jason told about some of the Christmases he'd spent in Utah with his dad and Alicia, which sparked me to ask him about Avery.

"She came home for Christmas too ... right?" I prompted

Jason shrugged. "Not too often."

"Why not?" Kelcie asked, surprised at his answer. "Didn't she want to come home from boarding school?"

"Obviously not," said Jason, "but she came other times when she had breaks from school. Of course, I wasn't there at those times."

"That does sound strange," commented Merle. He leaned back in his chair with his arms folded. "It's almost as if they couldn't handle both of you at the same time." He chuckled.

Jason scrunched up his face, then said, "You know... I've wondered about that several times myself. It seems almost as if they didn't want me to be around when Avery was there ... or vice versa."

"But why?" asked Kelcie. "Why would they want it that way?"

"You'd have to meet those two ... my dad and Alicia ... to understand what I'm talking about."

Kelcie looked at me. "Why did you get a divorce from Jason's dad, B.J.?"

Merle cleared his throat then and stood up from the table. "I'm going to help you do these dishes," he said to me, and then turned to the kids. "Then we'll see what are inside those packages under the tree."

No more was said about touchy subjects. Later, we enjoyed a pleasant evening with the presents and lighter conversation. When I asked Kelcie if she had heard anything from her dad, she replied that she hadn't been in touch with him since he left to take care of her grandmother.

When it grew later, Jason and Kelcie stood up. Jason said to me, "Mom, I'm sleeping over at Kelcie's tonight. That way Merle can have my room."

This time I did not object. I smiled and nodded my head while Merle looked at me in surprise. He had probably hoped that I was going to welcome him into my bed. Thank goodness my son had enough common sense to think ahead and plan accordingly. For someone 21 years old, Jason had a lot of things in life already figured out, and I was proud of him.

Christmas came and went. It was nothing spectacular for me that year. Jason and Kelcie went tobogganing at the Sand Dunes both Friday and Saturday, so Merle and I lounged around my apartment and talked about a number of things.

It was plain to see that he was greatly disappointed when I told him that I had developed an intimate relationship with Grant Tucker, who was coming back to Blanca Hills on Sunday evening. Merle had been convinced that he was going to rescue me and reclaim me and that things between us would be like they had once been.

I told him I had not yet made up my mind about quitting the shopper. I didn't want to rush into making that decision until I was sure the business could not hold its own any longer. I didn't plan to contribute any more of my house money toward the *Billboard,* and Merle agreed that I shouldn't.

"I've got a bit of savings," he told me. "I would like to be an investor."

"Merle, I can't ask you to do that."

"Why not?" he asked. "I could be a partner. I could even move here from Dexter."

It was obvious to me that Merle was not going to give up on winning me back into his life. I didn't want to hurt his feelings any more than I had, so I thanked him and said I would give it some thought and get back to him later. He seemed satisfied with that.

Merle left for Dexter on Sunday morning. Jason returned from Kelcie's and relaxed with video games after the activity of spending lots of time together. He found an opportunity to ask me about Merle when we were eating some leftovers at suppertime.

"Mom, tell me the real reason Merle was here," Jason prompted me.

"He and Janie broke up after Thanksgiving," I said. "Merle kind of wants me back in his life."

"But I thought Kelcie's father was in your life now."

I sighed and ran a hand through my hair. "It's complicated, Jason."

"What happened between you and Kelcie's father, anyway?" Then he added, "Does it have anything to do with the *Sentinel's* ad policy?"

"Partly," I said. "Jason, I'm not sure how much longer I can keep the *Billboard* going if we don't get enough ad revenue coming in."

"I figured as much," he mumbled. "Mom, please don't give it up. I love this job. Everyone who works for you loves their job. Colleen and Molly told me it's the best job they've ever had. You've got to keep it going."

"If I can't make the payments, what am I going to do?" I told him. "Start-ups are always risky, Jason. They don't always succeed."

"But the people of the valley love the shopper," Jason insisted. "I hear it everywhere I go." Then he asked, "When are you going to make up your mind?"

I couldn't give him an answer to that. "What are you planning to do with your week off?" I asked in order to change the subject.

"Hang out," he said. "Kelcie wants to go skiing at Aspen. I don't think we can afford it."

I laughed. "Jason, you sound like a grownup!"

"I am," he said with a smile. "I have to think ahead, Mom."

I nodded, proud of him. "I know."

Later that evening my cell phone rang. Sure that it was Grant having arrived home, I eagerly went to answer it, but there was a local number I didn't recognize.

"Mrs. Martin?"

"Yes?"

"I'm Sergeant Baca of the Valle Viento City Police."

"Yes, I remember you," I said, recalling that he had been the officer in charge of the investigation when we'd had the break-in at the shopper. "How can I help you?"

"We have someone in custody who was found inside your office about half an hour ago."

Another break-in? "Oh, my gosh! What happened?" I asked.

"Would you mind coming down to the station?" he replied. "We can explain everything then."

"Was there any damage? Did somebody steal something?"

"Everything appears to be fine," said the sergeant, "but we'd appreciate it if you could get here as soon as you can."

"Of course," I said and hung up. Then I called for Jason.

"Yeah, Mom?" He popped his head into the room.

I explained about the call and he insisted on coming along. "Should we take your car or mine?" he asked as he pulled his jacket out of the closet.

I grabbed my purse and keys. "No, we can take the rental car."

Five minutes later we were headed west on the highway from Blanca Hills to Valle Viento. The sky was a gorgeous brilliant red as the sun went down. I couldn't help but admire it, even in my frantic state of needing to get to the police station. We both were sure that the police had captured another thief.

It was dark by the time we got there. Sergeant Baca was called to the front office and he smiled at us in greeting. "Thanks for coming, Mrs. Martin. Please follow me." He led Jason and me to a room that I assumed was his office and told us to sit.

"Please tell us what happened," I begged.

"Well," said the sergeant, beckoning us to take a seat, "we got a call almost an hour ago from ..." He looked at a paper on the table and read the name ... "a Rodney Rankar?"

"Rodney!" I exclaimed. "He's one of my employees."

"Yes, he said he worked for you," said Sergeant Baca. "Rodney happened to be at the office this afternoon on his way back from visiting some relatives out of town. He said he had left some work that he wanted to pick up and take home. He was rummaging through his desk drawers when he heard a door opening. When he turned around, somebody stepped out of the bathroom next to the kitchen."

Jason and I looked at one another, very concerned. "Who was it?" I asked.

"A young lady," said the sergeant. "She screamed and started to run when she saw Rodney was there. Apparently this girl had been staying at your office and sleeping in your back room."

"Then what happened?" asked Jason.

"She tried to escape, but Rodney caught hold of her and held her down. He was much stronger than her. He had his cell phone on him and he called 9-1-1. We have the girl in custody and she wouldn't give her name. She didn't have any identification on her at the time, but one of our men found some of her belongings in that closet in your storage room. She didn't have any driver's license, but she did have a credit card and the name on the credit card was Dirk Martin."

"Avery!" Jason cried out.

"Can we see her?" I asked.

"Certainly." Sergeant Baca stood up and we got up and followed him out into the narrow hallway to the back of the station, where we entered through a security door into the jail. Valle Viento's jail was very small with only two cells. We saw the young lady with long dark hair, dressed in jeans and a baggy blue sweatshirt, sitting on the bench. She looked up as we approached and there was fear in her eyes.

"Avery!" Jason walked up to the bars in the cell. "What are you doing here?" He turned to the sergeant and said, "We know this girl. She's my stepsister."

Avery rose from the bench and shuffled over toward us, not smiling. Her eyes looked frightened. "Jason," she said, and then she stared at me. "What's going to happen to me?" she asked.

I turned to the sergeant and asked, "Are there any charges against her?"

"That's up to you." Sergeant Baca shrugged. It was obvious he didn't care one way or the other what we decided.

"Why were you staying in our office?" Jason asked Avery.

She shook her head and stared at the floor.

"Never mind that now," I told her, then looked at Sergeant Baca and said, "I'm not pressing any charges. Will you release her into our custody? We'll take her home with us."

Avery looked scared again and slowly shook her head from side to side.

"It's okay," Jason assured her. "Avery, you'll be safe with us. I don't know how or why you got here ... but I think you've been in the valley for a couple of months now."

"I'll have to have you sign some papers and then we'll release her." Sergeant Baca led us back through the security door into his inner office, where he gave me the documents to sign.

A little later we left the police department, along with the items the police had gathered from the storage room that they had assumed were Avery's. Jason climbed into the back seat, to let his stepsister sit in front next to me, and then we headed back to Blanca Hills.

Jason tried to ask questions, but Avery said she didn't want to talk about anything right now. I asked how she had gotten into the office and she said she had found out about the door from the enclosed alley. She also revealed that she had been staying there, in secret, for the last two weeks!

We were halfway to Blanca Hills when I noticed in my side mirrors that there was a car that was staying close behind us. I couldn't tell what kind of car it was because of the darkness, but its headlights were on bright and when I slowed down to give them an opportunity to pass, they didn't. The car continued to follow us.

Grant called me before we got home and I didn't want to answer it, mainly because I was driving, and also because I couldn't talk to him at the moment. I figured he had made it home and was letting me know.

My two young passengers didn't seem to notice that we were being tailed. I knew they were lost in their own thoughts and I wondered if Avery was going to open up to us once we got her home, and I also worried that she might try to run away again.

I had to find out why she had left home and what she was afraid of.

40

Once we reached our street, I didn't make the turn and kept going. Jason said, "Mom, you missed the turn."

I was aware of the car behind us still on our tail and decided to check them out, to see if it had only been my paranoid imagination. I made a sudden left turn onto another side street, and the car continued to follow us.

"What are you doing?" Jason asked me.

Avery turned around in the front seat. "Someone's following us," she said. It was the first thing she had spoken since we started out. She had a frightened look on her face.

I turned right at the next intersection and the car was still there. I decided to speed up. Heading for the main road through Blanca Hills, I hit the accelerator, my heart pounding now.

"Mom! Slow down!" cried Jason.

As soon as we got to the intersection, the light turned yellow and I impulsively shot across to the other side. Brakes screeched behind me, followed by a crash. Apparently the vehicle that was following me had run the red light, and someone had not seen them coming. Glancing at my mirror, I saw that there had been a collision.

Avery gasped and Jason swore out loud. I continued on and we drove directly back to Greenwood Street to our apartment complex. After pulling into the parking space, I leaned against the steering wheel in relief. Avery spoke again. "It's dangerous to have me staying with you. I should leave."

"And go where?" demanded Jason. He put his hand on his step-sister's shoulder and frowned at her.

"Come on, let's all go inside," I told them. "I'll make some hot chocolate. Avery, have you had anything to eat?"

The girl shook her head slowly and stared into her lap.

"Jason, help her," I directed. "I'll be right in." Then I added, "Don't let her out of your sight."

While my son helped Avery out of the car and held onto her as they made their way to the entrance, I pulled out my cell phone and looked to see if Grant had left me a voice mail. He had not. I decided it must not have been urgent. He had probably just gotten home and wanted to let me know. After things calmed down, I'd give him a call later.

Kelcie arrived at our door the same time I came in from the car. "Jason called me," she explained. "He thought you might need me to help."

"Thank you, Kelcie." I smiled and we both walked into the apartment. Avery was seated in a chair at the kitchen table while Jason was rummaging through the refrigerator, finding her something to eat. The girl stared, wide-eyed, at Kelcie.

"Hi," said Kelcie, approaching Avery cautiously but with a friendly smile.

I filled the teapot with hot water and got it going on the stove.

"What are you planning to do with me?" Avery asked as I opened the cupboard to find the cocoa.

"I don't know yet," I told her calmly. "It depends upon you." I looked at Jason, whose head was still in the refrigerator. "Jason, there's some left-over fried chicken in the meat drawer that you can warm up for her in the microwave."

"Gotcha," he said. "And I found some coleslaw. Is it still good?" He pulled a carton out to show me.

"Yes, Merle brought it," I said and took a seat at the table. Kelcie sat across from Avery while Jason went about fixing the food for his stepsister. "Now Avery, I want you to explain to me why you were staying in my office."

"It was the only safe place I knew of," she said, still looking frightened. "I ... I had nowhere else to go."

"What are you doing in Blanca Hills?" I asked. "Why did you come here?"

She lowered her eyes and hesitated. I noticed her lower lip trembling and reached over the table to touch her hand.

"It's okay, Avery. We know that you've been in the Lower Valley for quite a while. You came to the office one weekend asking for Jason. Why didn't you come back?"

Jason turned to her and said, "Yeah, and I saw you just last week at the gas station. I was gonna talk to you, but you suddenly ran out."

"I was afraid," she said.

"But why?" he asked.

I took a deep breath, then said, "Avery, we want to help you. Why did you run away from your mother and stepfather in Salt Lake?"

"Alicia," said Avery. "She's so mean. She hates me!"

Both Jason and I looked alarmed and stared at one another. Then I said to her, "But Avery, she's your mother. She doesn't hate you ..."

"*You* don't know!" Avery yelled. She glanced at Jason, then said, "And *he* doesn't know! He lived with *you*. I was sent away to a boarding school. They didn't want me around." She pouted.

"Did something happen to make you want to leave home?" I asked her.

Avery sniffled, trying to hold in her emotions. "My dad ..."

Jason had just put the chicken in the microwave and walked over. "I thought your dad died when you were a baby," he said.

"That's what they *told* us," said Avery.

"You mean ... he's not dead?" asked Jason. "Did you think he might be living here in Blanca Hills?"

"No." Avery shook her head. "No, that's not what I mean."

"What do you mean, Avery?" I asked gently. "It's okay ... you're safe here. Was someone after you? Is that why you were hiding in the shopper office?"

"I got into trouble when I arrived in Blanca Hills," she said, finally starting to open up to us. She looked around. "Could I please have a drink of water?"

"Jason ..." I gestured for him to get Avery something to drink. "Go on, Avery," I prompted her. "What do you mean you got into trouble? What kind of trouble?"

"I had no money," she said meekly. "I had the credit card they found. But I couldn't use it."

"Dirk didn't know you had his credit card?" I asked.

She nodded. "I didn't know what to do. Then this man talked to me, and he said he'd help me. His name was Javier. At first he was very kind. He bought me a meal at the café in Valle Viento. I knew that you and Jason had started a newspaper. I was going to talk to Jason ... but then I decided it wasn't a good idea."

"What were you going to talk to me about?" Jason handed her the glass of water.

"It was about my dad."

Jason and I looked at each other, puzzled.

"My dad ..." Avery couldn't hold it in any longer. "*My* dad ... is *your* dad!" She looked at Jason and suddenly burst into tears. "*Dirk* is my dad. I'm your *half sister* ..."

This came as a shock! Both Jason's and my mouths had fallen open as we sat there and watched this beautiful young girl break down into tears. How could this be? How could Dirk be Avery's father?

Kelcie moved closer to the dark-haired girl and put her hand on Avery's shoulder. "It's okay. Please tell us more. We need to know the whole truth."

Maybe it was because Kelcie was a kind stranger. Somehow Avery calmed down and smiled at the blonde girl. The microwave beeped, but Jason wasn't ready to get the food out. Like me, he was stunned at the news we'd just heard.

Finally, I took a breath. "And Alicia?" I asked. "Isn't she your mother?"

"No! She's *not* my mother," Avery insisted. "She's resented me from the very beginning."

"Well ... if Alicia's not ... then ... who is?" asked Jason, totally confused.

"I overheard an argument when I was home last September," Avery explained. She sipped at her water. "They were yelling at each other and didn't know I was able to hear them. Alicia said she'd had enough of the lies. She was angry at ... Dirk ... and she was frantic because she'd intercepted a phone call that was meant for him. The man, who was from Blanca Hills ... left a message, threatening to expose the truth about Liz Russo."

I gasped. "Oh my gosh!"

"Aunt Liz?" Jason's eyes were bulging.

"Go on," encouraged Kelcie.

The microwave beeped again, letting us know the food was waiting, but Avery continued her story. "I heard Alicia say that she wasn't going to cover for him anymore, that she was tired of people believing that *she* was my mother. She told Dirk he should have married Liz and that they should have raised their daughter together!"

Stunned, I had to get up from the table. With trembling hands I went to the microwave and took out Avery's meal. I fumbled for some silverware and a napkin, completely befuddled by Avery's story. We were all silent for the next couple of minutes as I set the food in front of Avery. She was apparently very hungry because despite all she had told us in the last few minutes, she began eating the food in front of her. I went to the sink and braced myself. It all was starting to make sense to me now.

Finally, Jason broke the silence. "So," he said in a calm voice, "it turns out that Aunt Liz became pregnant from my dad ... which makes you my cousin ... as well as my sister."

"Wow," breathed Kelcie and blinked her green eyes. "I don't know what to say."

The memory of that awful time in my life when I had found out Dirk and my sister were having an affair under my own roof brought it all home for me. Of course Dirk would have found a way to cover up his mistake. He was certainly not going to marry a drug addict, yet somehow he supported her through the pregnancy and then, when he married Alicia, conned her into saying that Avery was hers! That poor woman must have truly resented this innocent little girl, knowing that she was Dirk's, but having to pretend that she was the mother and that Avery was the result of adultery. The lies must have finally gotten to her, which also explained the yelling I'd heard when I'd listened to the conversation Jason had with his dad at Thanksgiving.

Kelcie had been thoughtful and suddenly asked, "You mentioned a man named Javier. You said he helped you?"

Avery nodded, taking another bite of chicken.

"And did you know his last name?" Kelcie asked.

"He's Mexican," said Avery. "I mean ... he's Hispanic. He made it clear he was not a Mexican, but his last name was Gallegos. I'm pretty sure that's what it was."

"There's a Javier Gallegos that works for my father." She looked me in the eye. "I'm wondering ..." She turned back to the girl. "Avery, what did this man do?"

"He protected me ... for a while," she admitted. "Then he wanted me to earn my keep." She held back a sob and put down her fork.

I was afraid to ask, but I had to. "What did he expect from you?"

"I was going to be forced into work I didn't want to do." She hung her head. "At first, he offered me a lot of money, so I thought, okay, maybe just this once ... because I needed some money." She gulped, tears welling up in her hazel eyes. "And they gave us stuff to make us wanna do it ..."

"Drugs?" I asked.

"Yes." Avery hung her head. "I hated it."

"Avery, were you a victim of human trafficking?"

Kelcie gasped. "Oh my *gosh*..."

"Yes ... but I managed to get away. That's why I hid in your office."

"How did you know about the door into our storage room off the alley?" I asked her.

"I was there when Javier told José where to break into your office."

"Who is José?" asked Jason.

"I believe he is the one who stole the money on Halloween night," I said. "He was caught and is serving time in jail." After a pause, I said, "But the thief didn't come through that door. He crashed through the bathroom wall and got in that way."

Avery shrugged. "It's a narrow opening. José is very big. I think he was too fat to enter through that door."

Now I knew that Javier was behind a lot of illegal activity and it frightened me that this could implicate Grant. For all I knew at that moment, Grant had knowledge of all this and had kept it from me. How could he do such a thing?

Kelcie suddenly broke down and buried her head in her arms. Jason stood up and wrapped his arms around her. "Oh no ... *oh no* ..." she sobbed. "I was afraid this would happen."

"What, Kelc?" asked Jason, trying to comfort her.

The tea kettle whistled, indicating that the hot water was ready for cocoa. I got up and turned it off. Hot chocolate was the least on our minds at the moment.

A knock on the door startled us. Avery immediately froze, her eyes wide with fear. We all waited a few seconds until the second knock sounded.

"Don't answer it, Jason," Kelcie cautioned.

I stood up and walked slowly toward the front door, after picking up a large cast iron frying pan that had been in the dish rack. I looked through the peep hole and breathed a sigh of relief. It was Grant. I opened the door and he stood, looking at me with a grin. But when he saw the cast iron skillet in my hand and the kids sitting at the kitchen table, obviously in distress, he stepped inside and stared at all of us.

"Bridget ... what's happened here?" He looked from one to the other us, then said, "Kelcie, why are you crying?"

Avery did not seem to recognize Grant, which made me breathe a sigh of relief. "Grant, please come in. Something very important is happening here."

He placed a small, gift-wrapped box on the chair next to the door and shook off his coat while I wandered back to the kitchen to replace the frying pan. Kelcie continued to sniffle while Jason comforted her. Avery had just finished her plate and pushed it aside, reaching for her glass of water.

"Grant, I'd like you to meet Jason's sister, Avery." I patted the empty chair beside me, across from the girl with the long dark hair. I now understood why she was almost the spitting image of my sister Liz.

"Hi, Avery." Grant smiled, then looked at the rest of us. "What's going on?" he asked.

"We were discussing Avery's arrival in Blanca Hills," I said. "It's a long story, and she has been through a lot. Avery, this is Kelcie's father, Grant Tucker."

"Pleased to meet you, sir," she said in a muffled voice.

He nodded, then looked at his daughter, who kept blinking and shaking her head at her dad. "Kelcie ... what's wrong?" he asked again.

"Dad!" Kelcie started shaking. "It's you! You're part of it! Don't you understand that's the reason I quit at the *Sentinel* and went to work for B.J.?"

"What are you talking about?" Jason asked his girlfriend.

Kelcie grew angry. "*The Mountain Sentinel* has ties with the mafia," she told us. "Everyone in this valley knows it. I couldn't bear to work there any longer when I found out. Dad, I'm sorry, but I just don't want to work for a company that is responsible for getting rich by turning people into drug addicts, or taking people like Avery and selling them as prostitutes to pedophiles!"

Grant was obviously astounded at her words. All of us were looking at Grant now and he was either putting on a great act of innocence, or he had been played for a fool. At first he was speechless, but then he looked his daughter in the eyes and slowly shook his head from side to side. "I will not pretend that I haven't heard this rumor before," he said in a calm voice, "but I am telling you all now that I have nothing to do with the so-called drug cartel that has allegedly infiltrated this part of Colorado."

Kelcie looked at her father and said, "It was that man who works for you, Dad—Javier Gallegos. Avery has spent the last two months in hiding because he and others like him tried to make a prostitute out of Avery. It was Javier, Dad! Javier Gallegos!"

I looked at Grant and nodded my head sadly. I didn't want to say *I told you so* because I already knew that Grant was not surprised to hear the news.

Grant stood up and pulled out his cell phone, then walked into the living room and punched in some numbers. The rest of us waited to see what he was going to do. Meanwhile, I got up and started fixing hot chocolate, simply because I couldn't stand any more bad drama.

"Avery, you'll sleep in Jason's room tonight," I said, "and Jason, you can stay with Kelcie or take the couch." My son nodded in agreement. He was still trying to comfort Kelcie, who was calming down after her angry outbursts.

"I'd like to take a bath," Avery said. "That is ... if you don't mind."

"Of course." I smiled at the girl and took her dishes to the sink. "You can take one now, if you like."

Without a word, she got up from the table and found her way down the hallway to the bathroom. Jason had brought in her few belongings, and Kelcie perked up suddenly and said she'd run back to her apartment to get Avery a nightgown and a change of clothes. She and Avery were similar in size.

"I'll help her." Jason ran out the door as well.

I was rinsing off Avery's dishes and glanced over at Grant, who was talking on his cell phone. He was far enough away that I couldn't hear him, but when he put his phone in his pocket, he turned to me with a stricken look on his face.

"Grant, what's wrong?" I was almost afraid to ask.

He walked over to me. "There's been an accident," he told me.

Right away I thought about the car crash after I had sped through the yellow light with the mystery car in pursuit. "Where?" I demanded.

"I just called Javier's cell," Grant explained. "He didn't answer, so I got hold of someone else at my paper ... Juan, my advertising manager." Grant's lower lip trembled. "His wife was killed when she ran a red light downtown."

"Oh, lord!" I wondered if it had been a woman driving the car following us. "Grant, please sit down. I have to explain what's happened here tonight."

"Bridget, I am not part of the cartel," Grant told me. "I don't know where Kelcie got that idea." He sighed as he took a seat at the kitchen table. We heard the water running in the bathroom down the hall. I brought two mugs of hot chocolate to the table and handed one of them to Grant. "All this time I thought she was angry with me over Samantha."

"No," I assured him. "I'm sure it had nothing to do with her mother." Then I took a deep breath and told him how I had received the call from the Valle Viento police late that afternoon, and how Jason and I had driven to the station and found Avery in custody. I explained how she had been sleeping in the storage room at the *Billboard's* office for the last couple of weeks, and how frightened she had been.

"This is the girl you were talking about ... the one you saw in Javier's red car," said Grant.

"Yes. She ran away from home. Apparently she overheard Dirk and Alicia talking about her, and she learned that Dirk is actually her father."

"What?" Grant stared at me. "You mean ..."

"Alicia is not Avery's mother," I said. "Avery is Dirk's and my sister Liz's daughter!"

Grant puzzled over this as he took a sip of the hot chocolate. "And she claims that Javier is running some kind of human trafficking! Why, that *scum!*"

"Avery said that Javier instigated the break-in at the *Billboard* office on Halloween night. That's how she knew there was a doorway from the enclosed alley into the closet of our store room."

"A doorway from the alley? Really?"

"Yes," I said. "I discovered it one night. Apparently, the man was too large to go through that way, so he busted through the wall of the restroom instead. Avery went in and out through that secret doorway. And Rodney showed up at the office this afternoon and discovered her there. He called the police and they arrested her."

"Bridget, you've been through a lot," said Grant, looking deeply into my eyes. "I'm so, so sorry that I couldn't be here for you."

"No, Grant. You had to help your mother." I paused to sip some cocoa, then asked, "Did your sister get back okay?"

"Yeah, she and Gail had a fine time. They wanted me to stay and visit another night, but I really wanted to get home to you." He smiled and reached for my hand.

I smiled, feeling the longing for him that had never left, but then remembered his phone conversation. "The accident," I said. "You didn't say *who* got killed. How did Juan know about it?"

Grant sighed. "This is the sad part. It was his wife ... Juan Espinoza's wife ..."

"Espinoza?" It suddenly struck me. " Certainly you don't mean ... it couldn't be ... Grant, my friend Peg is married to a Juan Espinoza. Oh, it couldn't be *her* ..."

"Yes, it was Peg," said Grant. "That's her name. She used to work in the advertising department several years ago ... before I took over the paper."

That was my breaking point. "*No!!*" I burst into tears. "She was my friend! How could she be my friend and she was *following* me ... chasing us!" I buried my head in my arms and sobbed.

Grant's cell phone rang and he answered it. I forced myself to stop crying and watched Grant's face as he listened. "Yup ... okay ... uh-huh ... don't worry ... I'll be right there." Then he hung up. Then he asked, "What were you talking about ... somebody following you? Chasing you?"

"Yes," I told him, grabbing a napkin to blow my nose. "When we left the police station, I noticed a car was following us really close. So when we got into Blanca Hills, I started taking other roads to see if the car would keep behind us ... and it did ... so then I accelerated and sped through a yellow light. The car behind me tried to speed through as well, but the light had already turned. Oh Grant ... what have I done? My God!"

He walked over and took me into his arms and held me while I cried on his shoulder. Jason and Kelcie came through the front door and stared at us. Without saying a word, they wandered back with a bag of clothes to Jason's bedroom. We heard Jason call into the bathroom,

"Avery, are you all right?" and she answered back, "I'm fine. Thanks."

"Bridget, I hate to leave you right now, but I've got to meet with the FBI. They just called. There's an investigator I've been working with when I started looking again into your sister's murder. He just called and has some important information to share. I'd ask you to come along, but I can see you have your hands full."

"Will you call me afterwards?" I asked. "I'll be up."

"I promise," he said and planted a kiss on my forehead. "Take care of the kids." He winked, then walked out the door. I noticed that he had left the gift for me on the chair. I picked it up and carried it over to the Christmas tree and set it down for later, when he would return.

When Kelcie and Jason came into the living room, I told them the tragic news about Peg. Kelcie burst into tears again and Jason sunk onto the couch, groaning. I prayed that this horrible night would end soon. There had to be another day … another sunset … and I wanted Grant to be part of my life.

41

It was a stressful evening. After Avery had her bath, she was exhausted and just wanted to sleep, so I put clean sheets on Jason's bed and made her as comfortable as I could.

"What should I call you?" Avery asked me as she slipped her feet underneath the covers.

I fluffed up the pillow and smiled. "Whatever you'd like," I said.

"I mean ... are you Aunt Bridget, or are you Aunt B.J.?" She smiled at me warmly. "I've never had an aunt before. As a matter of fact, I've never really had anyone."

I leaned over and gave Avery a hug. "Avery, you can call me Aunt B.J. ... or Beej, if you prefer."

"Thanks ... for everything." She reclined and pulled the sheet up to her chin, then rolled onto her side. "Goodnight, Aunt Beej."

I turned out the light and closed the door, then returned to the living room. Jason and Kelcie were sitting on the couch together, holding each other and looking very sad.

"Mom ... I can't get over Peg," said Jason.

"Me neither." Kelcie sighed.

I was probably more crushed than either of the kids. Peg had been my closest friend. I found it hard to believe that she had kept the truth from me about having worked at *The Mountain Sentinel*, and that her husband, Juan, was Grant's production manager. I asked Kelcie, "Didn't you know Peg when she worked at your dad's paper?"

Kelcie shook her head no. "It must have been before I returned after the university," she said. "I did know Juan, however. He was my supervisor."

"Mom ... do you really believe Peg was involved with the cartel?" Jason asked.

"I find it very hard to believe," I admitted.

"She never told you she'd worked at the *Sentinel?*" Kelcie's green eyes stared at me somberly.

"No," I replied.

Yet she had been following us. She had taken me into her confidence, and Peg had been obsessed with Liz's murder. Had she been trying to throw me off track? I remembered her telling me about Liz's boyfriend, Harvey Franken, whom she said had murdered my sister at the Blue Heron Motel. I recalled that Peg had told me Harvey was in jail.

Finally, the two kids left to go to Kelcie's apartment for the night. I decided to wait up until I heard from Grant. I picked up a book I was reading, but found it hard to concentrate. I must have drifted off in my chair because I suddenly woke up to the sound of a soft knock on my front door. When I saw that Grant was standing out there, I let him in and fell into his arms. He held me tight and I found comfort in the sensuous smell of him and his stubbly chin when he kissed me.

"What did you find out?" I asked after he took off his coat and we moved to the couch.

Grant explained that the FBI investigator had confirmed that his manager, Javier Gallegos, had been trafficking under-age teens, and had been aided and abetted by Juan Espinoza, who worked under him at the paper. Whether Peg, Juan's wife and my ex-employee, had been implicated in the crimes of the cartel, the FBI agent could not confirm.

"I suppose it's possible that Peg was following me to try and warn me," I suggested.

"It's doubtful," said Grant. "She wasn't completely truthful with you, now was she?"

"She convinced me that she was my friend." My voice trembled a bit and my eyes teared up.

"Maybe we'll know more when they arrest Javier," said Grant. "There's a warrant out for him. We have evidence, and we have the testimony of your niece."

"And Peg's husband?" I asked.

"Juan has already turned himself in. He feels responsible for Peg's death."

"You spoke to him?"

"No. The FBI agent told me." He sighed. "I've lost my two most valuable employees. This scandal is going to hurt the *Sentinel's* reputation."

"I'm so sorry, Grant. This whole thing is awful ... just awful." I didn't see how I was going to be able to sleep. "I wish I didn't have to be alone tonight. I'm afraid the dreams will come back."

"Bridget ..." Grant turned to me. "I'll stay here tonight."

"You will?" I smiled up at him. "Thank you."

"Maybe I won't have bad dreams either," he commented. "Together we can be dream chasers."

"I like that." I leaned over for another delicious kiss and giggled when his chin tickled mine.

"Oh!" He pulled away, suddenly remembering something. He stood up and looked around. "What did I do with it?"

"What?" I asked.

"Your Christmas present. I had it when I ..." He looked at the tree then and saw the little package with the bright green ribbon on it. "Ah, there it is." He went over and picked it up, then came back and offered it to me. "Merry Christmas, Bridget."

I hesitated, then asked, "Should I open it now?"

"If you wish."

We sat down together on the couch and he put his arm around me, caressing my hair with his fingers as I carefully took off the bow and removed the gift wrap. It looked like a velvet-lined jewelry box and my heart began to race as I slowly opened the lid and peered inside.

"Oh, Grant! You didn't!" I cried. Before me was a sparkling diamond ring with a rose gold band. "Is it ... is it a..." I was afraid to say it.

"A diamond it is," he said proudly. Then he smiled at me and looked into my eyes. "Bridget, will you do me the honor of becoming my wife?"

After everything that had happened that day, I would have thought receiving a marriage proposal would be the thing that did me in. But instead, I found myself grinning up at him and nodding my head. "Yes!" I told him. "Oh, yes ... I will be your wife." And then he grabbed me and kissed me until I had to tear away in order to catch my breath and wipe away my tears of joy.

He took the ring out of the little box and he lifted my left hand and carefully slid the ring onto my finger. "I didn't know your size," he said, "but we can get it adjusted. How does it feel?"

"It feels just right," I said, still smiling. I felt like I was in a fairytale. I didn't want to face all the loose ends that were in my life right now. My business ... my best friend turned enemy ... my ex-husband's scandalous secret ... a niece I had never known I had ... but at the moment I just pushed all of that aside and let myself drift off into a new dream ... a wonderful future with a man I had finally fallen in love with.

The next morning we woke up to snowy weather. I brewed coffee and was preparing to make breakfast when Jason and Kelcie returned. Avery had gotten up and was getting dressed. When Kelcie saw Grant sitting in the living room with just his pants and his undershirt, she gasped out loud.

"Dad!"

"Good morning, Kelc," he said as if it was nothing unusual to have spent the night in my apartment. "Did you two sleep well?"

Jason and Kelcie burst out laughing. She went over to give her father a hug, and Jason wandered into the kitchen to find his favorite mug. "Oh, are we having pancakes?" he asked.

"We are," I told him with a smile.

"Uh-oh!"

"What's wrong?" I asked.

"Kelcie, come here," Jason called. The blonde girl hurried into the kitchen to see what he wanted. "Mom's wearing an engagement ring."

"What!"

"That is what it is, right?" Jason pointed at my hand and Kelcie gasped again.

"Dad?" Kelcie turned to her father and this time he grinned and winked at her, then went back to reading the magazine he'd picked up off my coffee table. Kelcie squealed with joy, then gave me a hug. "Congratulations, B.J.!"

"You're gonna have to start calling her Mom now, like me," joked Jason.

I was frying bacon and starting the pancakes on the grill when Avery roamed into the room, looking perkier than she had yesterday, though she was still very shy. "Good morning," I called to her. "How did you sleep?"

"Fine," said the girl, taking in all of our faces. She wandered over to the living room window and looked out. "It's snowing!"

"Yup, it does that here in Colorado."

"I *know*," she retorted. The look she gave her brother reminded me so much of Liz that I had to smile.

"Hey, maybe we can all go to the Sand Dunes and go sledding again," Kelcie suggested.

"Would you like to go do that?" I asked Avery, who had sat down at the table.

"Sure," she said, half smiling.

"Do you want some coffee?" I asked.

She shook her head. "I don't drink caffeine. But I'll take some orange juice."

"I'll get it, Mom." Jason reached for a glass in the cupboard and opened the refrigerator.

"Yes, that's a fantastic idea," said Grant. He stood up and came to the table. "I think we could all go to the Dunes. There's supposed to be a full moon on New Year's Eve. If it's clear, I'd like to take the camera and get some pictures. That is … if it clears up by then."

We were eating breakfast a while later and Jason suddenly asked, "Mom, have you decided to keep the shopper?"

The question startled me and I almost dropped my fork. I caught Grant's look of surprise, but the two girls kept on eating as if the question wasn't important.

"Well …" I reached for my coffee mug. "No, Jason. I'm not yet sure what I'll do."

"You're not keeping the shopper?" Grant stared in confusion. "Why?"

Jason cleared his throat. "Hey … when you're done, Avery, maybe we can show you Kelcie's apartment. She's got some cool video games over there. Wanna join us?"

Avery glanced at me, uncertain. I nodded, and then she replied, "Sure." They had finished their food and all three got up and put on their coats to go have fun at Kelcie's. I knew Jason had done this so that Grant and I could talk alone.

42

The week passed swiftly. In fact, it was pretty much a blur. Looking back at those days now, it was more like a bad dream.

Grant and I had talked over my dilemma with the *Buffalo Billboard*. He suggested that once we were married, we could merge the two publications. Instead of being competitors, we would work together. He had the money to sustain the shopper until it was able to make a profit on its own without having to pour all of my life savings into it.

I had been ready to fold. I had planned to call each one of my employees that very day and tell them I was not going to publish any more issues. I was going to go visit Mr. Starkmore at the bank in Valle Viento and see what could be done about my loan. Then I would have had to contact Otto Breitbart and tell him I was breaking the lease on our building.

Then I would have called Merle to have him help move me back to Dexter. And every time I thought about that, and trying to convince myself that making a life with Merle wouldn't really be so awful, I knew I was kidding myself.

I called Dirk that afternoon, after Grant went home, and told him Avery was staying with us. Even though my ex-husband was usually arrogant and hard to get along with, this time he actually thanked me. He even broke down and stammered over the phone.

"She's s-safe. Thank God. I've been so w-worried." He admitted that he had almost flown to Colorado to look for her as he suspected she might return to Blanca Hills, since she had learned about the death of her birth mother.

"Dirk, I don't understand why you kept Avery a secret all these years. Why did you send her away to boarding school? If you cared about her ... and you apparently do in your own deranged way ... why didn't you raise her like you wanted to raise Jason?"

After he blew his nose, Dirk told me on the phone that Alicia had been okay with Avery when she was very young, but then the girl began to look more like Dirk ... and her resemblance to Liz had weirded her out to the point that she couldn't stand to have Avery around. Plus they didn't want anyone to suspect that Dirk was really Avery's father.

Then I understood why he had agreed to joint custody. He feared I would find out about Avery and the fact that she was Liz's child. He knew it would be grounds for me to take him back to court and demand more child support from him. Dirk had always put himself and his needs in front of what was best for others.

Before we hung up, I asked him if he would object to my becoming legal guardian of my sister's child until she was of legal age. He told me he agreed that it was best for all concerned, and he was more than willing to support her through college whenever she was ready to resume a normal life. With Dirk's blessing I hired an attorney to draw up the necessary papers to become Avery's guardian.

Jason was so relieved when he heard that the paper was going to continue. He still wanted to finish his degree, and he was planning to enroll at Blanca State next semester and try to get his courses completed by going part-time while still working for the shopper. All of my employees were also glad to hear that their jobs were secure, although Peg's fatal accident had put a major damper on everyone's holidays.

Javier Gallegos had finally been picked up after he tried to flee to New Mexico. Juan Espinoza, Grant's production manager at the *Sentinel*, was arraigned on conspiracy charges and was facing trial over fraud and drug trafficking. He would not admit that his wife, Peg, had been part of the cartel. He defended her in every way, yet could not explain why she had been killed in the car that had been chasing me two days after Christmas. I suspected that Peg knew Juan was involved.

On Wednesday I called Merle in Dexter. He had been eagerly awaiting my call as to whether I was going to continue my business and make him an investing partner. He was predictably disappointed when I told him I had agreed to marry Grant Tucker and that we were going to merge our papers.

"Well, Beej ... it sounds like you've made up your mind," he said glumly. "I'm happy for you ... and sorry for myself." After a long pause, he said, "I guess it was inevitable. I just hope we can always remain friends."

"Merle, we will," I insisted. "I don't know what I would have done without you. Thank you."

On Thursday of that week, Grant and I took all three of the young people to the Sand Dunes for an afternoon of sledding, tobogganing, and simply having a good time. The snowstorm had subsided two days before, and we were not the only ones celebrating the fresh powder. It was New Year's Eve and there were people on cross-country skis chugging up and down the dunes, and lots of parents with little ones on their sleds.

A thin man bundled up in an old Air Force parka, who had long grayish hair and wore sunglasses, was walking toward us with a German shepherd dog on a leash. As he passed us, he noticed us and stopped. "Hey!" he called out. "How's the shopper?"

Jason was the first to react. "Mom, it's The Captain."

We stopped and stared as the man from Rockcrest grinned at the two of us. He then reached out and shook Grant's hand, then mine. "Now look who's won the damsel in distress," he commented and laughed.

"Grant, this is the man who rescued Jason and me on our first press run," I explained.

"How are you?" Grant was a little perplexed, but decided to be friendly.

"Nice day to be walking in the Sand Dunes," said The Captain. The dog was sniffing the ground and pulling at the leash, so he waved at us and continued on down the path.

"That was The Captain," I giggled as Grant looked after the man and his dog.

"A little strange, but he seems like a pleasant enough guy." Grant squeezed my hand and we followed after the kids.

While Jason, Kelcie and Avery were having fun, Grant and I took a stroll. He had his camera bag with all his needed equipment hanging from his shoulder, and we held hands, bundled up in our parkas and wearing snow boots as the late-afternoon sky began to darken and maroon clouds gathered in the west. He was determined to get a beautiful shot of the sunset.

"When should we set the date?" Grant asked as we came to a protected area surrounded by huge rocks. "Have you thought about it?"

"With everything that's been happening, no, I haven't. What about you?"

He smiled down at me and said, "How about Valentines Day?"

"Valentines Day it is," I said and leaned up to kiss him. That's when I caught sight of the figure of a man standing about thirty yards away, watching us.

"What?" Grant was alert and turned to look, but the man had darted out of sight by then.

"A peeping tom," I chuckled, and we continued walking.

About twenty minutes later we stopped to rest, where we had a fabulous view of the western sky. Grant squatted down in the snow and started fumbling through his camera bag. I leaned against a big rock and hugged myself to keep warm. The late afternoon chill had settled in.

Grant tried taking a few shots, but he didn't seem satisfied. He turned to me and grunted. "I think I'm going to climb down this hill a little ways. I want to see if I can get a better shot. You coming?"

"No, I think I'll stay here. It's warmer," I said, bundling my scarf closer to my face.

"I won't be long," said Grant and started down the path that went around a hillside.

"Be careful," I called after him. Turning around, I could see far off in the distance the kids on the snowy slopes, still sledding and having a good time. Some of the families had already packed up and had left the park. I stood and contemplated my life and the good dreams I knew were coming true.

"So ... you won his heart." Liz's voice hadn't been in my head for several days. I tried to ignore her, but she wouldn't leave me alone. "Bridget, I'm not here to taunt you. You found Avery for me."

"Liz, you should never have given up your baby. Not even to Dirk," I told my sister.

"I wanted to keep her. I really did. But she was better off."

"I wish I had known about her all along. I could have helped. I would have raised her myself."

"*You always were the lucky one, Bridget. Now you've got it all. And what do I have?*"

"Stop it, Liz. You could have chosen another path."

"*You could have chosen to help me … when I needed help!*" she reminded me. "*Why didn't you? Because you didn't reach out to me when I asked … I'm stuck now. I'm stuck! Do you hear me?*"

The guilt hit me like a stab wound. "I'm sorry, Liz. I know. I should have called you. I was afraid. Afraid of what kind of trouble you were in. How could I have helped? You never would listen to me before."

"*You're right,*" she said mournfully. "*I probably wouldn't have done anything different. You were right to let me die. I could never do anything right in life. That's why I'm stuck now.*"

I felt sorry for her then. The voice in my head had never sounded remorseful like it did now. My heart softened toward my sister. "Liz, maybe it wasn't all your fault. And Avery is such a lovely girl. At least you got that part right."

"*And you're going to help her?*"

"Of course. Dirk sent her away, but I'm going to give her a real home and a real family. She's already a happier person."

"*Bridget, RUN!*" Liz screamed in my ear.

I didn't react soon enough. I heard a rustling sound and then, suddenly, a large hand had covered my mouth and I lost my balance. A man who was breathing hard, with puffs of carbon dioxide that stank of foul breath, knocked me to my knees. And then, still clutching me so that I couldn't break loose or scream, he began dragging me away behind the rocks. I struggled and fought with all my might, but he was overpowering me and I feared for my very life.

I heard Grant's voice in the distance, calling "Bridget! Come down here, you should see this."

The man who had grabbed me kept me from yelling and wrestled me to the snowy ground, where he sat on my chest and kept my mouth covered so I couldn't scream. I tried to kick. I tried to push him away, but he had a firm hold on me. He was dressed in dark clothing and was wearing a dark brown jacket with a hood. I saw a dark complexion and a scraggly black beard. He lifted a huge dagger that was in his gloved hand.

"You good-fer-nothin' little bitch," he cursed at me. "You'll pay! Just like your nasty little sister paid ... she got to be too nosy for her own good."

He wouldn't let me talk. I couldn't even ask what he meant by his words. Who was he? I had never seen the likes of this man before, but he was big and brusque and meant to kill me. I continued to struggle and squeal with my last breath.

Suddenly, out of the blue, a large heavy animal pounced on us! I rolled aside, face down in the snow, as the furry brute ran over the top of me and attacked my assailant. I thought a wolf or a mountain lion had jumped us. Then I heard the man scream and shriek in pain, while the animal growled ferociously and began tearing clothes and flesh on the man whose blood now melted the snow.

I managed to scramble aside and struggled to my feet. The sun was going down and we were losing light, but I saw that a large dog was on top of the man in the dark brown jacket, and there was blood everywhere. Too scared to run, I screamed and began yelling for Grant.

Within seconds, two figures appeared on the path in front of me. The first one was The Captain, whose dog it had been who was making mincemeat of the attacker. Behind him was Grant, stumbling to get to my side. The Captain motioned for Grant to wait until he could get his dog under control, which took another couple of minutes, and by then the man in the snow lay, dying in his own blood.

Finally, Grant scooped me up and pulled me away from the horrible scene. By then a small crowd had gathered from the snow sledders. Jason, Kelcie and Avery came running and stopped with their mouths wide open when they saw me, and then watched as The Captain secured his German shepherd on the leash and pulled a phone out of his pocket.

Grant set me down next to a rock near the gathering crowd, and the kids circled us. I was sobbing and clung to Grant. When I finally calmed down, he helped me stand up, and The Captain walked over to us and pulled out a badge. "Are you hurt? Do we need to call an ambulance, B.J.?"

I shook my head, even more confused as I stared at the badge he held in his gloved hand.

"What happened here?" asked Jason.

"I'm a Drug Enforcement agent," explained The Captain. "This man is Harvey Franken. We tracked him here."

"Harvey Franken?" I looked bewildered as I looked from Grant to The Captain. "Isn't he the one who killed my sister at the Blue Heron Motel?"

"Most likely that's true," said The Captain, nodding his head sadly.

"But I thought he was in jail," I said.

The Captain shook his head. "We've been searching for Franken for over two years."

"Then Peg ..."

"She lied to you, Mom," said Jason, putting his arm around me.

Kelcie grinned at The Captain. "You're a DEA agent? For real?"

"Yup, I am, as a matter of fact." The Captain turned his gaze on Grant and me. "Don't worry, if he survives, he's going to be put away for life," The Captain promised. He reached his hand out to Grant, and Grant shook it. "Better take your family home now, Mr. Tucker. We'll take it from here."

As we weaved through the gathering crowd of onlookers, a small group of law enforcement officers—I wasn't sure who they were exactly—hurried up the path toward us and joined The Captain. Avery linked her arm in mine and Grant clung to my other side as we all made our way back to the waiting car.

After everyone else got in except Grant, I hesitated and looked toward the sunset. It was another absolutely gorgeous orange, red and purple sky. I gazed at it in awe, and Grant walked over and put his arms around me as we watched it together.

"My God, Bridget ... I almost lost you." Grant's voice cracked with emotion.

"Just please tell me everything's going to be okay now." I was trembling and glanced over at the car as the three young people squeezed into the back seat. I could tell they were shaken as well. He held me and together we stared at the rosy sky in the west.

"Since I met you, Grant, I've really come to appreciate sunsets," I murmured as he nuzzled my cold nose.

He held my face and kissed me. "Let's go home now." Then he helped me to the car as the sleepy sun slipped behind the mountains of the Lower Valley.

Epilogue

It is springtime now in the Lower Valley. Grant and I exchanged our wedding vows on Valentine's Day in a small chapel, surrounded by our children, a few close friends, and many of our combined employees. The *Buffalo Billboard* continues and is thriving under the umbrella of *The Mountain Sentinel,* and I am ecstatic living in Grant's spacious house, which is our home.

Kelcie decided not to renew her lease and moved into the apartment with Jason. Avery has her own luxurious bedroom suite in our Blanca Hills home. She has already made a lot of friends at Blanca Hills High School, where she will graduate in just a matter of weeks. She has blossomed into a beautiful young woman with flowing dark hair and sparkling hazel eyes.

Avery still has a ways to go before she overcomes the childhood pain of rejection and being sent off to boarding schools. She wants to attend Blanca State, but prefers to live with us instead of in a dorm, to experience the kind of life that normal girls have lived. She understands about her mother and forgives her, as well as Dirk and Alicia. She knows they tried their best with the circumstances that had been given them.

My dreams of Liz have stopped. I feel she is at peace. Grant and I hiked the Sand Dunes this afternoon and visited the rocky area where Harvey Franken had attacked me. He survived, but has permanent injuries, and will spend the rest of his life in prison. As we stood watching the glorious sun setting over the mountains of the San Juans to the west, Grant lifted his camera and shot several pictures.

Then he drew me close and held me as we both watched the last bright red chunk of sun dip between the peaks. I looked into his face and those wonderful green eyes and said to him, "Another day, Grant ... and another sunset."

The Author

Ann Ulrich Miller enjoys writing romantic suspense. *The Dream Chasers* is her fourth novel in this genre. She has written and published Young Adult fiction under the name Ann Carol Ulrich, including a late '60s-era rural teen-age series (the Annette Vetter mysteries), of which there are seven. Number eight is coming out soon.

Writing has been her love her entire life, since she started pecking out her first story on an old Royal typewriter at the age of six, in the family's basement in Monona, Wisconsin. She received her Bachelor of Arts degree in Creative Writing from Michigan State University, and has worked most of her adult life in the newspaper business, with experience in every capacity.

Her memoirs include *Throughout All Time, A Cosmic Love Story*, which covers the twenty-year period in her life when she met and married her soul mate, Ethan Miller, and *Stepping Forth, An American Girl Coming of Age in the '60s*, which covers her years growing up as Ann Schumacher, until her marriage to her first husband, Jeff Ulrich, who was her high school sweetheart.

She has three grown sons and one grandson, and currently resides in Western Colorado. *The Dream Chasers* was inspired by her actual experience of starting a shopper in the San Luis Valley in southern Colorado in 2002. Many of the events in the story actually occurred. A few of the characters in the novel, though they are fictitious, were inspired by some of the people involved in the "Dream."

No one actually died in true life, and the mystery aspect is completely imaginary.

Be sure to read about her other published works on her website at *AnnUlrichMiller.com*.

With Thanks

There are several people to whom I owe thanks in writing this novel.

To my son Ryan, thanks for all the hard work and loving support you gave me during the months we produced our newspaper. We went through a lot and learned many lessons, and it was a huge step in both of our lives. You went back to college for a master's degree in Art and met your soul mate, Trish, through your involvement in theater at Adams State. And now I have a spectacular grandson.

I will never forget all the people who worked for me and their enthusiasm, without which we would never have even got off the ground. My time in the San Luis Valley was an experience I value, and I always loved that commute over Cochetopa Pass every week after the paper was out, when I got to go home to Paonia and spend weekends with my husband, Ethan Miller.

Without Ethan's encouragement and help at the most crucial times, we wouldn't have lasted as long as we did. We all miss him now. He passed away in 2008. He was the person who planted the seed when he asked me, "When are you going to start that shopper you've been talking about?"

To all of my First Readers, thank you for taking time out of your busy lives to read my manuscript and give pointers for making this a better story: Suzy, Donna, Lydia, Anna, Corean and Lisa Marie ... I value you as my librarian/writer/artist friends.

Doug, your patience with me is so appreciated. Writing is a labor of love that consumes a lot of time and effort. You are a most understanding partner and I am glad you are mine. Writing is a whole lot of fun, but so are you. Thanks for putting up with me and for understanding my need to work hard.

www.ingramcontent.com/pod-product-compliance
Lightning Source LLC
Chambersburg PA
CBHW071101250626
47159CB00002B/542